WARNING

This book contains sexually explicit scenes and adult language. It may be considered offensive to some readers. This book is for sale to adults ONLY.

* * * * * * * * * * * * * * * * * *

Please store your files wisely where they cannot be accessed by underage readers.

ISBN-13: 978-1988083773
ISBN-10: 198808377X

Other Books by Carla Coxwell:

<u>Fifty Recipes For Disaster New Adult Romance Series </u>(This series precedes "<u>Star Bright New Adult Romance Series</u>")

Trying to win a competition for best chef is cut-throat business. Kiara Sands has just won the opportunity of a lifetime. When she arrives at Fission, she has no idea just how much her life is going to change. She's immediately introduced to Jenny Foster and Robbs Martin, her competitors in the cut throat competition. The only thing Kiara finds more distracting than Robbs' hateful attitude is the handsome executive chef, Paul Weston. It doesn't help matters that Paul is quite taken by Kiara, and showers her with more attention than he gives her competitors.

<u>Torrid Exposure New Adult Romance Series</u>

April is finished with school and ready to build a career. Coming from a well-to-do family, she has decided to reboot her life completely. With family scars too deep to mend, April craves a fresh start. But the past is harder to shake than April ever would have imagined. At the center of it all is Bennett, an old family friend who is the heir to a billionaire media mogul company. Bennett and April haven't been able to stand each other since they were kids. But as the world shifts, the two of them discover the past might be the key to their future.

<u>Devil's Advocate BBW MC New Adult Romance Series</u>

When Kristie comes home from college, the last thing she is expecting is her world to be turned upside down by the appearance of her step-brother, Gray. Gray is rash, impulsive and breaks the law. Kristie's mom asks if she can try to befriend Gray, in hopes to get him on the straight and narrow. The plan backfires, however, as Kristie finds herself falling for Gray. Is it possible he feels the same way? The connection between them threatens to tear down everything Kristie has ever held dear.

<u>Obsessed Bounty Hunter Romance Series</u>

Jacqui Schneider couldn't help it. Every time the memories of her family's brutal murder haunted her, she had to escape. The only thing that could replace her sorrow was sex...and lots of it. Depressed and with no goal in sight, Jacqui continued on with her self-deprecating lifestyle until it all changed one day. Uncle Max, an old family friend, appeared unannounced. Jacqui was astonished when Uncle Max revealed a secret to her about her father. From those few words, Jacqui's world turned completely upside down. She really didn't know her own father. In fact, she didn't even know much about Uncle Max, except that he visited them for a few days at a time over the years.

Get the latest update on new releases from the author at:

https://www.carlacoxwell.com/newsletter

This book contains all the stories of the "<u>Star Bright New Adult Romance Series</u>"

Book 1

Torn between her feelings for her agent, Jon, and Rich, a charming bad boy who has ties in the movie industry, Jenny finds herself working through her own past to try to get a grip on her present. As she struggles to learn the lesson that in Hollywood not everyone is what they appear to be, Jenny tries to become a person that she can be proud of. Will she be able to find love and success in Hollywood? Or will she be dragged down by her past forever?

Book 2

Jenny finally feels that she is able to focus firmly on her future until a ghost from her past returns to ruin her present. Things are not always what they appear when dealing with rising fame. Jenny discovers love doesn't always work out the way that she plans and friends aren't always the people she thinks they are. With the walls closing in around her, will Jenny be able to face the fear head on, or will she merely sink and drown under the waves?

Book 3

Jenny finds herself lost in Hollywood, her personal life open to tabloid drama. She has fallen into the clutches of Rich, a man who wants nothing else from her but to ride her coat tails to fame and fortune. With Rich blackmailing her, Jenny feels her grasp on her own life fading.

Book 4

Time is running out for Jenny's chance of getting rid of
Rich, her blackmailer. While working out a plan to
escape his clutch, she uncovers details of his past that
explain why Rich is the man that he is today. As she
navigates her life and strives to leave her fear in the
past, will she lose everything she has worked hard to
achieve? Will Rich forever have control over her or will
Jenny break free and come into her own?

Star Bright New Adult Romance Series

Books One to Four

By Carla Coxwell

Copyright Revelry Publishing 2016

Table of Contents

Book One

Chapter One

THE SUNLIGHT creeps into my room. I groan and turn my head the other direction, trying to sleep through it. The last thing I feel like doing is getting up this morning. I never want to get up again. Everything I've done for the last few months has been robotic.

The holiday season is usually my favorite time of year. There is nothing I love more than browsing around the shops, looking for the best things to buy for my parents and friends.

That was before everything in my life went to hell. Now the thought of seeing anyone or even shopping makes me want to go back to sleep for the rest of the day.

Maggie… my daughter…

This would have been her first Christmas.

The thought comes to me quickly, before I can attempt to stop it. I try to stop all thoughts of her. Yet all it does is drive me into the pit of despair even faster. If I start thinking about her now, I will never get out of bed. I tell myself I will handle this morning the way I handle every other morning – with baby steps.

Open my eyes. It sounds ridiculous to make that a step but when I tell myself baby steps, I truly mean baby steps. If I think of what to do all at once – get up, shower, make coffee – it is all so overwhelming that I don't want to leave my bed.

The baby steps continue. Get out of bed. Walk to the bathroom. Brush my teeth. Open the shower door. Depression makes even the thought of getting in the shower to wash, only to do it all over again tomorrow, seem idiotic.

After my shower, I decide to go grocery shopping. I remember coming home last night and not finding anything substantial to eat. Instead I ate three slices of bread and went to bed. My stomach is growling loudly at me, demanding something decent to eat.

I slip on an oversized long-sleeved T-shirt and a pair of baggy jeans. Gone are the times when I cared about what I looked like. I don't want anyone to notice me ever again. It is safe to be by myself. I tell myself I can handle being alone.

Before I leave, I check my bank account on my phone. My savings are dwindling. I need to get a job. This can't last forever. When I quit my job, I figured something else would fall into my lap. But it's hard to have things fall in your lap when you never leave your bed. *I'm becoming pathetic.* I grab my purse and head out into the chilly morning.

A thin layer of snow covers the ground. The sun has now retreated behind a mass of gray clouds. They threaten a heavy snowfall. I wouldn't mind if it snowed everyone in. Sadly, Netflix is my new best friend.

The grocery store is brimming with families with their kids in tow, out of school for the holidays. I curse myself for not thinking of this before I left my apartment this morning. I wander around blindly, my list in hand, as my gaze falls on the kids around me. My heart beats quickly in my chest and my skin feels numb. All I want is to take Maggie's hand and walk through the store with her. I would kill to see her try to grab something off the shelf or plead with me to get her a doll in the small toy section.

Instead I am alone, a panic attack blooming on the brink. What is my trigger exactly? Happy kids? Couples who look down at their children and beam? I feel stupid as I park my basket in a random aisle and bolt into the restroom, which is thankfully empty. I go into one of the stalls then close my eyes tightly.

I can't live like this forever. Every time I decide to leave the house, I find myself overwhelmed by people or past memories. Everything seems to be trying to get my attention, telling me that my old dreams have died and I am letting life pass me by.

I have done things in my life that I am not proud of. I have terrible taste in men. I have a habit of only being attracted to assholes or drunks and I have had no issues cheating on people to be with someone else.

My skin feels hot and itchy as I try to avoid the panic attack that will knock me over. I focus on my breathing.

I am here. I am here. I am here.

I am nowhere else. What I have done in the past is in the past. I can't get Maggie back. I won't get Paul back after what I've done to him. I even feel like I deserve what Robbs has done to me.

Focusing on my breathing and repeating my mantra helps slow my heart rate down. I am glad no one else has come into the bathroom. The last thing I need is someone else thinking I am crazy.

After ten minutes, I am able to leave the stall. I splash some water on my face and look in the mirror. I hardly recognize myself. I have let myself go. I have to get a handle on my life but I have no idea how to do so. I have been hoping a sign will come to let me know what to do next. But what if that is just an excuse to give myself a pass on my shitty behavior? What if this is the sign – almost having a panic attack in a supermarket over happy children?

I leave the restroom, ready to get my grocery shopping done without further incident. By the time I leave the supermarket, I am feeling grounded again. Sometimes my head gets the best of me. I decide I'll brush it from my mind and go get a coffee. I haven't bought anything frozen, so I don't need to get home right away. My inner chef refuses to die, so the thought of making a frozen meal still does not appeal to me, even with how depressed I am.

It has been a while since I have treated myself to an overpriced iced coffee. But today is quickly becoming a day that is unlike the others so I head into the coffee shop, trying to ignore the small crowd standing in line to wait. I find myself lost in thought at the menu, which seems to have doubled in items since the last time I was here.

Someone taps on my shoulder, and I nearly jump out of my skin. I take a deep breath and turn around, fearing who it will be.

"I knew it was you! I wasn't 100 percent sure, but I just had to see!"

"Kathy?" I reply, my eyes widening.

Kathy smiles a toothy grin back at me. "Jenny! It's been so long!"

"It really has," I reply and then stiffen in surprise when she brings me in for a hug.

I haven't seen Kathy since high school. We took English class together our junior and senior year. We really mostly just slacked off or talked shit about the different people in class. We probably could have been in AP English but instead had opted for the regular class. Despite the fact that both of us had been lazy about school, at least Kathy was involved in drama club. I had watched her in the school play every Christmas. They were always terrible. I vividly remember the crazy drama teacher to this day and the fact that she never did a run through of her own work. The plays always ended up being over three hours long.

Near the end of senior year, Kathy and I had a falling out. She'd dated a guy she knew I had liked. Back then, that had been enough to end the friendship. We had lost touch. But now, instead of feeling dread at a social interaction, I feel relief. Here is someone who has no idea about what I have gone through with Kiara, Robbs or Paul. She doesn't know about Maggie either.

The relief of knowing I'm not going to have to answer uncomfortable questions makes me feel more warmly towards her than anyone else recently.

"How have you been?" she asks me.

I am cut off before I can reply because I am next in line. I order something with white chocolate, and Kathy orders something overly complicated. Before I know it, I am sitting across from her in a little table in the back of the shop. Her hair is up in a slick ponytail and her makeup looks as if it had taken hours to do. She is wearing an outfit that fits her like a glove. She looks absolutely stunning. Kathy was always a bit of a wallflower in social situations in the past. She only came alive in the terrible plays. But now it looks as if the sun is shining down directly on her.

"So, tell me what has been going on with you?" I prompt, not wanting to start the discussion with me going first.

"Oh, nothing in this boring old town. I'm planning on moving, actually."

My heart drops, which I know is stupid. I have just met her after years of no contact. Already I have apparently leapt ahead to having a friend here, someone I could reconnect with. The fact Kathy is moving shuts the door firmly in my face.

"Where are you moving to?"

"Hollywood!" Her eyes light up as she takes a sip of her coffee. "I got a new agent, and we agreed trying to bounce around for work in this town is a bad idea. Better to move to the heart of it. Just pack up and leave."

Just pack up and leave. The words roll across my brain. I have a mental image of packing up and just leaving. Somewhere where no one knows me. Paris. Hong Kong. London. It doesn't matter. Somewhere no one will see me or know my past.

"Hollywood, wow," I breathe, thinking of how the city never sleeps and there are always things to do. "That sounds amazing, really. So you're going for the big time then, huh?"

Kathy nods. "Sure am. I had one foot in my old world living here and another in Hollywood. But you can't have both. I realized you have to pick a world and stay in it. But why would I stay in the old world when I know for a fact that it doesn't make me happy?"

Her words resonate with me. I take a sip of my own coffee to stall for time before I respond. I don't want to say anything stupid. I am worried I'll look weird if I start to spill my heart out to Kathy. But her words are burrowing into my chest, heading toward my heart. *A foot in one world and a foot in another world.*

"What about you?" Kathy asks. "What are you up to?"

Lie. Make something up. Tell her you volunteer at the library or something. I try to take in a long deep breath only to let out a strange choked noise.

"Nothing," I reply, my voice strange and high pitched. "I'm not doing anything."

Chapter Two

I can't believe it. I feel like an ass. Here I am, literally blubbering about my life to a friend I haven't spoken to since high school. I was so thrilled at someone not knowing the baggage in my life. Yet for some reason Kathy asking me how I am doing and realizing I can tell someone who was on the outside about what I had gone through was enough for me to spill my guts.

I spew up the entire story. Kiara. Working as a server. Being with Paul and Robbs. Losing my baby and what Robbs did. By the time I finish, the ice in my coffee has melted, making it undrinkable. Some people are glancing over at me, as if trying to figure out why a woman is crying in the middle of the coffee shop.

To Kathy's credit, she didn't once look overwhelmed or put off by my sudden emotional outburst. She lets me talk without interrupting or getting up and walking off. How much of that is due to being polite and how much of that is because of how much she cares, I don't know. All I know is when I finally finish my tale of woe, I feel as if a giant bubble has burst inside of me. The bubble of negativity that I have been holding inside of me for what felt like ages is now gone.

However, I feel mortified. I can't believe I just blurted everything out to someone who is practically a stranger. I rub my eyes swiftly to stop more tears from coming.

"I am *so* sorry," I say, taking in a shuddering breath. "Oh my god, this is so… I can't believe… I'm so sorry." I bury my face into my hands and try to calm my sobbing.

But Kathy shakes her head, her brown eyes wide with concern. "No, Jenny, it's okay. You needed to talk. To really talk, by the looks of it. And what you told me – what you've gone through – makes my last rough period look like a vacation."

I feel ashamed. The last thing I want to do is trivialize anything someone else has gone through with my own bullshit. I open my mouth to say as much but Kathy speaks first.

"Listen, I need a roommate. I have the apartment I want all set up, but I can only live alone for about three months before I run out of savings. I was going to look for a roommate once I got to Hollywood, but why don't you come with me?"

I freeze. What she is suggesting is the last thing I expected her to say.

"No, no," I reply, shaking my head. "I couldn't possibly."

"Why not?" Kathy presses. "You said yourself that there's nothing left for you here. That's how I feel about living here too. Plus the amount of money I was spending on flying to Hollywood and back was stupid.

Two different worlds, remember? That's what's going on with you, too. You have a world where you're stuck in the past and a new one that I'm offering you. Come to Hollywood. Experience the world with me. You said yourself you don't want to be a chef anymore, so come on."

I suddenly feel in over my head. This all sounds too good to be true. I stand up suddenly, wanting nothing more than to get out of here.

"I need to go. Let me think about it, okay? When do you leave?"

"This Friday. Let me give you my number."

I log her number into my phone and then bolt, giving her a quick wave. Once I get back outside, the cold air smacks me in the face. I feel stupid for blurting everything out like that. There is no way Kathy could honestly mean for me to come with her, right? But as I get in my car, I remember the look on her face when she asked me. She truly did mean it.

But should I take her up on it?

That evening, the snow kicks up. The threatening gray skies finally open up. The white flakes come down heavily, covering everything like a blanket as I curl up on the couch watching TV. For the first time in ages, I make hot chocolate and do several loads of laundry. That, plus the grocery shopping and my conversation with Kathy, means this day has been one of the most productive I have had in ages.

It could be because the entire time I have been thinking about what Kathy has offered - moving to Hollywood. What would I do there? Wait on tables yet again? I don't want to get back in the same business, but my experience in other areas is lacking.

But haven't I been wishing about packing up and going where no one knows who I am? And now I have the option but I'm stumbling. I am stalling and trying to find a reason to say no. Kathy is right. I am afraid of moving forward. That and the thought of my dwindling savings makes me call her later that evening before bed.

"Did I wake you?" I blurt out before Kathy can even fully answer "Hello?". I cringe to myself at how I seem to have lost all proper manners lately.

"No, I'm usually up super late. What's up?"

"I was thinking… about your offer… the one to move to Hollywood." I am stalling, suddenly feeling unsure again.

"Listen, I know it was a lot to spring on you. I get like that sometimes, just so full of crazy ideas that I spew them out without thinking them all the way through. Of course you have a life here that you need to tend to. It'd be insane to expect you to just drop everything and go."

My heart falls. Is she retracting her offer? I suddenly realize that I *want* to go. That is what I truly want. Anything else is the fear talking, trying to hold me back in my depressive slump that I call my life.

"But," Kathy goes on, oblivious to my inner dialogue, "I still think you should consider it. I can give you the number to my old agent. He's excellent, but he had to drop off some clients because of a family emergency. I volunteered to be one and then just hopped to another agent he recommended because I didn't feel like waiting. I just don't want you to think I'm giving you someone shitty."

"An agent?" I reply, stumbling over my words. "Why would I need an agent?"

"You don't want to go after the dream of being a chef anymore. So why not try getting into show business?"

I swallow my laughter. I know Kathy is being serious. I don't want to seem as if I am pissing all over her idea. But honestly - acting? How can she be serious? I don't know the first thing about acting. I have a mental image of me in a commercial for a feminine hygiene product, jumping into the air to hit a volleyball or strolling along the beach, a big smile plastered on my face because of my brand of tampon.

"Kathy, I don't think I need an agent." I hope I don't sound like that was the craziest idea I have ever heard.

"You won't get anywhere without an agent, Jenny, trust me. Anyone who doesn't have one is filming low budget horror movies in ten-minute segments 'cause they can't afford filming permits anywhere." Something in her tone makes me think that she has had experience in this as she goes on. "Anyway, Jon is great. I'll give you his number."

"No, Kathy, I mean that I don't think acting is for me. I don't know the first thing about acting. I've never done that for a second in my life."

"Oh. Well listen, it could be a talent you don't even know you have! Think of it as an adventure!"

An adventure. I allow the words to sink into my head. If I am going to Hollywood, then why not go all the way? I have been slumping around here, fending off panic attacks over happy children and thinking about Robbs and Paul. I need to reinvent myself desperately. And even if acting turns out not to be my thing, it's Hollywood. I can find something else to do.

"Okay," I say. "Sounds good. Let's do this."

Kathy squeals, sounding relieved at having found a roommate already. "Great! That's great! I'll text you the information for the place I'm renting. I'll be leaving before you, but that's okay. I'll get everything set up. You just get things wrapped up on your end."

We talk a little more before I hang up the phone. I suddenly feel exhausted. Was it really this morning I had woken up, using baby steps to get myself into the shower? Now I'm moving to Hollywood. I look out the window.

Everything is going to change. Am I ready to reinvent myself?

Chapter Three

My heart is pounding in my chest. The taxi driver is ignoring me, lost in whatever terrible music he's listening to. I turn back to watch my apartment become smaller and smaller. Has it really only been two weeks since Kathy made me the offer to come with her to Hollywood?

I had to quickly sell my car. Settled for much less than what it was actually worth which bummed me out. The cost of living in Hollywood is much higher than here, and I needed the cash, especially since I have been using my savings to laze around. I had to pay a fee to end my lease early. Lastly, I told everyone on Christmas that I was leaving.

It hadn't gone as well as I would have liked it to. I understand it all seemed sudden. My family is worried I am making a rash decision and am having a lapse of lucid judgement. My words had failed me when I tried to explain to them that I need to get out of here and start somewhere new.

I sold everything I could and packed up my clothes. Before I know it, I'm riding toward the airport. Kathy has been there for a week already and tells me that her old agent, Jon, is waiting for my call.

That is something I haven't told anyone else – the possibility of acting. I know that everyone will shoot it down and with good reason. I have spent a ridiculous amount of time Googling stuff about acting. The chances of anything coming of this are slim to none. My previous notion of landing a tampon commercial is dreaming too high. I will be lucky if I get an audition.

I told Kathy as much, but she brushed off my concerns. She is overly positive for someone who, from what I can gather, has gotten only tiny roles here and there in commercials and bad movies. But I don't want to suddenly piss on her parade since we're going to be roommates and she'll be my only friend in an unfamiliar city.

By the time the taxi arrives at the airport, I have worked myself up in a frenzy. Part of me wants to stay in the taxi and turn back around, back to my apartment. Call the whole idea off. But I have nowhere to live here now. If I don't head to Hollywood, I'll just be homeless and jobless.

After spending what feels like an eternity getting through security and waiting for the plane, I finally locate my seat. I plop down into the window seat, hoping whoever sits next to me won't feel like talking. I decide I'll put on headphones and zone out with an inflight movie. I wish I brought something to read as well in case the movie options are horrible.

I press my head against the airplane window, which is cold to the touch. I am leaving, going to Hollywood and starting over. I shut my eyes and take in a deep breath. Will it be possible to move on from my past? To not wake up in the middle of the night and feel haunted by what had happened to Maggie?

All I can do is move forward and find out for myself.

<<◇>>

By the time I finally get to Hollywood, I'm feeling a strange mix of exhaustion and exhilaration. Every nerve in my body hums. I desperately want a shower. My face is glued to the window as we land. I am finally here.

Kathy is waiting for me by the baggage claim. She runs over to me, dressed as if she is going to a business meeting. Her hair is up in a bun, and she wears a dark brown pantsuit with a fabulous necklace. I feel frumpy in my sweatshirt and yoga pants. Everyone around me is dressed to the nines in clothes that I wish I owned. *Investing in a new wardrobe is something I hadn't considered.* It is true. Somehow in all of my planning, the fact that I am moving to Hollywood, where the young and rich come to play, had fallen out of my head.

"Hey!" Kathy shouts. "How was the flight?"

"Long. The layover felt even longer. But I'm here now! I could totally use a shower."

"Great. Let's get your stuff, and you can finally see your new home!"

Before I know it, we have my luggage and are stepping outside. I am bowled over by how humid it is. Suddenly I realize that I am the only person wearing a sweatshirt in the entire baggage claim. Now I understand why. I yank it off, revealing a baggy T-shirt I had thrown on in the last second before leaving.

I get in Kathy's car, and we zip out of the airport, heading toward her – no, *our* – new place.

"I have the apartment unpacked and set up but if you find you need anything we can just run out and buy it. I know you were bummed about selling your car, but feel free to use mine. I like to walk around Hollywood anyway, so you can use it unless I have an audition. You should call Jon tonight, too. He wants to get the ball rolling with you ASAP." Her tone is clipped and sharp, as if she has a mental list in her mind a mile long.

I nod mutely, still on sensory overload as we pull off the highway and into Hollywood. I look outside my window at all the palm trees. Even more people. The sky is a bright blue, as if we are in a marble. The buildings are tall, gleaming in the sunlight. Everything I look at makes it clear I am a far cry from back home.

"It's overwhelming when you first get here," Kathy says, clearly making note of my expression. "But you'll love it, truly."

I tear my eyes away from someone playing their guitar on a street corner and look at her. "Thanks for… all of this."

"Don't mention it. It isn't a problem. It works out for me too, since I needed a roommate."

"Are you nervous about living here full time?"

Kathy shakes her head as we hit traffic. "Nah. I'll never make it if I don't make the full jump."

"Does this old agent of yours…"

"Jon."

"Right, Jon. Does he know I've never acted a day in my life?"

"He's looking for new blood, Jenny. Someone with potential. That's you. You just have to unlock it in yourself."

I look back outside the window as we inch forward. *Unlock it myself.* I used to be able to do that. I used to be confident and look where it got me. *No*, I tell myself firmly, brushing thoughts of the past away. I am not going to fall down that hole. Not here.

It feels like it takes ages to get to the apartment. The traffic is unreal. There is even traffic on the smaller roads. It isn't until she makes a few more turns that the roads are clear of traffic and we are driving at a normal speed.

"Is it always like that?"

"The traffic?"

I nod. "Yeah, it's pretty brutal."

"Usually always bad, especially on weekdays. If you're going anywhere, make sure you factor in the traffic and learn to be patient."

I open my mouth to reply when we turn down another side street and pull into an apartment complex. It is a far cry from the luxurious high rise apartments that I saw back in the heart of the city. This apartment complex is four floors and looks as if the last time someone cleaned the roof was some time in the last century. One of the apartments on the bottom floor has a window that has been patched together with duct tape. The whole complex looks depressed, as if everyone who lives here has given up on their dreams.

"I know what it looks like."

I glance at Kathy and realize I must look horrified. I quickly shake my head.

"No, no, it looks fine," I lie. "Really."

I can tell Kathy doesn't believe me. The place looks like a dump. But I don't want to complain about the place we both are living in. I don't want to sound spoiled. So we get out of the car and grab my things. As we get closer to the complex, I can see that it looks even worse up close. The sidewalks are cracked and badly in need of some repairs. The paint on the doors is faded and chipped. It looks as if the entire complex let out one long sigh and then just gave up.

We tug my luggage up to the third floor. I am panting by the time we walk down the hallway. The staircase is rusted and creaks, which makes me paranoid enough to lean against the bannister as I wait for Kathy to unlock the front door. The last thing I need is to fall and break my neck. The apartment is facing the sad little parking lot and a taco shop across the street. No, it is not the height of glamor but at least tacos are close by.

Kathy gets the door open, and I yank my luggage in after her, closing the door with my foot. Then I look up to see where I am now living.

The living room is small and a little cramped but Kathy has clearly done her best to make it look "homey". The floor is tile but she has tossed down a deep red area rug to try to soften the room. A TV is against the wall. The couch has some throw pillows on it. Pictures of flowers hang on the wall. I am happy they aren't of her and her friends. I don't want to feel the urge to try to tack up old photos of my past so I don't look so pathetic.

Off to the left, I can see an even smaller dining area, with a table and two chairs. I can't see the kitchen, but my guess is it will be incredibly small as well.

"It's nice," I lie and plaster a smile on my face. "Where is my room?"

"Just off by the kitchen. That's one of the reasons I liked this floor plan so much. We each have our own space."

I trail after her. As I figured, the kitchen can barely fit the two of us. There is a hallway in between the dining room and kitchen. The bathroom is there and next to the bathroom is my room.

I step inside. Any silly bummed out feelings I have been having over the fact I don't have my own personal bathroom is wiped away by another concern.

"Wow," I breathe. "It's … quaint."

Microscopic is the actual word that jumped into my head but I brush it aside. My bed, which I have shipped ahead of time, takes up almost the entire room. It is a good thing I barely brought anything from my old apartment. It won't fit. I open the closet and examine how little space I have there as well. My mood darkens. This place is a fucking dollhouse. I should have asked for the master bedroom.

"I know it's small. But for our budget, it's the best we could get. And to be honest, it really isn't that bad. Yeah, it's a little out of the way and cramped, but we won't really be here much. We're going to be hitting the pavement and making our dreams come true!"

I bite my bottom lip, looking outside the window. I have a fantastic view of the parking lot and the taco shop. If I squint, I can see the high rises on the horizon. I could always stare at them and pretend that I was rich.

I know Kathy is waiting for me to tell her how I feel. But complaining about what she has managed to pull together, and even putting me in contact with her old agent on top of it, makes me feel like a bitch. She is right. Hollywood is expensive.

"It will take some getting used to. But you're right! This is Hollywood! I hope we won't be spending all day inside."

Kathy smiles, looking relieved. She turns to go get the rest of the suitcases, and I find myself staring back out the window. The self-doubt I felt on the airplane is back in full force. I shake my head, trying to clear my thoughts. At least now I have motivation not to lie around the apartment all day.

Chapter Four

Sleep doesn't come easily. Even though I am exhausted and in bed at eight o'clock because of the time difference, I end up just lying there. Tomorrow, I have plans to call Jon and see if he would be interested in representing me. A lot hinges on this meeting. If he declines, I have to triple my efforts to find a job. Kathy might be able to pay the bills with her acting alone, but I still need another job on top of looking for auditions.

The fear that I haven't thought this all the way through is still gnawing at me. Should I have looked for a job first? What if I don't find any work? In the end, I tell myself to stop overthinking it and focus on my breathing until I calm down and fall asleep.

When I open my eyes in the morning, the first sight is a different ceiling that isn't one I'm used to seeing. The cheap blinds that came with the room offer almost no protection from the sun. I make a mental note to buy better ones when I can. After yanking out clean clothes from my suitcase and stumbling into the bathroom, I manage to get into the shower.

There is a note on the counter when I get out of the shower from Kathy, saying she is running out to get some items for the apartment and she'll be back soon. I relax slightly. For some reason it makes me nervous to call Jon when she is around. It sounds silly, but I want to make this call alone.

"Hello, this is Jon," he says, answering on the first ring.

I clutch my phone tightly. I had thought the number was for his office, not his personal cell phone. For some reason, I feel thrown off. I had planned to put on my formal voice when I spoke to the receptionist but now find myself stumbling.

"Uh … hi? Hi! This is Jenny," I stumble through, cringing. "Kathy's friend," I add lamely.

"Oh! Hey, there." Jon's voice is smooth, as if he deals with idiots like me on a daily basis. "Kathy said you would be calling me soon."

"Yeah, I got in yesterday. Hope it isn't too late to discuss anything."

He is in his car, I can hear his AC blasting in the background. "No, not at all. Kathy was a great client. It was a shame to lose her, but family things just came up. I had to transfer a lot of clients."

"That sucks." I hate how boring I sound.

"Anyway, I have an opening today at around three. Last minute cancel. Do you think you could make it?"

I was hoping for tomorrow, honestly, if only to try to prepare myself mentally a bit more. But there is no way to say no to this. If I want to learn how to be a fully functioning human being again, throwing myself into things is going to be the best bet.

"Sounds great."

"See you then, Jenny."

We hang up, and I stare at the phone. *See you then, Jenny.* I like the way my name rolls off his tongue. He could do voice overs. I shake my head and shoot Kathy a text. Now it is time to get ready.

We hit traffic again. When Kathy had wanted to leave almost an hour early to get somewhere twenty minutes away, according to my phone's GPS, I had thought she was pulling my leg. But no, she is right, as usual. I should learn to stop doubting her when it comes to the traffic in Hollywood.

Kathy peppers me with advice and it makes my head feel crowded. I know she means well, but it is just making my nerves worse. I am grateful for her help with the outfit though. While I don't look as well dressed as most people in the city, at least I don't look like I did when I got off the plane yesterday.

"Jon is very direct," Kathy is saying to me and I try to focus on her as we hit another red light. "Some people can find it off putting, but I found it helpful."

"Why didn't you just go back to him when his family emergency was done?"

Something flickers across Kathy's face – it is so quick that I figure I must have imagined it because in the next second, she is smiling. "I had signed on with this new agent and it was just too much of a hassle to move back."

I nod, looking outside the window again. I miss my own car. I wish I hadn't had to sell it. *When you have enough money,* I promise myself, although I don't know when that will actually be. I run my fingers over my skirt, trying to recite Kathy's advice to me. As if sensing my nerves, she falls silent, too.

We pull up into an office building that looks about a hundred years old. It is only four floors. For some reason, I was imagining a skyscraper, housing celebrities and models with maybe even some paparazzi surrounding it.

"You were expecting something else, right?" Kathy says, a smile on her face.

"Honestly, yeah. Something a bit more glamorous." Where was the glamor in this city anyway?

"Most agents have plain boring offices like this."

I get out of the car. I wonder what else in Hollywood isn't going to be how I expected it. I guess a lot. I take a deep breath and follow Kathy into the main floor. We don't stop at the desk and instead go straight toward the elevator.

"Third floor," she says to me as I step inside.

"You're not coming with me?" I blurt nervously.

"Nah, I'll wait for you though. There's a coffee shop next door. Good luck!"

I was going to protest and tell her I need the support but before I get the chance, she reaches into the elevator and presses the button. The doors glide shut and the elevator is lifting upward. Is it stupid to wish Kathy had come with me? I guess so. But I still would feel better. Even with all her advice, it would be good to have her with me. *I have to do this alone,* I tell myself as the elevator doors open to the third floor.

I walk into a modern waiting area. There is a fish tank off to one side and lots of windows. A woman sits at a desk, the sound of her long nails clicking as she types. I walk over to her and clear my throat. She stops typing and smiles. Her teeth are so white, they're practically blinding, especially in contrast to her California-bronzed complexion. Her nails are a neon pink. She looks as though she could be an actress herself.

"Let me guess," she trills. "You must be Jenny."

"Yes," I clear my throat again, "I am."

"Have a seat. I'll let Jon know you are here. It shouldn't be long."

I nod and sit down on one of the chairs. I pull out my cellphone and start to fiddle with it. I can't believe how nervous I feel. I really want this guy to agree to represent me. I want to turn over a new leaf and start a career that no one would expect from me. This is my best shot. I take a deep breath and exhale slowly. My nerves lessen a little. I can't blow this. I have to be on my A game.

"Jenny?" I look up at the sound of my name. "Jon will see you now."

I stand up and follow the assistant down a small hallway. She stops at the door at the very end, smiles at me, and opens it. I step inside slowly. The office is as modern as the waiting room. The view is of the parking lot. A man turns around in his desk chair and smiles at me.

"Jenny, welcome," he says as he stands up and walks over to me.

My throat goes dry. I am knocked over by how handsome Jon is. I have heard that people in Hollywood are more attractive than everyone else. I had brushed that off as due to Botox and any other crazy anti-aging stuff famous people went through. But Jon is gorgeous. His black hair is slightly messy and falls into his eyes a little. His suit is well tailored and clings in all the right spots to make it obvious there are tight muscles underneath. *Oh no, he's hot!*

He holds out his hand to shake. His smile is bright and his teeth whiter than I ever thought possible.

I shake his hand. An electric shock goes through me. I hope I don't look like a deer caught in headlights. All the thoughts have emptied out of my head. His brown eyes remind me of warm coffee as I take a seat across from his desk. I find myself automatically checking for a wedding ring. No ring. *Stop it, you want this guy to represent you. You aren't supposed to find him hot.* It figures that the first man I find attractive in ages turns out to be my potential agent.

"It's nice to finally meet you," I manage to say.

"Same. Kathy has told me a lot about you. Do you want coffee or water to drink?"

I ask for water, and he goes over to a small mini-fridge in the corner of his office.

"Kathy said you're great. Said you helped her a lot before you had to drop some clients due to a family emergency." I cut myself off, hoping I haven't said too much.

Jon has gone still over by the fridge, as if I have caught him off guard. "Right. Luckily the family emergency is all squared away now."

"Great!" I chirp, my nerves getting the better of me.

Jon hands me a bottle of water and sits back down, opening his own. "Kathy say anything else?"

I take a sip of the water and shake my head. "Just that you are great at what you do."

Jon smiles and my knees go weak. I'm glad I'm sitting down.

"Well, she mentioned you didn't have any experience in acting, is that correct?"

I think about mentioning a fourth-grade play where I had been Merlin but decide against it. "That's right. Is that okay?"

"It will take a little longer to get you rolling but not a big deal. Most people who come by have a head shot and maybe a portfolio."

"Head shot?" I repeat stupidly.

"Just a picture of you that casting directors can use to see if you'd fit the part."

"I'm going to guess a selfie from last time I went to the beach wouldn't count."

Jon laughs. It sounds like music and I find myself smiling in return, feeling more relaxed.

"No, but we can get you set up with a photographer. You don't have a portfolio yet either, so we'll have to start off small. Get some audition demos out there. Do you have any acting training at all?"

"No. But I can thrill casting directors with tales of how I used to be in the restaurant business. I can even tell them how to make a great salad."

Jon smiles again. Maybe I am imagining it, but it feels as if his eyes rest on me for a few extra seconds before he looks at his computer.

"I think you'll do great on some test shots and an audition tape. I'll have to schedule you to come back so we can get everything all set up."

My heart skips a beat. "Does this mean that…?"

"I'll represent you. I'll have my assistant draw up a contract for you to review. Just sign it and bring it back next time we meet up."

I feel as if my heart is constricting. "Are you sure you want to sign me? I have nothing to offer." I am about to blow this. I bite my tongue to shut myself up.

"Okay, first lesson – try not to say that to anyone else." Jon laughs. "I know raw talent when I see it, Jenny."

Again, I like the way my name sounds from his mouth. I stand up as he does.

"I'm about to head out for the day," he says. "Why don't I walk you downstairs?"

I agree and we leave his office together after his assistant gives me a contract to sign. I grip it tightly in my hands, afraid that if I let it go it will fly away. In the elevator, I can smell Jon's cologne. It is subtle but makes my head swim. I try not to check him out.

"You and Kathy are roommates, right?" he says as the doors slide shut.

I nod. "That's right. Sort of whirlwind how it all happened but I wanted to get out of where I was living."

Jon looks at me, and I can feel goose bumps spring up along my skin, "You came to the perfect city to reinvent yourself then."

The elevator doors open, and we step out together into the lobby.

"Have you lived here long?" I ask Jon, wanting to keep the conversation going.

"Yes, a while now," he replies. "But I couldn't imagine going back to where I was before."

I was going to respond when I see Kathy heading over to me. I give her a wave, but she falters when she sees Jon.

"Hey," Kathy says as she walks up to us. "I finished grabbing what I needed at the store across the street so I was going to wait for you."

"I'm all done. Jon is going to represent me," I reply, beaming.

Kathy smiles, but it looks forced. Jon suddenly looks at his watch and then back at me.

"I have to head out. Have somewhere to be. See you later. Nice seeing you, Kathy."

Jon leaves us and heads toward his car. I watch him go, frowning. That seems sudden. I don't quite understand what has happened. I turn to look at Kathy, who is watching him leave. I close my mouth, deciding not to tell her about my meeting. She has a funny look on her face.

As if sensing me watching her, she turns to look back at me and forces a smile. "Want to grab a coffee? Tell me all about it?"

Maybe I just imagined it.

Chapter Five

That night, I can't sleep again. This time it isn't the fact I live in a dollhouse that is bothering me. Jon has called me to ask if I can come in tomorrow to get a head shot taken. He has been able to call in a favor so I can even get it done for free. *Is he this nice to all his clients?*

I want to ask Kathy, but after seeing how weird the two of them had been with each other, I decide against it. Maybe I am imagining it, but it feels as if there is some awkward tension between the two of them. Kathy had dropped me off and told me she was meeting some friends for dinner, so I didn't get to ask. Would I ask if I was able to?

Jon's voice on the phone gave me goose bumps again. It is naïve to think that he is being nice to me because we have some sort of connection. There is no connection – I just want to jump his bones. I sigh and roll over, covering my face with my pillow. In the distance, I can hear sirens. A few apartments down, I can sometimes hear people yelling. Not a dream home by any means.

Somewhere in this city is a nightlife that entire movies are based off of. Movie stars with no concerns are getting VIP bottle service and talking about their next blockbuster movie. There is no way that can be me, right?

Do agents say they see potential in all their clients or only when they truly mean it? It doesn't help that Jon is so attractive. There is absolutely no way I can violate our professional relationship in hopes for a date. I probably just need to get laid.

I finally fall asleep. I dream of my daughter. I wake up in the morning in a cold sweat.

"I want you to look as if you are gazing out in the horizon at your destiny."

"What?" I reply as the photographer snaps photos. "Is my destiny some tangible thing I can hold?"

We are thirty minutes into trying to get a decent head shot of me, and I am feeling over it. The photographer's directions for each picture are growing increasingly vague, and I feel out of my element. I had thought the entire thing was going to be quick, like having a high school photo taken.

Unfortunately, I was wrong. Jon has gotten a woman to do my makeup and hair. I feel unlike myself, as if I can be anyone I want to be. However, the photographer's ridiculous instructions are making me hyperaware of everything.

"Let's take five," he finally says, lowering his camera. "Your aura is all wrong."

"What the fuck is an aura?" I mumble to myself through clenched teeth.

Jon walks over. He is dressed casually compared to yesterday and has a bemused expression on his face. My heart does a flip.

"Jon, where did you find this guy?" I whisper.

"I called in a favor. He normally doesn't do head shots."

"You think?"

Jon laughs. "He's trying to make it big. He'll take what he can. We're going to get head shots plus some other photos I can use, too. It's a win-win, even if it doesn't feel like it."

"It does not feel like it."

"Come on, let's grab a coffee."

I follow him over to the small table that has been set up with some food. The guy who is doing the lighting is cramming a donut in his mouth as he talks on his phone. The makeup artist is gossiping to the photographer about seeing a celebrity at some club named Underwater Nosh last night. What a name.

I borrowed Kathy's car to get here. It took about an hour to get twenty minutes to the tiny studio. I had asked her if she wanted me to take a cab but she refused. I am pretty sure she is hung over from wherever she went to last night.

Lost in thought, I don't even hear people greet the man who has just come in. I pour myself my coffee, trying to shake off my tired state. I really need to sleep better. If I get regular acting jobs, I might have to get up at 4 a.m.

"Rich, I didn't expect to see you here," Jon says, although his tone sounds stiff.

"I heard someone was using my studio today for some new talent and I wanted to scope it out for myself."

"Did you." Jon replies. It is meant to be a question but comes out more like a tone of annoyance.

I realize just then that I am the "talent" and turn around to see who owns the studio. I am facing another handsome man. Is there any other kind in Hollywood? He is the polar opposite of Jon. His hair is a light blond and he wears a tan suit. His blue eyes are bright and gorgeous, reminding me of the ocean.

"I'm Rich."

"Jenny. Hi. You said you own the studio?"

We shake hands and he nods. "Yes. I own quite a few on this side of town."

"Among other things," Jon mumbles.

Rich either doesn't hear him or ignores him because he goes on, "I'm also a casting director. I used to work with Jon before we went our separate ways. You didn't tell me you had such a beautiful new client though."

I feel butterflies in my stomach. Is this guy *flirting* with me? In front of everyone? No way. He said he is a casting agent. Maybe he just likes what he sees. Maybe I'll even get lucky and he'll cast me in something.

"Jenny is new to the business but I think she has something real to offer the casting agents here. Something different."

Rich's eyes scan my body. "Looks like it."

I can feel heat rising to my cheeks. He is flirting. I open my mouth to respond when the photographer, apparently bored of hearing about Underwater Nosh, turns and claps his hands. "Back to work!"

I am back in front of the camera. Jon mumbles something in the photographer's ear, whose enthusiasm dims as he goes and gets a chair for me to sit in.

"Apparently we have enough shots for my own portfolio," he says in a low voice to me. "Sit. We'll get your head shot now."

I look over at Jon and mouth the words, "Thank you."

He winks in reply. I turn my head quickly, sitting down. He is just playing around with the wink, I tell myself, as my stomach gets butterflies again. I can feel Rich's eyes on me as well. Two good looking guys both watching me get my photo taken. It is perfect. If only I felt more confident in my poses.

It doesn't take long for the photographer to get my head shot. Apparently he cares more about building his portfolio rather than what he was actually hired to do. I can't blame him. I have gotten the head shot for free because of the favor Jon has called in. I *do* have extra photos on top of it.

Once we finish, I hesitate walking over to Jon. He seems to be in a serious conversation with Rich, who is cute and clearly interested in me. No matter how much Jon gives me the shivers and goose bumps, he is still my agent. Going after him would be foolish, given our professional relationship.

But Rich on the other hand? If he wants to flirt again, I am considering flirting back. He is super cute, after all, and focusing on a new guy might make any fantasies brewing in my head over Jon to vanish.

With all this in my mind, I decide to head over to the two of them. Jon sees me first and falls silent as Rich looks up.

"You did great," Jon says. "I'm going to get everything organized and start putting my feelers out there for an audition. I'll send you the photos, too."

"You should send her information my way, too," Rich says, his eyes still on me. "I might have something for her."

My heart thrums. "Really?"

"A beautiful thing like you? Be stupid not to."

"I'm heading out," Jon announces. "I'll talk to you later, Jenny."

I say "bye" and watch him go. Does he care about me talking to Rich or am I imagining that, like Kathy being odd?

"You looked great today."

I snap out of my thoughts to look at Rich and smile. "Thanks."

"You new in town?"

"Yes. Just moved here recently."

"How are you liking it?" He moves an inch closer to me and I feel a tingle go down my spine – something about him seems like a bad boy.

I can feel my old urges kicking up. *Bad Jenny.*

"I haven't really seen much of it," I admit, batting my eyelashes at him. "I heard the photographer and the make-up artist talking about some club named Underwater Nosh? I don't know what that is."

There is a noise behind me of someone coming back in the studio. Probably the photographer. Rich is looking directly at me, a slow smile spreading across his face.

"Underwater Nosh is the hottest club in the city right now. Highly exclusive."

"Oh," I reply. "I won't be getting in there any time soon then."

"Maybe not. Unless I take you."

My eyes widen. "You take me? Are you sure?"

"Of course. Consider it a date. I'll show you around and you can show me around."

Yes, clearly a bad boy. My type completely. *No*, I amend in my brain, *my old type*. I am not supposed to be into these sort of guys anymore. But would it really hurt seeing the hottest club in Hollywood?

"Great," I reply. "It's a date!"

Rich smiles. When I turn around, I see that it was Jon who has come into the studio again. His face is blank but it is obvious he has overheard us making plans. I snatch up my purse and head toward the bathroom, my face grows hot.

It doesn't matter. It doesn't matter. He is your agent.

Chapter Six

"Wow, Underwater Nosh? I probably couldn't even get twenty feet from the entrance," Kathy says, poking her head into my bedroom.

"Same here. It sounds so exciting. Actually seeing Hollywood, you know?"

"Rich – he used to work with Jon. If he likes you, I bet you can totally get a part."

I freeze. I am holding a dress in my hands but suddenly realize how ugly it is and toss it onto my bed. Get a part? That seems wrong somehow and is not what I am aiming for. Spurred on by what Kathy just said, I follow her to the tiny kitchen. She is making instant noodles.

"Get a part?" I echo.

"Yeah, that's right. I mean, he might think you're perfect for something and give you an audition, at the very least."

"Isn't that…" I grasp for the best word to describe it. "Cheating?"

Kathy laughs, looking at me over her shoulder. "That is not cheating, Jenny. That's Hollywood. It is all about connections, trust me. If he is really impressed with you, a part just might fall into your lap."

"That feels… wrong, somehow."

Kathy shakes her head. "It isn't wrong. It's Hollywood."

I take a taxi to meet Rich at Underground Nosh. He has offered to come pick me up but I actually feel embarrassed about him seeing the apartment. If he is rich enough to get me into this club, I blanch at the thought of what he would say about where I live.

I get to the entrance of the club five minutes early. Shoving money at the taxi driver, I get out, steeling myself. The line for the club wraps around the block. It looks as if waiting to get in would take hours, if you were even allowed inside. Kathy has told me this place is the hottest of the hottest. They probably let only a few nobodies inside. I can only imagine the bribes the bouncers saw nightly.

I wait along the sidewalk for Rich. I feel under-dressed. Everyone in line looks dressed to the nines. Some people are wearing fashions that look as if they cost thousands of dollars and here they are, wearing them out on the street. In comparison, my glittery night dress seems laughable. Not for the first time, I think to myself that I need a new wardrobe.

"There you are!"

I turn around and see Rich walking over to me. My heart skips a beat. He looks so *good.* He is wearing all black, which brings out his eyes, even in the neon colors from the sign. His hair is slicked back, and he oozes bad boy charm.

"Here I am," I reply, hoping he doesn't think I look as if I have moved here from Smalltown, U.S.A.

"I've been looking for you."

Confused, I reply with, "What? Isn't this the entrance?"

Rich laughs at my question and reaches for my hand. "For the regular people."

I take his hand and he escorts me away. Everyone is eyeing us, shooting us curious looks. Some people are downright glaring, as if they know where we are going. I sure as hell don't. We round the nearest corner and walk along the side of the club and some coffee shop. Music vibrates through the walls and along the sidewalk. Even here, people mill around, smoking cigarettes, as if just hanging out near the club was enough.

"Where are we going?" I ask as we turn another corner.

He doesn't have to reply. As soon as we round another corner, we find ourselves in a smaller line. Rich hands something to me – some sort of badge on a lanyard, which I put around my neck.

"Make sure you wear this till we get in. You need this to be in line."

"A badge to get in a line?" I feel very out of my element.

"VIP entrance. Otherwise this line would look like the one up front."

"Oh, VIP." I nudge him. "Impressive."

He grins at me and my mood lightens. As nervous as I am about getting into a high-end club like this, it feels like it will be okay when he smiles at me. The music is vibrating along the walls. I am suddenly anxious to get inside.

The line moves rapidly. Before I know it, we are staring at the bouncer.

"Mr. Dawkins!" the bouncer says, shaking his hand. "Nice to see you again. Come on inside."

I mouth, "Impressive."

Rich laughs and then we step inside the club. It is clearly the coat room, but I am amazed at the detail that went into it. There are lights that mimic being underwater along the walls and even the ceiling is painted to look as if we are underwater, looking up at the sun.

We walk past the coat check, continuing further along. I take a deep breath and step onto the main floor. I keep my mouth closed, even though my eyes widen in awe at the sight in front of us. The dance floor is absolutely jammed with people. It actually looks like an ocean wave, filled with people. They dance and move against each other, lost in the ear-splitting dub step beat that is playing. It is so loud that it feels as if it is worming into my brain.

The décor of the club is five steps further than the coat room. There are patterns of moving waves near the top of the club, but this time with lights, so it appears as if it is moving. Fish dart along the walls, swimming in giant aquariums. Something about them seems off, although I can't pinpoint what.

Rich leans over to me and gets close to my ear. "Fish are robotic!"

It makes sense, I think, as I watch one of the robot fish dart in its aquarium. Way easier to maintain. Plus fish will not appreciate the vibrations from the music. They look so lifelike though. Rich takes my hand again, and we move through the crowd. People bump into me non-stop, so I stop excusing myself and just focus on making sure not to lose Rich's hand. I feel as if I let go I'll be swallowed up by the human ocean.

We pass one of the bars, which is absolutely packed. We pass it and walk up a spiral staircase toward the second floor. There is a bouncer here as well. VIP entrance and now the VIP room? Rich knows how to spoil a girl on the first date. Our passes get us past the bouncer and into the VIP area.

This isn't as crowded, although it is just as lively. The floor is translucent as if I am standing on the ocean. If I look below my feet, I see more fake fish, as well as coral reefs and even a fake lobster. Above my head, the ceiling is made to mimic the look of sky, with a fake sun shining down on us. The sky is illuminated and changes colors with the music.

Entranced, I try to soak in the rest of the VIP area. I swear that I see at least two popular singers at one table. The dance floor is crowded here as well, with dancers in cages that mimic being underwater. The effects of the water elongate their features. They glow like jellyfish in the dance cages.

Rich pulls me toward one of the smaller tables and we sit down. A waitress comes by to take our drink orders almost instantly.

"Better than trying to get a drink at the bar downstairs," Rich says to me before he orders.

The waitress then turns to me, and I find myself stumbling over my own drink order, still entranced by the club. "Do you have anything that has alcohol in it but you can't actually taste the alcohol? I'm a lightweight."

"The house drink is the Jellyfish Juice. I swear you won't taste a thing."

"Sounds great."

I watch her go, thinking that Jellyfish Juice is a corny name for a drink. I'm relieved to notice that the music is a little softer by our table so we won't have to shout at one another.

Rich looks at me. "What do you think?"

"It's uh… overwhelming," I answer nervously. "I mean, the theme is effortless. It really feels like I'm partying in the Little Mermaid's mansion or something."

Rich chuckles. "It really is breathtaking. Of course, I'm sure in a year or two this place won't be nearly as packed."

"Why is that?"

"There is always another club that comes along and piques everyone's interest. You're hot till you're not, basically."

The waitress comes back with our drinks. Mine is overly decorated with a light up jellyfish hanging off the straw. I watch her leave, wondering what it must be like to work here day in and day out.

I turn back to look at Rich. "So, you must have been here for a while now, right?"

"About eight years. Moved here right out of high school. Wanted something new. Most people who end up moving here do."

"I hear you. That's why I did, too."

"There is so much to do in the city. This place is unlike anywhere else I've ever been. I feel like I'm really making something of myself here. You will, too."

I fiddle with the straw in my drink. "Will I? The odds are against me on every level, aren't they? No experience in acting and compared to everyone else, I feel like the ugly duckling."

Rich reaches across the table and holds my hand tightly, looking in my eyes. "You are anything but the ugly duckling. You'll find your way. I'll keep my eyes peeled for anything that might suit you."

"You haven't even seen me act," I reply, not wanting to point that out so clearly but having no choice.

"Jon said he's setting you up with some casting tapes later this week."

Jon had mentioned that at the photo shoot when I had first arrived. The thought makes me nervous, and I am trying not to think about it.

"Besides," Rich goes on, "I don't mind calling in favors for my girls."

I take a sip of my drink, smiling weakly at him. Calling in favors for his girls? Plural usage, by the way. What the hell did that mean? I think back to what Kathy has said about getting an audition from this date. I know she has said that is how things worked in Hollywood but it makes me feel… dirty. He didn't think I would sleep with him for an audition, did he? *This is why you were supposed to call off bad boys.*

I clear my throat. "Girls?"

Rich waves his hand at someone, yelling hello before looking back at me. "Don't look at me like that, sweetie. Come on, finish your drink and we'll go dancing."

I smile back uncertainly and take a sip of my drink.

Once we get out on the dance floor, all my concerns fly away. It has been ages since I have let loose like this. The music swirling in my head and Rich's body pressed against mine is all I need to let go of my concerns. Everything faded – living in the dollhouse, concerns about how I feel about Jon, concerns that Rich is out of my league, and concerns about my own taste in bad boys – go to the backdrop as we dance crazily together on the floor. It really does feel like I am dancing underwater.

We leave the club at close to two a.m. Too tired to take a taxi, I agree for Rich to drive me home. He pulls in front of my apartment complex but luckily doesn't say anything about how rundown it looks. Instead, he gets out of the car to walk me to the front door.

I wonder if he is going to try to kiss me. Dancing with Rich had been very sensual. We had lost ourselves to the music. It has been a long time since I have been with someone who was so good at dancing. His hands on my hips sparked a desire in me I had thought was dead. But his words of girls and auditions still rang in my ears. I like him but didn't know if the feeling is mutual.

We stop at the front door and Rich smiles at me. "I had a great time tonight."

"Me, too," I reply honestly. "That club was amazing."

"Can I call you again?"

"Yes," I reply, feeling as if every nerve in my body is wide awake waiting for him to touch me.

As if sensing this, Rich leans down and kisses me. I hesitate for only a moment before I kiss him back. I think back to his hands on me at the club, running down my hips and along my ass and I kiss him hard. He presses me against the door and kisses me hungrily. Then he pulls away from me, smiling.

"Goodnight," he says with a twinkle in his eye.

I watch him leave, feeling slightly confused. I'm so attracted to him. It feels as if he has a ton of secrets that I wish he would tell me. His hands on the dance floor had felt so good. Maybe I just need to get laid. But he's already driven away. Maybe he really isn't the bad boy I thought he was.

I suddenly need to catch my breath. I realize that maybe part of me wanted him to take things further.

Chapter Seven

A couple of days after my date with Rich, I head up to see Jon, who had called earlier and told me he had some news for me. I haven't heard from Rich yet, which makes me a little nervous. I had a nice time with him. Did he not feel the same? Maybe I am so blinded by my attraction to him that I didn't notice he had been bored.

My audition tape had been yesterday, and Jon had not been there. I couldn't help but be disappointed. He had only organized the meeting. The taping went okay. The director had me do a couple of readings and filmed it. At the end, he told me that I had a "natural love affair" with the camera, which I took as better than hearing I treat the camera like an ex-boyfriend.

I smooth out my hair in the rearview mirror. Kathy has let me take her car to see Jon. She asked me for non-stop details about Rich when she saw me but seemed to drop all conversation whenever I had brought up Jon. I am still convinced that something strange is going on.

I tell myself there is no need to be worried about seeing Jon. I clearly am not into him anymore, since I had such a great time with Rich. That is what I keep telling myself, anyway, as I walk down the hallway behind his assistant to his office.

Jon looks up from his computer. He is typing away, wearing glasses. My chest tightens. He looks amazing. I shake my head and step inside.

He looks up and smiles. "Jenny. Great, you're here."

"Hey, how are you?"

"Busy. But what else is new? Sorry I couldn't have been there yesterday, but I had a big event going on with one of my other clients."

I sit down. "No problem."

"Well, the director really loved you. Said you were a natural in front of the camera."

"That's good. Glad I have some sort of natural talent or else I'd have to be a waitress and tell everyone I really am an actor."

Jon laughs, and his eyes crinkle in an adorable way. "Well, I have some great news. I sent your video off to some different casting agents. One of them wants you to come in and do a reading."

"You're kidding!" I blurt out.

"Nope! I told you you're impressive, Jenny." His eyes stayed on me a beat too long and then he cleared his throat. "It's for a soap opera."

I try to recall the last time I had even watched a soap opera but nothing comes to mind. Don't they always have over-the-top plots with evil twin sisters or something?

I shrug. "Not a problem. I'll take what I can get."

"This is a big audition. I have to admit that I didn't think they'd call you in, due to your inexperience."

I think of Rich. Is he behind this? I want to ask but am afraid Jon will know instantly what I mean.

"Anyway," he goes on, "The audition is this Friday at two. You should make sure to bring your head shots and everything."

"You're not coming with me?"

Jon blinks. "That isn't the process normally."

"Oh." I say, disappointed.

"Are you okay?"

"I'm fine. I … I know sounds stupid, but I just didn't want to go alone."

Jon gets up from his desk and walks over to me, pulling a chair closer to mine and sitting back down. "Hey, don't worry about it. You'll be great. I can spot talent when I see it."

I smile a little back at him, aware at how close we are together. When he looks at me like this, he really does make me feel as if I can nail the audition.

"I didn't know you wore glasses," I say, pointing to his frames.

His hand goes to his face, and he looks embarrassed. "Oh, I didn't even realize I had them on. I usually wear contacts."

"They look good on you," I say without thinking.

Jon pauses for a moment and then smiles. "Sounds silly, but as a kid I was picked on for my glasses. So I stopped wearing them. I used to go to school and couldn't make out anything that was on the board. Stupid, right?"

"No, not stupid. I think everyone at that age really cared what kids in the class thought. I was bullied once for bringing this Barbie doll to school."

He frowns. "Wasn't that normal for little kids to do?"

I cringe. "It was actually in the eighth grade. I was completely mocked."

He laughs. "Well, I wouldn't have mocked you. Mostly because I wouldn't have been able to see you or your Barbie."

We laugh together this time, and I relax. He is easy to talk to. I'm glad I don't have some weird stuck up agent.

"So, what happened with your glasses?"

Jon leans back in his chair. "They sent a note home to my mom about my grades. I admitted the glasses story. She was so pissed. I told her about being teased but ultimately being grounded from video games was scarier. So I just dealt with it. Eventually the guys lost interest."

"How stupid. They're just glasses. Not exactly amazing bullying material."

"Are you saying your Barbie was?"

I wrinkle my nose. "My Barbie was flawless. They just didn't realize it."

A comfortable silence fills the room. I feel warm all over. I know there is absolutely no way that I should even read into my feelings for Jon. He is my agent. I'd had a fun date with Rich. But the ease of us swapping bullying stories and how confident Jon has sounded when he says I'd nail the audition makes my throat tighten.

"Who is the casting director on the soap?" I ask, trying to make my tone light.

But I can tell instantly that Jon knows what I am asking. "Not Rich. Why?"

"I was just curious," I lie, trying to back away from the subject. The last thing I want is for Jon to ask me about my date with him.

Jon looks at me closely. "Jenny, I'm your agent so I can't tell you how to live your life. But Rich is bad news."

"Why? Didn't you guys work together?"

"Yes. That's how I know he's bad news." He looks as if he wants to say more but cuts himself off.

"I'm being careful."

Jon nods and stands up, signaling the end of our personal conversation. "Remember, Friday is the audition. I'll text you with the details."

When I get home, Kathy is in the living room, painting her toe nails. She stands up when she sees me. She had looked exhausted this morning, having filmed some infomercial during the night, but now she looks excited.

"Guess what!"

"What?" I ask, pushing thoughts of Jon out of my head.

"I got an audition!"

"That's great! What's it for?"

"A soap opera," Kathy replies, and my heart drops. "Apparently for an actual role. I won't be Woman Drinking at Bar #4 this time."

My throat dries up. How do I tell her that I got the audition, too? It seems wrong, in a way, to be up for a part against Kathy. She is the entire reason that I am here, after all.

"Hey, why do you look like you just ate bad fish?"

"Nothing… nothing… it's just that… I'm up for that role, too."

To her credit, she only looks surprised for a moment before she smiles. "Really? Wow, that's great! I told you that Jon was a great agent. Plus with Rich working in casting that probably helped, too."

"Rich is in casting?" I echo as Kathy sits back down on the couch, her enthusiasm clearly dimmed.

"Oh yeah. He probably saw your audition tape."

"Jon said he wasn't part of casting."

"Oh, he's new to the soap. Started right before I sent my tape in."

"I'm sorry."

She looks up at me. "For what?"

"For getting this audition. Probably because I had a date with Rich. You deserve the part. I should call Jon and tell him that I won't do it."

But Kathy is already shaking her head. "No way, Jenny. Listen, I told you myself – Hollywood is all about who you know. Even if Rich got you this audition, you told me yourself that people think you have natural talent. So use it."

"But you deserve the part over me."

"All of us have equal shots at making this part. Apparently this soap opera wants fresh, new faces. It is all fair game to everyone auditioning."

I want to agree with her but I can't stop thinking about Rich. What if he gives me the part just because I went out on a date with him? I shouldn't have let him kiss me good-night. But being around him is so entrancing. He's dark and seductive and everything I like in a guy. Even now, just thinking about him, makes my skin warm.

I decide I will call him myself and see if he had any part in getting me the audition.

Chapter Eight

"I'm glad you wanted to see me again," Rich says with a smile.

"Thanks for picking me up," I reply, taking a sip of my iced coffee.

Rich ended up wanting to see me instead of talking on the phone. I had to admit it – I had wanted to see him again, too. Especially after the conversation in the office with Jon. I keep going back to it. The natural flow of our conversation. How easy sharing stories of our lame childhoods had gone. How handsome he looks.

Bad Jenny. Jon is my agent. To have feelings for him in any other regard is unprofessional. Anything I may have thought he feels about me is imagined. Agreeing to see Rich is dangerous, too, since I am paranoid about getting a part through dating him casually. But I decide it is less dangerous than actually thinking about Jon.

"Not a problem," Rich replies. "I'm thrilled to see you again. I'm sorry I didn't call you. I have been so busy with work since our date."

"I understand. Listen, I actually have a question. It probably sounds stupid since I'm new to all of this but I just have to know."

He waits. He is wearing a white button-up dress shirt today and black dress pants. I can tell he must work out on a regular basis. I catch myself wondering if he has a six pack underneath his clothes. I hope I'm not blushing.

"I got an audition for some soap opera," I rush on. "And so did my roommate. I was just making sure… I heard that… well, that Hollywood is all about who you know and…"

"Are you asking me if I'm the reason you got the audition?"

"Yes."

Rich laughs loudly, and a few people look over. "I am enchanted by how naïve you are to this business."

"Thanks. I think?"

"It's a compliment. Trust me." He reaches for my hand and holds it tightly. "You're different from most people in this town. I like that."

"That's great. Thanks." I am trying to say what I want to say perfectly. "But the audition…"

"Yes, I put in the good word when we got your tape."

I blanch, thinking of Kathy. She got the audition off of pure talent. I *have* gotten the audition because I had gone on a date with Rich.

Rich studies my face. "Why? Is that a problem? Normally people are very pleased when a connection gets them an audition."

"Right. I mean, I'm new to this. It just seems… wrong? I guess?" Under his gaze, I am stumbling over myself, suddenly unsure.

"Wrong? Honey, Hollywood is based all off of who you know. Surely someone has told you that before?"

He is right, someone has. Kathy. Her words echo in my brain. Maybe there truly is nothing to feel bad about, after all. Rich has gotten me the audition but it isn't as if he had gotten me the job. That will have to come from my pure talent. I probably won't get it, because I am so inexperienced.

"Yes, but my roommate is up for the part, too. And she said basically what you said – it's all about who you know."

"See? So no problem then." Rich smiles, taking a sip of his coffee.

"Right. No problem then."

Then why do I have such a strange feeling in my stomach?

Friday comes quicker than I expected. At night, I can hear Kathy reciting her lines in her room. I try to go over my own lines, but feel self-conscious. Kathy sounds so great in her room. Any time I speak out loud, I sound completely out of my element. I am the definition of cold feet.

As I get ready in the bathroom Friday morning, my phone goes off. To my relief, it is Jon. I want to word vomit up all my insecurities to someone and doing it to Kathy seems wrong, given that we are both going after the same audition.

"I'm so glad you called," I say by way of greeting.

"Hello to you, too, Jenny." I can hear the amusement in his voice.

"I am seriously freaking out. This is my first audition, and I feel 110 percent confident that I am going to blow it."

"You were fabulous in the tapes we sent out, Jenny. You have a raw talent. You just have to know how to get it to shine. Maybe I should look into some acting lessons for you."

"That's great, except that won't help me *now*. I thought you'd be like 'Jenny, you're great, don't sweat it,' but instead you're bringing up acting lessons. Does this confirm I am completely out of my element here?"

"I have faith in you," Jon replies, dodging the question. "You can do it. I just called to wish you good luck."

"I wish you would be there," I blurt out as I try to find a piece of jewelry that would look best.

There is a moment of silence and I wonder if I have gone too far when Jon replies, "Me, too. I'm sorry but I have meetings with clients all afternoon. Why don't you meet me for coffee this evening? Unless you don't drink coffee past six?"

"No, I do. I drink coffee whenever. All the time." *You're rambling, shut up.* "But that sounds good."

"I'll text you later. Good luck, Jenny."

After he hangs up, I find myself staring at the phone. *Just an agent meeting,* I tell myself sternly, *nothing more to it than that.*

"I didn't realize so many people would be here," I whisper to Kathy as we sit down in chairs in a corner of the waiting room.

"It's usually like this the first go around. It won't thin out until they do callbacks."

I look around the room. Fifty other women of all sizes, shapes and colors are waiting to audition. When they say they are looking for new talent, they apparently aren't kidding. They aren't just looking for the tall blonde Hollywood type. I relax slightly. I am not such a sore thumb after all.

The girl next to me looks on the verge of tears as she mumbles through her lines. Across from us is another woman who looks as if she has been up for a week straight. Her movements are jerky. But for every strange sight I see, there are tons of other women who looked polished and ready to go. Kathy is one of them. I probably look like a scared kid on her first day at a new school.

"You'll be fine," Kathy whispers to me. "Honestly. Just be yourself and give it your all."

"Everyone else looks so experienced. I know Rich was doing me a favor but maybe he shouldn't have."

"Don't be silly. Seriously, Jenny, you moved out here for this. Take this chance."

I look at Kathy closely. Anything sour she may have felt over me getting this audition is gone. Either she is a great actress or she truly is okay with it. In order to save my sanity, I decide to think of it as her being okay with it.

"I still think I'm going to blow it. Jon called while I was getting ready and didn't come right out to say it, but I can tell he isn't expecting me to get a callback either." I sigh. "I guess I can tell him how it goes when we meet for coffee."

"You're meeting with Jon for coffee?"

"Yeah, once he is done with his meetings for the day."

"How nice of him," Kathy replies, her tone curt.

I find myself studying her face. It is subtle but her features have definitely tightened. *I knew I wasn't imagining it.*

"Yeah," I reply slowly, wanting to change the subject. "Anyway, I'm sure I won't have much to say."

"Jon is very involved with his clients," Kathy says and then she looks at me, forcing a smile on her face. "He'll give you tips, I'm sure."

I open my mouth to reply when a name is called. The first woman, a perfectly polished redhead, goes in to the room, shutting the door behind her. I exhale and push thoughts of Kathy and Jon out of my head. Time to review my lines.

Kathy goes in before me. She texts me twenty minutes later to tell me she is waiting for me downstairs in the lobby. All I can do now is wait. I watch the other girls go in and not return. The girl next to me looks as though she might burst into tears when her name is called. *I wonder what her story is,* I think as I watch her go.

By the time my name is called, there are about ten of us left. My feet feel like lead as I make my way into the room. There are three people in the room.

A tall balding man in the middle waves at me. "Jenny, right?"

"Yes, sir," I reply meekly.

"I'm August Grant. I'm the producer. This is my assistant, Amanda Fields and the head casting director, Billy Arch."

A thin blonde woman smiles at me. Next to her, a gruff-looking man, obviously Billy, nods his head.

"It's nice to meet you." I try not to let the camera filming the audition make me nervous.

"Now, if you'd like to step to the middle of the room. We're going to start with the first scene, okay?"

I take a deep breath.

I press the elevator button, trying to control the sinking feeling in my gut. Part of me wants to cry. The other part of me just feels like an idiot. Why had I thought I could do this? I feel confident I have messed up the audition. The logical part of me is saying I didn't come off it as badly as I think I did. But the louder, nagging voice in my brain says I was terrible.

The first scene went okay. I ended up downplaying almost everything so it fell a little flat. I could tell Mr. Grant and his assistant were perplexed. But it was Billy Arch who was brutally honest with me.

"That was dull," he says, furrowing his thick eyebrows. "In this scene, your step-sister is in a coma and your boyfriend is accusing you of being the reason she almost died. We need to feel that from you – the horror that your boyfriend could accuse you of such a thing."

The next take is on the other end of the spectrum. Completely bonkers. But if my non-existent boyfriend had accused me of such a thing, of course I am going to completely flip out, right?

Wrong.

"Let's try it again," Billy says with a shake of his head. "But in the middle this time, Jenny. Less mentally unhinged, more aghast and horrified."

Trying not to act flustered, I go through the scene one more time. This time, Amanda writes something down on a sheet of paper and August nods at her.

"Okay, great. You've got a lot of energy," Billy says, looking at my head shot. "I can see that you're new to the rodeo. That's fine. We're looking for new talent. But you might want to figure out how to properly channel the energy you're feeling. You take any acting classes?"

"No, sir."

"You need to. Let's skip to scene three and run through it."

This scene was the overly dramatic one where my character decides that popping pills would solve all her problems. By this point, I am feeling so flustered, like I have fucked it all up, that I go through it without needing to glance at my paper once.

Yet their faces are blank when I finish. Billy ends the audition after that scene. There is no mention of a callback. There is nothing to read off their faces. I feel like a complete failure.

I try to tell myself it doesn't matter. There is no way that I would have gotten the part. I wouldn't have even gotten the audition if it hadn't been for Rich. I should start small. Back to my dream of a tampon commercial, I suppose. Oh well. Kathy deserves the part – more than I do.

I try to repeat that mantra as I step onto the main floor of the building we are in. I promptly stop. By the front desk is Kathy… and Jon. He is holding flowers in one hand. My heart skips a beat. Both of their faces are drawn tight and it looks as if they are bickering. That can't be correct. What could they possibly bicker about?

I steel myself and walk over. As soon as they see me, they both try to hide the expressions on their faces. I decide I will play dumb. I wave as I walk over, making sure to look like I haven't noticed anything peculiar.

"Hey," I say, smiling. "I thought you had meetings with clients."

Jon looks sheepish. "I do. But I wanted to swing by and see you. These are for you." He hands me the bouquet of flowers.

My face flushes. I didn't think that they were meant for me. I take the flowers gingerly.

"You didn't have to do that," I reply. "Really. I'm sure I bombed the audition."

"I'm sure you did fine," Kathy interjects.

I glance at her, trying to gauge her mood but her face is blank. "I don't know. When I left, they had no expression on their faces. I have no idea how they felt about my performance."

"It's your first audition. Don't be so hard on yourself," Kathy replies.

"How did it go with you?"

Kathy's gaze flicks to Jon. "Fine. Listen, I'll wait for you in the car, okay?"

I watch her leave, frowning. First, the two of them were bickering and now Kathy's sudden exit. I turn to look at Jon. "What was that about?"

"What?"

"I don't know," I lie. "She just seemed off, don't you think?"

"Did she? Anyway, I'm sure you did fine on the audition. I really wouldn't worry."

"Maybe," I reply, smelling the flowers. "You really didn't have to get me these though."

"Just think of it as an apology for not being able to be here for the audition. And the fact that something came up so I can't have coffee with you tonight."

I want to hide behind the flowers. I am pretty sure I am blushing. There is no way that agents usually bought their clients flowers, right? I wasn't sure. It seems like it wouldn't be the case. But it isn't as if I have a ton to go off of. I didn't want to read too much into something that isn't really there. Do I really deserve flowers because he had something come up?

"Well, they are beautiful. Thanks."

"No problem. I have to head out because I have another meeting, but I'm glad that I was able to catch you."

"Me, too."

"I'll call you once I hear something."

I nod and watch him leave. My heart beating loudly in my chest. I cling to the flowers, watching him depart. Coming all this way to see how I did. Giving me these flowers. Is it crazy that maybe he has a crush on me, or is it merely wishful thinking?

Chapter Nine

On the way home, Kathy makes small talk about the audition but doesn't mention Jon or the flowers. She is acting okay with me. If she is really mad at me for having Jon as my agent, wouldn't she say something?

In any case, when we get home, Kathy goes to her room, claiming she is going to have a nap. I decide to put the flowers in my room. When my phone goes off, I realize it is Rich.

"What are you doing tonight?" he asks when I pick up.

"Well, I had plans but they fell through."

"Come out with me."

"And do what?"

"What do you want to do? Clubbing? Dinner?"

"Honestly, I'm pretty tired. How about just a movie?"

We agree on a time for him to pick me up. I decide to let Kathy know that I am going to be leaving. When I come out, she is already in the living room with an overnight bag.

"Hey, what's going on?"

"My friend is having a birthday party in West Hollywood. I figured I'll probably be too drunk to drive so I'm just going to crash there. You okay for the night?"

I nod. "I'm seeing Rich tonight anyway."

Kathy's shoulders relax slightly. "Okay. Well, be safe."

"So, anything you wanted to see?" Rich asks as we pull up into the movie theater parking lot.

"I probably should have picked one out beforehand. Nothing sad, I know that."

"Okay. We'll just see what's playing."

Rich looks amazing tonight. His sandy blond hair falls in his eyes a little and he is wearing a black button-up shirt and dress pants. I keep thinking back to us on the dance floor from our last date. I want his hands on me. I can feel the energy vibrating between the two of us. He wants me, too.

"How did the audition go?" he asks casually.

I shrug. "Okay, I think. Hard to tell by their lack of facial expressions so I guess we'll just have to wait and see."

"I'm sure you did fine. They always keep blank faces. Treat it all so seriously."

"Why weren't you sitting in on the auditions?"

"I'm not the head casting director. I only have some say in what goes on there."

I think about Jon saying he is bad news. I wish I knew what had happened between the two of them.

"It's fine. My friend Kathy is up for the same spot. She deserves it."

"Whoa," he replies, grabbing my hand. "Don't say that. She doesn't deserve it any more than you do."

"I don't know. She's been in this business a lot longer than I have."

"But she isn't one of my girls. You are. You deserve it just as much as she does." He lets go of my hand. "Now, let's go see a movie."

As we walk up to the theater, I find myself turning his words over in my head. This isn't the first time he has mentioned his "girls". There is no way I should expect us to be exclusive – even I don't want to be thinking about that yet. But being lumped in with whoever else he is seeing, as if we are all part of his harem, rubs me the wrong way.

"Girls?" I say suddenly, stopping in my tracks.

Rich stops and looks at me. "What?"

"You said I'm one of your… girls. What does that mean exactly? How many women are you seeing?"

"Why?" He moves out of the way of people walking up to the theater and leans against the side of the building. "Do you want to be exclusive?"

"What?" I blurt out, feeling suddenly as if my words have come out all wrong. "No. No offense but we just started dating."

"Then why is it a problem if I see other women?"

"I guess just how you word it. Like we're all in some gang where you are our leader or something."

Rich leans close to me. I can faintly smell cigarette smoke on his breath. He trails his fingertips down my arms, which causes goose bumps to pop up along my body. I shiver in spite of myself.

"I'm sorry I made you feel that way. I won't say it again," he whispers, his eyes bright and yet somehow stormy at the same time. "Is that okay?"

"Yes, that's fine," I mumble as he wraps his arms around me and pulls me in for a kiss.

The kiss starts a heat deep inside of me. I can feel it start in my chest and then slowly roll out along the rest of my body as I push myself against him and kiss him back hard. Any time he touches me, all the thoughts in my brain simply fall out of my head.

Rich pulls away first. My chest is rising and falling quickly, and I try to steady myself. He smiles at me – a dark smile with a promise of things to come.

"Let's go into the movie now," he mumbles in my ear.

During the entire movie, I overthink everything on top of fighting my growing desire to throw myself at Rich. My body just melts when he touches me – it's been ages since I felt like that about anyone. I really want to sleep with him.

On the other hand, I am also attracted to Jon, even though I try to deny it. But I have no idea how Jon feels about me. I am terrified about reaching out for him. What if I am just misunderstanding the attention and our seeming connection to one another and end up rejected? After Paul and Robbs, I can't handle any rejection. It will cut me to my core. Can I risk ruining a professional relationship all because I think *maybe* Jon likes me, too?

But Rich is a sure thing. He feels strongly for me. There are no worries about rejection with him. He wants me, and I want him. I glance over at him in the darkness of the theater, my heart pounding in my chest. He is watching the movie, a somewhat bored expression on his face. He looks over at me and smiles. My heart constricts.

Rich drives me home in mostly silence. When he pulls up in my apartment complex, I look at him.

"My roommate is gone for the night. Would you like to come up?"

"I would love that," he replies.

We stumble into the apartment, our arms thrown around each other, kissing each other for dear life. The heat between us makes my heart race so fast that in any other situation I would have to lay down. Instead, I press myself harder against him. We are in the living room. He reaches for my shirt, and I suddenly get nervous and move away.

"Give me one second," I whisper, hoping I sound sexy as I turn to go into the bathroom.

Once in the bathroom, I take a deep breath. My skin is flushed and my face is red. I am burning up with desire. It is moving quickly, so I need a second to breathe. I am nervous about sleeping with someone again. I splash some water on my face and go back out into the living room.

"Sorry about that."

Rich is sitting on the couch and pats the spot next to him. I sit down and exhale. He leans over and kisses me gently along my neck. I catch my breath and my skin is tingling. Rich kisses down my neck and then gently tilts my face to his. His eyes are full of fire, like a blue storm, when he kisses me hard on the mouth.

I melt into him. All concerns about being nervous vanish away as I slip my tongue in his mouth and kiss him back. His hands are on my legs, inching up my skirt.

"You're so hot," he whispers in my ear as he kisses my neck. "So fucking sexy."

In reply, I start to unbutton his shirt. When it finally slips off, I see that I have been right about his six pack. My heart thuds as he removes my own shirt. The air in the apartment is cool to my skin. I am suddenly glad that I wore my nice black bra tonight. It pushes my breasts up to make nice cleavage.

Rich likes what he sees and begins to kiss my breasts. I moan softly, closing my eyes. I feel him unclasp my bra and then fondle my breasts, gently taking each nipple in his mouth and sucking on it. He gently pushes me back on the couch and moves my skirt up around my waist. Rich stands above me as he takes off his pants. I watch, wanting nothing more than for him to be inside of me as soon as he can.

He slides down his pants and his stiff manhood strains against his boxers. Rich pulls them off as well, stroking himself in front of me.

"Do you like this?" he asks.

"Yes," I breathe, "I like it."

"I'm going to fuck you," Rich says gruffly.

The words give me a thrill, and I nod as he slides over me. When our skin touches, I sigh in delight. He is giving off so much body heat. He nudges open my thighs and enters me.

I moan, closing my eyes as I take him inside of me. Rich bites and licks my nipples as he begins to thrust inside of me. He feels so good that I begin to moan louder, wrapping my legs around him in an effort to try to get him deeper inside of me. There is nothing else in my mind besides Rich fucking me. I rock my hips as I take him inside of me.

Rich thrusts hard and fast in me, moving one hand down to my clit. He moves his finger expertly over it, bringing my moans harder and stronger. I am sure the people in the apartments next to us can hear me but I don't care. The sensations of Rich inside of me as well as moving his finger along my clit is too much to take. I climax.

I cry out his name and shake against him as my orgasm rocks through me. It is so intense that I am panting. Rich is whispering my name in my ear, telling me how sexy I look as I climax.

When my climax subsides, he increases his thrusts. Rich rocks hard and fast inside of me. He looks so good as he fucks me. I cling to him until he grunts my name and pounds hard inside of me. His climax shudders through him as he comes hard.

When he finishes, he rests his head on my chest. We both are soaked in sweat, panting heavily with our limbs entwined. Slowly, Rich detangles himself from me.

"Where is your room?" he whispers. "Let's go to bed."

I lead him to my room.

Chapter Ten

I wake up the next morning from a terrible dream where I am falling down the stairs. Every time I hit the bottom, I am suddenly back at the top of the staircase with Robbs bearing down on me.

My skin is cold and clammy when I wake up. My heart races in my chest, spurned on from the fear of falling. The sunlight that comes in from my room gives me some comfort. If the room was pitch black, I would be panicking more.

Instead, I turn to my right. . I'm in my bed alone. For a second, I think maybe I have imagined the entire night with Rich. After we had sex on the couch, we stumbled to the bedroom, where he woke me up once in the middle of the night to have sex again. But there is a sheet of paper on the pillow, folded over, which lets me know it wasn't a dream after all.

I snatch the paper up and open it up to read:

I had a great time last night. I had a meeting this morning and couldn't bear to wake you up from your sleep.

Call you later,

Rich

I feel mildly disappointed that Rich hadn't woken me up to say goodbye. I lay back down, mulling over my thoughts. Sleeping with Rich was passionate and exciting. I enjoyed the time we spent together.

So why am I thinking about Jon?

Frustrated, I get up and grab clean clothes to take a shower. I make sure to get my clothes from the living room as well, so I don't have to deal with Kathy asking questions. Plus, she probably wouldn't want someone screwing on her couch.

I feel better after the shower. When I get out, I see that I have a voicemail on my phone from Jon. My grip on my phone tightens. I look at the flowers in my room and listen to the voicemail.

"Hey, Jenny. Call me back ASAP, okay?"

I wish he had left more details. I call back instantly, nervous about what he is going to say.

He answers on the second ring and sounds out of breath. "Hey! I'm so glad you called back!"

"What's up?" I try to sound casual.

"The casting director from the soap opera audition called me this morning."

My heart drops. I guess I'll be having my first official rejection today.

"You got a callback! This Monday!"

"What?" I stammer, certain I heard him wrong.

"You got a callback, Jenny. They liked how well you took direction. They want you to come back for the second round."

"Oh my god! I can't believe it!"

"I knew you'd do well! I told you!"

"Thank you, Jon. I can't believe it. I thought for sure that would never happen. I mean, just a callback is a reason to celebrate for me."

"It's amazing for your first audition, but you have the talent to pull through. You should celebrate."

I bite my tongue and then decide to go for it. "Why don't you celebrate with me? We could grab drinks somewhere."

Long pause. I suddenly feel like an idiot. I can try to pass this off as merely an agent/client meeting but something in the silence lets me know he knows I didn't mean it just as that.

Finally, Jon clears his throat. "That sounds great."

"Really?"

"Yeah. Are you free tonight around eight?"

We make plans to meet up at a place around the corner, so I don't have to borrow Kathy's car. Plus, I can make it sound as if it is just a quick meeting in case she asks anything. That is when I hear the front door shut. I walk out to say hi to her and see her beaming at me.

"I got a callback for the soap opera!" Kathy trills, looking excited.

"I did, too!" I manage to muster up some enthusiasm to match her good news.

I tense up, waiting for her to look irritated at me but all she does is look excited. She comes over and hugs me.

"Isn't this exciting?" she asks. "I hope it goes well for us."

I do, too. But there is a possibility of it only going well for one of us.

"Did you really think that was going to work?"

Jon laughs and shakes his head. "No, but I had no clue what I was doing."

I laugh and pop a chip into my mouth. It is a little after eight. Jon and I have settled down at a Mexican restaurant around the corner from my apartment. I am hoping that the conversation with Jon will wash away the one I had just had with Kathy.

She asked where I was going. Sensing that I should probably lie but not quite sure why I feel that way, I opted to tell her that I am going to see Jon to celebrate the callback.

Kathy stiffens and a dark cloud passes over her face.

"How nice of him to offer," she repeats, an earlier echo of the flower exchange.

"It was me," I say, trying to protect Jon from… I am not even sure what exactly. "I offered, since he helped me so much."

"Just be careful, Jenny. Don't get in over your head."

"What does that mean?"

But Kathy evades my question and heads to her room. The entire exchange has left a bad taste in my mouth. Obviously something besides a family emergency was the reason that Kathy has left Jon as her agent. But why recommend him to me?

"You okay?"

I snap out of my thoughts. Jon comes back into focus. He is wearing his glasses tonight, with a loose-fitting dress shirt and dress pants. His hair is a bit messy, but naturally messy, unlike when Rich tries to style it that way. His smile is easy going, and I feel relaxed just looking at it.

"Yeah, sorry… just… thinking about the callback," I lie, not wanting to ruin the moment by bringing up Kathy.

"You'll be great. I wouldn't worry about it. Even if you don't get the part, consider this experience under your belt."

"You're right. I know I should. I just don't want to fuck it up when I get in there."

"You won't. It'll be the same group as the last time, although Rich might be there," he says with a slight scowl.

"Rich?"

"Yeah, he had a hand in the selection for the callbacks."

"You mean I have to act in front of *Rich*?"

"Yes, why?" Something dawns on his face. "Did you really… I mean, are you seeing him, officially? I know I heard you guys mention a date before but…"

"We've seen each a couple of times," I reply, hoping I don't blush when I think about how we slept together. "But we aren't officially together or anything."

Jon shifts in his chair. "I know it isn't my business, but Rich is bad news."

"You've said that before, but haven't exactly given me anything specific," I point out.

The waitress comes by at this point and we order our food. When she departs, Jon runs his fingers through his hair.

"Rich and I used to work together. We opened my office together, actually. But I wasn't a fan of how he did business. He was shady. He used to openly hit on all our clients, even if they were married or seeing someone. I suspected him of sleeping with all the women and making promises to them of getting roles if they did so. So we fought, and he left the business. Went on to be a casting agent."

"Sleeping with women and giving them roles?" I ask for clarification, my brain buzzing.

"He's got that over-confidence a lot of women like. I get it, whatever. If that is your thing, it's cool. But Rich is more than a player. He's a sleaze. He's bad news. I never proved anything he did but I just don't trust him."

A cold feeling goes through my stomach. The chips and salsa suddenly taste bland in my mouth.

"I have to use the restroom, excuse me," I mumble and head toward the ladies' room.

Fortunately the restroom is empty – I lean against the sink and try to clear my head. I didn't sleep with Rich just so that he would give me something in return. I would have never thought to discuss such a thing. There was no mention of offers or exchanges. I had gotten that first audition due to connections, not because I was dating Rich.

I tell myself I am being silly. Jon has never proven Rich was sleeping with these women in exchange for roles. I just need to calm down. Enjoy whatever is happening between Jon and me. Think twice about seeing Rich again.

The rest of dinner flies by in record time. Jon thrills me with tales of his childhood and makes me laugh so hard my sides hurt. I find myself enchanted with the colorful way he tells stories and how easily it is to be attracted to him. By the time we leave the restaurant, I have butterflies in my stomach that I have never felt around Rich.

"Let me walk you home," Jon says, once we step outside. "It's just around the corner, right?"

I nod and we set off. Part of me wishes he would hold my hand. Another part of me is saying that I am falling hard for him and should back away.

"So, I never asked you what brought you to Hollywood. That's a big change to make."

Memories flash in my head, all of them bad. I fall silent for a moment, unsure of how to answer.

Jon speaks up again, "Did I say something wrong? You have a funny look on your face."

"No, no, I'm fine. Nothing good brought me to Hollywood. I just needed to get away from where I was."

"Bad memories?"

"You could say that," I reply. "I… I was pregnant… and then lost the baby."

I can't believe I said that. My mouth went dry as soon as the words left me. Saying it out loud brings back the nightmare of falling down the stairs, with Robbs' hands on my back, pushing me down.

"Wow, Jenny. That's horrible. I'm sorry. I don't even know what to say."

"It's okay. I'm sorry. You probably wanted some funny story and here I am blabbing out some nonsense."

"No," Jon replies firmly. "It isn't nonsense. I'm sorry that happened to you."

I don't feel like telling the rest of the story of how I lost my child so I just nod. We walk in silence. Jon looks as if he wants to hold my hand but at the last second he changes his mind and slips his hand into his pocket. I sink into my thoughts. Are we into each other or is he just seeing this as a client/agent meeting? The signs are so confusing.

We get to my apartment, and I unlock the front door. "Wait here, I'll get the money."

I had foolishly forgotten my wallet when I left to see him. I feel bad making Jon foot the entire bill and want to at least give him some cash so we are even. I dart into my bedroom for my wallet, grab some money and head back to the front door when I hear Kathy talking to Jon. I flatten myself against the wall in the kitchen, straining to hear.

"… tell her about us…" Kathy says, sounding irritated.

"There isn't anything going on with Jenny and me," Jon replies and my heart drops.

"Does she know that, Jon?" She is whispering, which makes it harder to hear. "Do you know that?"

"Of course…"

"Does she… that we used to be together?"

Wait, what?

"No," Jon replies.

"Are you going to… that we used to date?"

My heart thuds in my chest. They used to *date*? Everything snaps into place. How strange the two of them act around each other. How Kathy got so irritated when Jon brought me flowers. I suddenly feel stupid. Not only is Jon saying that he has no feelings for me but he dated Kathy. I am so stupid.

Turning on my heels, I go into the living room and shove the money at Jon. "Here you go. You can leave now."

Jon blanches. "Jenny, wait."

"Please leave," I say stiffly and close the door in his face.

I turn around and Kathy is fiddling with the buttons on her shirt. "Listen, Jenny. I didn't mean for you to overhear that."

"Well, I did!" I snap.

"I wanted to tell you the truth. That Jon and I had dated. I really did. But I didn't know a right time for it."

"Seriously? You couldn't find a right time in any of the times we were talking? Or when Jon was coming around? Or when you told me to call Jon to represent me? Why would you even do that, by the way? If you two used to date, why do something that would bother you?"

"Because it didn't bother me until Jon started hanging out with you," she admits, averting her eyes. "He shouldn't… he shouldn't go after clients. It's how we started dating and it just rubbed salt in the wound. I haven't seen anyone since… since we broke up." Kathy is stammering over her words now, looking upset. "So when he started flirting with you, it just pissed me off."

"So you're upset he was moving on?"

"No. Yes. I just didn't like him going after you. Where I would have to see it, Jenny. It has nothing to do with you."

"You heard what he said. He said he had no feelings for me in that way. So all of this is just him being friendly."

Kathy shakes her head. "No way. He's just trying to save my feelings. Listen, I know you're upset I wasn't honest with you. I get it. But it really isn't that big of a deal, Jenny, really."

The fact she is now trying to dictate my feelings is pissing me off. She has no idea how I feel. Trying to tell me that it is okay and not a big deal is simply invalidating my own emotions. It rubs me the wrong way, and I can feel myself closing up. I feel stupid. Knowing that Jon and Kathy had a history makes me feel as if I am just being used to make her jealous or something. Jon had declared that he didn't have feelings for me. I have misread everything and now look like a jackass. Is he trying to make Kathy jealous?

If he is, it seems to be working. She can tell me that it is because she doesn't want me to go through what she has gone through, but I don't fully believe it. Kathy doesn't like seeing Jon flirt with me. I am stuck in the middle of their mind games.

"Jon is a really good agent," Kathy goes on, not noticing my darkening mood. "I truly thought he would help you. And he has! It has nothing to do with you seeing him as an agent. I just don't think you two should see each other—"

"I don't care what you want," I snap, storming back to my room to get an overnight bag. "I don't appreciate getting pulled in the middle of your mind games with Jon."

"Jenny!"

I start shoving some things in my bag, wondering where I can go. I need to cool down. It isn't as if I know a lot of people in this city. The only person left for me is Rich. My reservations about him fly out the window. Jon probably lied about him at dinner as well.

I call Rich and wait for him to pick up. "Can I see you?"

Chapter Eleven

Rich drives me to a place I have only seen in movies and TV shows.

"You live in *Beverly Hills*?" I say, my face practically planted against the window of his car.

Rich chuckles. "It isn't a big deal."

"Are you kidding me? Of course it is. I bet my apartment fits into your closet."

Rich turns into a gated community, swiping a code that opens up the ornate gate. As we drive into the community, all thoughts of what has been stressing me out fly from my mind. The homes – make that mansions – are massive. I can't believe that people can actually afford something like this. We drive past them slowly with Rich obviously letting me take in the expansiveness of these enormous urban palaces.

"Mine isn't as big as some of these," he says. "I wouldn't get too excited."

I wave my hand in his direction, my eyes still glued to the window. "Whatever. When people say Hollywood, this is what everyone truly means." I pause for a moment and then look at him. "How did you get so successful anyway?"

"Ah, if you're thinking it is all from my job, I'm going to disappoint you. I was born into money."

"Lucky," I grumble, looking back out the window.

We turn another corner. This street has smaller houses, although they are still massive in relation to anything I've seen back home. Rich turns his car into one of the driveways of a spacious, well-maintained, two-story house. *A far cry from the dollhouse,* I muse as I get out of the car. Clutching my overnight bag, I trail after Rich toward the front door.

He holds open the door for me and I step inside. We are in a large foyer with low lighting. There is a painting on one wall and marble flooring underneath my feet. I think back to Underwater Nosh and how overwhelmed I had felt when I had merely stepped into the coat room. I feel the same thing now.

"Want a tour?" he asks.

"Oh, definitely!"

He leads me through the house. I marvel at how large his kitchen is – he could easily fit twenty people in the kitchen alone. The dining room has an oak table and windows that overlook the pool. The living room is modern, with all sorts of tech-savvy stuff I probably can't figure out on my own. He leads me up the stairs to the second floor. He stops in the guest room, which looks exactly like something I would see in a five-star hotel.

"This is where you can sleep tonight," Rich says, although his tone is overly light, as if he is suggesting I don't have to if I don't want to.

"Okay," I reply, keeping things vague on purpose.

I am still fuming over what Kathy has said and how I feel used by Jon. And no matter what anyone has said about Rich, he hasn't done anything to hurt me. Maybe I am a fool. Jon is obviously a bad guy wrapped up in a nice guy exterior. No one wants to be used to make someone jealous, including me.

I trail into the bathroom and for the first time since I stormed out of the apartment, I check my phone. I had put it on silent, not wanting to deal with it. There are two calls from Kathy and three from Jon. Two voicemails. Two text messages. I shove my phone back in my purse. I'm not interested in hearing anything they have to say right now. Not while Kathy tries to tell me how to feel and being used by Jon.

"Lost in the bathroom?" Rich peeks his head in.

I turn around, flustered. "Yeah. I mean, a rain shower in the guest room? What do your parents do anyway?"

"They're heavily involved in the stock market," Rich replies, motioning me to follow him out of the guest room.

"Damn, I should have gotten involved in that, too."

Rich walks past a billiards room and opens a door at the end of the hall. I step inside and look around, mouth agape. His bedroom is luxurious, all dark browns and reds. There are floor-to-ceiling windows on one side that open out onto the patio – I notice a hot tub. A big screen TV is on the wall across from the bed. There's an ensuite bathroom, which is probably massive as well.

"This is incredible," I breathe as Rich moves behind me, placing his hands on my shoulders.

"A soak in the hot tub would probably help you unwind, you know," Rich whispers in my ear.

I close my eyes. I briefly mention to him that I had gotten into a fight with Kathy over the audition and need to cool down. The thought of melting into a hot tub sounds perfect.

"I don't have a suit," I reply, opening my eyes at the sudden thought.

Rich smiles against my skin. "Do we really need suits?"

That flame of desire sparks up inside of me again. Not caring about anything to do with Kathy and Jon, I turn around and head toward the guest room to slip out of my clothes.

I let out a sigh of delight. The bubbles feel amazing against my skin. I lean back and close my eyes. I have told Rich I wanted to get in the hot tub first. I am nervous about strolling out onto the patio naked. He agreed, and is waiting for me to get settled. It has been ages since I relaxed in a hot tub.

"Are you ready?" he asks.

"All set."

I keep my eyes closed. It sounds silly, but the thought of seeing Rich naked and getting in the hot tub makes me blush. All this luxury and money… I am feeling out of my league. He probably can have models or celebrities. What in the world does he see in me, some newbie who hasn't even had a single role yet?

"Feels good, doesn't it?"

I open my eyes. He is across from me, looking out at the view. I swear that I can see what could be considered comparable to a waterpark in one of the mansions a ways off.

"Fantastic," I say lazily, finally starting to forget what was bothering me earlier. "I would soak in this every night if I could."

"I have to admit that I don't use it enough."

"That's a shame," I mumble, closing my eyes again.

We both fall silent, enjoying the bubbles. I try not to think about Rich's body and the skilled way he had made me orgasm the last time we had slept together. It is difficult to find a man who knows how to treat you in bed. Rich is very good at that.

"What are you thinking about?" he asks suddenly.

I hope he can't see me blushing as I open my eyes to look at him. "Nothing. Kathy, I guess," I lie.

"She needs to get over it. It's show business."

"Right."

"She shouldn't feel threatened by you. If she had confidence in her skills, she wouldn't be so concerned you got a callback."

"Yeah. I know, you're right," I reply, wanting to switch the subject.

"It's 'cause she probably has all these stupid ideas of how Hollywood works from Jon," he scoffs.

Intrigued, I decide to pursue this topic. "You worked with Jon, right?"

Rich eyes me. "He didn't say anything about me?"

I shake my head, hoping my face is blank. I am interested in what Rich has to say about Jon.

"He has his head in the clouds. He came to Hollywood with nothing. I was the one who hired him. His code of ethics doesn't match what goes on in this business. His ideals are so pure that while he is a great agent for people like you, new to the industry, I really have to suggest you dump him once you get some real work under your belt. I can suggest some people for you."

"So you left the company because you two just didn't see eye to eye?"

"Jon didn't want to get his hands dirty. Unless, you know, it was with his own clients. Although I'm sure you know all about Kathy and Jon."

"Oh, yeah. She mentioned it ages ago," I lie, fuming that Rich knows this and I have been left in the dark.

"You shouldn't date your own clients. They had that messy break up, and he lost a rising star because of his stupidity."

"Kathy was pretty vague on why they broke up." I can't help myself, I want to know every stupid detail. "Do you know why?"

"Kathy said he wouldn't commit. Jon said he just wasn't ready to settle down yet. Anyway, he harps on me for what I do or what he *thinks* I do, but he isn't that swell of a guy either."

I try to match up Rich's dark words against what I know about Jon. I even told Jon about Maggie, something that still torments me when I think about it. Opening up like that is rare for me. I have kept everything inside of me locked up so tightly yet I shared something so personal with him without even knowing him for very long. What will he do with this information? How can I keep him as my agent when I have feelings for him?

It is stupid to even think about the feelings I have for him. I have feelings for Rich, too, I tell myself as I look at him. He is handsome and well off and has great connections. So why am I so upset about Jon and his history with Kathy? I should just forget about him completely. Rich can help me find another agent.

"Let's not talk about those idiots anymore," Rich says roughly, sliding across the hot tub toward me.

He tilts his head down and kisses me. He tastes faintly of the water in the hot tub. I kiss him back, sinking into him. His hands go around my waist, holding me tightly against the side of the hot tub. I wrap my arms around his neck. Rich is the guy for me. I don't need to torment myself over Jon any longer.

We stay like that for a while, making out in the hot tub. His kisses are hot and slowly growing hungrier. Our bare bodies press against each other. I can feel the bubbles on our skin. The sun has fully set now, leaving us only guided by the lights from the hot tub. The whole thing feels as if I am in some sort of fever dream. All I focus on is holding onto Rich and kissing him.

Finally he breaks apart from me. "Want to come inside?"

"Won't we get the bed wet?" I mumble, feeling dazed.

He laughs and I blush. "The last thing on my mind right now is good housekeeping," he grins at me. I realize how ridiculous that must have sounded considering the moment. We get out of the hot tub, and he leads me to his giant bed. We stop in front of it, and he looks me over, drinking me in with his eyes.

"You're so sexy," Rich whispers.

"So are you," I reply, kissing him.

He kisses me back, and I lower myself to my knees, taking him in my mouth. He lets out a groan as I move my tongue up and down his length slowly, teasing him. Rich is stiff and warm, throbbing. I move my head up and down as I suck on him, rolling my tongue around the tip of his cock. He shudders and moans my name.

I work on him like this for a little bit, enjoying the feel of him inside my mouth. Rich has a nice cock and I like sucking on the tip and then taking the rest of it in my mouth.

Finally he moves away from me. "I need to fuck you," he says gruffly.

I am out of breath and my head feels light. I want it, too. I get on the bed but he shakes his head.

"I want you to ride me. I want to watch you."

Emboldened by how sexy he thinks I am, I straddle him after he lays down. I sink slowly down on his cock, moaning a little as he fully fills me. Once I got settled, I began to ride him. Rich reaches his hands up to my breasts.

My clit rubs against him, sending shivers of delight through me. I arch my back and ride him harder, liking the tremors that work through me. Rich is moaning loudly, gripping my breasts and squeezing them. Whenever our skin touches, I can feel how warm we are. The moonlight casts a light on us, and I rock against him so hard I can hear the bed moving slightly.

The sensations of riding him and feeling him inside me send me over the edge. I let out a gasp and cry his name as I come, shuddering hard. Suddenly, Rich takes hold of my hips and starts to pound inside of me, fucking me so hard that it only makes me peak harder. He is hitting my G-spot, I realize, as he fucks me. I cling to him as I come again. My moans have turned into screams of passion as Rich comes as well. He moans loudly, his orgasm rocking through him as though his entire body is vibrating.

When we finish, I collapse on top of him. We are
both covered in sweat. Sleep grabs a hold of me and
pulls me in. I don't resist.

Chapter Twelve

I go back home the next day. As incredible as it was escaping for a night with Rich, there is no way I can avoid these problems forever. Being with Rich has clarified what I need to do. Whatever feelings I have for Jon are not going to be reciprocated. I would be stupid to focus on what I have felt for him. He obviously isn't the type of person I thought he was.

As for Kathy, she still has given me a lot of help to get out of the spot where I had been depressed and lost. I am not pleased with the situation, but for the sake of us living together, I need to forgive her. I have to be the bigger person.

I also figure Kathy will give me another agent to call and see if I can switch agencies. I don't want to ask Rich for a favor like that yet, especially since he will ask why I want to switch. The last thing I feel like explaining to Rich is how I thought Jon and I could be something.

I walk in the front door of our apartment to see Kathy reading a book in the living room. I have readied myself for a conversation with her.

When she sees me, she jumps off the couch. "Oh my god, Jenny, I was so worried!"

"Why?"

"I didn't know where you were going or anything. I wanted to make sure you were okay! I didn't hear from you! Jon tried to contact you, too."

"Don't worry about it. I had my ringer turned off last night."

"Jenny, I'm so sorry," Kathy says, coming over to me. "I should have been upfront with you right away. I was stupid to hide it from you. I recommended Jon to you purely because he's a great agent. He helped me a lot with building up a solid body of work to go after actual roles, like this soap opera. And when I saw him bringing you flowers and being kind to you… it just brought up all these bad emotions," she goes on, rambling, her skin flushed. "I couldn't stand to think I had chased you off. I had the best intentions. I just messed up. I'm sorry."

I put my hand on her shoulder, trying to give her some comfort. "It's okay. Truly. I slept on it and I understand how… tangled emotions can get. But you helped me move forward when I didn't realize I needed to and would never have thought to. I can't hate you for being mad because you thought your ex was moving on. I shouldn't have thought of Jon as anything but an agent. Especially seeing as he didn't consider me as anything else but a client," I add, somewhat bitterly.

Kathy opened her mouth to say something but then shut it and shakes her head. "You should really speak to Jon. He called me, worried about you, trying to get a hold of you."

"It can wait. I should honestly find another agent."

"Oh, Jenny, please reconsider it."

I wave my hand. "If you know of anyone, let me know, okay? I should probably get ready for this audition. I've been so caught up in this stuff."

Kathy watches as I head to my room and calls out, "Jenny, please call Jon."

<<<◇>>>

I don't call Jon. I do listen to his voicemail though.

"Jenny. Please call me. I want to clear this up with you. What you heard... what happened with Kathy and me. Are you with Rich?"

The other voicemail is from Kathy. She has sent me two texts as well but there is nothing else from Jon. I try to push that from my mind and focus on my audition instead. If I nail this part, I can find another agent. They would want to represent someone on a show, surely? It puts a spark in me to keep trying my hardest.

When I am acting out the scenes in my room, this time not caring if Kathy hears me, I feel my mind wiped clean from worries. It is different than when I was with Rich. My mind is blank but fills with a desire to feel him and be around him. This is a pure focus on the words and the emotion I can put behind them. Even if Rich is in the audition, I won't let someone I know being there throw me off.

<<<◇>>>

As Kathy and I drive to the audition on Monday, I try not to let my nerves show. I have spent the entire weekend focusing purely on preparing for this audition.

I know I am going to see Jon as well as Rich. I can't let that ruin my focus.

"Are you nervous?" I ask Kathy, wondering if someone who's been through this several times already can still be nervous.

"Always, although I have managed to come up with ways to handle my nerves. When I first started out, it used to tear me down completely. The fear was insane."

"What did you do to fix it?"

"I thought of the worst moment in my life and just let it sink in me. Wash over me, really. I sat there in this shitty memory from my past and felt the fear from it. And then I began to grapple with it and fight with it. Instead of running from those emotions, I faced them head on and used them to my advantage . I fought my fear and I won. Now when I think of that memory, I feel in control of it. I take the essence of it and apply it to the auditions."

"Wow," I breathe. "That's impressive."

I wish I could do something like that. But anytime I let myself go back to that moment with my pregnant belly and Robbs looming over me, my entire brain shuts down. I don't think I could live in that moment. Going through it once was enough.

"It is terrible at first. But the power you get from it and the ability to put other aspects in control of your life is awesome."

I study Kathy, feeling curious. I realize that even though we live together, the two of us have been so wrapped up in our own lives that I don't even know a lot of what makes Kathy tick. I make myself a promise to find out more once this audition is over.

We pull into the same building as before. I brace myself and follow Kathy inside the first floor. A couple of other girls I recognize from the first audition head toward the elevator. I wonder how many out of the fifty original girls they have called back.

"Jenny!"

I turn around to see Jon over in a corner by the window, waving me over.

"I'll wait for you upstairs," Kathy replies tactfully. Before I can stop her, she darts off toward the elevator.

Knowing I can't avoid Jon anymore, I walk over to him. He has bags under his eyes and looks as if he has dressed in a hurry.

"I have to hurry. My audition is soon."

"I know. But I need to talk to you about what happened."

"Why? I know everything already. Listen, I'm probably going to try to find another agent."

Jon's eyes widen in surprise. "Jenny, please don't be rash."

"I'm not. I just don't feel like having a person represent me who tried to make their ex-girlfriend jealous."

Surprise flickers over his face and Jon suddenly laughs. "Jenny, you think…? Oh my god, I can't believe you think I was trying to make Kathy jealous."

His laughter pisses me off. I bristle and turn to leave.

"Glad you find it funny. Let me know how the audition goes, okay?"

"No, Jenny, I'm sorry, wait!"

But I ignore him and head toward the elevator. My heart pounds in my chest and it isn't because of the upcoming audition. I am shaken by how strongly I felt when I saw him. Yes, Jon laughing as if I am stupid and naïve has rubbed me the wrong way. But just seeing him again has dragged up my feelings for him. I hate myself for it. He doesn't feel the same. I have Rich. What is wrong with me? Why do I always get hung up on bad men?

The elevator doors open, and I decide I need to try to calm myself and focus. Not because I am going to have a panic attack, like that time at the grocery store that feels like centuries ago, but just because I want to make sure I'm not going to take this bad energy into the audition with me. I turn down a small hallway and head toward the ladies' restroom. At the same time, someone comes out of the men's room. I realize it is Rich.

"Jenny. Hey, the auditions start soon."

"Yeah, just have to use the restroom," I reply, pointing to the door.

"Well, it's great seeing you again. I had a great time last night."

I try not to blush and look over my shoulder. I don't want a bunch of people hearing that I slept with Rich last night and knowing he's partially involved with casting. Rich notices and he laughs.

"Jenny, I wouldn't worry about that. Everyone on the casting team knows they're doing me a solid."

I blink. "What?"

Rich shifts and lowers his voice. "You know, getting you a callback because of our status."

"What?" I repeat, feeling like an idiot.

"You know." He motions between the two of us. "Anyway, I'm sure you'll be great."

"Wait," I say slowly. "Are you saying they didn't want to call me back originally?"

"I just suggested they give you a callback. They were worried about your inexperience, but you take direction great. They could mold you. Anyway, I gotta go. Talk to you later."

Rich moves past me and heads down the hall. I watch him go, all my confidence drained. I *did* only get the callback because I'm seeing Rich. Another thought strikes me. Would I have even had a chance at all if I didn't get involved with him?

Eyes filling with tears, I slam my way into the restroom.

Chapter Thirteen

For the first time since I moved to Hollywood, I want to go back home. I don't want to stay here anymore. Despair clings to me as I sit in the stall, staring at the door. Confusion reigns inside of me. Part of me wants to blow off the audition completely. Another part of me wants to go in there and nail it. Show them that even if Rich did have hand in getting me a second audition, I deserve that spot.

I can't shake the thought that Rich has gotten me the callback because I slept with him. Kathy has told me multiple times that Hollywood is all about who you know and your connections. But I don't want to be known as the girl who has slept around for a spot on a fucking soap opera.

I close my eyes, feeling the familiar surge of anxiety rise in me. The whole thing with Jon still has me rattled. Seeing him today has made me so upset. And then after running into Rich and seeing how casually he tells me that the callback is due to him makes my heart ache.

My phone vibrates in my purse and I slip it out. There is a text from Kathy asking where I am. I bite my bottom lip. *I should just do the audition.* I put my phone away. Get it over with. I have practiced all weekend. It seems a shame to waste it because of what Rich has said. Then I'll decide if I am moving away afterward.

Taking a shuddering breath and trying to keep my emotions in check, I stand up. I am still going to try my best in this audition. I head out into the hallway and to the waiting room. There are about fifteen other hopefuls waiting, including the woman who looked on the verge of tears the first audition.

Kathy waves me over and I sit down. "Hey, you okay? They already called the first woman in."

"I'm fine," I lie and force a smile. "Just had to calm my nerves."

Kathy relaxes, obviously believing my story, which makes me feel a little better. If I can act well enough to fool Kathy, maybe I'm not as raw and terrible as I think I am. She doesn't ask about Jon, luckily, and instead goes back to reviewing her lines.

This time I am called before her. I give her hand a squeeze and head into the audition room. The same people are there from last time. Amanda gives me a small smile. Rich looks at me as though he doesn't know who I am. *What a professional.* I try to control my irritation. I am not sure yet if I even have a right to be mad at Rich, who probably just thinks he is helping me out. *Think about it after the audition.*

I try to block everyone else out. I throw myself into the first scene. The rest of the audition is a blur. I focus only on myself and what emotions I can put into the scene.

When I finish, Mr. Grant scribbles something down on a piece of paper and then looks up at me. "Thank you. That will be all for now."

Everyone has blank faces, including Rich. I leave the room, heading back toward the elevator. My heart is pounding. I have no idea how I did on the audition but I know that I have tried my very best. I have taken my swirling emotions and focused them. *I did all I could do, especially given the circumstances.* I step into the lobby to wait for Kathy.

<<<◇>>>

Finally getting back into the apartment, I let out a sigh. I suddenly feel exhausted. Waiting for Kathy took another hour. I am running on high emotions and want to nap. She looks tired, too.

"How long does it usually take to find out?" I ask her.

"Anywhere from three days to weeks. Not sure. All we can do is wait. I'm sure you did great though."

I fiddle with the skirt I am wearing as I sit down on the couch. "Kathy, can I ask you a question? It isn't about Jon and you," I add quickly when I see her face.

She relaxes a little and sits down. "Sure."

"It's about Rich. I know Jon and Rich had a falling out. But depending on who you ask, you hear different things. I wasn't sure who to listen to."

"I have to admit I didn't interact with Rich a lot. Jon was representing me right around the time Rich was leaving. So I can't really offer much of an unbiased opinion. Just what Jon told me about how he thought Rich took advantage of some of the clients or would have sex with them in exchange for parts."

"Do people really… I mean, do they do that on purpose? Have sex with someone for a part?"

Kathy leans back on the couch. "Oh, yeah. Anything to get ahead in this city," She looks at me. "Why, did Rich tell you he'd get you the soap opera part if you slept with him?"

I shake my head. "No. I guess I'm just a little wary about everything in this town. I'm thinking about maybe moving back home."

Her eyes widen in surprise. "What? Jenny, you can't! You're already doing so well!"

"Things just feel messy. I don't know if this life is for me after all."

Kathy reaches for my hand. "Jenny, I know you went through a lot of pain and torment before you moved out here. You've been doing so well since you got here, truly. If you're upset about Jon, then switch agents. I'll help. But you have talent. It seems like such a shame to leave right now when you seem so focused on things."

She has a point as much as I don't want to admit it. Ever since moving to Hollywood, I haven't been able to think about my previous pain. Seeing a child doesn't bring a panic attack like it did before. Besides some nightmares about Robbs, I have been completely focused on what life is handing out to me.

Kathy goes on, "If you don't want to keep going after acting, then don't. We'll find another job for you. At least think about it."

"I'll think about it," I concede.

Kathy smiles. "Great. I'm so glad. Maybe we'll go do something soon, just the two of us, to relax, okay? We deserve it."

"That sounds nice," I say and I mean it.

After we finish talking, I find myself curling up in bed. My head is ready to burst with so many thoughts. All I want is to sleep for a while.

After my nap, I find myself going over my bank account. If I keep slumming it like I am doing and focus on paying the basics, such as rent, I still can only go one more month without any sort of income. *If I don't get this role, I will definitely need to get a job on the side.*

My phone suddenly goes off. It's Rich. I bite my bottom lip, debate answering it or ignoring it. Finally, I decide to answer. I can't see Rich anymore. I am getting involved with him way too quickly. I don't want to be part of his "girls", getting auditions because of what I do with him.

Rich wants to see me, so I agree to meet him at a coffee shop close by. Kathy is curled up in bed, sleeping off what she calls her "audition hangover". I dress quickly and pull my hair up in a loose ponytail, throwing only a little makeup on. Is this a break-up? I am not sure what to think of it as. I just know I need to get everything back in control.

Rich is looking around the coffee shop distastefully when I step inside. It is very small and rundown. Probably not what he is used to in Beverly Hills. As I watch him look at the menu with a frown, I try to think of what I like so much about him. Everything I come up with seems to be linked to superficial things – his looks, his house, his air success. I shake my head to clear my thoughts and go over to him.

"There you are. Have you been here before? They don't even have soy milk," Rich says in a put-off tone, looking back at the menu.

"Yeah, they just sell regular coffee," I reply dryly.

We each order a coffee and sit down at one of the small tables in the back. The place is decorated with things that look like they came from a storage unit. Trip-hop plays over the speakers, giving the entire café a sort of dream vibe to it. I find myself enjoying it, even though Rich is hating every second.

"I'm glad you answered my call. I wanted to talk to you about the audition," Rich says as he dumps a sugar packet into his coffee.

"Me, too, actually."

Rich leans forward as if he is going to tell me a secret. "It's between you and Kathy."

I freeze. "What?"

"Yeah, they really loved the passion you brought to the audition. But your friend is polished and really on top of things. They liked that she had experience as well." He shrugs.

"Kathy deserves it," I say automatically.

"Do you really believe that? Listen, they are leaning toward Kathy. But I'd be more prone to helping you out if you, you know…"

I stare at him. "What?"

"If you'd like to come over and spend the night." He raises his eyebrows.

"Are you asking me to sleep with you for the part?" I reply, barely able to keep my voice to a whisper.

"What? Don't tell me you thought the other times were because we had slept together." He waves his hand. "No, I merely helped you out with getting a callback because we were hanging out."

"And what, this is a formal notice?" I reply icily.

"What's the big deal? I thought we had an understanding."

"How the hell did we have an understanding?"

Rich looks surprised. "I showed you around the city. I could tell you wanted to fuck. That's fine, I like throwing girls a bone every now and then." He grins. "But I mean… I just wanted to show you that we were friends with the callback. That wasn't because we slept together."

"But to get the part I have to sleep with you? That's what you're telling me?"

"I just mean I can scratch your back if you scratch mine."

The ice melts and rage overcomes me. *Stupid! So stupid to fall for this guy!* I stand up, wanting to throw my coffee at him, but he's not worth the effort. I am seeing red. He *threw me a bone* by fucking me the first time. Gave me the callback because we are "friends". But now if I want the part, I am supposed to sleep with him again?

"And what about the night at your home?" I ask him through clenched teeth.

"Fun between friends. I thought you knew we weren't exclusive."

"I know I was just one of your 'girls'. But I'm not sleeping with you to get a part. You misread everything that happened between us. I slept with you because I liked you. I wasn't expecting you to get a callback for me or do me any favors. And I am not sleeping with you for a role. Go fuck yourself."

I turn sharply on my heel and storm out of the coffee shop. Rich doesn't come after me. I am fuming! I agreed to see Rich to tell him I can't see him anymore. Instead, he tries to get me to fuck him for a soap opera role. My knuckles are turning white from my angry fists. Kathy deserves that role. If it comes down between sleeping with Rich to get it and Kathy getting it, then she needs to get that role.

I have taken care of Rich, even if it was in a way I hated. I am going to lose the soap opera role, which means I am going to need find a job soon and fast. Next, I have to figure out how to handle seeing Jon. He is still my agent. Do I want to keep him as an agent? Will I be able to move on from my feelings with him?

I decide I will give him a call.

Jon agrees to meet me at the cheap taco shop across the street from the apartment.

"Traffic is brutal today so I'll come to you to make things easier. I'm about to leave the office anyway," he says on the phone.

I have agreed because I feel that I may have been too rash with him the last time we had spoken. And with Rich being an absolute asshole, how can things get worse today? No, better to clear the air with Jon and see if I need a new agent.

I head over to the small taco shop. I can see Jon already inside, drinking a soda. He looks out the window and waves when he sees me. I step inside.

"Hey. I was waiting for you before I ordered anything," Jon says as he stands up, making his way to the counter.

As we order our food, I look at him out of the corner of my eye. Jon is wearing his glasses and just a T-shirt and jeans. I have never seen him look so casual before. He looks incredibly handsome. My chest tightens when I think about how I had been falling for him before everything had gotten so messy.

Once we get our food and sit down in the booth, Jon speaks first.

"I'm glad you called me. I feel like our wires have been crossed since the night we went to the restaurant down the street. I hadn't meant for things to happen like that."

"I could have handled it better myself," I admit. "Not been so hard on you and listened to you. I cut you off in the lobby, too. I shouldn't have."

"I understand why you did though. I know you overheard… Kathy and me talking about our past."

"I lost my cool. Completely. It was lame of me. What you went through with Kathy is your own past. Not mine."

"Right." Jon shifts in his seat. "But the other thing I said… about how I have no feelings for you…," Jon's voice almost trails off as he's gathering his thoughts.

Did I read everything wrong? I think to myself. I mean, I used to think that I could read guys pretty well. But I could have just fucked it all up.

"I just said that because Kathy had been so upset about me moving on from her. I just tried to diffuse the situation, and I handled it terribly. I'm sorry."

I peer up at him, my heart starting to beat quickly. "Does this mean that you're… you're saying you were lying?"

For the first time ever, I see Jon blush. "I was lying. I am interested in you. I have a great time with you. I want to see this how far it goes."

Relief sweeps through me. Jon *is* interested in me. I haven't misread the signs. I smile at him.

"That's great," I breathe. "I'm happy to hear that."

"You're…?"

"Interested… Yes. I still am interested."

Jon smiles and crams his mouth full of a bite from his burrito to try to hide it. When he swallows, he looks thoughtful.

"I probably shouldn't be your agent anymore. Conflict of interest."

"Yeah, I was thinking the same thing."

"We'll see what happens with this soap opera audition and then go from there."

Part of me wants to tell Jon what has happened with Rich. But at the last second, I change my mind. I feel stupid to tell him that I haven't listened to his warnings about Rich and had fallen into his arms not once, but twice. How could I have been blinded by someone like Rich? After what I have gone through with Paul and Robbs, I hoped I would avoid this sort of shit forever.

Telling Jon how badly I had fucked up makes me embarrassed. I can't bear to see the look on his face when I tell him I had been used by Rich. No, better just to let it fade away. When I don't get the audition, we can move on from the entire mess.

"Sounds good," I say, and I smile.

Chapter Fourteen

When my phone goes off early Monday morning, I jolt awake. I was having another nightmare. The same one as always. Robbs' hands on me and the stairs raising up to meet my face. The pain in my stomach. Then the dream melts into something else. Maggie is crying somewhere. I am running through a house that just seems to grow larger and larger. Every room I check is empty. All I can hear is her crying. Her cries grow louder and louder by the time I finally find a room that has a crib in it. As I run over to check the crib, I suddenly wake up.

My phone keeps ringing. My heart is pounding as I look around my tiny bedroom, trying to catch my breath. I am dripping with sweat, as if I have actually been running. I see it is Jon. I pick it up.

"Hello?" I try to calm myself down.

"Hey, did I wake you?"

"No," I lie. "What's up?" Breathing normally now.

"I heard from the soap opera today. They decided to go with someone else for the role. I'm sorry, Jenny. I know you tried your best. But they just wanted someone with more experience."

I already knew I wasn't going to get the role but tried to sound upset. "Well, I tried my hardest. Can't win them all. I'll call you later, okay?"

I hang up, trying to still my racing heart. The nightmare was so vivid. It feels as if I was actually running around trying to find out where my daughter is. I wish Jon had waited a few extra seconds before he ended up calling me. I want to know if Maggie was in the crib.

It doesn't matter, even if she was. She isn't here anymore, Jenny. I know that. I know I'll never see or hold my daughter. She is gone from this world. The closest I can get to her will be in dreams. I will fight to see her in dreams.

I think back to what Kathy has said about living in her fear and using it to get herself through the auditions. The thought of sinking into the bad memories of my past and going through them terrify me. It is easier to run from them and pretend that they never happened. The thought of facing them head on and living through them again is too much to bear.

I slink out of bed and into the shower, scrubbing myself so raw that my skin is bright red. I allow the hot water to roll over me. I imagine the dream is rolling off of me and going down the drain where I don't have to think about it anymore.

Once I feel okay, I finish the shower and step out, thinking about the audition. I knew I wasn't going to get it after I refused to sleep with Rich for the part. But I have to stop beating myself up over it as well. I fell into Rich's trap. I got lured in by his good looks and his charm. I ended things with him because I wanted to but I am refusing to let him suck me back in again. I haven't heard from him since I told him to fuck off anyway.

"Jenny? Jenny?" Kathy calls.

I quickly wrap a towel around me and poke my head out. Kathy is standing in the kitchen, positively glowing. I know the news before she says it.

"I got the part!" she squeals.

"You did? That's amazing!" I cry. "I would hug you but…," Kathy can see I got out of the shower, my wet hair dripping water all over the floor.

Kathy laughs. "It's okay. Finish getting ready."

I duck back into the bathroom. Kathy stands outside the door and tells me about how she has just gotten the call.

"Apparently it came down to me and one other girl. But one of the casting directors didn't think she would work well with the cast, so they picked me!"

I bite my tongue as I comb out my hair. Is that the bullshit Rich has told them? I feel unnerved by the entire experience. I know Mr. Grant and the others liked how well I took direction. But the entire audition and callback was only due to Rich. Am I really talented or just a complete flop? I feel insecure. But I refuse to let any of this ruin Kathy's moment.

"That's amazing!" I cry through the door. "You must be so thrilled!"

"This steady gig means I can take a break from the infomercials I kept getting cast in not to mention those terrible B-movies. My last one was about aliens who took over beavers' bodies. I mean, really?"

"Wow that does sound terrible," I reply, finally dressed and opening the door.

Kathy laughs. "I know!" Then her face falls. "Oh, honey, I'm sorry. Here I am blabbing away when that means you didn't get the part."

"I'm sure Jon will call me any minute to tell me. It's fine, honestly. You deserved it more than me."

"You have talent. I feel confident that you can do it."

"Well, they will probably make a sequel to your alien beaver movie, right? I can play your sister or something," I joke.

Upon seeing I wasn't angry, Kathy relaxes and pulls me in for a hug. I am truly happy for her. She deserves the part. My phone goes off again in my bedroom.

"It's probably Jon," I say.

Kathy nods, darting off, holding her phone and getting ready to call her family about the news.

It is Jon calling. I answer.

"Jenny," His tone is odd and my grasp on the phone tightens. "Can you come down here? Right away?"

"Right now? I can see —"

"Please hurry. At my office."

He hangs up. I find myself staring at the phone in confusion. I grab my purse and tell Kathy what is going on. She insists I use her car.

"I don't need it until two this afternoon," she says to me, covering her phone as she speaks to her parents. "So just have it back by then."

I say thanks and dart out toward her car. A sick feeling has formed in my stomach. Something about Jon's tone had seemed so different than usual. What could he possibly need to see me right away for? I try to think if there is something I am missing, something in the big picture that I should make sure to discuss with him but nothing comes to mind.

Naturally I hit traffic. Any Zen I have been feeling is quickly wiped away by rage as I wish people learned how to drive. It takes what feels like ages to get to his office. I try to imagine what would make Jon sound so stressed out but I am not sure what it can be. Maybe I am reading too much into his tone. It could be that he just wants to see me about the audition. I did sound strange on the phone when he called me the first time. My mind had still been in the nightmare. Someone could take that as me freaking out and wanting to be alone.

I finally get to his office building and park the car. I try to control my breathing but I can't shake the feeling that I am going to get bad news. *What else could get out of control?* With a racing heart, I make my way inside of the lobby. It is almost empty. There are a few other agents housed in the same building, and I see one girl in a corner, fighting with someone on her phone.

I get into the elevator and anxiously wait till the doors open for me to step out into the waiting room of his office.

His assistant is there, pink neon nails and big hair. She smiles at me. "Oh, I'll let him know you're here."

She buzzes in the back and nods a couple of times before lowering the phone. "He'll see you now."

I nod and follow her down the hallway. She doesn't seem stressed out. Maybe this isn't a big deal at all. Wouldn't she know if it is something truly bad? I know I am grasping at straws at this point.

I can't really think of anything else as I step inside his office. Jon is at the computer, a frown on his face. My heart is racing. I want to shake whatever he has to tell me out of him.

"Jenny," he says as his assistant leaves, shutting the door behind us.

"Hey. I came as quickly as I could. What's going on? Is this about the soap opera? Because I'm fine. I'm glad that Kathy got it." I barely finish what I'm saying when Jon cuts me off.

"It isn't about the soap opera. Sit down."

"Oh. Okay." I sit down, suddenly feeling like a school kid about to get in trouble from the principal.

"I got something in the mail today."

I nod, not following what in the world Jon is talking about.

"I wish you would have told me about this."

"Told you about what?" I ask, starting to feel incredibly stupid and slightly annoyed.

Jon sighs. "Jenny, please. Don't make me say it out loud."

"I honestly don't know what the hell you are talking about." I am starting to lose my temper now.

Jon rubs his eyes and suddenly I am terrified about what he is going to tell me.

"The sex tape, Jenny. I wish you would you have told me about the sex tape."

-To be continued in Book 2-

Book Two

Chapter One

THE FEAR crushes me. I feel it on my chest, alive and burrowing its way inside of me. I gasp for air and spin around. Robbs lurks behind me, somewhere in the shadows. He calls my name. His throat is raw and hoarse. He calls my name again, and I scream, kicking off the ground with my heels. The world spins around me, and all I can think about is my child. I have to protect Maggie.

But Robbs comes out of the darkness. His hands are outstretched. I scream again, wildly, hoping someone will come for me. But his hands press against my back, and the world swirls in different shades of red as I connect with the stairs. I fall down them, and pain lances through me like a sharp blade.

Suddenly I stop falling. My vision goes in and out. Someone cackles over me – a sick grin twisting their face. More faces appear, laughing at me. They are clowns, I realize, as the pain makes my stomach ache brutally.

One more face appears. Robbs looms over me with a sick grin. He lets out another loud laugh and suddenly everything fades to black.

I awaken with a start, jolting upright in my bed. My fingers are wrapped up in my T-shirt, and I am panting.

My entire body is covered in a cold sweat, my hair is stuck to my face. I let out a trembling breath, looking around the room in a panic, trying to remember where I am. A wild glance over at the night table shows me it is a little past three in the morning. I feel groggy and sick, as if I am going to vomit. My eyes land on chocolates on my dresser, and I remember Kathy gave them to me in an attempt to cheer me up.

Kathy. I am in Hollywood. I remember everything in quick flashing images. Moving to Hollywood to try my luck at acting. Meeting Jon and Rich and quickly becoming torn between the two of them. Jon and Kathy dating. Rich and I sleeping together. Losing out on a part in a soap opera only to find out that Kathy landed one. Jon calling me in to tell me he had received a sex tape from Robbs.

I shut my eyes tightly. I have been trying so hard to move on from my past. The terrible things that I have done to people, like Kiara and Paul. I remember how I used my pregnancy to get what I wanted out of them. I was a terrible person. Since Robbs pushed me down the stairs, I have been trying to be on the straight and narrow. Coming to terms with the fact I had suffered at the hands of an emotional and physical relationship is not easy. Yet it is even harder when that person returns to torment you.

I get out of bed, padding my way toward the bathroom. Kathy is fast asleep on the other side of our small apartment, which we've nicknamed "The Dollhouse". Her first day of shooting on the soap set is in the morning. A part of me wishes it was me who was heading to the studio, but it would have meant having to sleep with Rich for the part.

I step inside the bathroom and splash cold water on my face, trying to forget the nightmare. It is the same thing every night – the same terrible dream, a strange mix of memory and twisted horror movie imagery – that has kept me exhausted and out of sorts the past week. I look at myself in the mirror. The moon casts a shadow along the bathroom, making my features look haggard.

A week ago, Robbs returned to my life. The asshole had sent Jon a sex tape. He hadn't said anything to Jon, just sent the tape. But as soon as I looked over and saw a scene from it, briefly, in the privacy of my bedroom after Jon sent me the email, I threw up. The sight of Paul and I entangled together was too much to bear. The threat is clear – *I have this tape. I can ruin you at any moment. You thought you escaped but you will always be under my thumb.*

Robbs and I had been so pleased with the plan originally. It was the perfect way to set-up Paul and put Kiara in her place. I had detested her for so long. It clouded my judgement. But now that lapse in judgement was coming back to bite me in the ass, big time.

I splash more water on my face to keep a panic attack from blooming. I have been locked up in my room the past week. Finally, Kathy asked what was going on and I told her. She knows about Robbs and filling in the blanks is easier than telling Jon the entire story. How do I tell him that I slept with Paul in a scheme to get back at Kiara? Why don't you just paint *Terrible Person* on my head and be done with it? My feelings for Jon are so strong that if he decides not to speak to me anymore or drop me as a client, I would be heartbroken.

I turn off the faucet and sit down on the bathroom floor. The tiles are icy cold, and I draw my knees to my chest, closing my eyes. My past will forever haunt me. I could move anywhere in the world, and Robbs would be there, looming over me, a horrifying specter of my past.

I feel frozen, unsure how to plan out my next move. Rich had even called me yesterday although I can't fathom why. Last time we hung out, he told me I had to sleep with him again for a soap opera part, and I told him to fuck off. Part of me couldn't face Jon. I was unsure what to say to him or how to act around him. As my agent, he would want to discuss the tape. As a possible love interest, he would want to know more about the tape. It was a lose-lose situation.

I make my way back to bed. I tell myself I will call Rich in the morning. At least I won't have to explain anything to him. And if he is an asshole, then perhaps letting out my pent-up aggression on him might serve me well.

Chapter Two

"There you are. I almost didn't recognize you. You look…" Rich pauses, as though uncertain how to continue.

"Like a mess, I know," I think to myself, but he's in no position to comment on it.

I don't give him a verbal reply but give him a short nod "hello" instead as I take a seat.

Rich sits down across from me. It is mid-afternoon the following day, and the coffee shop we are sitting in is a far cry from the one where I had told him off. That place was a bit of a dive and had served run-of-the-mill coffee. This place was high-end with coffee names I can't even pronounce. I am also pretty sure I saw a famous reality star ordering in front of me when I came in earlier.

Rich looks great, as usual. My attraction to him, even though our last meeting had been so sour, is still strong. Today there seems to be something different about him. His suit looks new, and his eyes are a sparkling and bright, as if he is going to tell me something interesting.

"I wasn't sure if you were going to return my call." Rich takes a sip of his coffee.

"Me either," I admit. "But I've had a rough week so you caught me with my guard down."

He leans forward slightly, as if to tell me a secret. "Listen, I know our last meeting didn't go so well. And I understand why. I wasn't my best self then."

"No, you weren't," I reply crisply. "You were a total prick."

"I was. I see that now. I've missed you this week."

I make a non-committal noise. The last week I have been solely thinking about myself, Paul, Robbs and Kiara, lost in the ghosts of my past. There has been little thinking of Rich, despite his being a jerk.

He clears his throat. "I know things got a little messy there, near the end, with the soap opera audition. But this week has been pretty eventful for me, and I'd like to make it up to you."

"Make it up to me how?"

"There is this big blockbuster film about to hire some minor roles. Speaking roles and enough to get you noticed by some important players in town."

"And…?"

"Well, I thought about a role for you," Rich says. Is he being sincere? I wonder to myself. "I can get you an audition. I'm working on the hiring for the roles, too. It's about a ninety-percent guarantee I can get you this role, Jenny."

I stare at him, feeling unsure. On one hand, I want to jump at this chance. A role in a blockbuster film? That will bounce my income up considerably. Worrying about jobs will fade away quickly. On the other hand, what if Rich is going to tell me the other ten percent is only promised by sleeping with him? I bite my bottom lip, looking around the coffee shop, as if some answer will pop out at me.

"I know you are hesitant. I understand why. But think about it, at the very least. It is a big deal, after all."

"You'll have to go through my agent," I reply on a whim.

A shadow crosses Rich's face, briefly. "Go through Jon?"

"Yes, that's right. He's still my agent, and I want to go through the proper channels. You say this is a legit offer, right? So then this shouldn't be a problem."

"Right," Rich replies. "Of course. I'll go through Jon then."

I take a sip of my coffee and force a smile, knowing this means I'll have to talk to Jon. "Great."

Jon calls me a few hours later, leaving me a message to come in to see him to discuss an interesting offer that crossed his table. I dread the encounter. There is simply no way that Jon will not want to discuss the sex tape. I take a cab to see him and arrive ten minutes early with my heart pounding.

As I make my way to his office, I ask myself what I am so afraid of. I realize it is his judgement. If I begin to tell him why the sex tape exists, then I worry I will have to explain the rest. Drudging up the past is something I am avoiding. Yet it feels as if I soon will have no choice if I want to keep hope alive that Jon and I will be an item.

His assistant is at her desk. Her hair seems to grow larger each time I see her. Today it is swept up in a large bun. Her lips are bright pink to match the pink sunflower dress she's wearing. Her nails are a neon yellow, and she gives a wave when she sees me. I wonder where in the world Jon found her. She buzzes me in and leads me to the office.

I step inside, looking around. Jon is pouring himself a cup of coffee at the other side of the office. He looks up at me when I enter and smiles. His smile is guarded. He is unsure how to approach me. I give him a smile back, although I am sure it looks forced.

"Jenny. Long time no talk," he says.

The last time I was in here, he had asked me about the sex tape. I merely asked him to send me the email and then bolted, avoiding his calls ever since. Now he is looking at me and I feel naked. I wonder if he watched the video. I feel mortified.

"I got your call," I say, sitting down on the couch near his desk. I am hoping that if I keep this unofficial, he will not feel prone to lecture me about the tape. He sits down on the chair across from me, and my heart constricts. I hoped he would sit next to me. Now I feel as if I am about to be interviewed.

Jon quickly recounts hearing from Rich and the offer he and I discussed earlier. I pretend I have no knowledge of it and when Jon wraps up, I study him. He looks tired and his hair is messy. His glasses rest on the bridge of his nose. He is looking at me kindly, as if I am a wounded bird he wants to pick up and brush off. My heart skips a beat. I'm struck by how handsome he is and how much I still have feelings for him.

"That's an amazing offer," I reply slowly. "What do you make of it?"

"That depends. Am I still your agent? I know we had been discussing you possibly finding other representation but we haven't mentioned it since…" He trails off and I swallow my sense of worry.

"I think you should still represent me," I reply. "At least for now, if that is okay. I haven't exactly looked into going with anyone else."

"That's fine. I think we still have some things we need to discuss. We haven't talked about the email I got a week ago."

I shift in my chair, my skin suddenly itchy. "Do we have to?"

"If you get this role on this movie, and Rich isn't pulling our leg with how much press it could possibly give you, then this person who sent the tape could go to the press. He could leak the tape. If you know who sent it, then we should contact them. Maybe even get a lawyer now before it really does comes back to ruin any future opportunities for you."

I think of seeing Robbs in some court room, or a lawyer's office. I think of his grinning face as he leaks the video to the Internet. Everyone seeing me having sex. I shudder.

"If we poke this person, they could just fight back against us," I say. "It might be better if we just ignore it."

Jon's eyes widen slightly in surprise. "You don't want to do anything about this?"

"No, I think nothing will come of it," I say, avoiding his gaze.

How can I tell him that what I fear is seeing Robbs? I feel better sticking my head in the sand and hoping it goes away than actually dealing with it. The fear of reaching out and talking to Robbs is too much for me to bear. If I even see him, I fear falling on my face and sliding back into old habits. The grip he has on me and the things he could do to me…what if I get pulled back into his claws?

But the words die in my throat. I can feel Jon silently judging me for letting this sex tape float around out there and not wanting to reach out to the person who sent it. I shift in my seat, suddenly wanting to run out of the office.

"Anyway," I say, in an attempt to change the subject. "Should I let you set up the audition through Rich?"

"Jenny, I still feel like we need to seriously discuss this tape. As your agent, I have to be prepared to handle anything that comes your way. If it gets out there, we're going to have a scandal. The fact this person sent it already might be a blessing in disguise. We can take care of it before it gets out of hand."

I think of myself, bent over the bar, Paul buried inside of me and my face flushes. I feel torn between inaction and action. In response, my body feels as if it is simply shutting down instead. How can I face someone like Robbs?

"Hey," Jon says, his voice soft and he leans forward and rests his hand on my arm. "I don't mean to come at you like this. I'm just concerned…as a friend now, not your agent."

"I know." My voice cracks. "Just a lot going on, you know? Easier to avoid it."

"Why don't you come over to my place? We can talk it out in a more relaxed setting. Friend to friend," he proposes.

While I am touched at his offer, the fact he has made sure to mention the word friend twice in under thirty seconds concerns me. Just a week ago, we had been discussing becoming more than that due to our mutual feelings for each other. Now with this sex tape hanging over our heads, we have taken three steps back.

But I brush that concern from my mind. I could use someone to lean on. I crave being around Jon as well. He could be saying the friend line for my sake, I think to myself, so I don't feel pressured.

"That sounds nice," I answer and sigh quietly to myself.

Chapter Three

I grip the glass of iced tea that Jon gave me and sink into his plush couch. His apartment is nowhere near the lap of luxury that Rich lives in, but there was something comforting about it. It smelled like pine wood and was well decorated with old movie posters.

"Cliché, I know," Jon says as he spots me looking at a poster for an old B-movie. "Having all these movie posters around. But I have a weak spot for old films."

"Haven't really seen any of these," I admit. "I can't get over how cheesy they are."

He chuckles. "I guess it is fun to mock them. When I was little, my brother and I used to act them out. Only we added more fight scenes, of course, as an excuse to beat each other up."

I let out a small laugh. "I can't imagine that."

"What, you can't imagine me being strong and tough, beating up my brother?" he asks.

I shake my head. "No, not really. I imagine you sitting around, playing video games."

He pretends to be offended and then grins. "Maybe a little."

I look around the living room. There is a bookshelf lined with books. On a closer glance, it turns out they are art books from various movies and video games. His cat is making soft snoring noises on a cat bed on the other side of the room. I can see his bedroom from here. Everything is in dark colors and suddenly I feel sleepy.

"I like your place," I say suddenly. "It's very cozy unlike the place I have with Kathy. You would think it was cozy too because of its small size, but you actually just feel too large for it."

"Well, if you get this movie deal and with Kathy's soap opera earnings, you two could get a bigger place."

A sudden thought crosses my mind and I frown. "I'll feel bad if I get this movie deal, and she doesn't even get to audition."

Jon studies me for a moment and then takes a sip of his own drink, as if he is chewing on his thoughts. "Jenny, I know I've mentioned it before and probably so has Kathy but…you don't have to hold yourself back because you think someone else deserves it more. If you get this gig on this movie, you don't have to beat yourself up over it."

"I guess I feel bad because Kathy has been doing this a lot longer than me. I feel like I'm just coming in and taking her parts away."

"You haven't taken anything away though," Jon points out. "She got the soap opera role. Are you going to spend every audition thinking Kathy should have it? You have talent, too."

I fall silent. Jon is right, I realize, as I look at the ice in my glass. I can't look at every job that lands in my lap and reject it because I felt as if Kathy is more deserving. I wonder if the reason I want Kathy to get the roles is because she deserves it more as a decent person. Why would I get fame and fortune? I let out a sigh.

"What are you thinking about?" Jon asks. "I lost you for a second."

"Nothing," I mumble. "Just…nervous about the audition, I guess. I have a lot on my mind with everything going on."

"Like the tape."

"Right," I reply, hesitant to bring it up. "Like the tape."

"Do you want to talk about it?"

"I don't know," I admit, unsure if I should tell him Paul was just an ex-lover or go into more of the grisly details.

"Why don't we watch TV instead? And if you decide to talk, we can talk."

I agree. The next few hours is nothing but terrible reality TV and watching Jon's face as he tries to suffer through it in silence. At one point, I swore I saw an eye roll but he merely smiled at me when he caught me staring. Not once did he complain about what was on.

The feeling of being comfortable grew. Before I could think twice, my eyelids become heavy and I drift off into sleep.

When I wake up, I take a few seconds to try to get my bearings. The room is dark. The TV is off. Someone is snoring. For a moment, fear grips me. I wonder if I am having another one of my dreams. I slide my fingers to my other arm and pinch the skin. There is a brief flash of pain, and I relax. *You can't feel pain in dreams.* I shift my weight to look around.

It comes back to me quickly. Falling asleep watching TV with Jon. He is snoring softly next to me. His body is warm, and I notice how close we are. The clock above the TV shows it is close to midnight. I must have been exhausted. The last week had been rough and I've been having difficulty getting to sleep. But being around Jon relaxes me.

I find myself staring at his outline in the darkness. I can trace his jawline with my eyes. His glasses are slightly askew on his nose, making him look boyish. My heart skips a beat. A want to lean over and kiss him. See where it leads. But I think back to how he said the word *friends* twice and hadn't made a move on me all night. If he rejects me, I won't be able to stand it.

I move an inch away from him. He doesn't move. I wonder if I should leave. But the thought of going back to my bedroom in the Dollhouse makes me sad. What would be the harm in staying, asleep on the couch, next to him? Friends can sleep next to each other, right?

I lean back on the plush couch and before I can count to ten, I fall back into the embrace of sleep.

Chapter Four

The audition room for a big movie like *Recoil factor* - based off a popular 80's TV show that ended up as a franchise - is a lot different than the audition room for a soap opera. For one thing, it isn't nearly as crowded. The soap opera had over fifty women there. This movie one has only about five. Three of the women I recognize from magazine spreads as rising stars. The other woman next to me wasn't ringing any bells but her calm and collected demeanor makes it clear this isn't her first rodeo.

I am feeling much more nervous than I dare to admit to anyone. Kathy had wished me good luck, as had Jon, early this morning. As much as Rich has promised that the role is practically mine to make up for his shitty behavior, as I look at the women around me, I feel so nervous that I want to crawl under my chair and hide.

I have spent the last two days fully learning my lines for this role. The supporting role as the rebellious daughter of the male lead seems run of the mill to me. The film was special effects heavy, focusing more on giant battles between creatures that have escaped from the core of the planet rather than the actual characters. That is good and bad. On the plus side, people will see the movie, which meant people would see *me*. On the bad side, I am not feeling confident that anyone would *remember* me in the role.

As I wait to be called into the room, one of the girls I recognize from magazines goes in first. Her hair is long and platinum. She was obviously not born with that color. I try to take comfort in the fact that I am at least a natural blonde. I think back to Kathy telling me how she used her emotions from events in her past to tackle the auditions. At the time it terrified me to even consider such a thing. But now, on the cusp of an even bigger audition, I think about what I have been putting off.

Moving to Hollywood helped me run from my past. Prior to that, I punished myself for my deeds, living alone and shunning anyone I knew. I welcomed misery. Yet why bring the punishments on myself when Robbs is still clearly interested in doing it for me?

At the thought of Robbs, my mood sours. My taste in men is forever dismal, I think as another girl is called to the back room. I wonder dimly if maybe the first woman didn't do so well, which would explain why she was finished already. I wonder if Rich is going to be in there as well. I swear to myself that if he calls me after this audition and tells me to sleep with him for the part, I am going to clock him. I try to banish thoughts of Robbs from my brain. The last thing I need right now is to be tangled up in the past with Robbs, Paul and Kiara.

My name is finally called. I'm the last one. I take a deep breath and stand up, hoping I look presentable. I still feel out of my element with these auditions. The fact I am about to do one for a major film rattles me, but I promise myself not to let it show. I step inside the room and instantly see Rich. His hair is slicked back, and he is texting someone on his phone but looks up and smiles when he sees me. I smile back and stand in the middle of the room. In front of me is a short, stocky man with an assistant who looks like she could be a supermodel.

They all introduce themselves. The man is the director - Fredrick - and his assistant's name is Marina. Rich gives me a small wave and Fredrick nods as if he is thinking.

"Rich has spoken highly of you," Fredrick says. "He said that you have a raw talent that would do well in an action film like this."

I realize that I am supposed to sell myself and clear my throat. "I'm sure you have other actresses here who have a more impressive resume than I do. But if you are willing to take a chance on new talent, then I promise I won't fail to deliver. In fact, I'll probably work harder than they will, because I want to prove myself so much to you."

Fredrick gives a slight nod to Rich. "Okay. Let's run through some scenes."

The following half hour is mentally exhausting. Fredrick and Marina put me through my paces, going through scenes that I haven't even gone over because they weren't in the packet given to me. I try my best, hoping that even though I am reading lines, I am giving them what they are looking for. Everything fades away as I throw myself into the character. As I focus on the lines, any concerns about Robbs and the past are merely background noise. Instead, I focus on giving Fredrick what he is looking for – proving to him that I am made for his film and will make it interesting.

At the end of thirty minutes, Marina thanks me and promises me that they will be in touch. Before I leave, Rich gives me a wink. My hearts soars as I step out into the hallway. I am hoping that wink means I killed it. Suddenly I realize how much I want this job. If I forget about Kathy and my guilt about taking a job from someone I deem more worthy than me, I realize that I am ready to have this role. As I head downstairs to the lobby, I decide to call Jon and tell him that I think it has gone well.

I notice an email notification on my phone. I have not gotten an email in ages that wasn't spam. Curious, I read it. The email is from a sender I do not know and is titled *Instructions Within.* I suddenly feel nervous and sit down in a chair. The receptionist looks at me but I ignore her as I click the email open.

I find myself staring at a screenshot of me bent over the bar with Paul behind me. My breath catches as I scroll down to read the body of the email:

Jenny,

I have not heard from you yet. I originally sent the email to your agent. Maybe he declined to show you the video I so graciously sent to him. In any case, I am reaching out to you now. Please email me back agreeing to pay me $100,000 or the video is leaked to the public.

Robbs

For a second, my vision dims. My head goes light and I find myself staring at the email until the words blur together. I feel disgusting, as if I suddenly need to take a long shower. The words are seared onto my skin.

Pay him $100,000, I think numbly, lowering my phone to my lap. I don't have that sort of money. Even if I get this movie deal, will I even be paid anywhere near that much?

"Jenny, didn't think you would still be here."

I look up, still completely out of it. Rich is standing in front of me, concern etched along his face. I try to plaster a smile on my face but it fails. I end up giving him a soft grunt in reply instead.

Rich glances over his shoulder and then sits down in a chair next to me. "Jenny? What's wrong?"

"Nothing," I lie quickly and his eyebrows arch. "Nothing, I just... coming down from the audition. Did I do okay?"

"Yes, you were great. I'm sure you'll get it."

"Do you know how much it will pay?"

Rich's brow furrows. "No, Jenny. Not off the top of my head. I hope you aren't looking for some A-list movie star salary though. I understand that it'll be your first role and to be on a big-budget movie like this is a big deal, but you shouldn't go around asking about money to anyone else. It might rub people the wrong way."

"So you don't know?" I reply, tuning out the rest of his lecture.

"No. Sorry." He stands up, as if I have put him off and gives a small nod. "I'll talk to you later."

I watch him depart, feeling hopeless. I imagine everyone seeing the video, and I curse myself yet again for my stupidity. If I could go back in time and stop myself from making such a stupid mistake, I would do it in a heartbeat.

Feeling defeated and panicked, I stand up. I waver on the spot and for a second I think I might fall over. The receptionist is looking at me with an odd look on her face so I walk out of the building.

Before I second guess myself, I call Jon.

Chapter Five

Jon looks out the window of his apartment, biting the tip of his thumb, lost in thought. I sit at his kitchen table, taking a sip of tea. He kindly offered peppermint tea, claiming it helps with headaches and anxiety. Since headache pills weren't working, I am drinking the tea as if it is some sort of life-changing elixir.

"You can't pay him, obviously." Jon finally says.

The sky is overcast and threatening rain. Absentmindedly, I try to recall the last time I have seen rain. Not since I moved to Hollywood. "If I don't pay him, then he'll show everyone the video."

"And if you do pay him, everyone sees the video anyway and you're out $100,000," Jon counters.

I give a small shrug. "Does it matter? I don't have the money to begin with."

"I think you should tell him you have the money and meet with him."

"Are you nuts?"

Jon stiffens and turns to face me. "No. I'm not *nuts*, Jenny. This guy is always going to be there, holding this over your head. You have to face him."

"I can't," I mumble. "I can't."

Jon sits down next to me, studying my face. "Why? I know it's scary but—"

"Because he's the reason I lost my child."

The words hang in the air, heavy with their implication. Jon's eyes widen, and I look away. Jon isn't understanding the situation. He isn't understanding what Robbs can do and has done before. But that is my fault. I have told him before that I was pregnant and lost the child. But I never told him how.

"What?" Jon whispers as there is a sudden clap of thunder.

"We were an item. He pushed me down the stairs. I lost Maggie," I say in a monotone voice, as if I was merely stating the weather.

"Oh my god. Jenny…" His voice trails off, and he reaches out to touch me but I flinch and pull my arm away, standing up.

"So I can't go to him, okay? I just can't. It isn't just someone with a sex tape of me, Jon. I just want to pay him and make him go away."

"But Jenny, he won't go away. He'll just come back. What is to stop him from telling you that $100,000 isn't enough? What if he wants more after that? What if this movie does well and you end up in the spotlight? Why would he stop then?"

His questions are too much for me. I suddenly feel defensive, as if he is blaming me for what is going on.

The logical part of me tells me to calm down and listen but I still am in fight-or-flight mode. The thought of confronting Robbs puts me in a pure panic.

"Did you not listen to me?" I ask him. "I lost my child because of this man, Jon. You want me to go after a man who pushed me down a flight of stairs!"

"I understand all of that, Jenny. But he won't go away until you show him you aren't afraid."

"He just wants money," I say, wondering if I say it enough I will begin to believe it. "If I give him the money, he'll go away."

"I don't think so," Jon whispers.

I stand up, trying to control my breathing. "I have to find a way to pay him off. You have to try to get me at least $100,000 out of the movie."

"I'll see what I can do, but I don't know, Jenny. I have to be honest with you, I don't see that happening. This is your first role. If you get it, I can see maybe $30,000. I can fight for $35,000. But I don't see $100,000."

I put my hands against my forehead. My headache is pounding now, as if there is some sort of techno party going on in my head. I had been banking on getting $100,000 to make Robbs go away. It is how I saw myself getting out of this situation.

"Jenny, you need to relax," Jon was saying, although his voice sounded far away, "You need to tell Robbs you have the money and meet with him. I'll go with you. You can tell him you aren't giving him a cent.

Tell him you'll tell everyone about what he did to you and Maggie. Did you tell the police what he had done?"

"You have to understand, I need to get this money to him." Hysteria edged my voice and a cold sweat broke out along my back.

Jon reaches out for me but suddenly the apartment feels like its closing in. If I am not going to get the money through Jon, then I will have to find another way. Jon's idea of confronting Robbs is too terrifying to consider.

"I have to go," I mumble as the sky opens up and rain pounds against Jon's window.

"Jenny, wait!"

But I turn sharply and get to his front door before he can stop me. I walk out of his building and into the rain. I don't have a jacket and have been taking cabs everywhere. Shrugging it off, I walk out into the pouring rain, not caring about how soaked I am going to get.

As I walk along the streets of Hollywood, most likely getting myself lost in the process, I try to think about what to do next. How to get $100,000. Jon's warning that Robbs won't go away floats in my head. I feel desperate. If the tape gets out, I will be shunned and my blossoming career over before it truly begins. If I pay the money, Robbs will go away – unless Jon is right and he just demands more money.

The thought of meeting with Robbs and trying to put him in his place spurs me on to walk even faster. I get a couple of curious looks from tourists as I storm along the sidewalks. I don't care. *Jon doesn't understand. He has no idea what I have been through. I cannot meet with Robbs and look at him in the face.*

My phone goes off in my pocket. I duck under an awning and fumble for it, seeing Kathy's name. I don't feel like talking to her and hit ignore.

"You can't stand here unless you buy something," the man in a food truck next to me says, jabbing at the air with his finger.

One look at his hot dogs tells me I am not hungry. I duck back into the rain, not sure where I am. For the first time, this doesn't bother me. The streets and people blend together and I keep walking. My phone goes off again and it is Jon. But I don't have any desire to speak to him. He will just keep pressuring me to speak to Robbs.

I sit down on a bench outside a tacky souvenir shop that takes your photo and sticks it in famous movie scenes. A family of three is currently posing for one. The couple looks older, their son nearby. He looks around five years old and is clinging to an action figure I recognize from the movie I auditioned for.

If my sex tape gets out, his parents probably won't want me in any more of the movies. Maybe they'll start an Internet petition. Those were all the rage currently, letting anyone with a computer feel as if they are accomplishing something. It isn't as if I'm a well-respected actress already who could bounce back from it.

My fingers, now numb from the cold, fumble into my pocket to retrieve my phone. The screen is smeared with water as I use my purse to hide it from the falling rain. I look for Rich's name and before I can second guess myself, I hit send and hear it ringing.

He answers on the third ring.

Chapter Six

"I used to think having a fireplace in warmer climates was a total cliché but now I don't mind at all," I say, yanking the blanket over me and warming myself up to the fire in Rich's living room.

Rich's laugh is warm and throaty. I can smell the Scotch he is pouring on the other side of the room. Part of me wants to ask for some and part of me knows it won't do my headache any favors.

"Well, you need to warm up. You were positively drenched by the time I got to you. Looked like a lost puppy."

"I feel like a lost puppy," I mumble, although the fire is comforting.

On the drive over, I had told Rich what was going on. He had listened and taken me to his house. Now that we are here, however, I realize that it is time for me to broach why I have really called him. I suddenly regret not asking for a drink.

He sits down across from me, taking a sip of his Scotch. "What are you going to do? Are you going to listen to Jon?"

"What do you think I should do?"

"Pay him off, obviously."

"Why do you sound so sure? Jon says he'll just ask for more money."

"Listen, stars deal with this all the time. It'd be a lot simpler if everyone stopped filming themselves fucking but I don't see that stopping any time soon. This guy wants money. He's probably broke. Give him the money and get the tape. Then it's over with."

"You make it sound so simple," I mumble.

"Isn't it?"

"If you have $100,000."

I hold my breath, not daring to look up at Rich. I need him to lend me this money but coming right out and asking for it feels wrong.

"Why don't I let you borrow it?"

I look up, relief flooding through me. "What? You'd do that?"

"We're friends, right?" There is that dreaded word again. "And I told you that I would make it up to you for the soap opera audition."

"But haven't you? You're getting me this role on this blockbuster movie."

"Then consider it as friends helping out friends."

"I'll pay you back," I say, sitting up straighter.

"You can make it up to me, don't worry," Rich says, standing up. "Come on. Let's get you to the guest room."

I follow him upstairs where he leads me to the lavish guest bedroom. The last time I had been here, I had found out about Kathy and Jon dating. Rich and I had slept together in his room. This time, however, he doesn't try anything and shuts the door behind him. It is in the middle of the day, yet I feel exhausted. I peel off my wet clothes and go into the bathroom. I step in the shower and let the warm water flow over me.

Knowing that I will have the money to give to Robbs finally makes my headache lessen. *Pay him off, get the tape,* I repeat to myself as I soap up my body. Once I have the tape, he won't have anything else on me.

After my shower, I curl up in the giant California king-sized bed and drift off to sleep.

"You'll be at the table behind me, right?" I ask for the millionth time.

Rich nods. "Yes, Jenny. I promise. We are going to go in. You'll give Robbs the money and get the tape. Then we are done."

I exhale slowly and nod. I am so nervous that I can feel sweat on the back of my neck, underneath my ponytail. No matter how many times I tell myself that it will all be over soon, the fact that I am going to see Robbs makes me incredibly nervous.

I emailed Robbs, saying I had the money and would give it to him in exchange for the tape. He had emailed me back almost instantly with this address and a time. I had been wide awake ever since, unable to focus on anything else.

"It'll all be over soon," Rich repeats and squeezes my hand.

I look over at him, grateful to have his friendship. Knowing he truly wants to make amends for hitting me up for sex for a role has made our friendship even stronger. Unlike where I feel with Jon – suddenly back in the "friend" zone – I know Rich and I are solid.

"It's because of you that this is possible," I say to him. "I never would have been able to get him off my back if it weren't for you."

"Don't mention it," he replies, almost shrugging it off.

I look back at the small diner. It looks ancient, as if it is a relic from the actual fifties. Judging by the people going in and out, it is just rundown and a cheap place to eat.

"Be brave," Rich whispers and we get out of his car.

My heart is pounding in my chest. I worry that it might actually explode and I will going to collapse on the parking lot. The sky is still overcast from yesterday, and I wonder if it is going to rain yet again. As if in reply, I see a flash of lightning nearby.

I step inside the diner and look around. It is dingy inside with Elvis crooning over the tinny sound system, as if he is singing in a cave somewhere. A group of truckers is at the front of the diner and a family with five squalling children is at a booth on the other side.

I see him. My breath catches. Suddenly I want to turn around and leave. This is a terrible idea. At that moment, Robbs looks up. He sits up straighter and my feet begin to move automatically. I have no choice now. I need to get through this. I sit down across from him, taking a quick glance to make sure Rich has entered now. We had made sure to agree on him entering thirty seconds after me so Robbs wouldn't notice.

"Great, you're here," Robbs says and his voice is so familiar and yet different enough that it makes the hair on the back of my neck stand up.

The cheap vinyl seat sticks to my thighs. My tongue is stuck to the roof of my mouth as I look at him. There is a shifting motion behind me, which I take as Rich sliding into the booth behind me.

A tired-looking waitress comes over, putting a plate of pancakes in front of Robbs.

"What will you be having?" she asks me and when I don't reply, she repeats the question louder.

"She'll have water," Robbs suddenly says and the waitress gives a curt nod.

I hear her move over to ask Rich what he wants, and he orders a coffee. When she walks out of ear shot, Robbs leans forward over his pancakes.

"You have it?"

"Yes." I reply, finally unsticking my tongue from the roof of my mouth.

"Great, hand it over." He reaches for the purse next to me.

I pull away from him, as if he is trying to throw acid on me and clutch the purse in my lap. His expression does not change. He looks bored with me, as if I am not doing what he needs me to do and he expected it. The waitress comes back with my water, and I tell her I don't want to order anything. She moves on to Rich behind me, without questioning me further. I take a swig of the water and then fix my gaze on Robbs.

"No money till the tape," I say, holding out my hand for the flash drive. "Hand it over."

Robbs rolls his eyes and shoves his hand in his pocket before pulling out a light blue flash drive. I snatch it out of his hands and then push the purse across the table. Robbs unzips it halfway and peers inside.

"Since we have such a long history together, I'll trust it is all there," he says simply.

I stand up, smashing my knee on the bottom of the table in my panic and walk away as quickly as I can. I open the door of the diner, almost running into an old woman. I realize it is raining again as I make my way to Rich's car before remembering that Robbs cannot see I have any affiliation with him.

Instead I turn blindly around, jogging across the street and stepping inside a smoothie shop. It is mostly empty, except for a group of high school girls sitting in a booth. The man behind the counter looks up at me, and I stumble over and order the first drink I see.

Taking the smoothie, which ended up being a mix of blueberries and bananas, I sit down at a booth near a window. I can see the diner from here. My phone is vibrating and I pull it out, seeing Rich has texted me to tell me that he ordered a couple of pancakes. I tell him where I am and then lean back, watching the diner, going over what has happened.

I know if I tell Jon what I did, he will be angry. He will tell me I should have told Robbs to fuck off and then handle the fallout of the sex tape. But it shows how much he knows, since I currently have the it in my pocket. I owe Rich as many favors as he ever wants because of how he has helped me.

My phone goes off suddenly and it startles me. It is Jon, almost as if I conjured his call. I glance at the diner and then answer.

"Hey," I mumble.

"Jenny, hey. You fell off the radar, everything okay?"

"Wonderful."

Jon hesitates, as if he is trying to determine if he should ask more questions, and then he says, "Congratulations! You got the part of Sophie in the movie!"

Excitement fills me. I sit up straighter and clutch the phone. "Truly?"

"Truly. Can you come in tomorrow to go over the contract and the pay?"

"Yeah, of course. Sounds great. Listen, I have to go, okay?" I say quickly, seeing Robbs suddenly leave the diner.

Before Jon can say anything else, I hang up. I press my nose against the window, trying to see Robbs clearly through the rain. He is getting in a rental car, I realize, and jot down the license plate number on a napkin, just in case I need it. He pulls out of the parking lot and turns left. I lose him in the rain soon after.

I have been so focused on watching Robbs go that I didn't even see Rich enter the smoothie shop. He comes over and sits down across from me, startling me.

"I inhaled those pancakes," he says.

I let out a sigh of relief. "It's over then."

He nods and doesn't say anything in reply. I slump in the booth, suddenly wanting to crawl into bed again. I remember Jon's call and sit up a little.

"Jon called. I got the part!"

Something glints in Rich's eyes briefly and he leans over and grabs my hand, smiling warmly. "That's great!"

I let out a sigh of relief. I hope now the worst is over.

Chapter Seven

"Sort of feels like I'm a clown," I say to Marina, the assistant to the director, as she hovers behind the make-up artist.

"Has to be applied thickly so it shows up properly on camera," she replies, an iPad clutched firmly between perfectly polished fingernails.

"Gotcha," I reply.

It is my first day on set, and I am trying to be as amenable as possible. The entire thing is a new experience for me. Luckily Fredrick is cutting me a break and starting me off with a scene actually on a set, as opposed to the rest of my scenes in front of a green screen.

"So, remember," Marina says, clearly having been told to help me out throughout the day by Fredrick. "Today's scene is Sophie fighting with her father about dropping out of college."

"Right, right," I say, closing my eyes as the make-up artist puts eye shadow on me. "The whole 'it isn't my dream, Dad, it's yours' thing."

I open my eyes. The corners of Marina's mouth twitch, as if she was going to smile but at the last second thought better of it. Instead she just nods and then her phone goes off. She turns around to take the call, and I look at my reflection. I don't recognize myself. The color scheme for my character is vastly different than the one I would use. However, it works. The black eye shadow and red lipstick bring out my blonde hair, although it is still limp around my face. I haven't even gotten to my stylist yet or dressed for the scene.

"Enjoy these few scenes. I think the rest of them have you running from monsters," Rich says from behind me.

He looks like a million dollars. It has been a few days since I gave Robbs the money. I haven't seen Rich since that day. Seeing him now and knowing what he has done for me – giving me this role and giving me the money to pay off Robbs – gives me a warmth that spreads through me.

"I'm excited for that, too," I reply as the make-up artist starts applying my blush.

"Anyway, I just wanted to come by and wish you good luck." He stands behind me, placing his hand on my shoulder.

I am suddenly losing sight of just being friends with him. Things with Jon have taken yet another stall. I find myself unable to even tell him that Robbs is no longer a concern and that I have handled everything. Instead, our meeting over the contract was short and to the point. Part of me is avoiding him, suddenly back in a place I don't understand. I wonder if the sex tape put him off his interest in me. Ever since Jon had found it in his inbox, he had made sure to mention being friends a few times. There have been no more discussions about us as a couple. It is as if we somehow hit the pause button on our entire relationship. I felt unsure of how to proceed.

Like always, Rich is simpler. Yes, he had been an asshole when we were officially seeing one another. But since then, he has been making amends for his shitty behavior. I couldn't ignore it even if I truly wanted to. What he did with Robbs is something else I can't just forget. I am starting to think Rich has truly changed.

"Thank you," I reply and I truly mean it.

My first day ends up being lesson after lesson on acting and working on a set. I soak up everything that I can in an effort to learn more and improve. Like always, acting makes all the other thoughts in my brain stop. I find myself only focusing on my lines and how I can deliver them the best possible way. It is amazing how different being in costume changes my mindset as well. I genuinely felt as if I was Sophie. It was remarkable.

The day ends up going over twelve hours. I blanch at the thought of how long it will take once we begin working on the green screen. I try not to be star-struck by my co-workers – my "dad" is played by aging action star Kane Lucky and his love interest is Rebecca Pike, who is about ten years too young to ever be hooking up with Kane Lucky.

Luckily, I think I play off my nervousness okay. I don't even mention a word about how ridiculous the name Kane Lucky is. By the time we wrap for the day, I am exhausted and head home, thinking of how my bank account will soon swell by $30,000. Jon tried to get $15,000 ahead of time but since it is my first job, the producers don't want to take a chance on me. Not to mention having this film credit on my resume. They don't kill me off in this movie either, which means I can get some screen time in the inevitable sequel.

I stumble into the Dollhouse, letting out a yawn. It is past two am. Yet I am surprised to find Kathy in the living room, her feet up on the couch, watching a late night TV program. When she sees me, she sits up and smiles.

"I feel like I haven't seen you in ages," she says.

I flop down onto the couch next to her. "It's true. We've both been so busy."

I can tell Kathy wants to ask about the sex tape but thinks twice about it and just nods. "We really have been. You have to tell me all about your day on set!"

Even though I am exhausted, I spend the next hour talking with Kathy. Both of us share stories of our jobs. She makes me laugh with her stories about trying to keep a straight face through some of the more ham-fisted dialogue. I make her laugh with my stories about how Kane Lucky ducked out in the middle of shooting to go get Botox done on his face.

However, soon both of us are dozing off on the couch. As we get up and head off toward our respective rooms, I think that maybe for once everything has finally fallen into place.

<<<>>>

"No, no, it's my fault," I say, moving the bag of ice on my knee and wincing slightly. "I'm just clumsy."

The on-set medic looks at me. "You're okay. Just going to be a nasty bruise."

"Thank you for taking the time to look at it."

The medic, an older woman, smiles faintly. "That's my job, sweetie."

I feel like an idiot. It was my first scene dealing with practically only green screen. I instantly feel out of my element as I try to pretend to be terrified by one of the creatures coming out of a lake. However, nothing is there. It takes time getting used to something like that. By the time I finally do and I am feeling good about myself, I turn too sharply and fall off the box I was standing on, landing directly on my left knee.

I move the bag of ice and look at it. Yeah, it isn't going to be pretty. My face flushes with embarrassment. Filming has been halted until the medic gives the all clear. I am determined not to let this slow filming down. The last thing I want to be known for is fucking up production.

"Hey, you okay? I just heard."

I look up and see Rich coming over to me, looking concerned.

I nod. "I'm fine. I think the medic is going to give the all clear and then I can get back to work."

I point to the medic talking to Marina by the set. She is nodding often and glances over at me once or twice before looking down at her iPad, which I have yet to see her without.

"Is your knee okay?"

"It's fine. Might need make-up for it though. It hurts but I can work through it."

Rich sits down next to me, looking at my knee. "Are you sure?"

I nod. "Yeah, shouldn't be a problem, really."

He looks visibly relieved and then looks around quickly before lowering his voice. "Have you heard from Robbs?"

I stiffen. I have been on set for a week and a half now and have been trying my best not to think about Robbs. "No. I think we're in the clear."

A funny expression flies across his face but it is so fast that I swear I imagined it. "That's great. I'm glad. The last thing we want is to have to deal with him again. Did you destroy the tape?"

"Yeah. I deleted it from the flash drive and then dunked the flash drive in the sink for good measure. If I could have set it on fire, I would have, too."

"Great," he replies as his phone goes off. "I have to take this. Be careful."

I nod, and he helps me to my feet. Marina is bustling over as Rich walks off, answering his phone.

"What are you doing calling me on this number?" I
hear him demand but before I can think about it, Marina
is in my face.

"The medic gave the all clear. Can you continue?"

"Definitely," I tell her and she looks relieved.

"Let's get you on the set!" Marina trills.

I push all other thoughts of out of my mind. Time to
get back to work.

I'm home at a decent hour tonight. It is close to
eight as I get back home to the apartment. I can hear
Kathy in the kitchen talking to someone on the phone,
and I find myself hesitant to let her know I am home.
Her tone sounds pleading and urgent.

"I know what I said. But I miss you. Can't you
consider it?" She falls silent and I inch toward the
kitchen. "I thought nothing ended up happening with
you two. I'll even talk to Jenny about it." Another long
pause. "Fine. Fine. Goodnight."

I hear her sigh as she ends the call, and I dart back
to the front door and make a loud noise as I put my
purse on the end table.

Kathy sticks her head out and sees me. Her smile is
wan. "Hey, you're home early."

"Yeah, and I have the next couple of days off, too,"
I say, hoping my tone sounds even. "My character is
lost in the rubble of a city explosion."

I hope my face isn't betraying anything. I am not sure how to feel, knowing that Kathy was just speaking to Jon. She made it clear before that she didn't like Jon trying to woo me. She has told him that she will talk to me about it. So I decide to wait.

I plop down on our couch, squirming a little. It isn't nearly as top of the line as Jon's or Rich's couch. I yank a blanket over me, and Kathy sits next to me, looking stiff.

"How was your day?" I ask her.

"My call time was four am. I got home around one in the afternoon and napped way too long. I'll be up for hours."

Just mentioning a nap elicits a long yawn from me and I stretch out. "I hear that."

Kathy's eyes widen. "Your knee!"

"What? Oh, yeah." I sit up a little and look at my knee.

It is a good thing that I have the next couple of days off. My knee looks terrible. It hurts badly, too. It makes me wish I was an A-list celebrity so I could just call a doctor instantly and get some pain pills. Instead I try to shrug it off.

"My fault. Green screen filming is weird. I took a tumble."

"Are you okay?" She looks closely at the purple hue of my knee.

"I'm okay. I'll just rest up."

Silence falls over us, as I get lost in thought. I wait for her to bring up Jon while pretending I am just flipping through our ten TV channels with an avid interest.

Finally, Kathy clears her throat and shifts her weight to face me. "Listen, Jenny…" She takes a short breath and stumbles on, "I wanted to talk to you about Jon."

"Oh?"

"You know that he and I used to date. Obviously, you know this," she says, stopping herself before she starts rambling. "I know you had feelings for him at one point but lately…you two haven't been hanging out or anything. And I know you hang out with Rich on set from what you've told me and you seem really into him so…" Kathy trails off and looks at me.

I look back at her, unsure if she is expecting me to say something. She hasn't exactly given me a lot to go off.

I clear my throat. "Okay…" I trail off, thinking one word is better than no words at all.

Apparently it is, because Kathy takes this as permission to go on. "I was wondering if you'd be okay if I ask Jon out again."

"Have you talked to Jon about this?" I ask, mostly because I am curious if she is going to lie or not.

"Yes," she says. "I asked if he would consider going out with me but he refused me. Said it was because of what was going on with you. I told him I would talk to you about it and let him know what you said. Maybe he'd want to go out with me if he knows you're okay with it."

I look away from her, watching the local news. It is, as usual, covering a high speed chase. I think about how to answer Kathy's request. Part of me has feelings for Rich, especially after everything he has done for me and apologized for. Yet I still have feelings for Jon as well. I feel as if we never even got off the ground. As soon as we discussed having feelings for one another, the sex tape came up and wiped everything else away. I feel as if I have been placed back to just being friends with him. In my hesitation to discuss what has unfolded with Robbs and paying him off, I let things stagnate. Now I am going to lose my chance completely to see if Jon and I have a future together, all because I am too nervous to sit down and talk with him about my choices, which I know he will disprove of.

"Jenny?" Kathy asks, snapping me back to the present.

"I mean, I don't know," I reply, stalling for time and thinking about the best way to word it. "Jon and I haven't really gotten to discuss anything to do with us."

"Jon says you're avoiding him," Kathy replies quickly, as if she already has everything mapped out in her head. "He says that you two haven't talked about even going out on a date or anything. I told him you were into Rich."

"You told him *what*?" I say, louder than I had expected.

Kathy flinches, as if I have struck her. "I told him you were into Rich."

"Why did you do that?"

"Because you are. You told me yourself you were having feelings for him the other night."

"That was in confidence," I stutter, irritated. "Between two friends. Not for you to tell Jon in your quest to get a date from him."

"Well, you can't have both just waiting for you," Kathy replies stubbornly and in that moment I want to slap her. "You have Rich and Jon waiting on the sidelines for you and it isn't fair."

"Sounds like you already decided."

"I wanted to ask you if it was okay, Jenny, because I honestly thought you wouldn't have a problem with it. But you sit here and tell me that, what, you want both of them at your beck and call?" She stands up now, her brow furrowing. "It's bullshit."

"Fine, go out with Jon," I snap and turn back to look at the TV. "Have a nice time."

Kathy stares at me for a few seconds longer and then heads into her bedroom. I hear her lock the door with a soft *click* and I watch as the car chase on the news comes to an end. I am fuming, although I don't know why. Kathy has a point. I am expecting both Rich and Jon to stick around until I decide which one I want. And yes, I have been avoiding Jon because I am afraid of what he will say about paying off Robbs.

But Kathy has forced my hand. Through her actions, I have picked Rich, even if I am still unsure. I flip through the channels again as my knee throbs. *It's over with, it never truly began with Jon so just let it go.*

Yet as I stay up and watch some terrible B-movie about invisible brain-eating monsters, I can't help but feel as if I messed everything up somehow.

Chapter Eight

I duck behind the wall and glance over at Rich, who is unlocking his car, glancing over his shoulder.

"Hurry up!" I hiss.

The car unlocks, and he slides in the driver's seat. I dart around the car and get inside just as the paparazzi round the corner. The lights begin to go off from the flash as they take photos of me. I turn my face away from the two men as Rich pulls out of the parking lot of the theater. The men still trail after the car, taking photos the entire time, as if there is something interesting about the rear of Rich's car.

"I never expected to run into paparazzi," I say in shock as we make it out onto a main road, leaving the two men behind. "Why in the world are they following me?"

"Well, production wrapped on the movie. They probably have you pegged as a rising star. They want to be the first to follow you around. That way if you become successful, they can brag they pegged you first."

I let out a shudder. "I don't want to be 'pegged' first. That was weird."

"It'll only get worse if you climb up the fame ranks," Rich replies, heading toward his house although the traffic is heavy on a Saturday night. "Luckily the amount of CGI in the movie means you'll be waiting for it to come out for a while. Consider this your calm before the storm."

I let out a small sigh and rest my head against the window. The lights of the city are bright, with neon signs blinking for different clubs and different events. When I had seen the men trailing after me upon leaving the theater, I had been terrified. Rick had known instantly who the men were and had ushered me to the car. But he is right. If the movie does well and I get more roles in the meantime, the possibility of having that be my full time life will become more and more plausible.

I close my eyes and think back. My parts on the movie only took a month to film. My character goes missing halfway through the film, leaving her end ambiguous enough that if the producers and public end up liking me, I can be brought in for the sequel. The days of filming on set were like a boot camp in acting. I feel I learned a lot from working on set. It makes me eager for more work.

There had been other changes as well during the past month. Jon and Kathy have resumed dating, albeit incredibly slowly. Jon mentioned the sex tape only once. After filming had wrapped and he was combing the area for auditions for me to do, he asked what had come of it. I simply told him it had been taken care of.

As much as I regret missing my chance with Jon, I am content on being with Rich. I remind myself of that whenever I see Jon and my heart begins to beat quickly. Things just never worked out in our favor. Things with Rich have been nothing but perfect since we started dating again.

In the darkness of night, the tiny voice in my head comes alive, punishing me with its terrible words that I screwed it all up and I should be with Jon. I ignore it and by the morning light, it fades away, leaving me to focus on Rich.

"Don't think about it anymore," Rich offers, breaking my thoughts. "We'll be at my place soon."

I relax at the thought. Rich's house has become a safe haven. Even though I have enough money to move out of the Dollhouse, I haven't yet. Truth is, I haven't been spending enough time at the apartment to warrant even having a place of my own. I spend most of my time with Rich. Kathy hasn't said anything but we have fallen into mostly frosty conversations whenever we actually end up talking.

"I'm already nervous about my audition tomorrow," I say. "And now the paparazzi."

"Don't worry about it," Rich repeats. "You're going to be great."

The audition is for a movie that focuses much more on acting than CGI stunt work. It is a drama about an Amish community torn apart by a scandal. I am up for a supporting role as the main lead's daughter, which is quickly becoming familiar ground. Yet the role is meatier than my last and will offer me a chance to show more skills than just screaming and running. If given the chance, that is.

"I hope so. I still feel out of my element around these A-list stars. Do you know that Kane Lucky gets Botox in his *armpits* to help him stop sweating?" I muse aloud, still finding that baffling.

Rich chuckles and turns down the road toward his gated community. My phone buzzes and I look at it, seeing a text from Kathy asking if I am coming home tonight.

"Who is that?"

"Just Kathy," I reply. "We're still kind of on shaky ground."

"I still don't understand why. So she's dating Jon, who cares?" Rich's tone was bitter, a constant reminder that Jon is not a friend of his.

"It's just girl bullshit," I lie, trying to change the subject. "Anyway, I'm looking forward to getting into your hot tub."

Rich leers at me. "Without your suit, I hope."

I laugh. "Always without my suit."

Once we get to his mansion of a home, even if it is the smallest place on the block, I pour myself a drink. Rich follows, wrapping his arms around me from behind. I let out a small sigh of delight. Yes, things with Kathy and I are not perfect and I still feel haunted by letting Jon go. But my career is burning up faster than I ever thought it would. I have Rich on my arm. My nightmares have finally stopped. I haven't heard from Robbs.

Rich is kissing up along my neck, sending shivers down my spine. I close my eyes and take a sip of my drink. It is warm and shoots directly into my stomach, spreading the warmth along my body. Rich is still kissing along my neck as his hands slide up to my breasts. I press against him, my ass against his crotch, as he squeezes my breasts. His hands are as warm as the brandy I am sipping, and I can feel him hard against my back.

I stay there for a little bit, letting him grope me in the kitchen. Finally it becomes too much for him and he slips his hands under my top, gripping my breasts. The touch of his hands makes me sigh in delight as he pulls down my bra and begins to pinch and roll my nipples around in his hands.

"I'm going to fuck you right here," Rich says in a rough voice.

He yanks down my skirt and it falls down around my ankles. I'm still wearing my high heels as he moves my legs apart. I can hear him unzip his pants. He slides a finger inside of me. I moan in surprise as he works me, preparing me to take his cock. He fingers me for a couple of minutes and then shifts behind me.

Rich is thick and it always takes some time to adjust to him. I grip the sides of the counter, bend over it with my ass in the air. Finally he is fully inside of me and begins to fuck me in earnest. The thrill of being fucked in his kitchen is a new one. I find myself getting into it, making sure the length of his cock goes fully in and out.

Rich is grunting, mumbling something under his breath that I can't make out as he wraps his fingers in my hair and starts pounding me hard.

His other hand is on my hips, holding me down on the counter. I can feel my own orgasm building up. My moans are loud. I never have to worry about someone overhearing me here.

He suddenly pulls out of me, and I look behind me in surprise. He pulls me off the counter and takes my hand, going into the living room where he sits down in one of the comfortable lounge chairs. He strokes his cock in front of me and I understand. I get in his lap, taking the length of him inside of me.

The position in the chair feels amazing. His cock is hitting my G-spot with every thrust. I grind my pussy against his cock as my orgasm begins to mount. I cling to Rich as I suddenly toss my head back, letting out a loud moan. My climax rolls through me. Rich is coming at the same time now, gripping my thighs as he orgasms.

I close my eyes, riding the wave of pleasure shooting through me. Together we come down from our orgasms, holding each other in his chair. I am sweaty and tired. Rich holds me as he catches his breath.

"I'm ready for bed," I mumble in his ear.

He nods and laces his fingers through mine, taking me toward his bedroom. As we sink into his big bed, I wrap myself around him.

Rich shifts slightly and then clears his throat. "We'll have to discuss how you can pay me back for the loan."

I pause, baffled by his statement. I understood I would have to make it up to him somehow – he did give me $100,000 after all. But to bring it up now of all times seems crass. I shift slightly to reply but Rich is already snoring. Puzzled, I cozy up to him and decide to chalk up the remark to him being so tired. I quickly fall asleep myself without a second thought.

"How do you think the audition went?" Jon asks over the phone.

I roll over on my bed, back in my tiny apartment. "I think it went well.

"That's good," he replies but something in his tone makes me think he has something to add.

"What?" I prompt.

"Well, I noticed Rich works on this project as well."

"I told you he's slowly switching from casting to producing," I reply, trying to keep the irritation out of my voice. "And he's producing this film."

"Right, I just mean well…you two are dating. And you're only auditioning or getting hired for projects he is working on."

"What are you getting at?"

"We might want to broaden our scope. Look for projects that don't involve Rich. It isn't even my personal feelings for him. But it just looks as if he is hiring you for everything. People might not take you seriously."

He has a point and it is good advice. The last thing I want is for my budding career to be over because of my association with Rich.

"Okay. Sounds good."

"Great," Jon answers, sounding relieved. "I'll look for some new prospects right away."

"Thanks for your help."

He pauses and then clears his throat. "Jenny, we haven't caught up together in a while. Been over a month now since we spoke about anything."

I feel unsure how to respond. Part of me wants to agree instantly and hang out with him. But with Jon dating Kathy again and me with Rich, it feels wrong to see him outside of our professional relationship.

"I'm not sure we should hang out," I finally say.

"Is it because I'm seeing Kathy?"

"Well, of course it is. It just feels wrong for us to be hanging out when you're with her, don't you think?"

"Right." His tone is now clipped. "I understand. I'll call you back about auditions."

He hangs up before I can say anything. I sigh and shove my face in my pillow. Does he want us to be friends or is he interested in something more? Every conversation with Jon pulls my heart in ten different directions. My attraction to him, physically and mentally, always comes back. I try to keep everything as professional as possible but I can't deny the feelings for him ever went away.

What could we have become? If life had unfolded differently, would Jon and I be together? I am content with Rich but would I be happier with Jon? In the end, it doesn't matter. I backed off due to my fear over the sex tape. Jon didn't pursue. It's over with.

A few days later I am at Rich's yet again, this time laying by his pool. I know I am spending too much time around him but I can't help myself. I am being sucked up by the lap of luxury his home offers and the sense of comfort it gives me. As I tan by the pool, I hear Rich shuffling around in the kitchen. We opted to stay in today instead of go anywhere. Press has begun for my film, even though it is still in post-production, and I am nervous about running into paparazzi.

Rich comes out with a couple of drinks. I smile up at him and sit up on the cot, taking one. He sits down next to me. He is wearing only swim trunks and the sight of his well-toned body sends thrills through me.

"Thanks for the drink," I say before taking a sip.

"No problem." He lays down on the cot next to me, sliding sunglasses on his face.

I settle back in, exhaling. Is it wrong that I feel like every moment here is a vacation? I know I tell Rich I want to take things slowly but I am a sucker for staying here, drinking and sleeping with him. All other concerns fade away.

"So, have you come up with a way to pay me back?" Rich suddenly asks, breaking my peace of mind.

I turn to look at him but cannot read him since his eyes are covered by sunglasses. "No," I reply slowly. "It isn't as if I have $100,000 laying around yet. But I'm sure with jobs coming in, I will be able to get it to you."

"Soon, hopefully?"

I feel stumped. Rich is clearly not lacking for funds. His sudden need for this money seems out of nowhere. I wonder why he needs it so badly so suddenly but decide not to bring that up.

"I don't know," I admit. "It really depends on the work I am getting. But hey, listen, what if I give you some right now? I can't give you the whole amount right away, but I can give you a little." I tell him.

"Okay," he says but he sounds stiff.

I feel unsure what to say. I obviously want to pay him back but I thought I would have some more time before he asked me about paying him back. It isn't exactly as if I am rolling in money.

I try again, "What do you want? $10,000? I can give you more if you want."

Rich settles back in the cot and falls silent. Unsure what to say to him, I settle back in the cot as well. Yet panic is gripping tightly at my throat. I don't want him upset with me because I can't give him the full amount back at once.

Finally, he clears his throat, "$10,000 will be good."

I relax slightly, "Great. That's great."

I smile at him and Rich smiles back. But his face seems tight.

Jon's words about facing Robbs face to face and not paying him a cent come back to haunt me in the afternoon light.

Chapter Nine

My phone vibrates next to my head, jolting me out of my sleep. I breathe in sharply, trying to remember where I am. I am back in my bedroom. I must have dozed off earlier because my clock reads two in the morning. The blinds of my window are still pulled open, which is stupid since paparazzi could easily find the slum I live in. The screen of my phone is illuminated brightly in the darkness of my room. I look at it and to my surprise I see Jon's name.

"Jon?" I mumble into my phone, still bleary eyed.

"Thank god you're up," he says in reply. "I was trying to get to you first."

"What? What are you talking about?"

"Someone leaked the sex tape, Jenny."

I sit up straight in bed, suddenly wide awake. My palms go clammy, and I clutch the phone. "What the hell are you talking about?"

"You heard me. I couldn't sleep tonight so I was up just surfing around online and saw it reported on some tabloid. Now everyone has it on their site and people are downloading it."

It feels as if the entire room gets very hot, as if I have stepped into a furnace. A warm sweat breaks out along my body, and my stomach churns violently. For a moment, I worry that I am going to vomit but close my eyes tightly, willing it to pass.

"I thought you said this was taken care of," Jon says, although his tone is neutral and not accusatory at all.

"I did," I reply, my voice tiny to my ears.

"How, Jenny? You never told me."

I hesitate, now barreling into a conversation that I have been wanting to avoid. Not only have I been actively trying to avoid it but now that Jon and I are discussing it, it is clear that paying off Robbs has failed.

"I paid him off," I finally say.

Jon lets out a small sigh. "Didn't seem to work."

"He gave me the tape," I protested feebly. "I destroyed the flash drive."

"He clearly made copies."

I think back to destroying the flash drive and feeling so pleased with myself that it was taken care of. I fight down the urge to start crying.

"What are we going to do?"

"You don't have a publicist. We haven't even gotten to that stage yet. So I'll have to come up with some sort of statement on your behalf and release it to the press. It isn't major news, since your first film hasn't come out yet, but everyone will see you in your first movie as the 'girl with the sex tape'."

"This is a disaster. How can I be so fucking stupid?" I bemoan, wanting to sink into the ground.

"We'll figure it out, Jenny," he says softly. "Somehow. Listen, try to get some sleep. Do not go online, okay? I'll call you in the morning."

"Okay. Thanks for letting me know, Jon."

"Let me know if you need me," he says gently, and the call ends.

I stare at my phone for a few seconds before curling up into a ball. My fingers are itching to check the Internet but instead I shut my phone off completely. The last thing I need right now is to read the horrible comments from people. I can only imagine what they say from reading past stories of people having a sex tape leaked.

How naïve am I to assume Robbs would have truly gotten rid of the evidence? Now that it is leaked, it seems almost absurd that I ever thought the flash drive would have the only copy on it. Clearly Robbs had a backup. I groan, thinking about how I have wasted Rich's $100,000.

The thought of Rich and the $100,000 only makes things worse. He wants me to pay him back, and quickly, yet all I have been able to give him so far was $10,000. On top of that, his money was for nothing because Robbs has leaked the tape anyway.

It feels as if the walls are closing in on me. I have made nothing but endless mistakes and now they are coming back to haunt me, one by one. I try to roll over to get some sleep but I doubt it will ever come. Instead I stay awake and think about all the things that I have done.

"Jenny? Do you want me to make you some tea or something?"

I stick my head out from under the covers. Kathy is on the other side of the door, clearly concerned since I have been living in my room the past two days. Since the sex tape leaked, my phone has been blowing up. Reporters somehow found my number and have been calling me for interviews. I've gone from someone in a minor role in the film to a trending topic on Twitter. The movie studio is even giving my character her own poster now that everyone suddenly knows my name.

Yet for me, it has been mortifying. No movie poster in the world can make up for the fact that everyone has seen me with Paul, bent over a bar, having sex with him. I am now paranoid about hearing from Robbs again as well but so far he has not reached out to me. I program an app on my phone to block all calls and texts except for a select few. My voicemail is full. I haven't left the house.

"I'm okay," I call back to her and I hear her pause, as if she wants to say more before shuffling away.

My phone goes off, one of the few callers being allowed through. I glance at it and see that it is Rich. I haven't spoken to him since the sex tape leaked. I dread what he is going to say before I pick up.

"You answered! I've been trying to get through to you."

"I haven't really felt like talking to anyone."

"How are you holding up?"

"I am terrible. I haven't left my room. I think there are some paparazzi outside. No one gave a shit about the tape until the movie I am in started feeding into it. I swear they are using it to generate buzz, like giving my character her own poster."

"Of course they are," he says breezily. "They'd be stupid not to, from their stand point. They have to spin this somehow."

I groan. "I wish they wouldn't." I hesitate. "I haven't heard from Robbs. I guess he wanted more money than what I gave him by releasing the tape."

"Probably."

I push forward, even though I don't want to bring it up at all. "I'm sorry your money went to waste."

"It's okay," Rich replies. "We should have just called the police on the guy. I gave you bad advice. I'm sorry."

"It's okay. I really don't know when I will be able to pay you back now." I hold my breath, wondering how he will receive this information.

"Don't worry about it, Jenny," he replies casually. "Nothing to concern yourself with."

I frown, taken aback by this sudden change of heart on him about the money. "Are you sure?"

"Yeah, not a problem. So I am guessing you don't want to hang out tonight?"

"No, not really," I admit. "I am not ready for that yet."

"I'll call you later then. Hang in there."

I put the phone down, feeling more confused than ever. Did Rich take pity on me for the sex tape being leaked? It feels as if he went from needing the money back quickly to not being concerned at all. I flop back down on my bed, chewing on my bottom lip. That is when there is another knock on my door. I think about pretending to be asleep but then realize Kathy probably just heard me on the phone.

I get out of bed and open my bedroom door, preparing to be peppered with questions. I freeze. Jon is standing in front of me, looking sheepish. I am taken aback at seeing him here in the apartment. He is not wearing his glasses and is wearing a dress shirt and pants. He looks as if he has plans to go somewhere. With a start, I realize Jon is probably going to be going on a date somewhere with Kathy and he is checking up on me.

"Hey," I say, leaning against the doorway, trying to avoid his gaze.

"Hey. I know you're busy in there but I wanted to give you some good news."

"Not sure what could possibly be good right now but try me."

"You got the role in that Amish drama."

My eyebrows shoot up. I had thought for sure that the role was out the window once the tape leaked and say as much to Jon.

Jon runs his fingers through his hair. "The director thinks it is edgy to have someone surrounded in controversy in an Amish drama. He says it will get people interested."

My shoulders sag. "Controversy," *but not talent*, I think to myself. "Great."

"Hey," Jon says, resting his hand on my shoulder. "I know it isn't ideal. But this role is meaty. It will show people you have more to you than a sex tape and running from monsters."

The touch of his hand on my shoulder is comforting. I have been blocking everyone out from my life, fretting about what this horrible turn of events will do for me. While the press hasn't been as nuts as they are for an A-list celebrity sex tape, my connection with the monster film is enough to get me on the gossip sites. To see my name splashed around the headlines makes me uncomfortable. Knowing it was Robbs makes it even worse. Because of this, shutting everyone out has made the most sense. Jon coming to me and offering me words of comfort, plus a job, makes me feel human for the first time in days.

"You're right. Blessing in disguise, I guess," I say slowly, trying to mean it.

Jon smiles, which changes his face into the one I know so well. My heart skips a beat. I return the smile and try to ignore the butterflies in my stomach. *I chose Rich,* I tell myself sternly.

Kathy comes around the corner. She sees Jon's hand on my shoulder, which he quickly removes. The butterflies give one last flutter and die as he turns to face her.

"Ready?" he asks her.

"Yes. Let's head out. Let me know if you need anything, Jenny."

I nod and Jon looks over his shoulder toward me. "I'll call you with details about the contract and the pay. You're going to have to come to my office though."

"Shit," I mumble, watching him depart.

I hear the front door close and shuffle back to my bedroom. Knowing I have another job lifts my spirits a bit. I do really like how meaty the role is. Feeling better, I sit on my bed, mulling over how I feel about seeing Jon and Kathy together. It bothers me more than I like to admit.

Thinking about Jon makes me think of Rich. I am still perturbed by how he no longer cares about paying him back. Something in the back of my head nags me but I push it away.

It is time to get out of bed and move on with my career, no matter how much negative attention I may get.

Chapter Ten

I look over the contract but the words seem to swirl in front of my eyes. I close them tightly for a moment and then open them again, hoping it will make them clearer.

"Are you okay?" Jon asks.

I rub my eyes. "My eyes are still buzzing from the paparazzi cameras. It wasn't a ton, maybe three or four of them, but they are like dogs with a bone. I think they took a photo every millisecond."

"Yeah, those guys have been camped on and off outside the building since the tape leaked."

"I should have taken your advice and gone around the back. But I wanted to show them I wasn't afraid of them. Not sure if it worked though. I probably just looked incredibly overwhelmed."

"Well, we can get you out through the back."

"My car is parked in the front."

"Stacy can pull it around to the back," he replies, referring to his assistant.

I hesitate. My car is the first purchase I made with the money from the monster film. I paid for it in cash. It isn't anything high end, but a normal four-door car, but it is mine. Having someone else behind the wheel feels strange. But walking into the paparazzi again makes me blanch and I find myself nodding to let Jon move my car.

"So, press is slowly building up for the *Recoil Factor* movie," Jon says, changing the subject to my monster film. "Obviously since the film is based off a popular 80's cartoon series, there is already a fan base coming with it. People love monster films as well, so it has that going for it. The first trailer is coming out this week. A teaser, really."

I run my hands over the contract for the Amish film idly, thinking about the trailer. "Am I in the trailer?"

"Not sure, but I think you'll get two, maybe three seconds in it. Enough so people can see you. Like I said, the studio is turning the sex tape in their favor. Trying to drum up interest in a new starlet."

"Isn't having a sex tape at this point a cliché?"

Jon laughs. "Maybe a bit, yes. But it got you this Amish role."

"I know I should be grateful but I don't want all these roles because of the wrong reasons." Something else strikes me. "And I don't want Rich supplying my roles either. Any leads on other auditions?"

Jon nods, looking at his smart phone. "Yes, I have people interested in bringing you in for a couple. One is a drama. You look young, so you'd be the best friend of the main character in a high school setting. The other is a slasher film. You'd be killed off in the first thirty minutes but a paycheck is a paycheck. Are you interested?"

"Yeah, send me the details," I reply. "I can't afford to be picky. Especially with auditions."

Jon nods, typing away on his computer. "Great. Now this Amish film – *Beloved* – kind of a boring name but it might change. Anyway, it's a much smaller budget than the *Recoil Factor* film. So your salary will be $25,000. If you hold out for more, you'll start sounding like a diva."

"Sounds great to me," I reply instantly, still marveling at getting paid like this.

Jon nods again, typing away as I look down at the contract. I start to think about what I really should be doing with this money. I decide that since I have a car, getting my own place needs to happen next. Kathy and I are slowly drifting apart, and I would like to have my own space.

"Hey, do you know of a good place to look for rentals?" I suddenly ask, looking up from the contract.

"You're going to move out of the apartment? Does Kathy know?"

"I can afford it. It'd be nice to have my own space. Do you think she'll be mad?"

"I don't think so. With her soap opera income, she can afford the place on her own now."

I study him but his face is blank. As if just to make things worse for myself, I ask, "How are things with the two of you?"

Jon stiffens slightly in surprise, so quickly that if I hadn't studied him so well, I wouldn't have noticed it. It passes and he resumes typing on his computer. "It's okay."

"That's it? She seemed really gung-ho about seeing you again."

Jon shifts in his seat. "I know. And she is a great girl. Kathy is nice and has a bright future ahead of her."

"You sound like her teacher, not her boyfriend." I lean back in the chair, trying to still my beating heart.

The ends of his mouth quirk up, as if he is going to smile. "I guess I do."

I tell myself to stop asking questions. It isn't my business to find out what is going on with the two of them. But like picking a scab, I can't stop. I want to know how the two of them are doing. I want to know how Jon feels about Kathy, as if I am examining the cracks in a fossil, attempting to see if any of them are going to break wide open.

"I think she'll be okay if I move out. She has you."

"Jenny," Jon suddenly says and his tone is odd. "Are you still seeing Rich?"

I am slightly taken aback but I nod. "Yeah. Although I have to admit I don't know if we are official or not."

He frowns. "Why is that?"

Even though I have just been poking and prodding my way into Jon's relationship with Kathy, I find myself nervous at discussing my own. How do I explain to him that the reason I am holding off on becoming official with Rich is because I still find myself thinking about him in the middle of the night?

"I've just been busy and I am not sure if I want to commit to him right now. Rich is always busy, too. He has a lot going on."

"Yeah, he seems to be transitioning into a movie producer fine," Jon says, although he sounds a little bitter. "So kudos to him."

"Not like he even needs to. All that family money probably means he doesn't have to work a day in his life yet he still chooses to."

Jon's brow furrows. "Family money?"

I open my mouth to reply when his phone suddenly goes off. Jon looks down at it and picks it up.

"Hey, Kathy. No. No, just meeting with a…client," he finishes lamely, his eyes darting up at me. "I can't make it tonight. I have a dinner with some friends. I'll call you later. Okay. Bye."

He hangs up and an awkward silence fills the room. I am unsure what to say. He clearly omitted the fact he is meeting with me. I am not even sure if the story about meeting up with friends is true. In any case, it is clear that his feelings for Kathy aren't as strong as she would want them to be.

I shift in my seat, suddenly aware of the scent of his cologne and how his eyes are resting on me. "So, I guess I should sign this contract, right?"

"Right, right," he says, shaking his head at whatever he is thinking. "Need to get that sent over."

Jon grabs a pen and hands it to me. I reach over and take it. Our fingers touch briefly. It is only a moment's touch but it is enough to send an electric shock along my arm and down my spine. Goose bumps pop up along my skin. I quickly look down at the contract and sign my name. Did Jon feel that, too? I don't trust myself to look up at him. I don't trust myself around him any longer than I have to be. Every nerve in my body is screaming for him to touch me.

Not for the first time. The opportunity for any romance has been missed between the two of us.

I close the book I have been reading and glance over at Rich. He is in the kitchen. I can see him through the windows from the pool. He is talking to someone on his phone and he looks irritated.

With a small sigh, I look away. Rich invited me over to hang out by the pool and most likely more but my thoughts are full of Jon. Even being with Rich right now feels like a mistake. Once again, I am second guessing myself.

I pushed Jon away due to the sex tape but that ended up coming back to bite me in the ass. We had told each other how we felt and never acted on it. I keep thinking back to how we briefly touched in the office. Just the small touch elicited more of a response than anything I have done with Rich.

I glance back at the kitchen. Rich's face is dark. I wonder who he is fighting with. I realize he won't tell me. *Why aren't you two official yet?* Jon's words pop back into my head. I wonder if I *did* want to be official, if Rich would even agree to something like that. I wonder how many other girls he is seeing. I wonder why I don't really care.

At that moment, Rich comes out of the kitchen. He is holding a drink. He has forgotten to make mine but I don't want to point it out. He is clearly trying to hide whatever has pissed him off so much, and I don't want to stress him out more with asking questions.

Rich sits down and glances at me. "How is the book?"

"Kinda shitty actually," I reply, glancing at the cover. "This sort of over the top romance stuff isn't my thing."

"Why are you reading it then?" he replies in an accusing tone, as if he wrote the book himself.

"Well, everyone is reading it at the moment. I wanted to see what the fuss is all about."

Rich takes a sip of his drink. "They'll probably make a movie out of it. At least you know the source material."

"Good point," I reply, sliding my sunglasses back down on my face.

Rich settles down on the cot. As I look at the pool, I realize how bored I am. Since the sex tape leaked, I don't go out as much as I used to. That wouldn't be a problem if Rich and I did something different in his large house. However, all we do is sip drinks and sit by the pool. I had snagged the book from Kathy from sheer boredom. Catching a tan was only interesting for so long.

Rich is radiating negative energy, which I can't even tell him because I know he will be upset with me. I look down at the book but can't focus on the words. All I can think about is Jon. Is he going to break up with Kathy? If he does, should I break up with Rich and try to be with him instead?

"I'm going to use the bathroom," I suddenly mumble, standing up and heading toward the house.

"Use the pool bathroom," he says.

I can't very well tell him I need to get away from him so I look over my shoulder. "Tampon's in my bag."

Even though I'm not actually on my period, the mere mention of a menstrual cycle has Rich making a face and I safely head inside his house. I step into the kitchen, suddenly freezing from the change in temperature. My feet are cold on his marble flooring. For the first time, I notice how cold and unwelcoming the kitchen is. Everything in the house looks like it belongs in a hotel. There isn't anything that screams Rich. I look behind me briefly but he is engrossed in something on his phone and is no longer paying attention to me.

I pad out of the kitchen and into the living room. Even in here, there isn't anything personal. I briefly recall Jon's apartment, which had photos on the walls and a slew of blu-rays along the other wall. He also had posters of terrible movies. It was comforting. This just feels like Rich rents the home.

I head up the stairs toward the guest room, where I usually toss my things. He wants me to stay the night tonight and part of me wonders if I can get out of it and head back to the Dollhouse. I shut the door quietly behind me and sit down at the edge of the bed, looking at the luxury around me. Everything is beautiful and lovely to look at it. Yet nothing stirs me like Jon's apartment did.

I feel stupid, like a teenager with a crush. How many times am I going to waver back and forth about Jon? Our ships have passed in the night. There is no reclaiming it. *But if he breaks up with Kathy...*the small voice in the back of my head says. *But nothing,* I snap back to myself, *that doesn't mean it has anything to do with you.*

I hear my phone go off. I have kept it up in the guest room. I ended up changing my phone number to try to shake off reporters so when I see an unknown number on the caller ID, I frown. I decide to answer it anyway, in the mood to tell someone off if they want to start shit.

However, nothing prepares me for the voice on the other line.

"Jenny, great, you answered."

"How did you get this number?" I hiss through clenched teeth, feeling as if I had just been dunked into the pool.

Robbs gives a small chuckle on the other line. "Not hard. Not if you know who to speak to."

"What the fuck do you want?"

"Your money went a long way to helping me get things set up. However, I ran into a snag. I need some more."

I let out a dry laugh, amazed at the balls he has. "You're fucking kidding me, right?" I didn't feel scared this time, just pissed off.

"You have quite a tone today, Jenny," he said, his voice cool as ice. "I thought we were friends."

"I already gave you that money. And you leaked the tape anyway. Why would I give you a cent more?"

He clicked his tongue against the roof of his mouth. "I kept to our bargain, babe. I didn't leak the tape."

"Oh, really? I forgot I sent the tape to tons of other people to leak – oh wait, I didn't. You told me I had the only copy."

I can hear him in the background rustling with something. The fact he isn't paying his full attention to this conversation pisses me off. The fact he can just casually call me up and threaten me for more money and still fiddle around with something at the same time fills me with a cool rage that makes me want to throttle him through the phone.

"Okay, so I *did* lie about that being the only copy. But how in the world could you really think that was the only copy? I thought you were smarter than that, Jen."

I bristled. "Don't call me that. So you're trying to tell me that yes, you lied about the tape, but no, you didn't leak the tape."

"That is correct."

My grip on the phone tightens and for a second I think about throwing it against the wall and being done with the whole thing.

"So why the fuck would I give you another dime?"

"For information."

My voice catches in anger. "Information?"

"Yes, that's right. I know who leaked the tape. You pay me and I'll tell you. I'll even lower the amount. $15,000."

I close my eyes, trying to count to ten. I want to scream and cry at the same time. Give this guy $15,000 dollars to know who leaked the sex tape when I know it is him. How stupid does he think I am?

I decide that I am not going to give him another cent.

"No."

"What?"

"You heard me. No. I know you leaked my tape. I'm not giving you another dime, Robbs. Your control over me is done. I'm not some little girl you can fuck with anymore. I'm not buying into your bullshit, do you hear me?"

There is a long silence on the other line. It is so long that I wonder if he disconnected the call but one glance tells me the call is still connected.

"Fine," he finally replies, although his voice sounds dark and horrifying. "Have it your way, Jenny. When you find out who leaked the sex tape, feel free to think about me. I tried to help you."

"Fuck you, Robbs," I hiss and hang up.

I sit there on the bed, breathing hard. My body feels as if it is full of pure adrenaline. I want to punch something or scream my head off. Instead I grip the bedsheets, crumpling them up in tiny balls in my fists.

I feel relieved that I have told him off. Yet I am also frightened. What if he decides to come back with something else? If he doesn't bother to ask for money and just goes to the media instead? Or…

I remember him pushing me down the stairs. The pain of losing Maggie. What if he decides to come for me? I could wake up in the middle of the night with Robbs looming over me, ready to tear me down again. The fear grips me, and my throat tightens. I choke down a sob. Rich is probably wondering where I am.

I decide that I won't tell him what just happened. If he finds out that not only was his $100,000 a waste but Robbs demanded more, he might flip out. Especially since his mood is so terrible today. Better to hide it.

I'll tell Jon, I think to myself as I grab my phone, debating sending it via text. But at the last second, I change my mind. Better not to blab about it through texts. I'll tell him about it the next time I see him.

I take a deep breath, trying to calm myself down and stand up, getting ready to head back to the pool.

Chapter Eleven

Jon hands me a soda and I take it, saying thank you and sitting down on his couch. It's been twenty-four hours since Robbs called me, threatening me, and I finally am getting to talk to Jon about it. I curl up on the couch and tug for the blanket that is always nearby. His cat is sleeping on the other chair, letting out a soft snore. Jon sits down next to me, concern etched on his face.

I tell him about the phone call and telling Robbs off. Now silence reigns, as Jon thinks it over before he speaks.

"Well?" I finally say, too anxious to wait for him to speak.

"I can see why you are worried. But you did the right thing. Otherwise he would keep coming at you for money."

"Right, but now he just might come at me for other things."

"Have you thought about calling the police?"

As soon as it he says it, I wonder why I haven't thought about it before. But I worry about bringing the police into it. What will they uncover about me if I have them start looking at Robbs? And how will Robbs get back at me for involving the police? Not to mention at this point the press would be involved. I should have called the police at the start of this mess, not now.

I tell this all to Jon, who presses his lips together in a firm line. "I can see your point. But if you are afraid of him coming back and doing something, it could be better just to deal with what happens from the police."

"I need to move out of Kathy's. I'm sure he knows where I live by this point. And maybe you're right. Maybe I will call the police. Tell them I am afraid. I mean, that is their job, right? To protect people?"

"You can try to get a restraining order."

"Those never seem to help," I say doubtfully, my mind racing with stories of celebrities dealing with break-ins from crazy fans.

"But it'd be on the record at the very least. Listen, if you get more work lined up, you might want to consider a bodyguard."

I hold up my hand. "Okay, let's do baby steps. I'm not ready to start discussing bodyguards and everything quite yet."

Jon nods and looks over at his sleeping cat, named Doof for some inane reason, before speaking. "Then file for a restraining order. In the meantime, the press for *Recoil Factor* is kicking up. They've been showing test footage to some audiences early."

"And?"

He gives a small shrug. "Not as positive as they are hoping for."

"What does that mean for the film?" I ask, suddenly nervous.

Jon must see my face because he shakes his head. "Don't panic! I think they brought another editor on board. They paid the post-production company double to finish the CGI and effects ASAP. They might push the release date up. Probably embargo early reviews. Listen, let's be real. We know the movie is aimed to be a summer blockbuster. It probably isn't going to be the highest rated movie of the summer *but* it will be one of the biggest."

I feel a little better knowing at least the movie will be released, possibly even early. The last thing I want is to have my big break shelved. I think of the press coming up. I know I'll be going to an actual movie premiere. What if Robbs decides to do something there?

"Did you tell Rich what is going on?" Jon asks, his voice neutral.

"No," I admit. "He seems stressed out lately. I didn't want to add to it."

"You don't have to answer this if you don't want to," Jon says. "But how did you pay Robbs off?"

I shift in the couch, pulling the blanket around me. I glance at him and in that moment Jon knows I got the money from Rich. He doesn't say anything and instead looks at his phone, as if it has made a noise or something.

I decide to break the silence. "It was the only way I could get the money. I should have done what you said to do. Confront him and tell him off. But he'd just have skipped right to the threatening. Now he has $100,000 and is back to threatening me. I panicked. I know you disagree with paying him off but…it's over with now."

"The only thing I hate is that you got the money from Rich, of all people."

"He's not a bad guy," I tell him. "He can be a dick, sure, but he's been making it up to me. He helped me with the *Recoil Factor* movie. I got the Amish audition because of him. And he gave me the $100,000."

"He'll want something in return for it," Jon replies, his voice dark.

I think back to Rich pressuring me to pay him back already but decide not to tell him about it. There isn't a point. He has told me he no longer is concerned about being paid back right away.

"Listen, I know you two have bad blood but let's not talk about Rich right now. Will you come with me to the police station to put a restraining order on Robbs?"

"Of course." He stands up and holds out his hand toward me to help me get off the couch.

I hesitate for only the briefest of moments before taking his hand. Once again, our touch sends shockwaves through me. The touch only lasts a few seconds but I swear I can feel Jon's hand lingering on mine. His skin is warm and I can feel goosebumps along my skin. I curse myself for being stupid as I follow him outside of his apartment. We can only ever be friends. Yet my heart refuses to accept it.

The air is chilly by the time we leave the courthouse. The sun has set and the moon is high in the sky, covered by clouds. Even though spring has rolled in, it feels closer to a winter night as Jon walks me to my car. We arrived at the courthouse moments before they closed for the day. The sun is setting so early that it feels as if I had been in there for hours instead of thirty minutes.

"Sorry that took so long," I said to him. "I know the papers have to go through the system now and we have to hear from a court hearing date but that just makes it all worse somehow."

A chill goes through me, and I find myself running my fingers up and down my arms. I will have to see Robbs at the hearing. I will truly be standing up to him then, I realize as I stand outside my car.

"Hey, I'll be with you every step of the way," Jon says, resting his hand on my shoulder.

His touch jolts me back to the present, and I smile a little sadly. "Thank you. I'm just dreading it. What if the restraining order isn't granted? Then I've just pissed him off even more."

"Hey." Jon's tone is soft. "Don't be that way. We'll take it one step at a time, okay? We have to wait to hear from them about the hearing."

"I'm scared," I say into the night air.

The words hang there, in between us. It seems silly that I haven't been able to say them to anyone else, like Rich. But Rich's dark face looms up in my head and I realize I couldn't say it to him. He would never understand my fear of Robbs and what he has done to me.

Jon leans forward and suddenly kisses me.

For a moment, the world stops. All noise ceases. I don't hear the cars driving by or a club down the street starting to have a live band set up and play. Instead, all I can think about is Jon's lips on mine. My body feels as if it has been tossed into a pool. I am taken aback by him suddenly kissing me. We have yet to actually kiss. I have merely told myself it will never happen. Yet here I am, with Jon's lips on mine.

Suddenly, the thought of Rich and Kathy propels me away from him. I don't want to end the kiss. But the act of kissing him while we are still attached to other people – even if I am with Rich unofficially – is still wrong. I push off his chest and take a stumbling step back as a sudden gust of wind kicks up, blowing my hair around my face.

"Sorry," Jon says in a strangled voice. "I'm sorry. I shouldn't – I should have not –"

"I want to but I can't," I say over him, my voice high pitched to my ears. "With Kathy and Rich, you understand–"

"Yes, yes, of course." He runs his fingers through his hair. "Listen, I am going to go. I will call you later."

Before I can say anything, Jon turns around and heads off toward his car. I realize I am trembling, watching him go. I trail my fingertips over my lips, marveling at how they are still tingling from our brief touch. I get in my car and stare at the courthouse, my mind spinning.

I didn't expect him to kiss me. In hindsight, I see that I should have. His quiet tones, his glances at me and lying on the phone to Kathy about being with me all shows me that he is still interested in me. Did I stick my head in the sand intentionally? My heart is pounding in my chest.

But Kathy cares for him. She really wants to be with him. How in the world can I break them up? Jon has to be with her. Her words come back to me about keeping both Rich and Jon on the sidelines. I shake my head to myself. I can't let Jon leave Kathy for me. And how can I stop seeing Rich, after everything he has done for me?

I try to push the kiss from my mind as I head home. But I know I will have trouble falling asleep tonight.

Chapter Twelve

I trail my fingers over the new dress hanging in my closet. The fact that I didn't have to stress out about shopping for the perfect dress, but instead, a designer, has actually *lent* me a dress as fine as this to wear to the premiere of *Recoil Factor* seems like a dream.

With the movie fast tracked to be finished and released early, I am merely two weeks away from the premiere. Press is underway and I even attended the first junket last week in L.A. Filming starts on Monday for *Beloved,* the Amish film, which means I'll be missing most of the international premieres. I am still bummed out about that, truth be told, but the junket was filled with peering eyes and whispered stories about my scandal, so maybe it is better in the long run.

Since I am going to be able to attend the premiere in L.A., I try to look forward to it as much as possible. This means checking the dress in my closet every ten seconds, running my fingers over the fabric. The color is a pale pink, which I appreciate. Ever since reading some study online about red being tied to "seductress" in people's minds, I have been steering clear of the color. The pale pink makes me look almost innocent and brings out my blonde hair.

My phone bleats and I look at it. My real estate agent is calling. The last few days I have thrown myself in looking for a new apartment. Kathy seemed nonplussed when I told her I was looking to move out. Grateful that her soap opera was renewed for another season, she told me that she can cover the rent by herself.

"Jenny, great, how are you?" my agent trilled on the other line, constantly perky.

"Wonderful and yourself?"

"Great, great. I have some wonderful news! The apartment you were looking for is all yours! The paperwork cleared and so did the money. You can pick up the keys at my office at any time. The apartment is now leased to you for the next year!"

I sit down on my bed, almost vibrating with happiness. The apartment I am renting isn't over the top or too luxurious. I chose something modest, a one bedroom on the outskirts of Beverly Hills that I can forever call my own, even if my career dies. No rent – no worries. The only splurge was the fact the building has high security, which will hopefully offer me some comfort in regards to Robbs.

I thank her and hang up, a smile on my face. My own place. I take a look around my small bedroom, grateful that I will be getting a larger space to call my own. Not to mention putting space between Kathy and I.

Each time I hang around her, I feel as if my entire face tells the story of Jon's kiss. It has been a week, and I haven't heard from him outside a couple of texts to do with my schedule. Both of us are unsure of what to say to each other. Even thinking about it too much drops a load of guilt on me. The entire reason I even have my own place is because she suggested I move out here with her. Her feelings for Jon seem to run extremely deep. How can I ignore all of that and pursue him? We had our shot and both of us blew it.

On the other side of the issue is Rich, who gave me $100,000 to take care of Robbs and has helped me launch my career. Even if we aren't "official", he still clearly cares about me. To break up with him and date Jon seems like not only a jerk thing to do, but throwing it in the face of the person who helped me so much will surely burn an important bridge.

So instead, I waver between what to do. Like I did with Robbs, I feel myself stuck between following my heart and the fear of fucking everything up. Instead I opted to ignore the entire problem, finding a new apartment and planning out my premiere and filming *Beloved.* I went to the audition for the slasher flick and bombed the audition for the drama film in high school. Unable to remember how to act as a teenage girl, I didn't feel confident that I amazed anyone in that audition.

I snap out of my thoughts, realizing now I will have to pack my meager things and start the moving process. On top of that, I will have to go shopping to get some things to fill up the rest of the apartment with. My phone goes off again and I see Jon's name. My throat catches and I pick up.

"Hey, what's up?" I say, hoping I sound casual and not as if I have just been thinking about him again.

"Sorry to bother you. But I just had to call you. I was alerted to an item in the gossip magazines and wanted to call. Not to lecture, just to give you a heads up."

I frowned. "I don't know what that means."

"A gossip item on republiccelebrity.com," Jon says, mentioning the name of a gossip website even I am guilty of still going on sometimes. "Says that Kane Lucky gets Botox injections in his armpits to stop his sweating and that you were telling a friend at Underwater Nosh last week all about it."

"What? I haven't been to Underwater Nosh since my first date with Rich. There is no way in hell this could have happened."

"Kane Lucky's publicist called me, super pissed off. Apparently this was something very true and totally supposed to be on the down low. Now he is the laughing stock of the Internet – at least until a new meme pops up."

"I didn't tell anyone this –" I start to protest until the words die in my mouth.

Jon hasn't noticed. "I believe you, Jenny. But for whatever reason, the story is reported everywhere as you being the one gossiping about it in clubs."

"If you believe me, then why are you lecturing me about it?"

"Better safe than sorry, okay? I'll call you later." He hangs up before the conversation can turn to anything other than the armpits of Kane Lucky.

I slowly lower the phone, staring at the wall in my tiny bedroom, lost in thought. I told one person about Kane Lucky shooting Botox in his armpits because it was so ridiculous.

Rich.

"Jenny, over here!"

"Smile for us, Jenny!"

"Mind telling us if you'll be releasing another tape?"

"Is it true you've been fired from the sequel of *Recoil Factor* for what you said about Kane Lucky?"

The three paparazzi hound me the entire time I walk up to the restaurant where I am meeting Rich for dinner. It is the same three as last time, probably from low-level magazines, trying to find a good scoop so they don't have to cover my B-list celebrity ass anymore.

I ignore them, even though the last comment almost got me. No, I was not let go from the sequel of *Recoil factor*. I even sent Kane Lucky a package of high-end steaks through our agents as an apology for the lies being printed in the press and to ensure I haven't told a single soul.

I omitted the fact I had told Rich about it. It feels like ages since I told him about it. In fact, it was during the first night the paparazzi came after me that I had blurted it out in the car without thinking.

But now I was facing the fact that Rich has told someone else about it and it went to the gossip rags. I don't know why in the world he would have told someone about it. It is clearly something that should remain behind Hollywood doors. If Kane Lucky has problems controlling his sweat glands, it really shouldn't be smashed along the pages of the Internet.

I couldn't fathom why in the world Rich would tell anyone. When I called him up and suggested going out for dinner, it was an attempt to find out why. The paparazzi has caught me off guard and now I feel nervous as I step inside. The restaurant is French and I am completely out of my comfort zone but Rich is the one who has suggested it. I agree to pacify him, wanting him to be in a good mood when I bring Kane Lucky up.

The hostess takes me to a back room where privacy is given and I see Rich talking on the phone with someone. Once again, his face is dark and he looks pissed off. *Great,* I think to myself as I walk over. He sees me and barks something in the phone, hanging up and plastering a thin smile on his face. He looks tired, as if he has been on edge for days.

"Am I late? I have those same paparazzi assholes following me."

"You're fine," he replies as I sit down across from him.

"Everything okay? You looked angry on the phone just now."

Rich stiffens only for a moment and then shrugs. "Just idiots unable to follow orders."

"Yeah, I understand all about idiots." I decide to use this as my lead-in. "Like the paparazzi won't stop–"

Unfortunately, the waitress came over to take our drink orders. We each order something and Rich orders some appetizer I don't know the name of and then we are finally left alone.

"You have the movie premiere soon, don't you?" Rich says.

"Yes. Next week."

"Who are you taking?"

I blink. "Taking?"

"You're not planning on going stag to this thing, are you?" he asks, a grin on his face, as if I am a small child that needs tending to. "I mean, this is your first movie premiere, especially after your controversy."

I bristle at his tone. I am irritated that he is presuming to invite himself to be my date. I also dislike the fact he is bringing up the sex tape.

"I don't know who to ask," I lie, refusing to fall into line with his desires.

His eyebrows shoot up. "I thought we'd go together."

"Won't it look bad, me showing up with the casting producer to the film? Especially after my 'controversy'?" I reply, throwing his words back in his face.

They seemingly bounce off of him and he blinks. "Showing up stag just shows you are playing the field."

"I'm going alone," I announce, trying to show him the conversation is now over.

His mouth turns into a thin line. "Fine," he replies, looking down at the menu.

An awkward silence falls across the table, and I feel unsure how to go on. Broaching the subject of Kane Lucky seems like a harder task than it originally was going to be.

"Anyway, you don't want to get swept up with me at the premiere," I say, determined to go forward. "The paparazzi is all on me and Kane Lucky loathes me after someone lied and said I was gossiping about his armpit Botox at Underwater Nosh."

There is no change in expression on Rich's face. I realize I had been hoping for one. Something that will show me that he told someone else and realizes just now he fucked up.

But instead he takes a sip of his drink and replies, "Yes, I read about that in the papers. Shame it is everywhere."

"I don't know how they found out about that," I lower my voice. "I only told *you*, Rich."

There. There is a slight twitch on his pinky finger currently holding his glass. It is so brief that I wonder if I imagine it.

"Only me?"

"Yeah, that's right. I am not going to make it a habit to tell everyone about A-list celebrity bullshit. I am already on thin ice as it is."

His cool demeanor is back. "If you have only told me, it means my car is bugged."

My eyes widen. "What?"

Rich picks up his phone. "I have to get it searched. If you truly mean you only told me and no one else about this, then those asshole paparazzi have some explaining to do. I have a fucking bug in my car."

My mind spins. The last thing that has popped into my head is the fact Rich's car is bugged. It must show on my face because he hesitates on his texting.

"You didn't think that I told the press about that, did you?"

I open my mouth to reply but the words die in my throat.

"You did, didn't you? Oh my god, Jenny. That is really fucked up."

"I didn't think that," I lie. "I just didn't think they'd go as far as bugging your car. I thought maybe you slipped up and mentioned it to someone. I was going to ask for your discretion."

"My discretion," he deadpans, as if I said something stupid. "I think I know a lot about discretion, Jenny. More than you do, apparently, if you are just going to come in here and insult me to my face about talking to

the press. Do you really think I need a gossip magazine
to pay my bills?"

"No," I say, stumbling all over my words. "I didn't
mean that. Truly. I just thought–"

"Save it. Not interested," he snaps.

"Rich–"

"Let's enjoy the rest of the dinner, okay?"

I wonder how in the world we are going to be able
to do that.

I'm feeling wonderfully shitty by the time the date
with Rich ends. There is no invitation to his place
afterward and I find myself not driving to the Dollhouse
but to my new apartment, which I have plans to move
into this weekend. I park the car and step inside,
shutting the door quietly behind me.

I marvel at how quiet it is. There is no hum of traffic
or loud music blaring two apartments down. The place
is spacious yet still giving me a comfortable vibe that I
know will be even better once I have it decorated. I trail
my fingers along the countertops in the kitchen,
relishing the fact the entire place is mine.

I sit down on the floor of the living room. My hands
are dug into the plush carpet. My mind feels heavy with
thoughts. Lately it feels as if I so rarely have any time to
myself. Between the filming, the auditions, paparazzi
and juggling Robbs, Rich, Kathy and Jon, my brain
feels stuffed. It feels as if as the more my career takes

off, the more my personal life keeps getting struck. Like a Jeep stuck in mud, I spin my wheels and only lurch forward yet remain in the same spot.

I can't deny that Rich has rubbed me the wrong way tonight. His blasé attitude over assuming he is my date to the premiere combined with throwing my sex tape in my face pisses me off. On top of that, the rest of dinner was stilted conversations that resulted in mostly dead ends. He was so insulted when I told him I thought he leaked the story to the press, maybe he was serious about his car being bugged.

I lay down on the carpet, staring at the ceiling. The sky is clear and the sliver of the moon that is high in the sky tonight casts a dim light into the living room. I trace the light with my eyes. Would the paparazzi really bug his car? For me? I would understand that if I was someone of note, someone who truly mattered but I haven't even had a movie come out yet.

I know paparazzi are cutthroat and dying for advancement. An up-skirt shot of a female celebrity can probably pay their rent for months. But bugging cars? I bit my bottom lip. Would they really do something like that?

Something about the entire situation nags in the back of my head. I lay on the floor for another thirty minutes before I finally get up and to my car, heading back to the Dollhouse.

Chapter Thirteen

"This is the last box."

"Thank you again for all of your help. You really didn't have to do this," I say, meaning every word.

Jon looks bashful. "Not a problem. I actually had a free day today."

"And you spent it helping me *move*," I reply emphatically.

He shrugs slightly. "I wanted to see your place. See if it is better than mine."

I laugh, pulling a beer out for him from the kitchen and handing it to him. "It's smaller. But it's all mine."

"It's a good feeling, isn't it?"

"Completely."

Jon calling me early this morning and asking if I wanted help moving had knocked me off my feet. We still hadn't discussed the kiss or what it meant for our respective relationships. Even now, as the sun set and the movers had dropped off my new furniture, Jon and I have not really talked about anything serious.

Not that I didn't like his company. It is nice to spend an entire day with him, swapping stories and having an easy confidence with him that I do not have with anyone else. The only time things got awkward was when Kathy called and he hit the ignore button, not thinking I saw. I didn't bring it up. He helped only here in the apartment and not at the Dollhouse. It is clearly an unwritten rule that Kathy can't see us hanging out.

Now I am looking around my new place, feeling happy at finally being in my own space again. Actually *owning* my own place feels unreal and makes me even more happy. I open myself a beer as well, remembering to thank my real estate agent for getting me such an amazing deal.

"Not sure how much I'll get organized before filming starts on *Beloved*."

"And then the premiere at the end of the week, too."

"I'm super nervous about that."

"You taking Rich?" Jon asks and I wonder if it is a casual question or if there is more to it.

"No. I decided it'd look bad if I went with the casting director."

He looks relieved and I wonder how much of it is because Rich isn't coming. "That's a smart idea. I was going to suggest it but didn't want to look as if I was intruding."

"I think he was pissed but…" I shrug.

"Have you heard from the courthouse about the hearing for the restraining order?"

"Not yet. But they said it could take a couple of weeks to notify Robbs since he technically lives out of state. I still don't think they are going to grant me one."

"We'll cross that bridge if it happens."

I hesitate, debating if I should tell Jon about Rich and the debacle in the gossip magazines. Silence has filled the room and I feel a bead of sweat on my neck.

"Jenny," he says, shifting his weight to one foot. "I think I'm going to break up with Kathy."

My eyes widen. "Jon, why?"

"I can't be with her. Not when…" He clears his throat. "Not when I have feelings for you."

I am not sure if my eyes are able to widen anymore but I hear myself awkwardly say, "What?"

"We discussed it before, you know. You and I. We were so close to being together. And then the sex tape came out, and I wasn't sure how to act around you. I think I came at you too hard about confronting Robbs. I figured you'd want to be friends while you sorted everything out. All I did was push you away. Of course you went back to Rich. And when I saw you back with him, I realized I fucked it all up. I should have been with you. But instead I just…I got all mucked up. Between the bullshit from Robbs and Rich and me spouting off we should be friends, I fucked it all up."

My breath is caught in my throat. I am taken aback. I know we kissed but I am not expecting this. Part of me has been expecting us just to ignore what happened between the two of us. But I think back to us kissing in the moonlight and the butterflies take off in my stomach.

"But Kathy really likes you," I hear myself say. "You can't…I mean, she told me I couldn't keep you on the sidelines anymore. That I had to pick someone. And I felt so cornered and I just thought that you two deserved another shot." My words are tripping over themselves now. "And she seemed so keen on you. And she is the entire reason I moved here and now have these jobs coming in. How could I say no?"

"I know how she feels about me," Jon replies after a beat. "But I told her that I wasn't sure if we could be together because of you. And then she came to me, telling me that you told her you wanted to be with Rich. I realized we weren't going to make it together. So I've been trying to throw myself into this relationship with her but it isn't working out. We already were together once and broke up due to our differences. They aren't gone now."

I take a step back and I see Jon's face fall. But my mind is spinning as I think about what it will mean to Kathy if Jon dumps her and starts dating me. I want to kiss him again, more than anything, but I find myself hesitating.

"I owe her so much," I begin. "I mean, I was languishing where I used to live and she offered me to contact you as my agent and helped me get on my feet again. How can I hurt someone who has given me so much?"

"I understand that, Jenny, I really do. But even so…I don't feel the way I should for her and it isn't fair to Kathy when I…when I feel this way about you."

I lean against the wall in my kitchen, trying to slow my racing heart. My guilt over dating someone Kathy has feelings for is too strong for me to be able to agree to date Jon. On top of that, I will have to officially leave Rich before I attempt to do figure out what to do with Jon.

In a simple world, I'd toss my arms around him and kiss him. We would make love on the couch and everything would fall into place. However, it isn't that simple in my actual life so I merely attempt to clear my head.

"Things are so complicated right now," I say to him. "I owe Kathy so much. Everyone tells me this business isn't about owing people anything but granting each other favors. I get that. But Kathy did more than just help me from a business stand point. She helped me mentally. And she had a point. I was trying to keep both Rich and you around to see where my heart went. She deserved this second shot with you."

"Jenny…" But I hold up my hand to cut him off.

"No, let me finish," I plead. "Obviously you can't stay with her if you don't have feelings for her. I get that. But I can't just start dating you, Jon. I have things on my end I need to work out. Rich, for one. Even if we aren't official, I still owe him an explanation that I can no longer see him because of how I feel about you."

"So you feel the same way about me?" Jon asks, a hint of hope in his voice.

I take a nervous breath. "Yes. But please, I need to work out Rich first. And I need to see how I feel about dating you while Kathy is so keen on you. I can't start dating you if I feel like I am doing the wrong thing."

There is a long pause where every inch of me wants to run over and kiss Jon. But I hold back and he takes a long swig of his beer before finally nodding.

"I get it. You want to feel out things with Kathy first. You want to officially get rid of Rich."

Jon puts down the beer, unfinished and grabs his jacket. My heart is beating fast in my chest no matter how much I want to slow it down. As he slides his jacket on, his eyes land on mine. "I'm going to wait for you. This time I don't want things to get mucked up."

I nod, my throat dry and my tongue stuck to the roof of my mouth. Jon turns around and grabs his car keys, leaving me alone in my apartment. My body sags, like a balloon letting out air.

Jon declaring his feelings for me has me happier than I can remember. Of course, we have done this before, haven't we? I remember us telling each other we have feelings for one another in the taco shop before things got fucked up from the sex tape. This time I need it to be different.

Dumping Rich is the simple part. The harder part is knowing that I will have to tell Kathy that Jon and I are pursuing a relationship. She will be furious. I can feel it in my bones. I feel as if I am burning the bridge that got me here. I wish there was some way around it but I am not sure there is. I cannot make Jon love her.

I sit down on my new couch, idly tugging on a strand of my hair. While Kathy and I have never been the closest of friends, trying to explain this to her is going to ruin any hope of that.

I close my eyes, deciding that I am going to sleep. I will deal with Rich first and then figure out how to handle Kathy. Jon has to break up with her anyway. I head toward my bedroom, enjoying the size of the room as I slide into my bed.

I thought for sure I was going to be up for hours but before I knew it, sleep washes over me quickly.

Chapter Fourteen

"You look wonderful," Marina says to me over my shoulder as the make-up artist adds the finishing touches. "You're pretty much all set. How do you feel?"

I look at myself in the mirror, unsure who is staring back at me. My hair is swept up in a pretty bun with loose hair framing my face. My makeup is soft, matching the gentle pink hues of my dress. I have a diamond bracelet around my wrist that costs more than my apartment. My head feels light for a second as I take it in.

"Wow."

Marina smiles the first true smile I have ever seen and nods, looking down at her iPad. "You have about ten minutes before we are going to usher you back out the hotel to the limo, okay?"

"I'm nervous," I blurt out, although I don't know why I am telling her this.

She pats me on the shoulder. "Completely understandable. But you've been professional this entire time, Jenny. Truly. I've dealt with some people, let me tell you. It was a risk taking you on due to your inexperience. But Fredrick and I stand by you."

In spite of myself, my eyes have tears spring up. I feel like a stupid little kid for getting emotional over something that my boss is telling me. But I've felt so overwhelmed lately that actually getting a compliment knocks me off my feet.

Marina's eyes widen. "Oh, honey, don't. You'll mess up your makeup!" She hands me a tissue.

I nod, sniffling, and her phone goes off. The makeup artist is cleaning up her things. It is the night of the premiere, and I am incredibly nervous. We are at an expensive, high end hotel in downtown L.A., one block from where the premiere is being held. Everyone is being snuck out of the hotel at different times to be dropped off at the premiere. I find it silly that everyone gets ready so close to the premiere but Marina states usually they get ready in the same building and end up driving in a big circle.

I try to tell myself to enjoy this moment. The past week has been full of organizing my apartment and filming *Beloved.* This is going to be my moment to enjoy my very first and hopefully not my last Hollywood premiere. On top of that, I ended up getting the small role in the slasher film, which I find myself looking forward to filming mostly because it will be fun to act silly and terrified.

The only things that I have not been able to sort out has been my situations with Rich and Kathy. I know that Jon has broken up with her because I got a tearful voicemail a couple days ago from Kathy, asking if I knew anything about it. Busy and worried about telling her the truth, I have put off calling her.

I feel as if Rich has been avoiding me. I attempted to call him twice but he never returned my calls. I wonder if things will sort themselves out and if he will dump me because of the Kane Lucky accusation. Part of me is secretly hoping that is how it will work out.

I am quickly ushered into a limo. I slide inside, feeling completely out of my element yet again. The limo has a full bar and a TV showing coverage of the premiere on the movie's website, streaming online. I am itching for champagne.

"You look great."

I let out a yelp, the voice scaring the hell out of me as I turn quickly to the right. On the other side of the limo is, out of all the people, Rich. He is dressed in a tuxedo. His cologne wafts over to me and instead of enticing me to slide over to him, I feel put off.

"Rich!" I exclaim. "What are you doing here?"

"I know we had a little bit of a fight last weekend. But I couldn't bear to be apart from you anymore. I just wanted to see you and I thought this would be the perfect place to do so."

Instead of feeling happy at seeing him, I feel irritated. I had made it perfectly clear I wanted to attend the premiere by myself. Yet Rich, clearly under the guise of making up with me, has now shoved himself in my limo, giving me no choice but to make him my date. I try to push down the irritation surging through me. Part of me wants to tell him to get out but before I can, the doors shut and the limo moves on.

"You look beautiful," Rich says to me. "Pink looks good on you."

"Thank you," I reply, hoping I don't sound as irritated as I feel.

Rich doesn't seem to notice and instead grabs my hand. I think of Jon and how his touches always seem to bring me to life. I need to end things with Rich but how can I do that as we head toward the premiere? I'm going to have to get through tonight and then break up with him, which doesn't exactly sound any better.

"Are you nervous? The tabloid reporters will say things."

"I'm fine. Did you find out who bugged your car?" I ask, unable to resist the topic.

Rich's face looks guarded but he smiles anyway. "Not yet."

My phone vibrates in my evening bag and I move my hand away from Rich's. In spite of my better judgement, I set up a Google alert for my name. Most of the stuff I have been getting is in regards to terrible fashion choices or how I am a slut and I don't bother to look at them. But something in this headline makes me stop. It is from republiccelebrity.com again with a blaring headline: *Stalked? Restraining Order Taken Out on Innocent Man!*

"Jenny?"

"Just a second," I reply as I quickly scan the article.

In fact, a source close to the actress states that Robbs is merely an ex-lover who has tried to reconnect with her. "She's so self-centered and thinks everything is about her," the source says, "She filed for a restraining order but I'll be amazed if it gets granted. I think she used Robbs to try to drum up attention that someone cares enough to stalk her." In fact, Jenny, who is filming the Amish drama Beloved currently, is using all the tricks in her book to get to the A-list. "She'll crush anyone under her feet if it means she gets what she wants. Robbs is only the latest in a long line of conquests, starting with the man in the sex tape and more recently her roommate going against her for a role," the source confirms. In any case, it will be interesting to see just how long Jenny can keep up these attention grabbing antics!"

I feel cold all over. The story echoes around my brain. There are leaked photos of the restraining order I filed at the courthouse. The only person who knew about the restraining order against Robbs is Jon. I feel my throat constrict. The limo is stopping. There is no way Jon could have done that to me, could he?

"Jenny, we are about to head out if you want to get off your phone," Rich snaps, clearly annoyed with me.

I can't think about this right now. There is no way I really believe Jon would leak that story and say those terrible things. It could easily just have been someone else at the courthouse. I glance quickly at Rich. I could believe Rich telling the press about Kane Lucky but I can't for a moment believe Jon would do something like that to me.

The limo stops and Rich gets out of it first, soaking up the attention he has been nagging me for. Right before I follow him out, my phone vibrates again. I glance down quickly and open a text from Jon.

IT WASN'T ME!!

I shove my phone in my purse and take Rich's hand. The lights of the cameras go off all at once and it feels as if I am drowning.

Chapter Fifteen

I have spots flying in front of my eyes by the time we get inside the theater. The paparazzi, luckily, shouted mostly things like, "Hey, over here!" instead of being assholes. I posed for photos, hoping I looked beguiling and pretty and wasn't showing every conflicting emotion across my face.

Walking down a red carpet was something I never thought would actually happen to me. I take note of Rich's arm constantly on me in some way, as if to let everyone know that we have arrived together. When I am instructed to take photos on the red carpet without him, his face darkens and he waits like a petulant child. I feel a stab of annoyance. His entire behavior tonight rubs me the wrong way. He doesn't even want me to have a moment alone to soak up my sun.

The photos are taken non-stop, leaving no room to have my mask slip. I must have a smile on my face at all times. I've read enough gossip sites to know even the smallest thing can be transformed into a full blown news article.

By the time we make it inside the theater, Rich is itching for a drink and yanking at his tuxedo jacket, clearly waiting for the best time to remove it. I am still irritated at him for making himself my date by pretending that we are patching up after a fight. Now everyone will have seen me with the casting director. So much for my image.

I look around the room. The lobby is bright with gold paint everywhere. The bar is fully stocked and crowded. Rich looks like a kid in a candy store when his eyes fall on it. Marina is in one corner and gives me a small wave and then a thumbs-up. I suddenly appreciate her kindness. Even though the production had to handle my sex tape being leaked, Marina never treated me any differently. She begins to walk over to me.

Rich makes his way to the bar as I mingle with people far above me on the success totem pole. I try not to look star-struck as Marina introduces me to some A-list celebrities, twirling me around the room with an efficiency that shows in everything else she does. I am not surprised that she is great with people as she is with organizing everything and everyone.

"I loved this cartoon growing up!" an actor I've seen in numerous movie musicals says to me as he shakes my hand.

"Your dress is beautiful, who designed it?" an actress asks me, touching the fabric gently. It is the millionth time I have been asked that question tonight and it is already growing old.

Rich is by the bar, talking to someone in earnest. I make my way toward him, a smile plastered on my face. I finally get to him and tap him on the shoulder.

"Oh, there you are," he booms, wrapping his arm around me. "I was just telling Mr. Johnson here about your dedication to your craft."

Mr. Johnson gives me a curt nod. "Nice to meet you. But I think I see my date waving me over to her."

"Yeah, he seems amazed by me," I mumble, watching him dart away from me as if I will do something terrible right then and there before I face Rich. "Hey, listen–"

Rich is sliding off his tuxedo jacket and hands it to me, as if I am the person manning the coat room. "I have to use the men's room, be right back."

I watch him leave, holding his coat and feeling stupider by the second. It is clear now that Rich wanted to run around with the elite of Hollywood and used me as a pass to get in. I sit down at the bar and order a drink. Rich's jacket is in my lap and I feel the weight of his phone in the pocket. It is vibrating. I roll my eyes and slide it out of the pocket, ready to throw it at Rich's head.

But I stop. The phone in my hand isn't Rich's phone. Rich has some state of the art smart phone that isn't even on the market yet. He treats it like his baby and I find it hard to believe it isn't permanently attached to him. But this phone in my hand is some tiny 2004 Nokia looking thing.

And I know the number on the screen.

The call is missed and goes to voicemail but nothing is left. With a glance over my shoulder at the direction of the restroom, I pull out my own phone and scroll to the last time he called me.

The numbers match.

"Fuck," I whisper and see an old lady glare at me as she totters off on her high heels.

I see Rich returning and before I can second guess myself, I shove the Nokia into my own purse. He comes back and I smile.

"My turn!" I trill.

"Hurry up, it's about to start," he says to me as the theater doors open.

I nod and take off, fighting against the crowd of people. For the first time in my life, the ladies' room is empty minus an attendant who looks bored in the corner. I step inside one of the stalls, and slide out Rich's Nokia.

The idiot didn't put a lock on it, clearly thinking it would never be out of his sight. I am not sure how long it will be before he realizes it is missing. I go to the texts, hoping against hope there are things there.

There are.

Tons of them.

With my vision blurring, I read the latest text from Robbs, *Story is supposed to go up right before the premiere.*

Because the phone is so old, I have to switch between the Inbox and the Sent to see what Rich is saying back. None of it is good. Random texts flash in front of my face.

She says she can't pay me back the $100,000. When I spoke to you in the diner about us doing more business transactions together, you swore you'd be able to double the money I let her borrow. Now I am out $100,000 and you can't find anyone who cares enough to buy the sex tape off of you, Rich had texted, the dates matching up with the week he was pressuring me to pay him back quickly.

*I thought I'd get $300,000 for the tape but she isn't well known enough. I am doing all I can. Please keep in mind that **you** approached **me** in the diner after she left about working together. I didn't approach you at all,* Robbs retorted and my heart slammed in my chest.

She isn't going to get the role in the Amish film. But I feel confident the sex tape will have the directors change their mind. This guy wants something to spark up some outrage and discussion. An actress with a sex tape playing an Amish woman is just the thing. Leak the tape and she'll get the role, Rich had sent to Robbs and my heart plummets in my chest knowing I have only gotten the role on *Beloved* because of my sex tape.

I leaked the tape, are you happy now? Robbs had sent the next day. *I get fucking nothing out of this, by the way. If your plan is to use her rising fame to leech off her money, then you better fucking share or I'm going wide with this.*

Don't worry, Rich texted back almost instantly. *Her star rising means more money for me and therefore for you. I've attached myself to her. She needs me.*

I feel tears spring to my eyes as I look over the text messages. There are messages about how Rich leaked the story about Kane Lucky for some quick cash and that I was onto him at dinner. A week of Robbs and Rich going back to forth about how Robbs has been contacted about the restraining order and has gone underground to shake off the courts. He leaks the story about the restraining order to get some quick money, timing it with the premiere to make me look the worst.

Rich and Robbs working together. My worst nightmare coming true. The fact that Rich went to Robbs at the diner to ask him to work together cuts like a knife. Had he planned that the entire time? I remember coming to him for help. Had he seen a way in at that very moment? Or was it only when he sat down in the diner behind me that Rich decided to team up with Robbs?

I let out a shuddering gasp, choking down a sob. The attendant is shuffling toward the door, clearly concerned.

"Ma'am, are you okay?" she asks.

"Yes, sorry," I squeak out at her before falling silent again.

The attendant pauses a moment before sitting back down at her chair and I burst from the stall. I am trying so hard not to cry that my face is turning red and my reflection in the mirror looks like I am going to turn into a tomato at any moment. I am paranoid the attendant will know who I am and tell the gossip magazines about me. I am terrified of everything.

I leave the restroom. My palms feel clammy. The phone is back in my purse and each breath I take hurts my chest. Do I go back to the theater? Do I get the phone out of here? But to where? I think about going to the police with the phone. The texts prove that Rich and Robbs leaked the sex tape. It will be enough to get them charged.

I turn to face the theater room doors. I can hear the movie already underway. My big debut and here I am, trying not to cry in the lobby. The doors open and to my chagrin, Rich comes out of the theater.

His eyes fall on me in the middle of the lobby, my cheeks sucked in from trying not to cry and my face a bright red that isn't flattering at all.

His gaze is cold and chills me to the bone.

He knows.

Chapter Sixteen

Rich crosses the lobby quickly and swiftly. The only person around is the bartender who is busy texting on his phone and not paying attention to a massive gossip scoop unfolding in front of him. Rich grabs my arm tightly, and I clamp my mouth shut so I don't cry out.

"You're missing the movie," he hisses and practically drags me into the theater, snatching my purse away from me to get his phone out of it.

I try to grab my purse back but he finds the Nokia and shoves it in his tuxedo jacket before throwing my purse back at me, narrowly missing my face.

I can't pay attention during the movie. Even when I am on screen, larger than life, with flawless makeup in spite of the fact monsters are doing battle in the city, I don't even enjoy it. My brain feels stuffed full of betrayal and self-loathing.

How stupid and idiotic am I that I fell back into Rich's arms? This is the same man who tried to get me to sleep with him for a role. How could I really believe that he knew it was wrong and was going to make amends for it?

Robbs leaked the news about the restraining order, but in my haste to get the full story, I was not able to read all of the texts. I still don't know if Rich has managed to get the legal documents leaked somehow. My guess is they paid someone off in the courthouse. I know Rich is involved in the nasty comments about me since he mentioned Kathy and trying to get the soap opera role over her.

The darkness of the theater is oppressive. I feel surrounded by bodies, none of which I can trust. Rich is next to me. He says nothing and does not glance at me as the film plays. This is supposed to be my moment yet all I can feel is fear. The air feels almost suffocating. My chest is tight and my vision blurs at the edges. I can feel a storm rising in me, a panic attack that I have not had in ages. I want to do whatever I can to stop it but I don't know how.

I focus on the bright Exit sign in the corner of the theater. I spend the rest of the film staring at it, lost in thought. When Robbs called me and told me to pay him off so he could tell me who had leaked the tape, he was trying to sell out Rich. But I refused and told him off. If I had found out then, what would I have done?

The fact Robbs had tried to sell out Rich is something I file away. There are cracks in their scheming. Each of them do not think they are getting the best deal. Rich wants to cling to me and raise up in Hollywood stardom with me as his ticket. Robbs wants money, plain and simple. Eventually that will tear them apart.

What will happen now that Rich knows I am aware of his doings? I am fearful of the man next to me. It feels like a new level of nightmare I cannot even begin to wrap my head around.

By the time film ends, I have watched about ten seconds of it. Applause fills the room. I am not that stupid. The film is summer blockbuster garbage but it will make a ton of money. The cast is called up to stand on the stage in front of everyone. I make my way past Rich, whose eyes are heavy on me. People's faces blur together. In my mind, none of them are friendly. All of them are out to get me.

I wish Jon was here. In fact, as soon as I can, I need to get to him and tell him everything. I need him to know. Now, more than ever, I want his arms around me to tell me it will be okay and I will pull through this. I want to feel safe.

I think of Jon as I step onto the stage with my co-stars. Fredrick is talking about the film at length at a small podium. There are flashes from newspapers taking photos. I hope my smile is convincing.

Even through the haze of Fredrick talking, people whispering to one another and photographers clicking away, I can feel Rich's gaze on me. It is heavy and sullen, taking me down with it.

I can't help but worry about what is going to happen next.

**-*To be continued in Book 3 -*

Book Three

Chapter One

"**JENNY, CAN** you smile a little wider? You look like you are at school picture day."

"Uh, yes, I'm sorry. Sorry," I say, giving a small wave of my hand, as if it will banish my dark thoughts.

The photographer nods and ducks back behind her camera, asking Kane Lucky to look "fatherly" toward me. It's been a week since the film premiere for *Fear Recoil* and the movie opens this Friday. A popular movie magazine is having the cast on the cover for this week's issue. Normally I would have been thrilled. But with everything that has unfolded over the last week, all I want to do is take a tub of cookie dough, curl up in bed and watch bad movies until the end of time.

Instead, I plaster a smile on my face that hopefully looks enchanting and stare at the camera. Kane Lucky tries to look fatherly, although I doubt he knows how, judging by the age of his dating history. Behind me, Marina is assisting the cast to get ready to move outside for the rest of the shots. I know it means I will be taken off to hair and makeup yet again. Photo shoots are exhausting.

"Okay, perfect. Let's take a twenty-minute break and then get everyone ready for the second round of photos."

I nod and everyone wanders off. I see one of my co-stars, Libby Montant, sneak outside to have a cigarette. I had been planning to sneak outside as well but Libby constantly acts as if her shit doesn't stink and I don't feel like being around that right now.

So instead I dart through the people working on the shoot, hoping to avoid any conversations and duck inside the bathroom, locking the door behind me. I exhale a little, my head throbbing. I was supposed to be enjoying this. This was my big break. My career was going to explode after this movie. Or at least that is what everyone is telling me. Filming on *Beloved* is almost complete. My small role on a slasher film will start soon after. I have people calling Jon for auditions instead of the other way around. I was on the brink of really becoming *someone.*

My phone, which I had snatched right as break was announced, gives out a soft ping. I unlock it and look at the screen, knowing I honestly needed to turn off Google Alerts for my name. But as much as I want to, I can't. Not when my boyfriend is the one feeding the rumor mill. This time the alert was simply for an article asking if I was the next big thing or simply a girl with a leaked sex tape.

I let out a sigh of frustration, wishing I could call them up and tell them off. *First off, I am a woman, not a girl, and secondly, I am talented and more than just a leaked sex tape.*

Yet the small voice in the back of my head began to taunt me – *are you really, Jenny?* I try to ignore it. The last thing I need right now is to feed into it. That is just what it wants. But the voice becomes louder. *You only got the role on Beloved because Robbs and Rich leaked the sex tape of you...*

"I am not listening to this right now," I say out loud to my reflection.

I half expect my reflection to reply but there is nothing forthcoming from it. My phone vibrates, and I look down to see Rich has texted me. A sour feeling grows in my stomach as I open it.

You done soon? Remember we have dinner tonight with some investors.

I don't reply. I know he will be furious with me for not replying but I am feeling rebellious. How can I be civil to him when I wouldn't mind bashing his face in with my own fists? I close my eyes and tell myself to calm down. Rage won't suit me. I need to focus on how I will keep my career as well as get away from Rich.

Rich – my boyfriend, officially, only because I am not sure how to get away from him with my dignity intact and my career still blooming. Rich – a slime ball I escaped from once before and then stupidly believed had turned over a new leaf. All he really wants to do is attach himself to my rising star and use me for money and fame. A fame leech - one of the worst kind. Rich wants me all to himself and he will destroy me if I don't give him what he wants.

I scowl and turn away from the mirror, trying to push Rich from my thoughts. He's just a new version of Robbs, and this came to fruition all because I had been too much of a coward to tell Robbs to fuck off in the first place when he slinked back into my life to blackmail me.

I leave the bathroom, getting ready to head back into makeup and put on a new outfit. This is my first real magazine shoot and while I like being all dolled up in pretty dresses, it isn't nearly as glamorous as it appears to the general public. For one thing, most of the outfits don't actually fit. Sure, it looks gorgeous in the photos, but the back of the dress is a mess of clothespins pinning the dress in just the right angles. Not as completely glamorous as I had assumed growing up.

Soon the cast is outside in a large field. We are using a mansion on the outskirts of Hollywood for the photo shoot. I don't know who the house actually belongs to, but it looks old fashioned. I wish I had more time to explore it. But as the sun is at the perfect height, we are all ushered out by the pool for more photographs. Libby is grumbling next to me about what the sun will do to her fair skin. She is awfully pale, which I suppose is part of her appeal. Lucky, who has more experience in photo shoots than the rest of us put together, is hitting on one of the young assistants. It would be funny if it weren't so gross.

As the photos are taken of us, either together or separate, I try to focus. The cast is about ten people, both major and minor roles, and we try to look natural, as if we all have chemistry with each other.

But my mind is far off. It feels as if it is full to bursting. I cannot enjoy anything anymore and I am not sure if I am ever going to be able to.

Chapter Two

"I hope you are calling me because you are heading back here," Rich says over the phone.

"Yes, I am. I couldn't have my phone with me on set. You know that."

"I don't want to be late to this dinner, Jenny. You know that if I can get these investors interested, they'll help me start my own production company. That means more roles for you, too." His voice is curt and cold, the way it has been since I found out what he was doing to me behind my back.

"Yes, we've been over this. I know. I'll get ready and meet you there at the restaurant, okay? I won't be able to meet you at your house."

"Fine," Rich replies and hangs up.

His tone hasn't been warm or inviting since I discovered how he worked with Robbs to leak my sex tape to the public. Since I stole his Nokia phone and discovered the truth the night of the movie premiere, Rich treats me like a business transaction instead of anyone he cares about. And why would he? Rich does not care about me. He wants fame and fortune, although he already has fortune. Why does he need me?

The production company idea had been announced to me earlier in the week. Rich apparently is no longer content to play as a casting director. Now that he has found me, he wants to aim higher. If he can have his own production company, then all projects will go through him. If it is successful, not only will he make money but he will be rubbing elbows with the Hollywood elite.

By the time I get home to my new apartment, I am in a foul mood. The idea of playing nice to some would-be investors and using my fledging star power to get Rich what he wants makes me sick. Not for the first time, I fight down the urge to cry. How stupid am I that I am always getting myself in these fucked up situations? I never listen to my gut feeling over men. I ignore it and look where it gets me.

I flop down on my couch, knowing I am supposed to be getting ready. But my limbs feel like they are each fifty pounds and all I want to do is fall asleep. My phone goes off, the ringtone breaking the silence that has settled over my apartment and I glance at it.

Jon.

My throat seizes up tightly. Jon, who I have feelings for, who declared his feelings for me and broke up with my old roommate, Kathy. Yet like two ships passing in the night, life gets in the way and I keep losing my chance to be with him. First Robbs and the sex tape. And now Rich.

Once again, I find myself pressing the ignore button on his call. If it is about audition or casting business, Jon will leave a voicemail. He is still professional toward me, even if our personal relationship is constantly in the shitter. The phone stops ringing and I wait to see if he's left a voicemail message. Nothing. So it was personal then.

I know I should talk to Jon. I want to tell him everything going on. I want to tell him how Rich has been spying on me, leaking information about me to gossip magazines for some quick cash and how he demands I date him or he will make things worse for me. But then Jon will ask how Rich will make things worse and I don't have the heart to tell him what Rich has over me.

At the thought of that, I manage to get off the couch, trying to push thoughts of Jon out of my head. What would Jon be able to do for me anyway? He will tell me to go to the police or even the press. But like with Robbs, the fear grips me tightly. Fighting against Rich terrifies me. I seem to only be able to function if I am struggling under someone's thumb.

"Fuck," I mumble loudly, hating myself at the moment with every fiber of my being.

Why am I such a fuck-up? In the back of my head, I think that I would have been a terrible mother. The thought brings tears to my eyes. I brush my eyes furiously, walking into my bedroom. I'll find some way out of Rich's claws. But the first thing to do is to get ready for this dinner.

I am back to taking baby steps to get through the day.

<<<>>>

"I think I can find some raw talent out there. Something that Hollywood hasn't seen before," Rich is saying as he refills my champagne glass. He must think I drank my last one quickly when I actually just dumped it in the fake plant next to the table when no one was looking. That last thing I need tonight is to be plied with alcohol.

One of the investors, an old man named Greg whose skin looks sallow, lets out a chuckle. "No offense, Rich, but we've heard that a lot around these parts. Everyone promises that."

"But very few people deliver," says Manson, the man next to Greg, an aging African-American man with very white teeth.

Dinner is not going as smoothly as Rich planned. I can see it on his face. He probably thought these men would be amazed by his speeches and his penchant for flattery. But these men are clearly from old Hollywood and have seen it all. I cannot help but feel some smug satisfaction at the fact that this is turning out poorly for him.

Rich tries to do damage control. "Gentlemen, I am sure you have heard it all before but this isn't just some speech I am spitting up for you to listen to."

"How will you be different from all other production companies? They are a dime a dozen in this town," Greg asks, leaning forward slightly.

I take a bite of the lobster I ordered – the only true highlight of this night. Whatever Rich had been hoping by bringing me to dinner has seemingly crashed and burned. Greg and Manson have no idea who I am, including the release of my tape. I am simply not well known enough to land on their radar. When Rich had commented that I am in the new *Fear Recoil* movie, the two men seemed unimpressed.

As Rich babbles on to them, trying to make a case for himself to be worthy of investing in, I find myself spacing out. Hopefully the men just say no soon and we can all go home. My phone vibrates in my purse and I sneak a peek at it, seeing that it is Kathy, of all people, texting me.

Kathy and I have not spoken much since I moved out of the apartment we shared. Our last real conversation had been her demanding I pick someone to date, Rich or Jon, and that I couldn't have both. I wonder if she is texting just to blame me for Jon breaking up with her.

I open the text message and read it quickly. *Call me!*

I slide my phone back in my purse, not interested in whatever she feels she needs to tell me. I am not in the mood to suddenly have to sit through a lecture from Kathy about Jon.

"Jenny." Rich's voice snaps me out of my thoughts and I look up at the table, "I was just explaining to Manson about your upcoming work on *Beloved*."

"Yes, yes. It is an Amish drama. I'm very honored to be getting some dramatic roles under my belt," I reply.

"Yes, but Rich has nothing to do with that project, is that true?" Greg chimes up, his eyes resting on me.

It is true but I balk at saying so. For some reason, I know that if I do, that will be the final nail in the coffin in regards to this deal going through. I had originally auditioned for *Beloved* because I was too nervous about relying on only roles through Rich. That's funny, considering my current circumstances.

"It's true that Rich is not working on the film," I say, wondering how much of a white lie I can craft. "But he suggested I try out for the film in order to downplay any claims of favoritism since we are dating."

Rich glances at me but I cannot read his expression. Not sure if I have said the right thing, I smile at the two men. Greg merely nods and Manson glances over at his friend.

"Well, we will let you know in the next few days what we decide," Greg says, standing up.

Rich stands up as well, bumbling over his words, "Gentlemen, it was lovely seeing you! I hope to hear from you soon!" He holds out his hand for a handshake but neither man gives him one. Instead, they say goodbye and make their way to the front doors of the restaurant.

Rich sits back down and turns on me, glaring. "Really, Jenny?"

"What? What did I do wrong now?"

"You should have just lied," he mumbles, looking furious. "You basically told them you didn't want to work with me."

I scowl. "How did you get that from what I said?
Why would I lie? These men would know I was lying
and how would that do you any favors? If I lied, they
would have said no on the spot."

"They're going to say no regardless," he snaps.
"How does it make me look when my girlfriend is
working with other production companies?"

"Sorry, Rich, I didn't realize I was supposed to
follow you around like a puppy on a leash for whatever
it is you want me to do. Why would I only work for
you? It looks even worse than if I went out and
discovered my own auditions. I still have an agent."

"For now."

The words make me freeze. Rich does not say
anything else to me, merely takes a swig of his
champagne and stands up.

"What do you mean by that?" I ask.

"It doesn't matter."

He pays the bill and I follow him out into the
parking lot. It is humid, even with the moon high in the
sky. There are no paparazzi around. I am hoping they
are losing interest in me about the scandal.

Rich's words about Jon bother me. I know there is
bad blood between the two of them but he cannot make
me drop Jon as my agent. Panic seizes me. It sounds
silly, but knowing Jon is still representing me has been
something that I have been clinging to in order to get
through the current mess I am in.

"What did you mean about Jon?" I demand as I stop in front of his car.

Rich spins on me and grabs my arm tightly, lowering his voice. "I said it doesn't matter. Are you hard of hearing? It doesn't matter because you fucked up the production meeting. I'm going to have to try other investors now."

I swallow my fear. "Why are you trying to make this happen so quickly anyway? Be more patient."

This only seems to piss him off more as he replies, "Because I need this. Because things need to happen quickly because my own personal timer is running out. And if *you* keep fucking it up, I will leak the fucking sex tapes of us, do you understand? I will cash in on you and leave you out to dry."

My breath catches. I have been trying so hard to keep the fact Rich has sex tapes he filmed without me knowing, out of my brain. If I think about it, I feel dirty all over, as if my skin is crawling. He told me the night I found out about him at the movie premiere. He had been so pleased with himself, too, telling me that he filmed us when I had sex with him on the couch in my old apartment and again in his bedroom the night I found out about the history between Jon and Kathy.

The fact Rich has filmed those moments make me sick. When I had ducked into the bathroom before the first time we had slept together, he had set up a tiny camera. He already had one set up in his bedroom. My career can survive one sex tape but two more and I will be finished.

"Why would you do that already? Then you won't get your production office. You won't get nearly as much money from me if you just leak the tapes."

"You think I will stick around in Hollywood after I leak the tapes? I'd take the money and run. Try again somewhere else. You're so stupid, Jenny."

"But," I falter, "Your parents—"

Rich lets out a dry laugh and finally releases my arm. Without saying anything to me, he gets in his car and pulls out of the parking lot, leaving me alone.

My chest is heaving and my brain is aching. Tears spring to my eyes as I curse myself for being so stupid. I head to my car, avoiding the eyes of an old couple squinting at me, as if they know where I am from.

For one wild second, I think about calling Jon and telling him about Rich's threat to blackmail me. But the thought dies as soon as I sit in my car. I couldn't handle him looking at me and thinking I was a shitty person. I wouldn't be able to handle him saying something cruel. I am not sure if he even would say something cruel or if I am just projecting.

I pull out of the parking lot, eager to try to forget the entire night.

Chapter Three

Between juggling interviews from the press for the upcoming film release and filming *Beloved,* it isn't until Wednesday that Jon calls and leaves me a voicemail, asking me to come into his office.

Feeling a mixture of both dread and excitement at seeing Jon again, I dress to impress and head off toward his office. There has not been a peep out of Rich since the botched dinner with Greg and Manson. Part of me hopes he is losing interest in me but with the movie being released on Friday, I know that it is a pipe dream.

I am in the waiting room, idly playing some game on my phone, when I hear Jon's laughter from down the hall. I look up but his assistant, clad in bright pink again today, is at her computer, typing away with her long fake nails. I hear a female voice and then Jon is saying goodbye.

The sound of high heels grows louder until a woman turns around the corner, stepping into the waiting room. She has long black hair that flows over her shoulders and down her back. It looks like silk. She is Asian and her eyes have dark makeup on them. On me, it would make me look like a terrible bitch. But on her it works with her skin complexion, creating a look with her red dress shirt and black pencil skirt that all melds together effortlessly. I wish I could create a look like that.

Jon's assistant smiles up at her. "All set, Miss Ryan?"

"Yes, thank you," she replies, her voice light and lilting.

"See you next time!" the assistant replies and the woman walks past me without a second glance, stepping into the elevator.

A million questions pop into my head and all of them are stupid. Of course Jon has other clients but I have never actually seen them at his office. It is like he times his appointments to never run over, so the clients never see one another.

The other thing bothering me is the woman was stunning. I mean, *super model* stunning. I cannot help but feel jealous that someone this gorgeous can talk to him at any time.

"Ready, Jenny?"

"Yes, sorry," I mumble, standing up and trailing after his assistant, who constantly smells like bubble gum, toward Jon's office.

She lets me step inside and shuts the door behind me. Jon is behind his desk, typing away quickly. He is wearing his glasses, which kicks up the butterflies in my stomach. His white dress shirt makes him look more professional than I have ever seen him before. I wonder if it is because of Miss Ryan and then quickly bar the thought.

"Hey, Jenny. Have a seat," Jon says and I sit across from him at his desk.

"How are you?" I ask, although I am dreading having to talk about our last conversation together.

"Getting by."

"Busy?" I hear myself ask, hoping I sound casual.

"Very busy. You probably saw Ayumi leaving. She's a long time client of mine but recently just came back from family business in Japan. Trying to get her career back on track."

I make a noncommittal noise, not caring a lick what Ayumi Ryan is doing back here in Jon's office. It is silly and I know it but I am still feeling jealous. Jon leans back slightly in his chair, studying me.

I speak first, "So, what's going on?"

"I know you have a busy week ahead of you. Just wanted to tell you that I have a film company interested in a big role for you."

I perk up. "Are you serious?"

Jon nods and looks at his computer. "It's a leading role for a big drama film named *Flower Queen*."

"Why do they want me? You mean I don't even have to audition?"

"That's right. If you agree to the terms and the script, it's yours." He slides a brown envelope over to me and my heart begins to pound.

I grab the envelope. "Why me? I mean, I'm psyched to read the script but come on. My first film isn't even out yet."

"They want to take a chance on you. You'd be working with some great people, Jenny. They've heard about your work ethic on *Fear Recoil* and *Beloved.* Which reminds me, you have to sign the paperwork for that slasher film, too…what is it called again?" he mumbles as he rummages through a drawer.

"*Silence Dolls,*" I reply instantly, reciting the ridiculous plot off the top of my head only because it sounds so fun to film. "Girls being kidnapped and turned into murderous dolls."

Jon lets out a small laugh. "Yeah, that. Sounds like a gem."

"Hey, it'll be fun. I loved watching that terrible junk as a kid. I seem to remember someone else having bad B-movie posters on their walls."

"Guilty. Just don't make slasher films a habit, okay?"

"Promise," I reply with a small smile.

There it is again – that easy confidence that we can slip in and out of without a second thought. Everything I do with Jon always feels so natural and relaxing. I never seem to question myself or every word I say.

But as soon as I think that, our last conversation comes to the front of both of our minds. Jon shifts in his chair and suddenly avoids my gaze. I know why. We never spoke again about him declaring his feelings for me. Like the first time we told each other we had feelings for each other, this has also withered and died and it is all my fault.

Jon shifts in his seat. "Listen, Jenny, we never really talked about our last discussion."

"Talking about talking?" I try to joke but it comes out dry and lifeless.

"You know I broke up with Kathy. And I was thinking about you and me but then I heard that you are officially dating Rich?"

Shit. I had somehow not even realized how terrible that makes me look. I have been so caught up in dealing with Rich and his threats that I didn't even stop to think about what Jon would be lead to believe once he heard about dating Rich.

"It's complicated," I say lamely.

Jon furrows his brow. "If you decided you didn't want to date me, that's okay. I mean, it sucks. But if you want me to back off…" He trails off.

I swallow hard. It isn't fair to Jon to tell him to keep chasing after me, especially with my own personal issues mounting. Part of me is urging just to tell him what is going on but once again I balk at him finding out Rich taped me having sex with him. And if Rich leaks those tapes, my career is dead in the water. What would Jon want with someone like me?

"Maybe we should just be friends," I say and the words feel as if they are poisoning me.

To his credit, Jon masks his confusion and merely nods at me before turning back to his computer. "Okay."

I feel like I need to keep talking because I can't just let it end there. "Jon, it isn't you. There is just so much going on with me right now and I am trying to sort it out."

But he holds up a hand as if to silence me, clearly either disinterested in what I am babbling about or how much it hurts that I am talking about it. I fall silent and Jon clears his throat.

"Let's talk business, okay?"

I nod and I feel my heart take another hit.

Chapter Four

I look at the contract again and let out a sigh. I lean back in my bed and turn on the small TV I bought for my bedroom, hoping for a distraction. In order to get out of Jon's office as quickly as possible, I took the contracts and a couple of scripts home with me, promising Jon that I would go over it at home and get back to him.

But the words seem to swirl in front of my eyes and make my head ache even worse. One of the smaller films that wants me to look over the script seems to have me naked in every other scene, as if my exposed humiliation means I have no problem taking my clothes off for films. The other film, the big drama *Flower Queen* that Jon has mentioned to me, looks great but has a clause in the contract stating that if anything sexual in nature or involving nudity of mine is shown to the press, I get fired.

I don't know what I am expecting. Of course companies aren't all going to think of my sex tape as a boon, such as the director of *Beloved.* But in the same token, other companies might very well take it as a free for all to get me to do nude scenes for their film. I am not interested in making my name off of my scandal so the film that wants me naked is out of the question. I shove the script away and look at the other script.

Normally the idea of getting fired over my unfortunate mishap would no longer concern me. With Robbs leaking the tape, my dirty laundry is out in the open. But Rich has ruined all of that. If I agree to this film, then I will have to toe the line with Rich until I figure out a way to get away from him. If I upset him, he will cut his losses and leak the new videos. Two more sex tapes will be the end of me.

I let out a groan, stretching out in bed, and close my eyes. As always, the thought of Rich casts a dark cloud over me. On top of that, I think of having to tell Jon I just wanted to be friends. I wish I could call him and tell him I lied. I wish I could tell him I am in over my head and need help but once again, the fear of him judging me beats out calling him for help.

Instead I curl up and read the script for *Flower Queen*. I don't want to miss out on this chance all because of Rich. If I can snag a role like this, it would show everyone that I can be a leading lady. It seems too good to pass up.

I try to shove all the thoughts out of my mind and focus on the story instead.

<<◇>>

"I don't want to go to this," I mumble as I look in the mirror, fumbling with my eye liner.

Behind me, Rich is picking out a tie. He gives me a small shrug, as if my complaints are pointless. He doesn't even bother to reply, which just irritates me more. I turn back to the mirror. I hate applying eye liner. I feel like it always comes out messy. Today is no exception. My frustration with Rich bubbles over and I curse as I mess it up, scrambling to find my makeup remover.

Fear Recoil opened in theaters today. There is a big party at Kane Lucky's house to celebrate. I had been formally invited by Marina. I had wanted to say no and stay at home, watch TV and shut out the world. But somehow Rich got wind of it and invited himself along. He refused to take no for an answer. Feeling powerless, I agreed and was currently getting ready to go.

"Rich," I say, my frustrations getting the best of me, "I do not want to go to this party."

Rich, finally called me early this morning just to tell me we will be attending the party, glares at me. "You know Greg and Manson said no to giving me funding for the production company."

I am taken aback, not because I thought they would have agreed but because Rich looks so angry. "Sorry." I reply, even though I do not mean it.

"This party is with the Hollywood elite. It is in Kane Lucky's fucking house. We are going to this, Jenny. It's not about you, it's about making connections."

"Fine," I mumble in response, giving in because I know if I protest again he will just threaten me with the tapes.

I turn back to the mirror and hide my guilty face. The truth is that I have also accepted the offer on *Flower Queen* with the no sex scandal and nudity clause and have yet to tell Rich. I know he will be displeased that I have taken on another film that has nothing to do with him. I am hoping he will not find out for a while, giving me more time to figure out how to find the tapes and get rid of them.

Rich does not notice my thoughts as he finishes up putting on his tie. He is anxious for this party to go well. I can tell by the look on his face. Not for the first time, I wonder how much he has lied to me about things. For instance, if he is so well off, then why blackmail me like this? Why work so hard to get a production company going? This house is clearly gorgeous and lavish. Where did the money come from? I know for a fact he works on projects, since he helped me with landing me jobs and was always around during castings.

So many questions yet no time to solve them. What I really need to do was start asking around about Rich. Surely people have dirt on him. Feeling motivated at having a plan at the party, I turn around and smile, my eyeliner finally on to my liking.

"Great," he says, barely glancing at me. "Let's head out. Limo will be here soon."

His house, which once offered me comfort and a place where I felt secure, now feels like a prison. We leave it behind as we get into the limo and ride in silence toward Kane Lucky's mansion. It isn't too far away, on a hill that overlooks other homes that look like tiny versions of Versailles. I have yet to see an A-lister's house and even though I still wish I was home in bed, I look forward to seeing how the elite live.

Rich barely masks his excitement as we enter the grounds of the house. Even though Kane's last three movies have been box office bombs, it has not affected his quality of life in the least. The gates open and we are stuck behind a line of limos. Apparently this party will not have a small guest list. I am hoping this means I can lose Rich in the crowd.

I spot a tennis court and what appears to be a small water park off to one side. I cannot imagine why someone would need a water park but I imagine after you hit a certain amount of money people just start adding things they do not need. But soon the tennis court and water park is whipped out of my view as the limo pulls in front of the massive mansion.

A man opens the door and Rich steps out first, forgetting to even help me out of the limo. Out of all the things he has done for me, this is minor but still incredibly irritating. We make our way up small steps toward the front doors of the house, which have been thrown open as if to welcome everyone.

Inside the foyer is a flurry of activity. Celebrities are making their way inside, past a large bookshelf crammed with books, I feel fairly confident, are only there for show. I cannot imagine Kane sitting down and reading one of them. We make our way through the foyer before stepping out into one of the main rooms. I try not to let my jaw go slack as I stare at the opulence. Kane clearly does not subscribe to the minimalist look. Instead this room is full to bursting with gaudy artwork and decorations that somehow make the entire room feel claustrophobic.

People are milling around, sipping on drinks and talking in small huddled groups. Music is playing but it is soft and classical. In fact, the whole thing looks less like a party and more of a soiree. I cannot help but feel disappointed at how dull the affair appears.

"Don't worry," says a voice from behind me. "These parties tend to pick up in the evening."

I turn around and see Marina there. She is dressed up, a rarity for her, and there is no iPad in sight. She looks pretty, with her black hair swept up in a bun and her dress fitting her perfectly. Marina glitters like a jewel and I smile, relieved at seeing someone I know.

"That's a relief. Not that I was expecting this to be like spring break but it seems so low key," I whisper, glancing over my shoulder to see Rich quickly depart into the crowd.

"Kane is always a big fan of throwing these mature parties. Every time he does, he swears it is going to be low key and mature. But by the time night time rolls around, everyone is drunk off their ass, blaring top forty and hopping into his massive pool."

I can't help but grin. "Sounds wicked."

"Don't be diving into any pools, Jenny," she replies, taking on a mock lecturing tone.

I put my hands up, as if I am completely innocent. "I'm here to discuss his art." I neglect to mention I want everyone, including Rich, to get smashing drunk so I can start asking questions about him without alerting anyone.

"Are you here with Rich?" she asks, as if she can sense my thoughts.

"Yes," I reply, hoping my tone sounds neutral. "Guess he's so excited he wandered off already."

"Right," Marina answers, although something in her tone makes me look at her twice.

"You made it! Wonderful!" a booming voice announces.

I turn around and see Kane making his way over to us. He is clearly in hosting mode. His face, which looks slightly puffy, as if he got some Botox done on his face and not just his armpits, breaks out into a well-rehearsed smile. While we have put the gossip story of his armpit Botox behind us, I know Kane is not my biggest fan. But anyone watching would never be able to tell from how he is acting.

Marina smiles as well. "You know I never miss one of your get-togethers."

"Ah, you are merely flattering me," Kane replies, although he is clearly eating it up.

"You have an absolutely amazing place," I remark.

His smile grows, this time with a touch of honesty to it. "I have spent years getting this house exactly right. I am proud of it. I'd love to show you around myself but I am so very busy with the guests. Marina," he says, facing her again. "Can you show Jenny around?"

"It would be my pleasure," she replies, although I am not sure how she feels about being delegated on her day off.

With a flurry of promises that he will check up on us later, Kane is gone, off to speak to a celebrity who has just entered that I am pretty sure is releasing a tell all book soon.

I look at Marina. "You don't need to show me around. Just enjoy the party."

She lowers her voice. "This place is a freak show, are you kidding? His house is insane, too." She gives me a grin and a quick wink.

I feel relieved that not only is Marina going to hang out with me but that her friendly nature wasn't an act while she helped me on the set of *Fear Recoil*. She grabs us each a drink from a passing waiter and we dive into the crowd.

The main room we are in opens up to another massive sitting room. This one is overly decorated as well. People are sitting around daintily, drinking and talking in soft voices. I have never been to such a quiet party before. I glance at Marina who jerks her head near a small door.

"Is that Rich?"

I look over. It is Rich. He is talking up an older man who sort of looks like a raisin. By the way he is laughing, I can tell he is trying to win the man over about something. Before I can ask Marina who he is, Rich spots me and waves me over.

"I'll be back," I mumble to her, hoping that whatever this is going to be will end quickly.

I make my way over to him and he grabs my hand quickly, feigning the happy couple routine. "Jenny, this is Mr. Smithson. He runs Bunny Hop Productions on the east side of town."

"Nice to meet you," I say, shaking his hand.

"I was just telling him how you were in *Fear Recoil* but wanted to get some TV work under your belt."

I try not to glare at Rich for his obvious lie. I have not once mentioned working in television. Not because I have anything against it but because I don't want to tie myself down to a TV show at the moment. But Rich's face is blank and I cannot read what angle he is trying to swing.

Mr. Smithson nods and gives me a toothy grin. "Television is in right now. A lot of people are trying it out."

"Right," I say. "Well, I'm just looking for the perfect project. I'm very picky."

Rich rests his hand on my shoulder. "If you have anything in mind, you should send it my way."

This irritates me and without thinking I reply, "Or through my agent."

Mr. Smithson glances at Rich. "I thought you were her agent?"

"I think Marina is calling me. Nice meeting you," I lie and give a small wave, darting off through the crowd before Rich can lecture me about messing something else up.

I feel irritated and swig the rest of my champagne. How am I supposed to keep up with all of his idiotic lies? I trail through the sitting room and end up in a hallway where the crowd isn't as thick. I lean against the wall, watching famous people I've seen on TV chatting. The hallway is littered with paintings along the walls. I can't imagine how much Kane has put into this place.

"There you are."

I look up and see Marina heading toward me, concern etched along her face. I try to look calm and swallow my irritation.

"Yeah, sorry, I couldn't find you. This place is like a labyrinth."

She is studying me now and I shift under her gaze. "You okay?"

"I'm fine," I say quickly. "Just overwhelmed by the party."

"Let's go by the pool and get some fresh air," she offers and I nod in agreement.

I follow her out through the hallway, out into yet another room, which has two televisions for some reason, and then outside. The pool is huge with a gorgeous waterfall flowing down over it. Foliage offers privacy from the rest of the lawn, where I can see the tennis courts and the small water park. People are chatting and one person is swimming in the pool. I realize it is Libby and she is already drunk.

"You didn't tell me you were back in town!" a woman says loudly, naturally drawing my gaze.

My heart plummets when I see that the woman, someone I am pretty sure is a model, is talking to Ayumi Ryan. Ayumi looks drop dead gorgeous, with her hair pulled up into a sleek ponytail. She is wearing a black form-fitting dress with silver jewelry. She is the last person I was expecting to see at this party. I am suddenly annoyed by the sight of her.

"Just came back from Japan," Ayumi says, hugging the model.

"Hopefully to take this place by storm."

"You know it," Ayumi replies with a small laugh.

I turn away from her, trying to focus on hanging out with Marina instead. I wish for the millionth time that I was home in bed instead of here.

Chapter Five

Marina ended up being right. By nine, the party was something I had only seen in movies or rock videos. The classical music was now blaring trance remixes of top forty music. People were swimming in the pool, sometimes naked, as other people did shots and stuffed their faces in the kitchen. The mansion was somehow even more crowded by the time it hit nine. Bodies crammed the rooms, dancing and talking loudly. My guess would be party crashers, seeing as everyone is too drunk to notice people coming in.

It is the perfect time for me to start asking around about Rich. Since the conversation with Mr. Smithson, I only saw him briefly, flirting with a model in the kitchen when I was going to get Marina another drink. Luckily he hadn't noticed me and I managed to get out before dealing with him again.

Now I am sipping only my second glass of champagne as Marina drunkenly talks to a man next to us at the pool. The music is so loud that I cannot make out what she is saying and the air is thick with mixture of chlorine and perfume. I'm pretty sure the body I can see passed out in a bush nearby is Libby. Everyone causally steps over her, as if this is a regular occurrence.

"You look so glum!" Marina has turned to me and is shouting in my direction, holding onto her drink.

"I'm fine!" I shout back, trying to be heard over the music.

"Where's Rich?"

I shrug in reply, not caring where he is. Ayumi trails by, talking with a group of people. It sounds petty to admit that I've had my eye on her most of the night. For some reason, I have a bad feeling in my gut when it comes to her but I'm not sure why. It is like I am waiting for something to happen either from her or because of her.

Marina grabs my arm and drags me toward a small alcove by the pool, with a couple of tables for people to sit and drink at. The tables are covered in empty glasses and one couple making out in the corner.

"I have to be honest with you," Marina says, clearly drunk. "I don't think you should be with Rich."

Eagerly I lean forward. "Why is that?"

"He has a terrible reputation. Really just no good."

"How so?" I press.

Marina looks off in the distance vacantly before waving at someone and then looks back at me. "He sleeps around a lot. And he is apparently really possessive."

"Where did you hear that?"

"Around." She waves her hands around, spilling some of her drink on herself, "Everyone thinks so. Also he tends to attach himself to some younger girls."

"Yeah, so I've heard," I mumble, slouching slightly, if only because I know all of this already.

"Anyway, I shouldn't be insulting your boyfriend. Hey, oh my god, are those mini-sliders?" Marina exclaims suddenly, eying a waiter with a tray. "I have to get one. Or twenty."

I watch her toddle off in her high heels and debate going after her. But something about what she has said about Rich has me frazzled. Of course I knew the rumors about him. And now I am stuck in his claws, trying to decide if it is worth giving up my career and becoming a hermit just so he'll leak the tapes and leave me alone or staying and fighting him for my freedom.

I leave the alcove, suddenly spurred on to find Rich. I weave in and out of the crowd, which has turned mostly into just drinking and dancing by this point. I step inside the kitchen, which is crowded and smells of cigarette smoke. I am almost mowed down by a man chugging a beer and manage to dart out of the way at the last second. I see Mr. Smithson flirting with a woman half his age. Freaked out, I duck into a small hallway near the kitchen and walk through it.

To my surprise, I end up in a bowling alley, which I remember Marina telling me about once we settled down by the pool. She also told me no one is allowed upstairs during these parties. Understandable, I had thought at the time, since people will probably sneak up there and do heavens only knows what.

However, it seems the bowling alley is full of nothing but people making out. A small group of four people are actually bowling on one of the two lanes.

Neon lights are flashing and even here the music is blaring. It reminds me of Underwater Nosh only I am not enjoying myself at all.

The mix of sweat, cigarette smoke and expensive perfume makes my head swim. I am about to leave when a neon light flashes brightly over the group at the bowling alley and I stop. The light illuminates the four people bowling. I don't recognize two of the people. But the other two, their faces close together as they yell in each other's ears, are none other than Jon and Ayumi.

For a second, my breath catches, as if I have caught Jon in the act of doing something wrong. It takes a few seconds for me to realize that Jon is doing nothing wrong. I was the one who told him we had to just be friends. Not only that, but he is merely hanging out with Ayumi. It isn't as if he is making out with her like everyone else in the room.

Still I feel my stomach turn. Wildly, I turn on my heels and leave the small room. Tears have sprung to my eyes, and I wipe them away furiously, feeling foolish. How can I be upset? Yet my bitter jealously sits heavy in my chest.

Even though I am in one of the large sitting rooms, the packed crowd starts to feel like they are closing in on me and it takes almost all I have to shove down my rising panic. Out of the corner of my eye, I see Rich. He is also drunk, sitting on a couch in the corner of the room, in a discussion with another guy dressed in a business suit. Even drunk, Rich is trying to make money. *I need to find out why he needs money so badly and so quickly.* I try to focus on something other than Ayumi and Jon.

I try to make my way through the room but it is slow going. I am not even sure where I am headed at this point. I debate just leaving but fear Rich being furious with me. I turn sharply to the left and step inside yet another room. This one has a large projector screen showing one of Kane's own movies. The scent of fresh popcorn from an old-fashioned popcorn machine wafts over. Mr. Smithson has walked in as well from the kitchen entrance, his eyes glazed over from drinking too much.

I make my way over to him and smile brightly, "Mr. Smithson! Lovely to see you again."

His eyes land on me and it takes a second for him to remember me before he nods, "Jenny, right? Rich's girl?"

I hide my annoyance at being called that and instead nod. "Yup. Given any thought to Rich's offer?"

Mr. Smithson looks as if I have caught him. I know he is not going to give Rich a dime for his dreams of a production company but I pretend I think it is a no-brainer. My smile is so bright that it is hurting the muscles in my face.

He clears his throat as an explosion goes off on the movie playing, "Maybe you can tell him for me that I think I am going to have to pass."

I let my face fall. "Why, sir?"

His eyes dart around, as if checking for Rich, and he leans forward. I can smell the wine on his breath.

"Rich is new to the area. Only came here a couple of years ago with high recommendations from Justin. So naturally we all want to help out someone *Justin* recommends to us," Mr. Smithson says in a way that I am supposed to know who Justin is. "But Rich is new money. I don't trust him. Especially the way he runs through his female clients. Disgusting." Seemingly realizing he is talking to Rich's girlfriend, Mr. Smithson's eyes widen. "Sorry, my dear, loose lips. Been drinking."

"Not a problem," I say quickly, leaning forward closer as a group of irritating men barrel through the room, loudly asking for a keg. "You said Justin recommended him to move to the city?"

"Yes, that's right, dear. Justin himself. Even helped him move from what I've heard. Although I cannot fathom why."

I open my mouth to ask what Justin's last name is but Mr. Smithson's eyes light up. I glance over my shoulder to see a model has stepped into the room.

"Talk to you later, dear," he says to me, stepping past me in a stench cloud of wine toward the model.

"Gross," I mumble, disgusted at how many old men are leering at young women here.

I move out of the way of a group coming through and flatten myself against the wall. On the movie projector, Kane is running through a jungle with his hapless heroine. I doubt anyone is paying attention to it anymore. If every Hollywood party is like this, I need to start faking sick.

I wiggle out the nearest door, spilling out onto a second patio. This is a little more low-key. The few tables here are filled with people but they are speaking in hushed voices instead of yelling over loud music. At this point it feels as if everyone in Hollywood has shown up here, invited or not.

Mercifully, I spy an empty bench nearby. I sit down on it and try to collect my thoughts. Mr. Smithson said that a man named Justin basically was Rich's ticket into Hollywood society. The way he spoke of him clearly showed that Justin was notable enough that no one would question Rich's credentials.

But without a last name I still was floating adrift in the sea. Did Justin really think Rich was great enough to work in Hollywood or had Rich scammed him somehow? I bit my bottom lip, lost in thought. The name is more than I had even an hour ago. It is something I can go off of. I still have access to Rich's house, after all. Surely there is something in the house that will let me know who Justin is and if I can get in touch with him.

Even outside, the air smells of sweat, perfume and booze. My headache is throbbing. I close my eyes, trying to collect myself when I hear someone call my name.

Surprised, I open my eyes and my heart plummets to my stomach. Jon has come outside onto the small patio. Behind him is Ayumi. They are not touching but are standing close together. The two others who had been with them at the bowling alley are not with them.

"Jon." I say, wishing I could get away from this moment.

"I didn't know you were here," he says, now standing in front of me.

"Crazy party, isn't it?" I ask, trying to sound light and casual.

"Kane's always are. I wasn't even invited but Ayumi got me in."

Ayumi smiles at me and holds out her hand, introducing herself. I shake her hand, noting that her skin is so smooth it is like silk.

"Having fun?" I ask her.

"Sort of. Japan was pretty quiet. This is a lot louder."

"Sort of reminds me of high school," Jon says. "I can't believe the amount of people here and how crazy this house is."

"Kane is constantly trying to hang onto his youth," Ayumi replies.

"Do you know him well?" I can't help but ask, curious.

Ayumi's eyes dart around quickly, as if seeing if anyone is standing close enough to overhear. Then she leans forward. I smell her perfume – a mix of jasmine and bergamot.

"I was his beard for about six months."

She then straightens herself out. I try to wrap my mind around what she has just told me. Ayumi has a scandalous expression on her face, as if she has just told me a major secret.

"Wait, you're saying—"

"Don't say it out loud!" She exclaims, looking over her shoulder before turning back to me, "It is like the worst kept secret. It was never officially stated to me but…it was made pretty clear."

"Wow," I breathe.

"We're going to head out now," Jon says. "I have an early meeting. Get home safely, okay?" His gaze lingers on me a beat too long before he looks away.

"Have a good night," I say to the two of them but the words are hollow.

I watch as Jon and Ayumi turn around, stopping one more time so she can chat to a woman at one of the tables, before going back in the house. I sit on the bench, feeling depressed. Were they leaving together just as friends or something more? As soon as the thought enters my brain, I wish I could shut my brain up.

I can't help but dwell on the fact that Jon and Ayumi are leaving the party together. Ayumi was nothing but cordial to me, which makes the fact I feel so jealous, ridiculous. It wasn't as if she even knew what was going on between Jon and me. She probably only sees him as a friend.

I think of the way Jon's eyes rested on me too long. That was the only indication that he was still thinking about me in that way. *I have to take care of things on my end before I can even consider coming to you,* I tell him mentally. But what if I sort everything out and Jon has moved on? It isn't as if I can blame him for that. I am the one who told him we are just friends.

My head is pounding harder now. I stand up, feeling dizzy for a moment. The heavy scents in the air get to me. The panicked sensation I felt in the bowling alley returns to me. It feels as if someone is sitting on my chest, slowly caving it in. It is hard to breathe.

I stumble back inside the house. I am back in the room with the projector. It is past 10 P.M. and it feels as if the party is just kicking up. I weave through the crowds and get turned around in the crush of people. Someone is trying to make a speech in the kitchen. I cannot tell who it is but it must be someone very famous because people are all trying to head there in one surge. I press against the crowd, the sensation of the walls closing in on me only growing stronger.

I let out a gasp for air, knowing that the last thing I need to do right now is have a panic attack in the middle of the party. I press against the crowd and finally burst through the edge of the cluster of people trying to shove into the kitchen.

I am in a small room filled with paintings and statues. There is a large window overlooking the grounds of the house and bookshelves along one wall. Next to me is a staircase. Remembering Marina's warning that the upstairs is supposed to be off limits, I glance over my shoulder. No one is looking at me. All of them are trying to hear the drunken celebrity's speech.

I lower my head and duck behind the small red ribbon that has marked the staircase off limits. Quickly I dart up the stairs and turn around a corner, exhaling. It is almost as if the party has turned off downstairs. I cannot hear anything from down below. The floor looks as if it is made from mahogany with a plush red carpet along the middle. At the end of the hallway are two people making out. They see me and look like cats caught in the act of doing something wrong. Quickly they dart off into a bedroom, shutting the door behind them. Apparently I am not the only one to sneak up here.

I walk down the hallway slowly, focusing on my breathing. I decide once I calm down I am going to leave. Rich be damned. I cannot take another second at this party, wondering if Jon and Ayumi are just going to be hanging out afterward or going to their own respective homes. My head feels full to bursting.

I turn down a smaller hallway and wander down it, looking at the photos on the walls. Suddenly I hear a laugh I know too well – Kane. Panicked, I look around. He is coming down the main hallway with someone. The last thing I need is for him to see I snuck upstairs. Maybe he would be understanding if he didn't already dislike me for what he believes was me blabbing his personal things around town.

I duck into the nearest room and close the door quietly. It is just in time because not even a couple of seconds later I hear Kane go into the bedroom next door. I exhale softly and wonder how long I should wait before heading downstairs. The crushing sensation in my chest has been replaced with a panic of being caught trespassing.

I turn around and look at what room I darted into. It is nothing more than a guest bedroom. I let out a small sigh. Just my luck to be sneaking around Kane Lucky's house. Not for the first time I wonder why my life is such a mess. I am about to leave and try to sneak downstairs when a photo on the dresser catches my eye.

As I can faintly hear Kane talking from the room on the other side of the wall, I tiptoe over to the dresser for a closer look at the photo. I see that Kane is leaning in next to an older man with slicked back hair. They are both extremely tan and a beach is behind them, crystal clear with a piece of a blue sky at the top. There is a signature on the photo that reads: *Great to see you! Hope we keep in touch! Justin Longhorn.*

I pick up the photo and study it closely. There are a million people named Justin in the world. There is no promise that this is the same man Mr. Smithson was meaning. But a girl can dream.

But I will dream later. Right now I need to bolt. I go to leave but stop for one second before pressing my ear against the wall. Last thing I need is to burst out of the bedroom and run right into Kane.

I hear Kane speaking in a low murmur but whoever is with him has no idea how to whisper because I hear through the wall, "I have wanted to kiss you all night."

I take a step back from the wall, quickly thinking back to what Ayumi claimed about Kane earlier in the night. *No business of mine,* I think before opening the door and stepping out into the hallway.

I move down the hallway quickly and down the stairs, toward the front door. I figure Rich can find his own way home. I will get the limo to myself tonight.

Chapter Six

It is Monday evening and I have just gotten home from filming *Beloved* for the day. Rich called me almost instantly, asking that I come over.

"The tabloids have noticed you are never near me," he had said on the phone. "They ask why we are only ever seen at events together."

"So what?" I had asked him, not following why he should care what those rags are saying.

He had sighed, as if I was very dim. "I need them to believe we are a happy couple, Jenny."

I had relented, if only because I secretly want to snoop around his house and see if I can find anything about Justin. If it turns out that the Justin Mr. Smithson mentioned at the party and the Justin Longhorn in Kane's photo are the same person, then I have something I can start working with.

I got off the phone with him and begrudgingly started getting ready to head over to his place.

"Jenny?" Jon's voice snaps me out of my thoughts and I throw the shirt I was holding onto my bed.

"Yeah, sorry. What did you say?" Jon had called shortly after Rich called so I had been on the phone with him and had totally spaced out.

"I was running down your schedule for the week but I doubt you heard a word I said."

"Sorry," I mumble. "My mind was somewhere else."

"Are you okay?"

Sensing that answering that question could lead to a conversation I could not safely have without broaching real feelings, I try to duck it and reply with, "Yeah, just tired."

"You seemed sort of…overwhelmed at Kane's party on Friday."

"Did I?" I ask and then keep talking, not waiting for him to reply, "Did you get home okay?"

"Yeah. Grabbed some food with Ayumi and was fast asleep by midnight."

At the mention of Ayumi, my stomach knots itself. I think of the two of them eating dinner together at some late night diner in Hollywood. A sour feeling sits in my gut as I try to swallow my jealousy.

"Great. Listen, I have to go see Rich so just email me the schedule, okay?" I say quickly before wishing him a good evening and hanging up.

Once the call is finished, I stare at the phone. It feels like dead weight in my hand. I fight the urge to toss it against the wall. If I think about myself too much, I feel an overwhelming feeling of self-loathing wash over me. It is my fault that I fucked up things with Jon both times we grew distant. It is my fault I was too scared to face down Robbs and make sure I had all the copies of the tape. I can't help but think I deserve to be in this situation.

But as soon as I think that, I tell myself it isn't true. I have made mistakes and maybe I have terrible judgment. My personal history is muddled and chaotic. But it is in the past. If I want to get rid of Rich's inky tendrils clinging to me then I must do it myself. If I lose Jon completely in the process then that is the price I will have to pay.

My phone vibrates in my hand. It is a text from Kathy. All it simply says is to call her. I ignore it. No time. I am already running late to meet Rich. Quickly I dress and then make my way to his place. I am ready to be charming and kind tonight, to throw him off and to have him lower his guard so I can snoop around his house.

The sun is starting to set by the time I get to Rich's house. The sky is a murky mix of black and orange, as if the sun has spilled over and is leaking into the rest of the sky. The air is humid and feels almost thick when I step out of the car. True to Rich's word, there is a lone paparazzi car across the street, trying to snap photos of me. I take my time, letting them take shots. I half expect Rich to come out and greet me into his home since he is so desperate for the media to believe we are dating.

Luckily he doesn't and when I step inside, I exhale. It is freezing in the house, a welcome respite from the humidity outside. His maid is just leaving, giving me a curt nod as she walks out the side door. I make a mental

note to be here when she is working so I can ask her
questions.

"Did they see you?" Rich asks as a greeting as he
comes out of his kitchen.

I nod. "Yeah, I lingered so they took a couple of
shots."

"Great. I need them to think we are seriously
involved, Jenny. I want this production company."

"Why?" I can't help but ask, unsure why this
production company means so much to him.

He sits down on the couch and I remain standing. I
don't feel like sitting next to him and taking another
chair might piss him.

Rich looks lost in thought for a moment before
replying, "Acting as casting director makes solid
money. I know that. But I could make so much more if I
had my own company."

"So it's about money," I deadpan.

"Everything is about money, Jenny. Casting
directors are a dime a dozen in this place. I want to be
more than that. I want to have my own production
company. Finding the talent, finding the projects that
matter. Making money on those projects. I've been
working as a casting director for two years now. I want
more."

I wonder how much, if anything, of what he is
telling me is a bunch of bullshit. "And you need me to
do this."

"You're a rising star. You made your acting debut in a franchise, yeah, but that sex tape still launched some curious faces your way. People know who you are. You got that movie coming out. The Amish one," he says with a wave of his hand like he can barely remember what I am doing. "And that slasher film, *Silence Dolls.*"

I remain silent. I debate telling him how I signed on for *Flower Queen.* Surely he will find out soon on his own anyway and it might be better if he hears it from me. He might even think I am turning over a new leaf in our agreement if I word it properly.

I take a deep breath and sit down on a chair across from him, still not ready to sit near him. "And *Flower Queen.*"

His eyes narrow. "What?"

Quickly I tell him about the film, slyly mentioning the clause in the contract against any leaked sex scandals and nude photos connected to me. At first he looks furious over what I have done but that starts to abate as I mention the money attached to the film. By the time I finish my tale, in a sweet voice, I have spun it in such a manner that I think Rich is convinced he was the one who told me to take on the movie.

"This is a big role," Rich says, mostly to himself. "I mean, you have the lead. Studio backing. They just offered you this?"

I nod. "Apparently the director wants to work with some new blood. I had my first phone call with him yesterday on the set of *Beloved.* He made it clear taking me on is a gamble. But how I handled myself on *Fear Recoil* set was apparently impressive and word got around." I gave a small shrug, silently blessing my good luck in at least the movie arena.

"Don't blow this, Jenny," Rich says sternly, as if I have been doing nothing but drugs since my first paycheck. "This can make or break you, you know that, don't you?"

"Actually," I reply slowly, as if the thought has just struck me. "You could."

Rich doesn't seem to understand and I wonder if he is really stupid and I am overthinking his intelligence when I reply, "The tapes, Rich."

"Oh." Understanding dawns on his face. "I told you – as long as you don't fuck this up for me, they'll stay sealed."

Not the answer I am hoping for. I had been hoping he would slip up on where he has the tapes and the back-ups for them. Instead he stands up.

"I ordered Chinese food, c'mon."

I follow him into the kitchen, where we sit at the breakfast bar with the TV near the fridge on, watching a sitcom. I will play nice until Rich falls asleep, I decide. He glances over at me and I smile.

By 10 P.M., Rich is yawning. Our fake date is boring him and I can tell he wants me to leave. Yet he keeps checking the window, to see if the paparazzi are there. If they are, I have no doubt he will ask me to stay the night in the guest room, to keep our illusion going.

Luckily he looks back at me. "I think they are gone. I'm going to head to bed now."

"Okay. I'll get my stuff and go."

He nods, knowing better than to ever suggest us sleeping together anymore. I move slowly as I gather my purse and then frown.

"Have you seen my phone?"

Rich casts a lazy look around the living room. "No."

I managed to hide it in a drawer in the downstairs bathroom and use it as a ruse to look around later, trying to find it. Rich watches me with a blank expression on his face.

"Just let yourself out when you find it, okay?" he says, not even offering to call it to hear it ring.

I watch him turn and head toward the stairs. I pretend to look around some more to lag around as Rich got into bed. He always can fall asleep almost instantly and I am banking on that tonight.

I shuffle around the house, pretending to look for it. Finally after fifteen minutes of searching, I pause and walk to the bottom of the staircase, trying to see if I can still hear him. There is only silence. I back up and take my phone out of the bathroom before going back and creeping up the stairs. I stop in the hallway, holding my phone out in case Rich demands to know what I am doing upstairs. I can lie and say I am just letting him know I found my phone.

But the incredibly loud snoring that is coming through his closed bedroom door lets me know that Rich has already fallen asleep. I am envious of how quickly he can doze off. Lately it takes me ages to be able to calm down enough to fall asleep.

I head back downstairs. The first room I want to check is his office next to the kitchen. He could have evidence in his bedroom but his office is a better bet. Throwing one last glance over my shoulder, I head into the kitchen and then into the office.

This is the first time I have been in here. Rich has it sparsely decorated probably due to the fact that he is strictly fixated on his business or whatever life he is thinking about ruining. I sit down at his desk. There are no photos. Like the rest of the house, it feels as if I am in a hotel instead of someone's home. There is nothing personal to be had anywhere in the house, this office included.

I am unsure what I am looking for. His computer is password locked and I have no idea what it could be. Even though Rich is asleep I know from our previous dating history that he can wake up and come downstairs for a drink of water after a vivid dream. I cannot take my sweet time looking around the office.

Even though I am confident the computer probably holds the sex tapes and I could even access his cloud account to get the back-ups, I decide I will have to tackle that another night. Instead I start opening drawers to see what I can find, if anything.

The first couple of drawers are filled with regular things like bank statements and policies on insurance.

There is nothing of note. Another drawer is filled with blank notebooks. Not pegging Rich for a writer, I flip through a couple but they are both blank. My hands go to pull open the third drawer yet it does not budge. I try again but it is locked.

Whatever is in this drawer has to be important if Rich has locked it. I bite my bottom lip, wondering where he would put the key. I run my fingers along the bottom of the desk. In the middle of the desk my fingers brush against something. I pull it down and stare at the small gold key with tape around it. *Key taped to the underside of the desk – this is the man I am allowing to outsmart me?* I can't decide if Rich is dumb or just lazy.

I slip the key in the lock and it clicks open. I pull open the drawer slowly. There is a pile of papers in here. I begin to leaf through them, my breathing coming a little faster now. I skim them, waiting for something to jump out at me. A name finally catches my attention – Justin.

I pull out the piece of paper and quickly read the body of the email:

Justin,

I am awaiting, per our discussion, the recommendation letter you are writing to ensure my transition to Hollywood goes smoothly. Once the letter is received, the documents I have from your personal assistant will be released to you and you can consider this transaction complete. Please remember I am not to see you in Hollywood for five years after my move.

Rich

I look at the email a couple of times before noting
the last name in the email address: Longhorn. So Kane
does know the same Justin. I file that information away.
I quickly type in Justin's email into my contact list in
my phone. I glance at the email again. Reading in
between the lines coupled with what I know about Rich
makes it clear that Rich blackmailed Justin for a letter
of recommendation to get him into Hollywood.

I am about to go through the rest of the papers when
I hear a shuffling noise.

"*Shit,*" I hiss through clenched teeth.

Rich must have woken up already and is coming
down for a drink of water. I thought I would have had
way more time. I shove the papers back in the drawer
and put the key hastily back underneath the drawer. I
hear Rich coming down the stairs, emitting a loud
yawn.

Quickly, I duck underneath the desk. I have left the
door to his office open. It is usually always closed. My
only hope is he is too tired to notice that it is open. I
crawl underneath the desk, bringing my feet to my chest
and holding my breath.

I hear him step onto the marble flooring in the living
room. I focus on the steps he is taking toward the
kitchen and squeeze my eyes shut. *Please keep walking.*
I am not sure what Rich will do if he catches me
snooping around in his office.

But the footsteps stop. He has noticed. I wish I
could curse out loud but I remain silent. The door to his
office makes a small squeak as Rich pushes it open

wider. I try to make myself as small as possible. His desk is large so even if he steps in front of it he will not see me unless he looks underneath it.

I can hear Rich breathing, soft and slowly, as if he thinks he is still sleeping. I should have thrown a bottle of water at his head before he went upstairs to keep him from having to come down later. Rich pads forward and I can see his feet coming around the desk. I hope I am as small as I can be. He stops in front of his desk and I hear a couple of things click. I hear the computer make a shut off noise. Seemingly satisfied, Rich turns and walks away, shutting the office door behind him.

I wait, straining my ears to hear him through the walls. I stay perfectly still and wait ten minutes until I finally untangle myself and crawl out from underneath the desk. I have Justin Longhorn's email address. That might be all I will be able to get tonight.

I peek outside the office door. The house is silent again. Quickly I dart across the living room, hearing Rich snoring upstairs. When I finally get in my car and pull out of the driveway, I feel relief at breathing in the night air.

Chapter Seven

The wrap party for *Beloved* is a small affair, although I suppose everything can be considered a small affair after Kane Lucky's party. It is no way like that bash. I end up inviting Marina anyway and while we are there she apologizes for what she said about Rich.

"I was so drunk. I really crossed a line, Jenny. I should have just kept my mouth shut," she says as she sips her glass of water.

The party, which is only about thirty people, is at a lounge bar in the middle of the city. *Beloved* had been a low-key shoot and I had enjoyed putting my best foot forward in it. I had two days of filming *Silence Dolls* and then a little time off before production on *Flower Queen* began. I am nervous about *Flower Queen*. The director, Matt Baylock, is a rising star with the support of some older directors and producers giving it funding. I am meeting him for the first time tomorrow morning before reporting to the set of *Silence Dolls*.

While I am grateful someone rising wants to take a chance on casting another rising star in the lead of the drama, I am still worried it will somehow blow up in my face. If Rich still decides to leak the sex tapes before I can find them or get him out of my life, then I will lose the role.

I try not to think about Rich tonight. In fact, I am trying not to think about any of my worries or concerns tonight. Tonight is to celebrate *Beloved* and I am determined to enjoy it.

I focus my attention back at Marina. "Don't worry about it. Believe me, you weren't the only one who blabbed to me about Rich that night."

Her eyes widen. "Really?"

"Yeah. It's fine. I know about how he apparently was dating girls new to town and everything."

"It isn't that I think he is terrible," Marina says and leans forward. "But you seem great, Jenny. I've been in this business almost ten years and you have this fresh talent. And it shines through. I think that is why Matt offered you the deal on *Flower Queen.*"

"That isn't official yet," I lie.

"Right, of course," she says quickly.

That is another reason I am trying to forget about Rich tonight. Gossip magazines have started reporting that I have been cast in Matt Baylock's film before it was officially announced. I feel confident that it was Rich who has leaked that news, for his usual scheming reasons. It was a risk I took when I told him about the news but I figured if he found out at the official announcement, it would just make things worse for the two of us.

"Listen, I hate to show my newbie experience here but at Kane's party, I kept hearing people talk about a Justin Longhorn guy."

Marina frowns. "Really? He's been absent from the scene for a good two years. Apparently lives in some hermit house in Jamaica somewhere."

"Yeah, no idea, everyone was pretty drunk so I think they were all just shooting the shit," I lie, hoping I sound convincing.

"Justin Longhorn was a pretty prominent producer and writer for a while here. He left two years ago. He might still have a Wikipedia page up. Anyway, he was a bigwig for a while. He left pretty suddenly…" Marina trails off, as if she just remembered something.

Someone accidently bumps into me and I manage to wave them off with a smile before turning back to her. "What is it?"

"Well, I heard this rumor that shortly before he announced that he was leaving town that Rich came into town with this glowing recommendation letter from Justin. It was unheard of because Justin has never done that for anyone before and no one had ever seen or even heard of Rich in the industry prior to that." Her eyes widen a little and she shakes her head. "I'm sorry. I can't believe I'm talking about Rich again. I'm a terrible friend."

Something propels me forward toward her and I grab her arm, lowering my face. "Marina, I need to know everything you know about Rich."

Her eyes widen, bright and green, at my sudden shift. But before she can reply, there is a chorus of cheers at the front door to the lounge. My own eyes shift upward and my heart skips a beat. Marina turns around to see who is coming in as well. I know who it is before I can even see her.

Ayumi strolls in, wearing a cute pink sundress, her hair swept up in a loose bun and a matching purse swinging on her wrist. She looks adorable, as if she has just gotten back from the beach and decided to swing by. In fact, I wouldn't be surprised if that was the truth.

However, I cannot believe she is *here*. It is like we are constantly bumping into each other at every event since she has come back from Japan. I cannot believe my luck. Marina must feel my grip tighten on her because she sends me one curious look.

"She's friends with the director, didn't you know?"

"She's friends with everyone apparently," I reply darkly.

Marina looks as if she is going to reply but at that second someone else comes in next to Ayumi. My heart tightens hard and then lurches as Ayumi pulls the person forward before grabbing their hand.

Jon.

"Fuck," I mumble, feeling as if someone has reached into my brain and scrambled it with a spoon.

I cannot let Jon see me. He is looking around almost bashfully. He knows this is my wrap party. Ayumi's hand is holding onto Jon's – a declaration that they have moved past the friend stage. I cannot stand it. I turn around, tears springing to my eyes as I make my way to the outside patio of the lounge. I push through a small cluster of people and step out into the night air.

It is humid and the patio is covered with roses. Their perfume fills the air as I move toward a corner of the patio, sitting down, wishing I could melt into the cracks in the stones. Once again, I try to tell myself that I told Jon to move on. I can't be mad at him for actually taking my advice. But it still hurts because I brought this on myself. If only I hadn't been so stupid as to let Robbs and Rich pull one over me, I could be with Jon at this party myself.

"Jenny?" I hear Marina following me, probably confused as to why I stormed out here.

She sits next to me and I wipe the tears from my face, glad I wore waterproof mascara tonight. Marina is looking at me, concerned.

"Sorry," I say, wiping my cheeks free of the tears. "I'm so stupid."

Marina hands me her glass of water and I take a sip. She doesn't say anything but I can tell by her gaze that some things are clicking into place. I feel silly for exposing myself to her. The last thing I want is for her to say something cruel to me.

But as I lower my glass, she lets out a small sigh. "I had no idea. I should have guessed. At Kane's party you seemed freaked out at seeing Ayumi there."

"I'm sure she's great," I mumble. "I'm just being a bitch."

"How long have you had feelings for him?"

I give her a small shrug. "It doesn't matter. I told him we had to be friends."

"Why did you tell him that?" she asks with a small frown.

I let out a desperate sigh, unsure how to even begin to tell the story. But something about the way Marina is looking at me, like a friend instead of a business acquaintance, makes me want to open up to her. No one else knows what Rich is putting me through and the burden is a heavy one.

There is a laughter from inside and with a quick glance I see Ayumi throwing her head back at a hilarious joke. My gut twists and I turn back to Marina. Slowly, in careful words as to not to alarm her too much, I explain to her about Jon and I missing each other due to our disagreement over how to handle the sex tape. My embarrassment at being too afraid to stand up to Robbs and ensure all copies of the tape were destroyed only made things worse. Coupled with wanting to make Kathy happy and dating Rich, we have now missed each other.

Marina blinks. "But why are you with Rich if you are clearly into Jon? Not that I am judging you," she says hastily, afraid of offending me. "But it doesn't seem fair to Rich."

A dry laugh emits from me. I can't help it. Anything being unfair to Rich strikes me as funny. My laughter only confuses Marina more. I shake my head, as if I am trying to clear my mind.

"I'm not dating Rich because I care about him. I'm dating him because he's blackmailing me."

"What?" she exclaims, her eyes so wide that I am afraid they will pop out of their sockets.

I tell her about the tapes and how Rich is holding them over my head. By the time I finish, I feel as if a burden has been lifted off of my shoulders. Telling someone else, even though I am embarrassed by my current situation, makes me feel a lot better. The crushing sensation on my chest eases a little, although the pain of seeing Ayumi and Jon together is still aching.

Marina's face has drained of color. She covers her mouth with her hand, in shock. I am betting whatever rumors she has heard about Rich have ill prepared her for what I have just told her.

"Oh my god, Jenny. You have to…I mean, we have to do something about this. You can't let this happen."

"What am I supposed to do?" I say to her, lowering my voice as a couple of people stroll out on the patio, lighting up cigarettes.

"Go to the police or something!"

I shake my head. "No way. Are you kidding? Rich will just release the tapes and then vanish. I don't want to risk it. I'll lose my career, Marina. This new way of life, as stressful as it is—" My voice catches and I am unable to put into words how messed up things were before I moved out here.

She rests her hand on mine. "We'll figure it out together, okay? Somehow. We'll get those tapes and get Rich in serious fucking trouble."

I smile wanly at her, not sure if I completely believe such a thing can happen but wanting to put my faith in

Marina anyway. Having told someone fills me with some lightness that I haven't felt in ages. I want to tell her what I have discovered and how I am debating contacting Justin Longhorn. But before I can the patio door slides open and Ayumi and Jon step out of the lounge into our area.

She still has her hand in his and is chatting with him. Their heads are bent together. Jon looks relaxed, an easy smile on his face. There is no tight posture like he usually has when he is trying to navigate the waters around our muddled relationship. Even his clothes are casual. I note that he isn't wearing his glasses though and I miss them on him.

Jon looks around at the patio and when his eyes land on me, he shifts weight on his feet. He knows I would have been here at the wrap party. He is still my agent, after all, although I am starting to think it would be easier to get a new person to represent me. I am debating a clean break with Jon as he walks over to me, leaving Ayumi talking to someone in the corner. Marina tightens her grip on my wrist in a show of support.

"Jenny, hey, how are you?" he asks.

"Why are you here?" Marina asks, although her tone is light. "Neither of you worked on the film."

An awkward look crosses Jon's face. "Ayumi knows the director. And I wanted to tell you congrats too, Jenny."

"Thanks. It was a good crew," I reply, hoping I don't sound stiff.

Jon nods again and runs his fingers through his hair. I wonder if he has come here just to show me that he is dating Ayumi.

"No glasses tonight," I point out.

"What? Oh yeah. I put in contacts," he replies.

"Is Ayumi your date? She's quite a catch making quite the splash since coming back from Japan. I thought you were representing her," Marina says rapid-fire.

"We decided she will work with another agent since we are seeing each other. Just seems proper."

"Proper," I echo, feeling sick at his confirmation that the two of them are seeing each other.

Before Jon can reply, Ayumi comes over, all smiles. "Jenny. Congrats on the film. I heard about *Flower Queen* as well. That's amazing. Matt Baylock is the director to watch right now. He's on the rise. If you become his muse, you are set."

I force myself to smile and I nod. "I only hope he is impressed with my performance."

"No doubt he will be," Jon replies, looking at me earnestly.

I realize that he is looking for a sign that we can truly be friends. It seems wrong of me to tell him that we cannot be together and then be pissed off that he is seeing someone new. Jon must sense my energy being off about the whole thing. He is looking for me to show him I am okay with this development. To be fair to him, he sees me being happy with Rich and now he is dating Ayumi.

I take in a deep breath and smile at him. "Thanks, Jon. Listen, I forgot the entire schedule again from our last phone call. Can you email it to me again?"

Jon visibly relaxes. My heart is aching the entire time but I know I cannot fault him for doing exactly what I told him to do — move on.

"Oh, Jon, let's grab a slice of their cheesecake before we go," Ayumi says, her attention back toward the lounge. "It's amazing."

"I'll email you with the details," Jon calls with a wave as they head back inside.

I try to relax but my muscles still feel tight.

Marina glances at me. "Way more mature than I could be."

"I told him to move on," I say with a strangled voice. "How can I then treat him like shit for it?"

"True. Do you want to head out of here? Grab something to eat?"

I shake my head. "Honestly, I want to go home. But call me, okay?"

Marina nods, still looking uncertain about letting me leave. But I give her a comforting smile and head back inside the lounge. I glance one last time at Ayumi and Jon, sitting in a booth, laughing. My heart feels as if it is going to pop. I wave good-bye to everyone and duck back into the night air, fighting off tears.

<<◇>>

"Shit, really?" Marina asks, pulling my phone screen closer to her face.

"Yeah," I reply, slumping back in my chair.

It is lunch time the next day. That afternoon I have to report to the studio for a group interview promoting *Fear Recoil*. I had called Marina to give her an update on my attempt to contact Justin Longhorn. I had emailed him last night, as a way to distract myself from feeling shitty about Ayumi and Jon. Instantly, the email address came back as undeliverable and my dreams of reaching out to Justin Longhorn hit a major setback.

Marina chews on her bottom lip. "Listen, you said Kane knows this guy, right? But it isn't as if you are Kane's best friend."

"No, not since Armpit Gate," I joke, taking a sip of my coffee, trying to ignore a couple of young guys trying to sneakily take a photo of me with their phones.

"Well, I'll be there with Fredrick today at the interview with the rest of you guys. Let me talk to him."

"How are you going to get any information out of Kane about Justin?"

"I've worked with Kane on and off throughout a lot of movies. He'd be more prone to open up to me than to you. No offense."

"None taken. If you want to try first, be my guest. But…" I hesitate, unsure how to word how I am feeling. "You really don't have to do all of this for me."

313

"It isn't as if I am going off to war with you. Just think of it as something friends do for one another." She shrugs. "I'm only talking to Kane."

I think back to how I overheard Kane with a guy in one of the bedrooms at his party but decide not to bring it up. Ayumi had said it was the worst kept secret in Hollywood so I am sure that Marina is aware of it. Besides it wasn't as if I was going to try to blackmail him just to get Justin's contact information.

I just couldn't help but feel that if I were able to reach out to Justin about Rich, I would find out information that would help me put a stop to this entire mess. Justin living like a hermit in Jamaica, giving Rich that letter so Hollywood's elite would hire him – whatever Rich had on him had to have been good.

"Okay," I relent. "But I'm buying you lunch next time."

"Sounds good," Marina says with a smile.

It feels great to have someone on my side during all of this.

The interview takes place at a huge TV studio in Burbank. It is for an entertainment show, *Holly's Time,* and will be all superficial questions. I am in hair and makeup, nervous even though I know it isn't as if they will bring up anything they shouldn't. Shortly before arriving, the official announcement of me being cast in the lead of *Flower Queen* was made.

Already I could feel a difference in the way that people are looking at me. The stares are longer and not full of malice that I use to imagine were being directed to me due to my leaked sex tape. It makes me realize that this movie role is going to propel me to the A-list if we turn out a good project. Everyone has eyes on this film and the fact Matt has cast a relative newbie to the film is drawing up the rumor mill.

I realize that I want this. I want people to respect me, not talk about my horrible mistakes behind my back. If I let Rich release the tapes, then I will lose my career. I play with the hem of my skirt nervously. The court had called on my way over here and told me the court date on my restraining order against Robbs. As much as I dread facing him and concerned I won't actually be granted the restraining order, it feels like a lifetime away since I had originally filed it. Besides, I realize ruefully, my bigger concern was now Rich.

Out of the corner of my eye, I see Marina slouched over, talking to Kane. Today he is dressed in a well-tailored suit. They are standing next to each other and I realize that he is taller than Marina. I know that isn't true. Marina is 5'9 and Kane is on the short side. *Must wear lifts in his shoes.* I am amused at figuring out yet another secret about him.

"All set," announces the woman doing my makeup.

I thank her and slide out of the chair, glimpsing myself in the mirror. I don't recognize myself again. I am wearing a simple summer dress in a light blue that brings out my hair, swept up in a loose twist. The heels of my shoes are quite high, making me look much taller than I actually am. Around my wrist is a single blue bracelet. I let out a puff of breath, feeling incredibly nervous.

My phone, clutched in my hand, begins to vibrate. It is Jon. My stomach twists. I flash back to him holding onto Ayumi's hand.

"Jon, hey," I answer, hoping I sound chipper.

"Great, I caught you before the interview," he replies, all business. "Listen, I figured with you getting signed to the Matt Baylock film it is about time to get a publicist working for us. I have a great one in mind and she wants to meet with you. Amanda Lang."

"A publicist? Wow, big time. Sounds good. Set it up."

"Great. You're doing the Holly interview right now, correct?"

"Correct. I'm kind of nervous. Silly I know because I'm just a supporting role but…"

Jon's voice comes out on the other line, soothing, "You're great once you relax. Don't worry about it. They'll love you."

I relax a little. "Thanks, Jon."

"No problem," he replies, although his voice sounds off now. "I'll call you later."

I stare at the phone, lost in thought. Hearing Jon's voice is painful. Hearing Jon address me as a friend hurts even more. I close my eyes and try to let the sick feeling in my stomach fade away.

"Five minutes!" the set director shouts.

I exhale and hear the sound of someone's heels clicking come up behind me. I turn around and see Marina. She is grinning.

"What?" I whisper as she glances behind her.

"I just had to smooth talk my way into Kane opening up about Justin Longhorn. Kane finally listened to how I wanted to ask Justin for career advice, blah blah blah. Anyway, he gave me his phone number but I am supposed to lie about how I got it."

"I love you," I blurt out, thrilled. "That's great."

She grins. "I'll text it to you. But in the meantime, it's show time for you."

Thrilled at the fact that Marina got Justin Longhorn's phone number, I turn to face the stage, ready for the interview.

Chapter Eight

I am self-conscious with Jon so close to me. I fiddle with my cellphone, pretending to check the news although I have read the main stories about ten times already. The piped in music into the high end smoothie shop plays a song I don't know. The colors of the building are jarring and my kale smoothie looks a sort of putrid green that isn't exactly appetizing to me right now.

"Not a fan of your smoothie?" Jon asks.

I wrinkle my nose. "I'm afraid to try it. I know kale is all the rage right now but it looks kinda…gross."

"It does look gross," he admits. "But it doesn't taste gross." As if to prove a point, Jon takes a sip of his own smoothie.

"I figured Amanda would want to meet at some stuffy place to grab lunch or something," I tell him. "Not a smoothie shop."

"But this place is the hottest smoothie shop in town! You and I got basic smoothies. But they can make some crazy combinations of flavors that everyone is jumping all over."

I glance at the menu, wrinkling my nose. "Like the sushi-flavored smoothie?"

"It actually has sushi blended into it."

"Gross."

"Yeah, it isn't that good."

"You *tried* it?" I ask him, stifling down a laugh.

Jon smiles that lop-sided grin that I know so well and my stomach explodes into butterflies. "Yeah. I was trying to fit in. I admit it."

In spite of myself, I laugh. As usual, even though we are waiting for Amanda to show up and I was worried about how awkward it would be, the conversation flows naturally and easily. Yesterday the interview had gone smoothly and I was feeling more confident in how I held myself. Because of that, when Jon had told me he was showing up to the meeting as well, I decided I wouldn't back out, even though I was nervous.

Now, as we're waiting for Amanda, I wonder if Jon and I can really be just friends. My heart has been fluttering ever since I laid eyes on him in the shop. He is wearing his glasses today and dressed in a nice button up shirt. I can see the curves of his muscles underneath the fabric whenever he moves and I wonder if he has been working out.

"There she is," he says, waving to a woman who has just entered.

I turn my head to see a woman in a bright red blouse and a navy blue skirt. Her hair is red, a shade darker than her shirt, and is pulled up in a tight ponytail. As she heads over to us in towering high heels, she gives off a chaotic vibe of energy. Her cellphone is gripped in one hand as her blue nails shine under the lights of the store. In her other hand is an iPad with her purse dangling off her wrist. Amanda looks prepared and I find myself relaxing ever so slightly at the sight of her.

"I'm on time, right?" Amanda says, glancing at her phone.

"Yeah, I'm just always early," I say, holding out my hand. "Jenny."

"Jenny, great, so great to meet you," she says, shaking my hand after she puts her iPad down on the table. "Been hearing a lot about you in the papers lately."

"Amanda, can I get you anything?" Jon asks her.

"Yes, love, one of those sushi smoothies but I want kale in it, too."

Jon shoots me a look that says *see, told you people drink this stuff,* and heads off to the counter to get her it. I stifle my giggle and Amanda and I sit down.

"Sorry we couldn't meet at some fancy restaurant or something but I'm booked solid this week," Amanda says in a fast-clipped tone. I get the feeling if I look at her iPad calendar for this date next year she would already have things scheduled.

"No problem. The fact you called is wonderful in itself."

"You have an interesting arc, Jenny. The role in *Fear Recoil* and then the sex tape leak. Anyone else would say 'oh, just another starlet trying to make a name for herself' but there was something honest about you in that time period. In those paparazzi shots, there was an honesty on your face that made me look twice. Like maybe you didn't leak it for fame."

"I didn't," I say quickly, although I have no idea how I looked honest in paparazzi shots – I mostly looked like a mess.

"I kept hearing through the grapevine what a solid worker you were. No tantrums on the set. You were kind to everyone. People were talking about you but it wasn't about the tape anymore. It was about how you carried yourself," Amanda says, as if she hasn't heard me. "And then, of course, the news about *Flower Queen*. Ah, thanks, love, great." She directs this to Jon, who has returned with her disgusting-looking smoothie.

"Not a problem. How is everything going?"

Amanda takes a sip and then replies, "Great, just letting Jenny know why I am interested in being her publicist."

"She's a rising star," Jon replies confidently and I try to ignore the way his eyes land on me.

"Listen, I can spin whatever story comes your way. The sex tape still is a strike against you. Middle America isn't a huge fan of that sort of thing. Millennials don't care as much as baby boomers but you still want to have a wide fan base." Amanda says all of this rapidly, like a machine gun, and I find myself trying to keep up.

"We never addressed the tape," Jon says. "It seemed almost…arrogant to make a big announcement or speech about it when her first film hadn't ever been released yet."

"At this point, I'm thinking a sit down interview with someone of note," Amanda says to the two of us. "The public can get to know you. More than just the scandal."

"Am I going to have to talk about the whole mess of what happened?" I ask, cringing at the thought of everyone seeing me bent over the bar with Paul.

"Yes, but I'll screen the questions beforehand. But it is important to discuss it, at least a little."

"Sure, okay," I concede, although I suddenly feel nervous.

We spend the next thirty minutes discussing details and other plans before Amanda's phone goes off with an alarm. She looks at it and stands up.

"I have a dinner meeting with another client in forty minutes. Listen, if you are interested, let's work together."

Jon glances at me, waiting for my answer before I reply. I nod my assent and Amanda smiles.

"Great. Jon, I'll have my assistant contact yours. Jenny, walk me out?"

"Uhm, sure," I reply, standing up and shrugging at Jon.

We step outside. The sky is a bright blue. Across the street is a movie theater. I see the *Fear Recoil* poster. I'm not on the main poster but my head still swims at seeing a poster for a film I am in. The road is blocked with traffic and Amanda heads toward her car, a beautifully clean and bright blue Lexus. She stops in front of it, slipping on a pair of Chanel sunglasses.

"I didn't want to bring this up in front of your agent. Thought it could be just between us girls."

"What?" I ask her, curious.

"You two – have a history?"

"What?" I repeat, like a broken doll.

"The way you two were looking at each other. I've been around way too long not to have seen it before," Amanda says, glancing at her phone to check the time. "But listen, I need to know the history between you two and if you have any skeletons still laying around in your closet."

In a flash, I see the stairs and that sick swooping feeling in my stomach as Robbs pushed me down them. I see Rich grinning as he told me about how he had filmed us having sex.

"Nothing happened between Jon and me."

"Physically, I take it? Listen, we'll have a one-on-one meeting soon."

I watch her get in the car. She gives me a small wave and backs up out of the spot, before waiting for a car to let her into the traffic. I watch her go, feeling someone behind me and knowing that it is Jon.

I turn around, hoping Amanda's words aren't etched on my skin. "Hey. She just left."

"What do you think of her?" he asks, oblivious to the fact that Amanda picked up our feelings for each other so easily.

"She seems great. Very professional and she has a plan for the future. I'm eager to work with her."

Jon smiles. "Perfect. Funny how quickly things are moving along, huh?"

"Extremely."

Now that the meeting is over and it is just the two of us on the side street, I feel acutely aware of us being alone together. Unlike earlier, where it was easy talking to him in the smoothie store, now it feels awkward. I realize Amanda so quickly spotting our feelings for each other has me feeling vulnerable.

"How is Ayumi?" I find myself asking, as if to steer the conversation out of troubled waters.

Jon runs his fingers through his hair. "Good. She's good."

"Great. Well, I need to go. I can finally have a night in."

"Yeah, okay," Jon says, taking a step back as if to ward me off. "I'll call you soon."

I nod and give him a small wave. I watch him cross the street to head toward where he parked. With a sigh, I head back to my own car. Behind the wheel, I close my eyes, focusing on my breathing.

Every time I think I have a handle on things, it ends up feeling messy. Rich still has a tight control on me. For a spilt second I debate telling Jon what is going on. But as I stare out at the traffic, I hesitate. I am so terrified of opening up to him and exposing what Rich has done to me that it holds me back. Like always, my instinct of covering my head and going through it on my own kicks in. If I tell Jon and he says anything negative…

No, Jon deserves to be with Ayumi and to be happy with her. I need to call Justin and see what I can find out about him. He could hold the key to figuring out what to do with Rich.

With that in mind, I decide to head home, pushing thoughts from Jon out of my head.

Chapter Nine

The TV is playing an old reality show. It is dated, everyone holding flip phones as if they are the biggest thing going. I barely notice. I am nervous about calling Justin. There are many ways to handle the conversation but none of them subtle. I am convinced that Rich is nothing but a glorified scam artist that must be dumping his money into gambling or some other vice. It explains why he needed the $100,000 back so quickly and suddenly before just leaking the tape. It explains why he is so hell bent on this production company and attaching himself to me like a parasite to make some cash.

I know I cannot be the only one he has treated this way. There *must* be others. And Justin has to be one of them. The signs point to it. If I can only get him to talk to me, to tell me something meaningful that I can use against Rich.

I sit down on the couch and take a deep breath and dial Justin's number. It is an international number, which means he probably settled down for good in Jamaica. Whatever happened, he seems to be seriously heeding to Rich about staying away from Hollywood for five years.

Just as I am convinced it will go to voicemail, a man answers, "Hello?"

My breath catches. For a second my brain goes blank with everything I should be saying.

"Hello?" he repeats, irritated.

"Hello, hi!" I say, sounding so chipper that I cringe. "Is this Mr. Longhorn? Justin, I mean." I am speaking rapidly and try to catch myself.

"Who is this?" the man demands. "How did you get this number?"

"Marina Madison," I reply – it is true, somewhat, and it makes sure that Kane's name isn't given.

"Marina Madison," the man repeats, as if he is letting the name soak in his brain. "The production director?"

"Yes, that's right," I reply, relieved he remembers her.

"How did she get this number? Never mind, it doesn't matter. This is Justin. Who is this?" His voice is low, as if he is out somewhere and trying to keep from being overheard.

"I'm Jenny. A friend of Marina's. I'm calling about someone we might have in common."

"Someone we might have in common?" Justin echoes, sounding confused.

I let out a sigh, irritated at myself for being so bad at trying to sneakily hint about Rich. I try again.

"I understand you left Hollywood two years ago."

"Yes, everyone knows that."

"Are you going to come back?"

"You called me to ask me if I am coming back," he deadpans. "We don't even know each other."

"I know, but—"

"I'm done with this call."

Panicked, I blurt out, "It's about Rich. The guy who told you to not come back to Hollywood."

There is a long pause. For a second I think that Justin has hung up but when I glance at my phone I see the call is still connected. If I strain my ears, I can hear his soft breathing on the other line.

"We can't discuss this on the phone," he says and when I don't instantly reply, Justin adds, "We have to discuss it in person."

"Okay. When can you get here?"

"No. When can you get here?"

When can I get *there*? I think about flying to Jamaica just to meet Justin and wonder how insane I would sound if I told someone like Jon what I was doing.

"I don't know," I admit. "I have a packed schedule."

"Clear it, if you can," Justin replies briskly. "I'll text you my address. Let me know when you are coming."

The call ends. I find myself staring at the TV, watching a commercial idly. Go to Jamaica? I pull up

my calendar on my phone. I have two days on set with
Silence Dolls and then a meeting with Amanda and Jon
on Friday that I am going to have to push back. I have
to meet Justin and see what he knows. Determined, I
head to my laptop to book the tickets that will take me
to Jamaica for the weekend.

<<◇>>

When I touch down in Montego Bay, Jamaica, at
eight at night, I feel exhausted. My body feels dirty and
I am pretty sure my hair is oily and stringy. The flight
had been roughly thirteen hours long and I feel
exhausted.

But stepping out into the humid evening air sends a
streak of excitement through me. I'm here and am going
to see Justin tomorrow. That thought alone spurs me
into a cab where I give them my hotel address and sit in
the back seat.

Montego Bay, a hugely popular tourist destination,
burns like an ember as the sun is setting. I find myself
taken aback by the juxtaposition of the quaint buildings
of the locals versus the luxury resorts I can see in the
distance near the beach. My own hotel is the closest I
could get to Justin's address and is off the beaten path
of the tourist area. I quickly pay the cabbie, although
judging by his face I probably have given him a tip that
far outweighs the drive, and duck into the front entrance
of the hotel.

The lobby is quiet. There is a bird perched in a cage
nearby, eying me with its beady eyes, as if it knows
exactly why I am here. The room is etched in color –
colorful rugs along the floor with furniture all in a

rainbow of colors, making the place feel like a child's coloring book.

I check in and am given a room on the far end of the small hotel. By the time I make it inside my room, I want nothing more than to sleep for ages. The jet lag isn't awful, seeing as Jamaica is two hours behind California, but coupled with the flying, I feel as if I have not slept in days.

I text Marina and Jon to let them know I have settled in safely. Whereas Marina knows why I am here, I have told him I was visiting family back home. If he knew my plans for coming here, he would have wanted to come along. But I am determined to settle things with Rich on my own, not wanting to run from him anymore like I did with Robbs. Also, I couldn't handle being in close proximity with him in a hotel room.

In Rich's case, I ended up lying and telling him the same thing I told Jon. I told him I was going back home to see my parents. He was disinterested, asking that I return soon so we can have a public date again because he needed me to drum up interest for backers for his production company. I doubt he will bother me while I am out of town.

The water of the shower is a welcome respite from the gross feeling from flying all day and the humid air outside. I let it fall down my skin, trickling down my back and down the drain. For a brief moment, I let myself think about if Jon was in the shower with me. I catch myself before I can let the image go too far. I need to get Jon out of my head for good. *He is with Ayumi now,* I chide myself, *what you really need is a fling.* Maybe I can fit one in here on my trip. I let myself laugh. As if I will have the time.

After the shower, I crawl into bed, sinking into the plush sheets and pillows. The window nearby gives me a view of nothing but thick foliage. If I pretend hard enough, I can even trick myself that I am in a jungle somewhere, away from anyone who wishes to bother me.

Before I know it, I am fast asleep in bed, sleeping like a baby.

The next morning I change into something presentable and head out. Justin had texted me earlier on, asking to meet him at a restaurant down the street for breakfast. I find myself feeling nervous about meeting him. I'm aware that it is crazy to fly this far just to meet someone who may or may not have useful information on Rich. But the thought of the possibility that Justin could help me end this guides my feet and before I know it, I am stepping into an open air restaurant overlooking a beach.

It is bustling. This is quite obviously a tourist stop, judging by how crowded it is and all the people in ugly, tacky colored shirts. I hesitate at the entrance, scanning the crowd for the face I recognize from the picture in Kane's house.

But he sees me first. He asked me to wear the color red and my summer dress is a dark red, contrasting with all the Hawaiian shirts in the area, even though we aren't even in Hawaii.

Justin waves me over. He is at a table near the edge of the restaurant, directly next to the hill that overlooks the beach. I weave my way through the crowd and then sit down across from him, feeling nervous.

He does not look how I expected him to look. For some reason, I had been picturing someone haggard from dealing with Rich, sent to exile in Jamaica, with bags under their eyes and sallow skin. Yet Justin looks to be only a little bit older than myself with dark hair that is combed back and a white T-shirt and khaki pants on. He is extremely tanned, as if he spends all day outside – although judging by the view, why wouldn't he? His eyes are a dark brown and he studies me carefully.

"Justin, I hope," I say. "Otherwise I am making a stranger uncomfortable."

Justin does not smile and instead just nods. "Jenny, right?"

I extend my hand for him and instead of shaking it, he gives it a kiss. The touch of someone else is electric and I feel the hairs on the back of my neck stand up. As I pull my hand away, I tell myself to get a grip.

"Nice to finally meet you. This view is amazing," I blabber, nervous and unsure if I just bring Rich up instantly.

"Did you sleep well?"

"Yes, like a baby," I reply as a waiter comes over.

We both order breakfast and then after the waiter leaves, silence covers the table. Justin seems fine to let

the silence soak over us but it makes me nervous. I feel
a bead of sweat fall down the back of my neck. It is
ninety degrees here and humid. I avoid Justin's eyes and
look out at the beach.

"Will you have time to go to one of the beaches?"

"Maybe. Not sure yet." Honestly I am not sure how
much time talking to Justin will actually take – he does
not seem very forthcoming.

"I can suggest some lovely places to go," he replies
and I think I detect a hint of an accent although I cannot
pinpoint from where. "You might as well see a little bit
of the town while you are here."

"Sure, that sounds great. Not sure when I will be
able to come back, after all."

Justin nods and another long silence fills the table. I
wonder if he is doing it on purpose. Is he waiting for me
to bring up Rich first? If so, I have no qualms about
bringing it up right now.

"Listen, Justin—"

"Not yet," he cuts me off abruptly, glancing behind
me as if Rich is going to magically appear there.

I fall silent instantly. The look in Justin's eyes
seems haunted and I realize it is one I have seen before
– in my own eyes. He is looking over his shoulder,
terrified of Rich, as if Rich is a monster that can lunge
at any moment. *Is that what I look like?* I think to
myself as the waiter comes back with our food. I had
been so fixated on getting Robbs out of my life that I
didn't even stop to think about back-ups of the tapes.

Robbs was like a ghost clawing its way back to me, sending me in a panic that I would end up back in clutches. In my terrified behavior I allowed myself to slip up and now Rich holds the reigns.

Maybe Justin and I are not so different in the end.

"How is Marina?" Justin finally asks as I dig into my eggs and toast.

"She's great. She's been really helpful as I get adjusted to Hollywood life."

"Yes, I heard about you landing the lead in *Flower Queen*," Justin replies, "Congratulations."

I'm guessing he must have looked me up on Google after I called him out of the blue to talk about Rich.

"Thank you," I say and smile. "I'm nervous as hell though. Everything else before this was child's play. And it feels like a house of cards, honestly. As if any moment it can come crashing down…" I trail off, feeling my gut twist.

Justin picks up on my mood change and takes a sip of his orange juice. "It is a quiet life out here. Packed with tourists, yes, but I keep to myself."

"Do you ever miss Hollywood?"

"I used to. Near the beginning of living here. Not so much anymore."

The rest of the meal is filled with casual conversation about the weather and the major differences living here in the bay. Justin asks once or twice about Hollywood but for the most part steers clear of the subject. I get the feeling he is gauging me, probing for weakness in my story or my personality. I get the feeling he is paranoid. Whatever Rich has on him must be massive and he probably thinks I am here to check up on him on behalf of Rich.

We leave the restaurant and stop along the sidewalk. Across the street is a small tea shop and behind me is a tacky tourist shop selling more of those hideous Hawaiian T-shirts.

"We're not even in Hawaii," I muse aloud.

"What?" Justin asks, blinking.

I point to the display window, a garish blend of tropical hues that makes my eyes hurt. Justin actually smiles, a lop-sided grin that makes my heart skip a beat.

"We're in the tropics so they just assume no one will care and buy it anyway."

"True. Seems to be working," I reply as a large man saunters by in a shirt that looks exactly like the one in the display window.

"Listen, Jenny, I have some business to attend to. But if you could come over for dinner tonight, we can discuss other matters."

I pick up that he wants to discuss Rich. Whatever test he had me jump through at breakfast to make sure I was legit I seemingly have passed.

"Sounds great," I reply.

Justin holds out his hand for a handshake and I comply. Once again, I get goose bumps when our skin touches. As he turns around, I can't help but notice how his muscles move underneath his T-shirt and it sends a thrill through me. I ignore it and turn back around, trying to figure out how I am supposed to spend my day around town now.

Chapter Ten

I end up taking Justin up on his advice and head to a beach. Even though it will be crowded with tourists, I cannot help but be lured to Doctor's Cave Beach. I find myself settled down on a patch of warm sand, with a couple of cheap beach towels I bought on the way over. With my big floppy hat and big sunglasses, I hope that no one will notice me from *Fear Recoil.* I doubt it and for once I am glad that I am not an A-list star.

The water is so blue that I can see the bottom. The waves are calm and the breeze rolls in off the ocean. For the first time in what feels like ages, I feel relaxed. I lay down on my towel and close my eyes.

The rest of the day passes by in a leisurely haze of snacking on local food and curling up with a tawdry paperback I purchase at lunch. I find that I do not mind being alone. It is nice to be away from the hustle and bustle of Hollywood, especially without Rich breathing down my neck. *There are worse places to exile yourself to,* I think at one point but then I remember Justin's haunted look as he stared me down and I think twice of it.

Evening spreads out across the town, sending up sparks of orange across the sky. I remember Jon's confusion at my telling him I needed a few days off to regroup by myself and how quiet he got. I try not to think about Jon and avert my gaze from the sky, which is reminding me of Hollywood.

Justin's house is only a ten-minute walk from my hotel, although it seems miles away from the crush of tourist attractions. The street is quiet, albeit cramped, and at first I pass by his house. I back track and stop in front of it, eying it. It is two stories and narrow. It looks more Western than any of the other homes on the street and is clearly the newest one on the block. I wonder if he had it custom built. I doubt he is ever planning to return to Hollywood.

I steel myself and knock on the door. I can hear a TV inside and someone shuffling toward the door. The door opens and Justin is there. His eyes land on mine and then quickly he scans my body, as if I wouldn't notice. I am wearing yet another simple dress, this time in yellow, and the straps of my bikini are exposed. I ended up running late to get here, having lost myself at the beach and barely had time to change.

"Great, you're here," he says, moving to the side to allow me to enter.

I step inside a modest-sized living room. The décor is all modern and in cream colors. The television is tuned to the Weather Channel and it looks like a waiting room for some sort of office building. Yet pictures line the wall behind the TV. I think I can make out Kane in one of them. There are more pictures on the coffee table. Once I see the pictures, I relax a little, the waiting room vibe now gone.

"It's nice," I say, taking a step farther into the house.

I instantly smell food cooking in the kitchen. As if in reply, my stomach grumbles and I blush. Justin lets out a laugh.

"Glad you're hungry. It should be about done. It isn't anything amazing. I am *not* a great cook."

"No problem. You probably have more cooking skills than I do."

I trail after him into the spacious kitchen. The dining room is painted yellow, giving off a warm feeling to the room. Justin pulls out my seat and I sit down, watching him head back into the kitchen. His posture seems slightly more relaxed than this morning. His hair is messy, some of it falling into his eyes as he pulls out plates. He is wearing a short-sleeved shirt that shows off his muscles and I avert my gaze, a blush rising to my cheeks.

When Justin comes back, he puts down a plate of pasta with homemade garlic bread. It looks delicious and once he settles into his chair, I dig in.

"This garlic bread is amazing," I gush as I grab another piece.

"Oh, thanks. About the only thing I can make."

We eat in silence for a little bit and then Justin clears his throat. "You mentioned Rich on the phone."

"Yes." I pause for a moment, thinking about how to word my sentence. "From what I've pieced together, I thought it would be best to reach out to you."

Justin's brown eyes fall on me and they seem heavy, as if he is thinking back to something before he looks away from me. "What have you pieced together?"

"That I think you moved here because Rich has something on you. I found an email," I explain quickly when he looks back up at me. "Where Rich said you can't come back to Hollywood and that he wanted a recommendation letter for himself."

"Do you know why he told me to move?" Justin presses.

I shake my head. "No. But I just assume he has something on you."

"And he has something on you, is that it?"

I hesitate briefly before I nod again. "Yes."

Justin leans forward slightly. "Why are you here?"

The question takes me aback. I'm here because he asked me to come. No, I'm here because I want answers. I'm here because I want to break free from Rich and stop fucking up because I am terrified.

I look at him levelly. "Because you could have information I need so I don't end up hiding out in some country or stuck under his thumb the rest of my life."

Justin lets out a laugh but it is a dry laugh. There is no humor to be found in it. It is the laugh of a man who thinks I am being silly. And frankly I am sick of people laughing at me because they find me silly.

"What is it?" I snap.

"Whatever Rich has on you, he won't be afraid to use it."

"Then why even invite me here? Why tell me to come here if you think it is so hopeless?" I say, bristling.

Justin falls silent again and clears his throat. "I thought you were going to ask me how to handle Rich so he goes easy on you. Not how to get untangled from him."

"Are you *serious*?" My irritation is getting the best of me now. "You think I came to Jamaica to ask how better to please Rich so he'll go easy on me?"

"There is no getting away from what he wants of you. He knows what he wants and it is always money. It is always power and it is always to serve his own purposes. If you fall underneath him, you either let him pull you along or you get trampled. I got lucky."

"You call this lucky?"

Justin's brow furrows. "What about it do you not consider lucky? I have a beautiful home here on a beautiful island."

"You have a pretty prison," I counter. "You left your job because of Rich. You left Hollywood because of Rich. And you are probably so afraid of what he will do if you come back that even after five years you'll stay here in a self-imposed exile."

Justin looks indignant. "I hardly think this is a prison."

"Well, I do. And if you aren't going to tell me your story or help me in any way then it was a mistake coming here." I throw my napkin down and stand up, done with this conversation.

My chest is burning with rage and sadness. As I storm out of Justin's house, I wonder if this is my fate. If I bow to everyone who fucks with me and mentally abuses me. If I will forever cower under their behavior, letting them control me. I let Robbs, didn't I? I had thought Justin would show me the way but maybe I am forever a fool.

I make it down to the road when I hear Justin calling me. I ignore him and keep walking. When he calls me a second time, something in his tone of voice makes me hesitate. He sounds desperate.

I turn around and watch him jog toward me. He looks embarrassed.

"Don't go," he says. "I'm sorry. You're right. Please come back inside."

I glance at the house, weighing my options and then nod. I trail after him back into the house. We sit down at the dining room table again, as if nothing has happened. Yet it is hard to get back into dinner after our little fight. Justin's face looks heavy and long and in that moment I see myself.

Justin has let Rich win. Didn't I let Robbs win with the sex tape? If I refuse to stand up to Rich, this is how my life will end up. Living under Rich's shadow. I picture him controlling my every move, like a puppet. At any moment, he can release the other two tapes, destroying my life and my blossoming career. Justin lives under this shadow as well.

As I nibble on a piece of garlic bread, I think back to what Jon said about facing down Robbs. How quickly I dismissed him and found the idea of it terrifying. How the shadow of Robbs bore down on me and made me cower. If I had faced my tormentor, where would I be now?

"You want to know what Rich did to me," Justin states.

I nod.

He clears his throat. "My story is probably no different than yours. Rich seemed like a nice guy. He had known my brother back when he was alive, and we had met briefly in passing. I was producing a film I had written and was visiting the set in Louisiana. They have great filming incentives there. Anyway, he had been hanging around set on the arms of one of the women working there. We all went out drinking one night and we hit it off. Went golfing a few times after that. I think we bonded over stories to do with my brother."

Justin stops talking, as if he is trying to come up with the best way to bring up the next part of his story. I wait patiently for him to keep talking.

"Anyway, about two months in our friendship, he meets me in Hollywood one night for drinks. Says he has big news for me. We meet and about halfway through the second drink, he slides over the folder."

My heart sinks. I know this all too well. After Rich told me about the tapes he had of me, I called him a liar. It was then he had pressed play on the TV in the living room and I had been treated with images of us in his bedroom. My skin crawls at remembering seeing the proof with my own eyes.

"Inside of it was…it was enough to end my career with nothing but negativity surrounding me. Become not only a Hollywood pariah but one in all the magazines as well."

"What did he say?"

"Everything he had was legit proof. I have no idea how he got it unless he systematically worked through my past to find it. I couldn't refute it. I asked how much he wanted for it to all go away. He said he wanted more than that. He wanted me to introduce him to Hollywood, get him a job so he could start making his own money there. I refused."

Justin looks sad as he recounts his story. My heart goes out to him. It must have been easier to agree to what Rich has on him and hide out here. It is what I am doing, isn't it? Ultimately I am letting Rich control my life because I am afraid of him, just like I let Robbs do.

"Rich applied the pressure. He even put something in a gossip magazine as an anonymous source, hinting about some big scoop about me. I balked. I told him that I didn't think he could make it in Hollywood. But Rich alluded to having some major debts to be paying off. Whatever money he has he must burn through quickly and is always looking for more. So I said that I want all the proof, I'd give him the letter, put him up in

Hollywood. But he wanted me out of Hollywood as well."

"What then?" I press.

"I gave Rich the letter of recommendation he wanted. I agreed to leave Hollywood. I even paid for the house he's living in now."

"What?" I exclaim.

"It isn't his. What did he tell you?"

"His parents have a lot of money."

"I don't think he's spoken to his parents in ages," Justin says with a small shake of his head. "I paid for the house."

"How did you make sure you really got all the proof?"

"I watched Rich delete it from the cloud. We burned the pages he did have. And then I pushed into getting his computer."

"You took his *computer*?"

"I bought him a new one. But I didn't trust him to delete the files on his own. He didn't care. He had gotten everything he wanted from me at that point so he gave me the laptop."

"Do you still have it? Did you go through it?"

"I went through it but there really isn't anything of note on there. Some emails with other women but he probably has a regular daily use laptop. That one was just for fucking people over," he replies with a small shrug.

"So then you just moved here."

"That's right. I haven't heard from him since but I saw him in the news a couple of times about projects he was casting director on. And then of course when I Googled you."

I sigh and lean back in my chair, going through the information Justin told me. "The laptop. Can I have it?"

Justin shifts in his chair, suddenly nervous. "I'll let you look at it and back up whatever you want from it, sure. But I can't give it to you. If Rich sees it in your hands…"

"Fine, fine," I relent.

"Like I said, Rich was serious about taking me to the cleaners. I got the sense he has a lot of debt but he could just be a scam artist. I wasn't the first person he fucked over. You probably won't be the last. I appreciate you coming out here to try to look for clues but that's all I can give you."

"I appreciate you telling me your story," I say and I mean it.

Justin nods and in that moment the two of us are united against Rich and what he has done to us. I slowly go over Justin's story in my head. I remind myself to buy flash drives to back up the laptop Justin took and go through it. I hope to find something that Justin may have missed. He is still terrified of Rich and probably barely looked at the laptop just out of pure fear.

When dinner is finished, Justin walks me back to the hotel. We walk in silence, soaking in the sights of the bay. At one point, his hand accidently brushes against me and I feel that warmth again spread across my body. We stop in the lobby where the bird squawks at us.

"I'll let you go here," Justin says and I nod.

"Thank you for dinner."

"You're welcome. You are here tomorrow as well, right? Why don't we have breakfast?"

"Sure. Sounds good."

Justin nods and gives me a small wave. I watch him leave the hotel lobby, different feelings swirling around in my stomach. Once I am back in my room, I crawl into bed, looking out the window. I think about what Rich could have on him but in the end, whatever it was, was enough to drive Justin here. I wonder if I will find anything on the laptop or if I will find anything helpful at all here.

I am disappointed. I don't know why I thought I would find all the answers here but I did. Will I actually find something on the laptop that Justin missed? I bring my knees up to my chest, trying to plot out my next move. If I keep thinking and keep moving, then the feeling of suffocation I get from being around Rich might stay at bay. If I stop for a minute, it surges back to me, crushing my chest in.

I fall asleep like this but quickly fall into another nightmare. This time Rich is laughing over me after I hit the bottom of the stairs. His mouth is slick with what looks like blood and I find myself trying to crawl away from him as he laughs. I can hear him breathing down my neck as I crawl away from him, my nails breaking against the floorboards as pain shoots down my back.

I wake up with the sheets tied up around my legs and my body covered in sweat. My chest is heaving as I try to suck in the air. Dizzily, I forget where I am. I look around and it all comes back to me, rapidly. I am in Jamaica. I saw Justin yesterday and he told me about Rich. I am trying to break free from Rich's clutches.

I run my fingers over the bed sheets in an effort to calm down. The sun is shining into my hotel room. Early tomorrow morning I go back to Hollywood. I remember I am supposed to meet Justin for breakfast.

In the shower, I start to calm down from the vivid nightmare. I think about Justin, the bags under his eyes that probably have been around since Rich toyed with him. I think about how Justin demanded to have Rich's entire laptop given to him.

Could Rich have made a serious error in giving him the laptop? Originally I figured he had everything on his desktop at home, but it makes sense for Justin to sit and watch him delete things from the cloud and take the laptop with him to Jamaica. I'm guessing Rich didn't care about losing one laptop compared to having a house bought for him and handed jobs in Hollywood.

I get out of the shower. The water dribbles down my back to the mat underneath my feet. I am trying not to lose hope. So Justin didn't have a slew of evidence to give me. But backing up the laptop means I might find something after all.

Justin seems well rested when we meet for breakfast at a small hole in the wall eatery. He does not bring up Rich and I do not prod him to. He spends the rest of the day showing me the island, tourist and non-tourist spots alike.

Talking with Justin is easy. There isn't any ulterior motives with him. Once or twice I catch him staring at me a beat too long. Anytime our fingers brush against one another I get a warmth shooting through me. It is when the sun is setting that I think to myself I wouldn't care so much if he tried to make a move on me.

We finish dinner on the beach in a small restaurant that has fresh seafood. Afterward, we walk along the dark beach and I find myself looking up at the stars.

"You can't see them in Hollywood," Justin says when he catches me looking.

"True. They're so bright here. I don't think I've ever seen them this bright before."

"When I first moved here, I used to lay out on the beach at night and watch them. They used to lull me to sleep. I had these thoughts like…what if I had stood up to Rich? What if I had faced him down? But there was no point."

I pause for a second before asking the question that has been on my mind, "What did he have on you?"

Justin falls silent. We have been growing closer throughout the day, the tension between us rising. The two of us are in the same boat and I can feel the heat between us. Have I gone too far?

But just as I am doubting myself for asking him it, Justin replies in a soft voice, "I didn't write my first two screenplays."

I stop walking. "What?"

Justin's first two screenplays put him on the map, according to what I read online. They were about love lost and ripped apart by the ravages of times. The themes united them and the fantastic acting and direction made them instant hits. To discover that he didn't write the two screenplays made perfect sense for why Rich would have latched onto this secret.

"My best friend's brother had passed away. We were going through his things and I found them wedged in the back of a dresser. They were so good. It felt like a shame that something like that – those two stories that were so well crafted – should rot in a drawer somewhere. So I took them and I tweaked them just a little, to fix up anything messy about them. They had a raw energy to them. Once I tweaked them, I tried selling them around town. And when I got a deal from them, it was on the tip of my tongue to tell everyone I didn't write them. It was. But…"

He trails off. Like before, I wait, letting the silence settle around us. The only thing I hear is the soft lapping of the waves close by and Justin's soft breathing, a little haggard, as if this is the first time he has spoken these words aloud.

"Everyone was looking at me as if I was talented. I had written stories often as a kid. I had loved to write but it hadn't amounted to anything. But everyone liked *these* stories. And the way my parents were so pleased…I never spoke up. I let them think they were mine."

"What proof did Rich have?" I ask him, curious now.

"He had somehow found the original transcripts. Maybe my brother had told him he had been working on the stories. Rich must have known about them and snooped around on me to find out about the storage unit. I had taken them and put them in there and Rich must have been following me. After Rich showed me what he had, I went to the storage unit but they were gone. I don't know how he got in. I don't know if he just decided to break into it and see if there was anything of value in there. But that proof would destroy me. Destroy what people thought of me. I couldn't let it out."

"So that's why you took his laptop?"

"He had made scans of the scripts. I burned the originals and he watched with me. Then I watched him delete them from his cloud and then he gave me the laptop. He was so thrilled with what he had gone and done that he didn't care about the laptop. I barely looked at it, Jenny. I can't even be bothered."

"I'm going to make a back-up of what's on it," I tell him, "In case there is something I can find that you missed."

Justin gives me a small shrug, as if what I am doing is pointless. "I doubt he has left anything on there."

"Well, I can't just not look at it," I counter as we resume walking.

We walk in silence. Justin seems to be burdened by what he has just told me. I wait for him to ask me what Rich has on me in return but he doesn't. In the end, I guess it does not really matter to Justin. We are connected through Rich. What Rich has done to me and what Rich has already done to Justin.

We stop at an alcove in the beach. I pause in front of it and peer inside. It offers shelter from anyone walking by and in one corner I make out a collection of beer cans. There is a sudden breeze and goose bumps pop up along my skin. I run my fingers through my hair, feeling the salt from the ocean caked through it.

Justin is behind me. I turn around and I can tell what he wants to do. I lean forward first and kiss him. He kisses me back passionately, and his hands slide around my hips. I wrap my arms around his neck and together we hit the side of the alcove. The cave stone here is smooth, weathered down from the wind from the ocean. Justin presses himself against me and we hold onto each other.

There is something pulling us together in this moment. Drawn together by Rich, we cling to each other like lifeboats at sea. No one else in my life knows what it feels like to go through what I am going through. Meanwhile, I know Justin has not told anyone else before about Rich and what he has done. Together, in this one moment on the beach under the stars, we are one.

Justin pulls away and in a gravelly voices he whispers, "Jenny."

My throat catches and I press my lips against his, not wanting to talk at all. All I want is to feel him. His hands travel down my back and his lips move down my neck, leaving kisses in their wake. My own hands are tugging at his hair as I am pinned against the side of the cave. If someone walks by and decides to look in, they will see us and we will be caught, two lovers under the stars. It gives me a thrill to think of it.

Justin's hands claw at the bottom of my sun dress as he yanks it up just enough that he can run his fingers along my panties. It sends a shiver down my spine. He moves them to one side and he slides a finger inside my wet pussy. I cling to him as he fingers me, slowly, almost torturously, against the side of the cave.

As he fingers me, I beg him for more in a hushed, rough voice. Justin pulls his finger out of me and I hear him unzip his shorts. He presses me hard against the side of the cave as I wrap my legs around his waist. Before I know it, I can feel Justin's cock entering me.

Our fucking is fast and hurried, knowing that at any time we can be caught. The heat that started yesterday has reached its apex between the two of us. Justin is grunting in my ear as he thrusts inside of me. I look out at the beach, the thrill of being caught at any moment, having a fling like this in the alcove, makes the sex even more amazing. I can feel my own orgasm mounting as he bucks into me.

I cling to him as if my life depends on it. With his one free hand, Justin yanks down the front of my dress, exposing my breasts to the night air. He gropes my tits, squeezing them hard with his hand, rolling and pinching my nipples with the tips of his fingers as he fucks me.

Finally I cannot take it anymore. I bite into his shoulder in an attempt to be silent. Down the beach, voices carry from a band of tourists. My climax rocks through me and I cling to him, grinding against him as I come against his cock. This sends Justin over the edge. With a final thrust, he groans in my ear, panting my name on the tip of his tongue as he comes. I rock against him, letting my orgasm roll through me. The warmth makes my cheeks flush as we both finally come down from our climaxes together.

The voices are louder now. The group is coming closer to the alcove. Hurriedly, Justin pulls out of me, zipping up his shorts as I yank my dress back in order. We sit down in the sand, attempting to look casual, as if we are merely hanging out in the alcove. At the last possible second of covering my breasts back up, the group comes into view.

I pretend to be looking intently at the beach. Justin fiddles with his cellphone. We probably look like two teenagers caught making out in their bedroom. The group wanders by with a quick glance at us.

After they pass by, Justin walks me back to his house. We step inside and he leads me to his office. Justin opens a small closet off to the side and rummages around in the back. I can smell the ocean and his scent on me as I wait. Finally he removes the laptop and sets it on his desk.

"You can back it up if you still want to."

I nod and Justin leaves the office. I boot up the computer, pulling out my flash drives. The laptop is almost barebones and does not have much on it. But I want to go through everything with a fine-tooth comb, just in case. I back it up quickly and then wander back out to the living room.

Justin is having a drink of whiskey and glances at me when I come back.

"I backed it up," I tell him. "Although it wasn't much. Guess we'll see."

"Do you want to spend the night?" he asks me suddenly.

"My things are at my hotel room."

Justin nods and looks back out the window. I can see how tight his muscles are under his shirt and I want to explore more of him. I know I will probably not see him again after this trip. Having someone to sleep with casually, especially someone who knows what I am going through, is pleasing to me. I think back to the other day about how I wanted a fling.

"What if you come to my hotel room?" I offer instead.

Chapter Eleven

I let out a stifled moan, burying my face in the pillow. Justin pumps harder inside me. His hands are on my hips as I take his cock. It is hours later, back in my hotel room, nearing two in the morning, and I am on all fours. We are on round three by this point. Our desires, a mixture of loneliness, desperation and fear of the future, has us thrown together sexually again.

I bounce back against him, making sure to take the length of his thick cock as he slides in and out of me. At one point he spanks me, which makes me moan even harder. Earlier we had gotten in the shower together, trying to wash the ocean off each other but instead ending up tasting each other. It resulted in us on the bed, me on top of him, riding his shaft to climax.

Justin grabs my hair and gives it a tug. He uses this as momentum to fuck me harder and deeper. I close my eyes, bouncing back as hard as I can. In this moment, I am not thinking about anything. All I am thinking about is taking Justin's dick and getting my orgasm out of it. All that matters is this small hotel room and our passion.

Justin grunts and then moans my name, sliding his hand from my hair. He leans forward so he can still thrust in me but rubs his finger along my clit. The stimulation is overwhelming. I can feel my body twitch from the pleasure of it all. I wiggle against him, feeling his girth buried inside of me and his fingers working my clit. I squeeze my eyes shut.

We are both sweaty and exhausted. Every muscle in my body is sore. All of sudden he pulls out of me and flips me over. I look up at him as he positions himself to enter me again.

"I want to watch you finish," he says in a rough voice.

Again he is fucking me hard, one hand on my clit. I cannot take it anymore. Our bodies are slick with sweat and rubbing against each other. My hips buck wildly as I climax. I arch my hips and moan. It is too loud of a moan and I am sure someone down the hall can hear me.

Justin's voice is hoarse as he moans my name. His thick cock is deep inside of me as he orgasms at the same time. His fingertips dig into my soft flesh as he clings to me.

Finally, he slides out and we lay on the bed, exhausted. We both smell of sex and the beach. Our limbs are entwined. I look at him out of the corner of my eye. Sweat shines at the top of his brow. It is so wonderful to be sleeping with someone who is not Rich. Thinking about Rich and how he touched me makes my skin crawl. It is also wonderful to be sleeping with someone and not think about Jon, miles away.

I roll over and he slings his arm around me. My eyelids are heavy, about to close. Even if I wanted to go for another round, there is no way I will be able to stay awake. Right before I doze off, I hear Justin speak.

"I'm glad you visited."

<<◇>>

I wake up with a start. My vision is blurry. My mouth tastes gross, like I need to drink water. The shutter on the airplane window has been pulled down and I rest my head against it. It feels as if time stops on long flights. I am just in some strange in between zone of the future and the past, colliding into one.

The man next to me is fast asleep, snoring a little. I stretch out the best I can and try to get my bearings. My guess is I will be landing back in Hollywood in the next couple of hours. I try to plan out what I need to do next.

I have a busy week ahead with pre-production work on *Flower Queen*. Amanda will want to meet to set up my first one-on-one interview. I will be around Jon and Ayumi again. At the thought of Jon, I close my eyes briefly. A small part of me was hoping that my short tryst with Justin would make it so the aching in my heart would cease when I thought of Jon. I ignore it and move on to my next big issue – Rich, of course.

My fingers itch. I want to grab the flash drives and go through them as soon as I can. I'm hoping there will be some clue that I can use. I will take anything I can to pin Rich down and get him to leave me alone. *If not, then I need to get into his computer. Delete the tapes from his cloud. Track down copies. I have to ensure it is all gone.* The thought of facing down Rich is still terrifying but when I think about Justin, living alone on an island, I realize I cannot let that happen to me.

I bring my blanket close to my face, just underneath my chin, and try to fall back asleep.

"Back in the land of the living." Marina quips as she heaves my one suitcase into her backseat.

"Thanks again for coming to get me. I could have taken a cab."

"No way. Besides, I want you to fill me in on everything," she replies as we get into her car.

I marvel at how clean the inside of her car is. In fact, it still smells brand new even though she's had it for five years now. Marina hands me a water bottle and I take a swig, trying to think of how to quickly sum up what I discovered.

There really isn't need to sum it up, in the end, because we hit massive traffic due to an accident just outside the city. So I recount every detail, including my hook-up with Justin, which Marina gets a kick out of.

"Oh, c'mon. Who wouldn't want a lover when they are in the tropics?" she says matter of fact and I wonder if it is something she has done before.

By the time I finish, we are finally inching along Hollywood Blvd. Marina glances at me.

"So, please tell me you're going to go through this stuff right away."

"Yeah, but I'm not hopeful," I reply with a shrug. "I think Justin would have seen something on there. Or Rich wouldn't have been so careless as to give a laptop with his secrets on it to Justin."

Marina chews on her bottom lip. "Yeah, you're probably right."

The rest of the ride goes by with Marina catching me up on the last couple of days. By the time she drops me off at home, I can't wait to grab a shower and then go through the files. I am exhausted from the last few days but there is no time to relax.

Before I go into the shower, my phone goes off. It is Rich. He had only tried to call me once in Jamaica and I had texted him back, telling him that I had a family dinner to go to. I pick up the phone, getting ready to deal with him again.

"Are you back yet?" he says instead of any sort of greeting.

"Yes, hi, Rich. I just got home."

"Perfect. I need you to come out with me tonight to this dinner—"

"Rich," I reply, irritated at him making demands as soon as I get my foot in the door, "I'm exhausted. I was busy the entire trip and frankly, I need to shower and go to bed."

"I don't care, Jenny," he snaps.

I bite my bottom lip and decided to readjust how I am approaching this. "Rich," I reply in a sweet voice, "I'd look like shit tonight anyway. Do you really want me looking like shit on your arm? Wouldn't that look bad? I just need to go to bed early and then I'll be all set. We can even go out tomorrow night."

There is a brief pause and then a grunt. "Fine. Tomorrow then. Goodnight."

Rich hangs up and relief sweeps through me. I hop in the shower, scrubbing the airline grubbiness from me and then settle down in front of my laptop. The first flash drive, the smaller of the two, is clutched tightly in my hand. I exhale and plug it in my laptop.

My machine whirs for a couple of seconds and then opens the flash drive. It is mostly word documents with some images. I go through the images first. They are all generic shots. Some of them are even stock photos of flowers and trees. I can't tell if they came with the computer and Rich was too lazy to delete them or what. There is one photo I pause on.

It is a picture of Justin and Rich. Justin looks youthful in the photo. He has no tan in the picture and is wearing a suit and tie. Rich has his arm slung around Justin as if they are the best of friends. They are at some party. Just out of the frame is a slightly blurry face of a woman. She looks familiar but I cannot pinpoint where I have seen her before.

I stare at the photo for a while and then click through the rest. There is nothing else of interest. There are a couple more photos of flowers and trees.

Nothing good is exposed. Maybe part of me deep down had been hoping to see something truly wicked, plastered on the computer screen for all eyes to see. But like I guessed earlier, Rich isn't stupid enough to let a computer with incriminating photos go to the person he has blackmailed.

I switch to the other flash drive to look at the word documents I pulled. Most of them make no sense to me. A lot of them only have one word on them. Nothing jumps out at me. By the time I finish looking at them, I feel disheartened. I realize just how much I have been hoping there was going to be something on there that would snap everything in place.

With a sigh, I give up and crawl into bed. I try not to taste the bitter disappointment in the back of my throat.

The sound of the doorbell ringing awakens me the next morning. I pad out of my bedroom and look through the peephole before I open the door. It is a delivery man who hands me a package to sign off on. Puzzled, I take the package and set it down on my kitchen table. I rub the sleep from my eyes and open it up.

I stop. It is Rich's laptop from Justin's house. I glance over my shoulder, as if Rich is going to burst in at any moment and see me with it. I scoop the laptop up and go to my bedroom, unfolding the small note that came with it.

Jenny,

I overnighted this to you. I don't want it anymore. It is just a reminder of what I cannot face. Maybe you will find some use for it.

It isn't signed. I take the laptop and bury it in some clothes in the back of my closet. I need to get going to meet Amanda for our meeting and cannot look at it now. I wonder why Justin sent it to me. Did our meeting make him regret not trying harder to fight against Rich?

Does he really think I can do something to stop him?

Chapter Twelve

Even though I have been careful throughout the trip to Jamaica to put on sunblock, I am still paranoid that Amanda or Jon will take one look at me and see right through me. However Jon is on the phone when I arrive at the restaurant and Amanda is typing away on her phone. Her nails are a bright blue and shine under the morning light. I still feel tired and instantly order the largest coffee they have.

Amanda looks up after I order. "All done with your sudden family business?"

"Yes," I reply.

The way she looks at me lets me know she doesn't believe for a second I went back home. I am hoping she won't press it in front of Jon, whose eyes are darting between the two of us. He looks tired but otherwise the same. I ignore the constricting of my heart when I see him. I quickly switch to business mode and refuse to give into my feelings.

"Well, now that we got that out of the way," Amanda says curtly. "Let's run down what we are going to do."

My phone goes off. The volume has been turned up and it blares through Amanda's words. She glares at me and I grow flustered. I look through my purse for it and

see it is Kathy calling. I remember how I haven't
returned her texts and I hit ignore on the phone,
remembering I have to call her back later.

I shove my phone deep in my purse and turn my
attention to the meeting.

It turns out Amanda talks long and furiously. I
almost wish I had brought a notebook to the meeting.
Since hiring her, Amanda has come up with a plan for
my career to make a splash. At one point, Jon shoots me
a wry smile and I feel my stomach do flips.

And just like that, Amanda wraps up and is gone in
a cloud of perfume and promises to call soon. I feel as if
my head is spinning. Jon walks with me out of the
restaurant.

"Have a nice trip?" he asks me as we step outside.

"Yes. Nice seeing everyone," I lie, hoping he won't
press the topic.

But something strange flashes across his face and I
turn around. Ayumi is waiting for him, long legged and
gorgeous.

She sees him and heads over, smiling. "Hey!
Thought we could go shopping since I need a dress for
my friend's wedding."

That sour feeling comes back to my stomach, and
Jon looks cornered by seeing Ayumi here.

"I have to go meet a friend for lunch. Nice seeing you again, Ayumi," I lie, even though lunch isn't for another hour.

She waves at me and Jon opens his mouth as if he is going to say something. But the words die on his lips and I head to my car, ignoring the burning feeling in my chest.

When I get back in the car, I call Kathy back.

"Hey, what's up?"

"Jenny! Finally, I get a hold of you. Can I please meet you? Like ASAP?"

"Is everything okay?" I reply, frowning.

"Please, for lunch or something."

I have no idea what in the world she could want to see me about. Things were left on a bit of a sour note after she wanted to date Jon again.

"Uhm, sure, okay," I relent, curious as to why she needs to see me so badly.

"I'll text you where to go," she replies and then hangs up.

When I get to where Kathy wanted to meet up, I cannot help but feel curious as to what was so urgent she needed to see me so fast. I suppose I have forgotten to text her back both times she tried. No wonder she called me.

Hesitant, I park my car and head inside. Kathy is at the bar and waves me over. I sit down next to her. She looks great. I know the soap opera has been picked up for another season. Her smile is kind and I relax.

"I'm so sorry I never texted you back," I say, "Things have been just absolutely mental since I moved out."

"I'm sorry to call you and demand to see you so quickly. But there is something I have to tell you and I just wanted to tell you first because I don't think anyone else knows."

I frown, wondering what in the world Kathy could know that involved me. She takes a sip of the drink she has ordered and looks me in the eyes.

"Jenny," she says, as if she is about to tell me something terrible. "Rich is a father. He has at least one daughter he is trying to hide from everyone."

**-*To be continued in Book 4 -*

Book Four

Chapter One

I AM pretty sure I heard Kathy wrong. I blink and look at her, wondering if this is her idea of some sort of joke.

"What?"

Kathy shifts in her chair, glancing over her shoulder as if someone will be hovering nearby. "Rich has a child."

I feel, just for a moment, as if the ground is going to open up and swallow me whole. Mixed emotions are swirling through me. I can't seem to pinpoint the one that is the most horrifying. Is it because I am shocked at the fact that Rich has a child? Is it because I can't believe something like this has been under my nose the entire time and I had no idea? Or is it the look on Kathy's face, as if she thinks this is delivering a death blow to my feelings for Rich?

"How do you know this?" I finally ask her.

"I tried to tell you right away," she says quickly. "Remember? I texted you twice. I should have called you, but I was so busy."

"Hey, it's okay," I tell her, realizing Kathy is afraid I will take out my feelings on her. "I should have contacted you back. I've just been so busy lately."

She gives me a small nod and then runs her fingers through her hair. "I was on break from filming an episode. I thought if I ended up going to the café on the studio grounds one more time, I was totally going to flip. So I walked down the street to this other coffee shop I had been wanting to try out. Anyway, I was in the corner, eating a sandwich and having my coffee, when this woman storms into the building. She looked flat out exhausted. But I looked back at my phone 'cause I didn't think much of it. It wasn't until she was suddenly looming over me that I looked back up."

I order a drink at this point, feeling nervous.

"She asks me if I work on the soap and I tell her yes," Kathy continued. "I'm thinking maybe she is a fan. But then she asks if Rich ever visits the set. When I tell her no, she looks so upset that I invite her to sit with me because I am afraid she is going to start crying. She sits down across from me, and I offer to buy her a coffee but she turns it down." Kathy takes a sip of her drink. "She asked me if I can tell Rich that she was here. Says her name is Sarah. I ask her what it is about, and she says that she is sick of Rich being behind on his child support."

"She just said that?" I blurt out, my eyes widening.

"Yeah! I couldn't believe it either. But Sarah seemed *so* angry, as if she had come down here just to find Rich to make him pay the money. She tells me she had been trying to corner him and the last she heard he worked on the soap opera. She said she got the idea after she saw him in the press, dating you."

I cringe. Even though it is Rich who is being an asshole, I feel guilty for dating a guy who is apparently behind on child support.

Kathy leans forward, lowering her voice. "She said that she recognized him even after his plastic surgeries and that his name change hadn't fooled her. She knew who it was."

I let this sink in. Plastic surgery? Name change? Of course I knew by this point Rich was a slime ball, but it never occurred to me that he would have changed so much and ran off so that the mother of his child had to track him down.

"So I just asked her like, why doesn't she report him to the police or something for non-payment instead of tracking him down? Sarah got irritated, I think she was on edge to begin with, and said that she had tried but she didn't want to go into it further. So she came to Hollywood once she saw him online but no luck so far."

"Did she say anything… anything about the child?"

"Sarah said that her daughter is fourteen now. She had her when she was sixteen and struggled as a single parent without Rich – sorry, she said his name was Doug, actually – to help or offer any support. He popped up when her daughter was young but faded off but at least made the payments. About four years ago, he vanished and Sarah has been trying to raise her daughter on her own but she needs Rich's financial support."

I lean forward eagerly. "Do you have any contact information for her?"

"Yeah," Kathy replies slowly. "I have her phone number. But why do you want to call her? Listen, Jenny, this guy sounds like a creep, honestly. I know things got weird over Jon and stuff, but I still don't want you getting hurt."

I find myself appreciating Kathy's concern. I want to tell her that I am working on it and that with each tidbit of information that lands in my lap I become more determined to put Rich in his place. But I don't want someone else to know what I am up to and instead smile at her.

"I appreciate the concern. Maybe I can help the two of them meet up? If I have her number, I can reach out to her. Get things settled."

Kathy nods and then pulls out her phone, texting me Sarah's number. I feel thrilled at this chance to talk to someone who knew Rich way back when. It feels like a breakthrough I can actually use, unlike the laptop sitting in the back of my closet.

"Listen, be careful, okay?" Kathy says. "She asked me to contact her whenever I hear from Rich, but I didn't say anything about giving her number to you. She seems really stressed out and might not want to talk to you."

"I'll try, at the very least. If she says no, then I can give the message to Rich."

"Okay." She nods and finishes her drink, standing up. "I'm sorry to drop this on you. Are you mad?"

"No. Thank you for telling me about this."

Kathy relaxes slightly and nods. She gives me a hug goodbye and I watch her go, my mind swirling. *Rich has a daughter*. Part of me isn't that surprised. It is clear that Rich is nothing but an asshole who uses people to get money and whatever else he desires.

As I sip my drink, I realize that I have to reach out to Sarah and see what I can find out. It would be stupid not to.

Chapter Two

"I'm nervous," I admit to Marina.

She hands me my favorite white chocolate iced coffee and smiles. "Don't be. Matt is really nice. You'll shine in this pre-production meeting."

"I wish you were working on this," I admit.

For some reason, even though I am thrilled to be working on *Flower Queen,* this first pre-production meeting has me incredibly nervous. Maybe it is because I didn't have to audition for this. Matt, a rising director in his own right, has given me this role without any audition or reading. What if we start going over the script and he decides I'm not a good fit? My mind is getting the best of me in spite of how I am trying to calm down.

Marina met up with me to wish me good luck before I headed toward the studio and I am grateful for her kind words. I realize that through everything, I have made an actual friend who is standing by my side, which means more to me than she will ever know.

"I've seen you on set, Jenny. A big production, on top of that. Everyone on the crew loved you. You were sweet to everyone, even people who usually get ignored. You were a hard worker and didn't even let your bruised knee stop you. People talked about you so much that Matt gave you this role," Marina repeated, a speech she has given me often the last couple of days.

I take a deep breath. "You're right. It's just hard for me not to get hung up on my insecurities, at least in my head. Like, what if everyone is giggling about my sex tape behind my back?"

Marina takes a sip of her coffee and looks thoughtful. "Fuck them."

I let out a laugh and feel a little bit better. Marina smiles at me, and we leave the coffee shop together. Before we depart, she stops and lowers her voice.

"When are you calling you-know-who?"

"Marina, it isn't Voldemort, you can say her name," I point out to her. "And maybe tonight. I'm nervous about that, too. I don't want to come across like a weirdo, but I really want to see what I can find out."

"You'll be okay. She probably won't have any qualms bashing on him. She sounds pretty pissed off."

"True. Well, I better get going. I'll text you."

As I get into my car, giving Marina a wave, my phone goes off. I see that it is Jon. My heart gives a hard thump, which I try to ignore as I answer.

"Hey, what's up?"

"I just wanted to wish you good luck today," Jon says. "I know you have your first pre-production meeting today."

"Thank you for calling. I'm really nervous but Marina treated me to a coffee and I'm feeling a bit better now."

"You'll do great, Jenny. You always make a positive impression with people. And Matt wants you on this project. I wouldn't be too worried. Just be yourself."

His voice is soft and kind, and I try to ignore the way my heart races. I wish every time I spoke to him, I felt nothing but friendship for him. It feels as if I am constantly reminding myself why I have lied and told him we have to be friends. I don't want him trying to save me from Rich and getting sucked into Rich's twisted world.

"Thanks, Jon," I reply gently, hoping my voice sounds even.

Jon clears his throat. "Call me afterward? If you want, I mean."

"I will, thanks. I better go or I'll be late."

We say goodbye and I hang up the call, an empty feeling settling over me. I ignore it, telling myself now isn't the time to fall into a negative headspace. I want to make a good impression at this pre-production meeting.

"We're wrapping up casting on that role," Matt says to me as we go through the script. "We'll have the neighbor casting finished soon."

I nod and make a note. My script is covered in notes. Originally, I had thought the meeting would be about production and a few things about the script. But Matt has us go through the script line by line, going over ideas and other things about production. I am glad I brought a small notebook with me, even though everyone else is writing in their iPads. I suppose I am old fashioned in that respect – I like writing on the script and my notebook instead.

"Okay, great," I reply, as I scan the page.

The neighbor is a minor role that I only interact with a couple of times, so the fact that it is not being casted yet doesn't really bother me. The rest of the cast is mostly in place. Matt launches into an explanation for what he wants for the next scene and I find myself listening to him closely. I can see why he is rising quickly.

Matt didn't look like I thought he was going to. He is incredibly skinny, as if he rarely eats and when he does it isn't anything more than a salad. His hair is messy from how he runs his fingers through it constantly when speaking. He also looks exhausted, as if he hasn't slept in ages. From the amount of thought that he has put into the script, I can easily see him up all night, thinking about the next scene. He is clearly dedicated and considers this film important in his career.

By the time we finish going through everything with the rest of the cast, it is four hours later and my stomach is growling. I dart my eyes around but no one seems to notice how loud it is. As people file out, Matt calls me back to him. I head over and sit back down across from him. Once the room is empty, he clears his throat.

"I'm glad you signed on for this film. I feel like both of us are on the rise, and I wanted to make this film together," he says, and I feel excited that he sees me in the same boat as him.

"I really love the script. And your past films really struck a chord with me."

I had made sure to watch his last two films before meeting with Matt today. It seemed only proper to know exactly who I was working with. His slow style and wide shots to illustrate the character's loneliness seem to hit a note with me and I found myself adoring them. The script for *Flower Queen* is a little wider in scope with themes but the core theme of loneliness and fear of rejection is one I can relate to all too well.

Matt smiles. "I'm thrilled you took the time to see my other films. Listen, if you have any ideas on your own character, I always want to hear them. I don't want you to think this is just a role where you come in and recite your lines and you're done with it. I really want you to get into it."

"I will. Thank you again for this chance," I say as we shake hands and leave the room.

A bubble of happiness rises in my chest. I am thrilled to be getting a role I can truly dig my teeth into. My previous roles hadn't allowed anything like that. *Beloved* was meatier but the director had a set vision for my character. Knowing I can explore my character on *Flower Queen* and even pitch my own thoughts has me massively excited.

I'm going to put my heart and soul into this, I think excitedly as I get into my car.

Chapter Three

It is a little after seven by the time I get home and eat some instant ramen, too lazy to actually cook anything. I plop down on the couch and find myself staring at my phone. I had told Marina I was going to call Sarah tonight but now that the moment is before me, I find myself nervous at the thought.

You're being stupid. You called Justin no problem and then went to Jamaica to see him, Jenny. I can't decide which reason makes me the most nervous for calling Sarah. Maybe because there is a child involved, and I don't want to come across like a stalker for calling her up and possibly lying about talking to Rich about her.

The truth is that the thought of lying to Sarah about Rich – claiming that maybe he will pay child support and I am meeting with her on his behalf – leaves a sour taste in my mouth. I can't lie to someone about something like that. How does that make me any different than Rich, lying to get what I want? No, if I call Sarah, I have to be honest with her.

With this in mind, I dial her number. It rings for what feels like ages before it goes to voicemail. My heart drops.

"Hi, this is Sarah. I'm busy and can't make it to the phone. Please leave a message. Thank you and have a nice day!" Her voice is chipper and airy. In that moment, I feel bad for leaving a message on her voicemail.

"Sarah, hi. This is Jenny. Rich's girlfriend." I take a breath, realizing I sound like a robot. "I was wondering if you can give me a call back. I have some things to talk to you about in regards to him. I think we have some mutual things to discuss. Anyway, I hope to hear from you. Thanks."

I hang up, wishing she had picked up. I worry I sounded stupid in the voice mail. I sink back in my couch, eating my ramen and trying to distract myself with the TV, but my thoughts are drifting. When my phone rings ten minutes later, I practically leap out of my seat to grab it off my coffee table.

It is Jon again. I remember he said he was going to check in with how the production meeting went and so I answer.

"Jon, hey. The meeting went great," I gush. "Matt really wants me to dig into my character, and I am so excited to try that out. No other role has offered me that, you know? I'm so excited."

"That's great, Jenny," he replies, and I stop speaking. His tone is off and I know it.

"So," I say after a long beat of silence, "I'm looking forward to working with him. I think it is going to be a great fit, the two of us working on this project together."

"I'm really excited for you. I'm glad that this is all falling into place for you," he says but he still sounds a little distant. "Listen, I'm calling to see how it went and also to tell you about casting news I found out today."

"Um, okay," I reply, wondering what in the world it could be.

"Ayumi got a small role in the film. She called me just now to let me know, since I don't represent her anymore. But I just wanted you to know because I didn't want it to seem like I was hiding it from you."

"Oh."

I wasn't sure what to say. I wasn't sure why he felt the need to tell me this, unless he thought I would think that he worked on giving Ayumi the role. The thought of working with her fills me with dread. Not because she has been anything but kind to me but because I know she is dating Jon and I will feel weird being around the person he is with.

Jon keeps talking, taking my silence for something bad. "She auditioned last week and it took them a while to pick someone for the role. I know she wanted to branch out from modeling and saw this as a way of stepping into it. I know we are dating, but I didn't want you to think I was springing it on you on purpose. Because of our past," he added at the end, as if I was not following him.

It is the first time that Jon has made mention of the night he helped me move and told me his feelings for me. Like the first time we confided in one another, I screwed it all up. The last thing I feel like doing is dragging it back up now. I know Jon would never have helped Ayumi land a role to upset me.

"Jon, it's okay," I tell him. "Congrats to Ayumi. I'm looking forward to working with her." The last part is a lie but there is no way I am going to look like a petty child over his relationship after I was the one who told him to move on.

The relief is clear on the other line when Jon replies, "Okay. Great. I just didn't want you to – you know with what happened – and I just – "

"It's okay," I repeat, and he stops rambling.

"Okay. I'll talk to you later. Goodnight."

I stare at the phone. It was nice of Jon to call me and warn me about Ayumi. I would have been taken aback to hear it tomorrow. I tell myself I handled the call the best way that I could and to try to relax.

Yet the rest of the night, I stare at my phone, willing for it to ring and be Sarah on the other end. It isn't until I am getting ready to get into bed at around eleven that it rings. I dart across my bedroom toward my phone and see it is Sarah. I snatch it up and answer.

"Hello?"

"Is this Jenny?" Sarah's voice sounds as if she is out somewhere.

"Yes. Hi. Sarah?"

"Sorry it took me so long to call you back. I have a lot going on."

"No, that's fine." I sit down on the bed. "I'm sorry to bother you."

"I am wondering if we can meet for lunch tomorrow. I don't know where would work best for you. I don't know much about Hollywood."

I feel relieved. I had been worried she would demand to know more about why I was calling. But it sounds as if she has been expecting my call.

"Yes, I have tomorrow off actually. Is one P.M. okay?"

When Sarah agrees, I give her the name of a diner to meet at and we hang up. With those plans in motion, I curl up in bed, telling myself all will be fixed soon. As long as I can stay focused.

Chapter Four

"I can't," I tell Rich the next morning. "I have some interview thing to film on Friday."

Rich practically demanded that I come out and have breakfast with him at a spot where paparazzi can easily take photos. It is stupid and silly but I agree. I am hoping if he gets his stupid paparazzi shots in, he won't bother me till this weekend.

But instantly he asks if I can come to some luncheon event so he can suck up to more people and drag me around on his arm. Amanda had emailed me early this morning with details about my first one-on-one interview on Friday and there is no way I am going to miss it for Rich's event.

Rich scowls at me. For a second, I wonder if he is going to throw the tapes in my face but he thinks better of it as what I said settles in.

"Interview?"

"Yeah with Rosie McGriffin." I try to say it casually, but his eyes light up at the name.

"How the fuck did Amanda get you on her show?"

Rosie McGriffin was young and appealed directly to millennials. Her show was always a combination of social media and her own questions. It is a new show, and she isn't interviewing A-list celebrities yet but the fact she tapped into social media means that I could gain access to a young audience. Of course, Rich would have known who she was and saw a chance for more exposure. I want to groan out loud but instead take a bite of my bacon.

I shrug. "Not sure. She has connections, I guess."

"I'll come with you to the filming."

I put down my piece of toast, trying not to gawk at him. "What? What about the luncheon?"

Rich leans forward. "Are you kidding me? This is way bigger than some luncheon."

"I don't understand."

Rich waves his hand at me, as if I am a small child asking stupid questions. "Just make sure I am on the list."

Breakfast ends soon after that. I want to tell Rich to fuck off. In fact, every inch of me wants to tell him to fuck off. But I temper myself. I am so close to finding out enough dirt to bury him that I know I need to hold back. I am itching to escape his clutches. But Rich needs to think I am still the scared girl from before in order for this to work. Anything else would be hasty and stupid.

I tell myself this as he makes sure one lone paparazzi cares enough to snap our photo as he kisses me before I get in my car. As much as Rich would like to fool himself that I am his fast ticket into the Hollywood elite, I am nowhere near there myself. While the *Flower Queen* casting landed me on the radar, along with my sex tape, it still is nowhere near A-list level.

As I drive away, I look at him in my mirror. He has no idea that I am going to meet the mother of his child in a few hours. I am itching to be rid of him.

The diner I asked Sarah to meet me at was old and run down. I had read about it in an article online for having apparently amazing omelets that no one knew about. When I pull up in front of it, I can see why. The diner looks as if it has been through a world war and is somehow still standing. I know no one I know would be caught dead here.

I step inside the diner and look around. There is a couple in one corner and a man at the countertop eating a stack of pancakes. In the right hand corner is a woman with brown hair pulled up in a ponytail, her fingers drumming on the table. When she sees me, she waves me toward her.

I sit down across from her, and she holds out her hand. "I'm Sarah. I recognized you from online."

"It's nice to meet you," I reply, hoping I do not look too awkward.

A bored-looking waitress comes over and we order our drinks and look at the menu. I pretend to be focused on the menu but sneak looks at Sarah. She is plain upon first glance but her hair is a dark chestnut brown. She has dark brown doe eyes and her clothing is simple. Not the traditional Hollywood type by any means but I can see why Rich would find her attractive.

"Do you know what you're getting?" she suddenly asks, glancing up at me.

I dart my eyes down toward the menu, hoping she has not caught me staring. "No. Not yet. Maybe just a burger."

"A burger?" She sounds surprised, and I look back up to see her blushing. "Sorry, that sounded rude. I didn't think Hollywood types ate burgers."

"I'm not really a Hollywood type. I moved here recently and just kinda got lucky with the roles I fell in."

"Oh," she replies, fiddling with the corner of the menu. "Was it a big change?"

"Yeah. I still hate the traffic, honestly."

"I cannot believe the traffic here. I am happy I left Elizabeth back home. She isn't very patient right now. It would have driven her nuts."

At the mention of her daughter, an awkward silence falls across the table. I can tell Sarah is worried that she has offended me. The mere fact she is worried that she has upset me over the daughter she had with Rich lets me know she isn't here to be mean to me. She is here because Rich owes her child support and she wants him to pay.

The waitress comes back with our drinks. I quickly order a burger and Sarah is still scanning over the menu, unsure of what to order.

"I heard the omelets here are amazing," I offer.

"I'll take a cheese omelet then," Sarah orders and the waitress leaves.

"Are you here long?" I ask.

"Until Sunday. That's how long my parents could watch Elizabeth. She was so upset about me not letting her come but if I did end up running into Doug, I didn't want it to be upsetting for her."

"When was the last time she saw Rich – I mean, Doug, sorry," I amend quickly.

"Ages ago," Sarah replies, her guard up. "What has Doug said about her?"

An awkward beat passes as I try to find the best way to word what I want to tell her. How do I tell Sarah he has never even mentioned *having* a daughter? That he has a fake name and is nothing more than a con artist?

But I don't have to say anything because Sarah must read it on my face. Her shoulders slump, as if she has been unplugged from an outlet.

"He hasn't said anything," she says, a statement instead of a question.

"No. I'm sorry. I heard through my friend Kathy," I admit.

"I don't know why I am surprised. I should know better." Her tone is bitter, and she looks away from me, out the window.

"When was the last time you spoke to him?"

"It's been years now. I've tried to get in touch with him. But he changes his number constantly. And goes by different names, lives in different areas. I had given up but then when I was on a gossip site online I saw him with you. Yeah, he had a lot of work done to his face so I guess most people from our hometown wouldn't know it was him. But I recognized it in his eyes. I knew it was him. So I came here to try to get to him. He owes back child support. There are warrants out on him but he will never come back home and he isn't stupid enough to get arrested now so…" She trails off and gives me a small shrug. "Do you think you can talk to him for me?"

"I don't think he would listen to me," I reply honestly.

A frown crosses Sarah's face quickly. "Why not?"

I bite my bottom lip. "Rich and I aren't on good terms right now."

While I want to tell Sarah everything, I am still hesitant. If she happens to speak to Rich and makes any mention of the fact that she knows he is blackmailing me or even a minor detail about our relationship, it might result in my house of cards crumbling around me. I want to be honest but I don't want to go into details, which means I am now in a balancing act.

"Oh, I'm sorry to hear that. Doug can be so difficult. I'm sorry. Rich, I mean. I'm not used to calling him that."

"It's okay. I wanted to meet with you to hear your side of things, honestly. I obviously do not want to bad mouth the father of your daughter. But if he didn't tell me about Elizabeth, what else could he be hiding?"

Sarah sits back in her seat. The vinyl seating is cheap, and I can feel it sticking to my thighs. It is humid outside and a perfect beach day. Yet here I am, in this rundown diner, trying to find out what I can about Rich, while making a mental note to make sure I pin Rich against the wall for not taking care of his own daughter.

"I was sixteen and so stupid. Doug was popular in high school. A golden boy on the fast track to becoming a college favorite in football. I mean colleges were bickering over him already and he was only sixteen. A sophomore but on the varsity football team. It sounds so cliché now but I was just this shy girl who blended into the background. I never thought he would notice me."

Sarah is cut off as the waitress comes back with our food. I pick gingerly at the burger, wondering how many stories of Rich being a terrible person I will have to sit through before I can somehow outsmart him and be free of his dark shadow.

When the waitress leaves, Sarah looks embarrassed. "I sound so stupid. Like I am telling you the plot of some teenage romantic comedy. But there was a party one night and my best friend at the time convinced me to go. She was always more outgoing than I was. I finally agreed to go. And Doug was there, and I had been harboring this stupid crush on him for ages. One of those crushes where the guy doesn't even know you exist."

"Oh, I know those all too well," I reply, thinking back to my own awkward crushes as a teenager.

Sarah gives me a small smile. "Most girls do, I think. In any case, it was nearing midnight and I had to get home. I was always so paranoid about being late for curfew. But my friend had gotten drunk and I had no way to get home. I was outside the house, panicked about getting home. I hadn't told my parents we were going to the party, you see. They'd be furious at me for going."

"Let me guess. Rich saved the day?"

"He saw me panicking on the driveway and offered to take me home. Of course I let him because it was Doug. It felt like the perfect twist in my story. I was so excited that night I couldn't sleep. We had talked the entire drive and I felt as if he understood me in those few moments. So stupid of me."

Sarah closes her eyes briefly, as if she is lost in her memories. I take a bite of my burger, not wanting to rush her.

Finally she opens her eyes again and blushes. "Sorry. I hate telling this story."

"You don't have to tell it to me," I tell her quickly. "I know I sound insane. Technically being his girlfriend and asking you for your personal stories."

"No, it's okay. My guess is if things aren't going so well between you that he is still the same old Doug."

She takes a bite of her omelet, and we eat for a few minutes in silence.

Finally, Sarah speaks again. "He started seeing me on the side. Like I said, I was blown away that he was interested in me at all so even though he asked me not to tell anyone, I agreed. I swore it was our secret. He pretended not to know me in any school or social situations and I just let him. He said his coach would be mad at him if he was dating anyone because he had to focus on the game."

I wrinkled my nose in disgust, knowing that just meant that he was a cheat and didn't want anyone to know.

"We went on like this for about three or four months. Then during a local championship game, Doug got injured. He blew out his knee really badly on a play. In one fell swoop, his dreams of a college picking him and then maybe going pro went up in smoke. Slowly but surely, over the next three months, he changed. In public, he was still the guy everyone loved. But as people forgot about him as a football player, he just got… angry."

I think about Rich, so close to the success he still so badly craves. It now makes sense why he is still trying so hard to become rich and famous. He probably felt as if his entire life had been sucked out from underneath him.

"Instead of channeling his rage into something else, it just felt like every little thing I did was grounds for yelling at me. My parents could tell something was going on with me but I didn't ever tell them about Doug. I was convinced he loved me and he needed my support now more than ever. When he finally struck me one night, I still didn't leave. It was all my fault. I had pissed him off, I had asked a stupid question, I had bothered him. It was always me. So I stayed and hid the bruises."

"Oh my god," I breathe. "That's horrible."

Sarah averts her eyes, as if too ashamed to look at me. I know Rich is an asshole and a master of manipulating people, but for some reason I never thought he was capable of hitting a woman.

"I found out I was pregnant shortly before our high school graduation. I was still able to finish school and get my diploma so I am lucky in that regard. When I told Doug, he absolutely freaked. I was terrified he was going to beat me to death that night. I finally managed to escape and had to tell my parents everything. They wanted to go to the police but I refused to turn him in. When they took me to the hospital, I still refused to tell them who had done this to me."

"Was Elizabeth okay?"

"Yes, thank God," Sarah exhales. "But Doug left in the night. I mean, he was gone. He told his parents that he was going out of town with some friends. But I knew he wasn't going to come back. He was terrified I was going to turn him in for what he did to me, plus he had no desire to raise Elizabeth. So once he settled down out of town, he told his parents he wasn't coming back."

By this time I am sitting back in the booth, my burger untouched. I feel disgusted, as if my skin is crawling with everything Sarah has just told me. Every time I think Rich cannot be more disgusting, I turn over more stones and find more horrible things about him underneath.

"He tried a few times over the years to get in touch with me," Sarah goes on. "Claimed he wanted to meet Elizabeth and get to know her. He only saw her twice. That's all I let him see her because he was refusing to pay any sort of child support, and I didn't want her around someone who had beaten me. By that point, I realized what an emotionally and physically abusive bastard he was. I didn't want Elizabeth around that. Eventually he agreed he would leave Elizabeth alone and make payments. But they were never forth coming."

"How is Elizabeth now… about her dad, I mean?"

"I think sometimes it bothers her that her father is not around. I try to explain to her the best I can about why Doug is gone. It just makes me so angry that he won't even pay child support. He ignored me while we dated and pretended we weren't but I cannot allow him to get away without paying child support for our daughter. I knew it was a long shot coming here but…" Sarah gives me a small shrug.

"I understand. You had to try, for your daughter."

"Yes, that's right. I owed it to Elizabeth to try. But I've had no luck getting him to even talk to me. And the fact you are meeting me instead of him shows me that you are stuck with him as well."

"Yes," I reply slowly. "You could say that. Although I have to ask… why not just call the police on him? You know he is here. You can call the cops."

"I don't want to include the police. I know it sounds stupid but if he is behind bars, then I won't get any money at all, will I? Plus if he is alerted to the police then I am afraid he'll vanish again and slip away from me."

"Sounds a little naïve." I don't mean to sound harsh but if I were in Sarah's position, I'd call the cops. Although I am not in any position to judge, seeing the situation I have gotten myself into.

"True, I suppose. I guess I can't bear to send Elizabeth's father to prison or get him in legal trouble. I just want the money owed to her."

"Rich seems pretty stubborn. And smart," I say, although it is mostly to myself.

Sarah gives a small shake of her head. "My advice is to get out as quickly as you can. Whatever he is telling you or whatever promises he might be giving you, there is a dark man underneath all of it."

I lean forward a little. "Sort of a weird question but do you have any photos or anything of him from back then?"

"I might be able to dig some up. I used to scrapbook our relationship, only it is the saddest thing in my entire life. It's literally just local newspaper articles about him since we did nothing publicly together. I have one photo of us together and he was asleep during it." Her face flushes, and I can tell she feels silly for this admission.

"That would be great. I promise I won't judge you for it."

Sarah smiles a little. "I'll get it to you when I get back home. In the meantime, if you can in any way tell him about me safely, please let me know."

We finish up lunch, although it is basically untouched. I wave goodbye to Sarah as she hops into a cab. My mind is spinning with new information. *All this information yet no way out.* I feel frustrated.

I know Rich is a liar. I know where he came from. I know what he did to Sarah. I know he lost his future on the football field. I know what he did to Justin and what he is doing to me. At first, I had been wanting just to escape from him. But even if I do, what is to stop him from doing this to someone else?

It is becoming clear to me that to do the right thing means more than just freeing myself from Rich's grasp.

Chapter Five

"I wish you would have told me Rich was going to be here," Amanda says to me, looking cross.

"I'm sorry. He sort of just shoved his way in," I mumble, hoping I am not blushing.

Amanda looks over her shoulder. Rich is talking to someone on his cellphone. He is animated, clearly trying to win someone over. My stomach clenches. Ever since I spoke to Sarah, I feel disgusted at the mere thought of Rich. Not only did he beat Sarah, he beat her when she was pregnant. There are few things more disgusting than that.

I turn my face away from him. I feel sick. It is from the nerves of having Rich around me as well as the nerves of being interviewed by Rosie soon. Amanda has helped me prepare the last couple of days but I still feel jittery, as if I have been drinking energy drinks all morning.

Rich is in good spirits. Besides the fact he is here on set of the set of Rosie's show, trying to win the producers over, he apparently has some bigwig interested in meeting with him next week. Because of this, he is overly chatty and I am trying not to let it irritate me.

"You want a bottle of water?" Amanda asks me.

I run my fingers down my skirt and exhale. "I wish this wasn't live TV."

"Why? It's just a daytime talk show. I wouldn't be too concerned. I think this is a good first step."

"Yeah, but she is going to take questions from Twitter and stuff. What if it is just about how much I suck?"

"Just relax," Amanda says, her phone going off in her hand.

She turns to take the call, and I watch as Rosie interviews someone who is apparently an up-and-coming chef. I feel someone gently tug on my arm and I turn around, prepared to see Rich.

Instead it is Jon. I am surprised to see him here. We have not spoken since he called me about Ayumi's casting, which I found out officially the next day. I wasn't sure if he was going to show up here or not.

"Hey, just wanted to stop bye and wish you good luck."

"Thanks. I'm so nervous. I feel like I tell you that every time we talk," I reply.

Jon smiles at me. He looks incredibly handsome today and I feel my heart thump against my chest.

"I guess we do repeat ourselves a lot," he admits, running his fingers through his hair. "But I still mean it. I know it is your first live TV interview and all."

"How are things on your end?" I ask.

"You're getting a lot of producers calling but no solid offers. I think some are just trying to feel you out and see if they should consider you for things. I am fielding them as we go. I know you said you didn't want any projects sent to you because you are working so hard on *Flower Queen* but you might want to strike when the iron is hot…What?"

I cover my mouth in an attempt to hide my laughter. "I meant, how are you doing with things in your life, Jon. While I am touched you jumped right to my business, I meant *you*."

"Oh." He looks embarrassed. "I'm okay. I'm pretty swamped with work and I've been trying to help Ayumi with her role."

"How is she?"

"She's excited for it. She doesn't want to model anymore. Sort of lost interest in it while she was in Japan."

I find it curious he made no remark about their relationship but before I can say anything, I see Rich walking over. My mood instantly darkens. I feel Jon stiffen next to me. The bad blood between them is well known.

"Jon," Rich says. "Why are you here?"

"Wishing Jenny good luck."

Rich wraps his arm around my waist, staring at Jon. "She has me. She will be fine."

"Didn't realize she needed you in order to figure out this interview."

Rich's eyes narrow at Jon, and I can feel the tension radiating off of him. "Do you come by for all your clients and wish them good luck?"

Jon straightens up and his eyes widen slightly. He is clearly taken aback by Rich so openly suggesting he has feelings for me, and frankly, so am I. I feel my own muscles tighten as I think of a way to separate the two of them without it coming to blows.

"Jenny, you're up next," the set director says, coming over to me.

I quickly detangle myself from Rich and give Jon a look as the set director ushers me off to the side. I try to slow my breathing but my nerves are on edge. The last thing I need is Rich and Jon fighting backstage as I do this live interview. Not only is the audience going to be watching me but anyone else who is watching the show online and tweeting about it.

They announce me and I step out, waving at the crowd and plastering a smile on my face. My anxiety is at an all-time high. I am worried about somehow fucking this up or something going horribly wrong. Rosie welcomes me, and I sit down across from her on the fake living room set.

Instantly she gives a quick recap to the audience about who I am. She has a cheesy way of talking and it suddenly strikes me that maybe she is so popular with millennials because she looks and talks like a walking Internet meme. The thought does nothing to ease my mind.

"Jenny, we are so glad that you are with us today," she says, finally turning to face me.

"Thank you. It is a pleasure to be here as well," I say, hoping my voice sounds even and professional.

The interview starts off on a good note. The questions are easy, if a little boring, and I find myself settling into the seat and relaxing a little. Even the Twitter questions are mostly regarding what it is like to find fame so quickly. The audience laughs at the right spots to my corny jokes and Rosie's fake smile starts to look like a real one five minutes in.

Of course there is going to be a bump in the road. The fact I believe for a moment it is going to keep at this pace shows that I am still too naïve for my own good when it comes to new situations like this.

So when Rosie looks at me and asks, "Now, I know you had an unfortunate tape of a sexual nature leaked recently," I can feel myself tense.

Amanda thought it would be wise to speak about the tape for the first time to clear the air and look professional. I am expecting to discuss the tape. Even with my accelerating heart rate, I launch into the answer that I have prepared beforehand.

When I finish, Rosie looks at her cheat sheet and leans forward, as if we are two friends gossiping at lunch. "What about Rich?"

I am taken aback. The last thing I want to discuss, of all people, is Rich. I am pretty sure Amanda didn't put that on the list of topics to discuss as well.

"What about him?" I reply.

"Well, you two were dating during the leak. It must have been nice to have that support system there."

"Yes, yes," I reply quickly. "It was great."

Rosie nods. "Rich is a rising producer, sort of like how you are rising star in your own right. What is in the future for the two of you? Marriage?"

I balk at this, wondering why in the world all these questions about Rich are being asked. I don't want to look like a bitch but I feel as if the interview is quickly slipping off the rails. It is becoming more about Rich, who only leaves a bad feeling in my stomach, instead of about myself and my career.

"I honestly don't know what the future will have in store for us," I reply and smile at her, hoping she can sense that I want her to drop it.

"It's great he was so understanding about the sex tape being leaked like that. We look forward to what the future holds for the two of you."

After that, Rosie turns to the camera, and a commercial starts. I look over at Amanda, my eyes wide, as the set director takes my mic off. Amanda comes over to me, a stern look on her face as she pulls Rosie aside.

I wait for her off stage, quietly fuming. While I think I handled the interview okay, I still do not understand why Rich was brought up at all. I look around for him, positive that he will be thrilled by this turn of events but I can't spot him.

Amanda comes back five minutes later, looking irritated. "Someone gave Rosie this cue card with everything identical except for bringing up Rich."

"What?" I replied, taking the cue card out of her hand.

"They asked the intern who gave it to them but he said he didn't know. Couldn't find him. Where is Rich anyway? Listen, Jenny, no offense, but I don't want your boyfriend going over my head like this. We had a set plan and topics that we wanted to discuss. Whoever wrote this new cue card up removed the plug for *Beloved* you were supposed to drop just to discuss *Rich*."

I look down at the card, irritation growing stronger in my chest. I feel positive that it was Rich who changed out the card. No wonder he was in such a great mood.

Amanda is typing away on her phone. "The producers of *Beloved* really wanted this plug. Fuck." She wanders off and I watch her go.

As I step out into the crisp air of the afternoon day, the anger in my chest is hot and bright. I am furious that Rich has done this. I know no one else would have done such a thing. I don't blame Amanda for being upset either. She has everything on a tight schedule and wants my image portrayed a certain way. A transition from my sex tape to my boyfriend is terrible.

When I get to my car, I stop short. Jon is there, leaning against it, looking at something on his phone. For some reason I thought he would have taken off early on in the interview. The last thing I was expecting was for him to stick around and wait for me.

I take a step forward and he hears me. He looks up and smiles a little.

"Hey," I say, "I thought you left."

Jon slides his phone in his back pocket and runs his fingers through his hair. "I just wanted to talk to you."

"What's up?"

"I know I'm probably overstepping again. But I can't keep quiet. I don't think you should be with Rich, Jenny. He's not the guy you think he is. And I don't want to seem like a jerk, telling you what to do, but you honestly deserve better than him."

I shift uncomfortably, acutely aware of the fact Jon has moved an inch closer to me. I don't know how to reply to what he is saying. I honestly was not expecting him to even still be here.

"What brought this on?" I finally ask.

"Nothing 'brought it on'. I've always thought this," he replies. "Rich isn't a good guy, Jenny. I think he has the wool pulled over your eyes."

"Why isn't he a good guy, Jon? I know you told me about what he was doing with girls but was that it? What else do you know about him?"

Jon's eyebrows move up an inch, as if he is surprised by my sudden onslaught of questions. "Like if he has done anything else besides take advantage of people who moved here? I don't know. He said his parents died a few years back but I don't really take that as an explanation for why he is such a dick. I don't mean to sound like an asshole, Jenny, but something about him just doesn't sit right with me."

"I appreciate your concern," I tell him, moving a step closer. "I really do." I wish I could say more but I stop myself.

We are almost touching and my breath catches when I realize how close we are to one another. As much as I want to fall into his arms, I tell myself that I cannot. He is dating Ayumi and I cannot justify giving him mixed signals.

"I didn't think Amanda even wanted to discuss Rich in the interview," he says to me, his voice low.

"It wasn't the plan. Cue cards got messed up somehow. Have you seen Rich since you two talked?"

Jon shakes his head. "No. He made some dipshit comment to me about you and sauntered off. Is it true he is getting his own production company?"

"Where did you hear that?"

"Just around." He shrugged. "I guess someone is interested in backing him. I don't know."

"Well, thanks again for the heads up," I tell him, taking a step back which broke the spell we were quickly falling under. A funny expression crosses Jon's face and he rubs his chin a little before walking away from my car.

"Jenny," he says, before he leaves, "I know that you don't have to listen to me. But I don't understand why you are with him."

"It's complicated." It is as close as I can get to the truth.

Jon nods and then gives me a wave. I watch him depart, my heart aching after him. I get in my car and try to push thoughts of Jon out of my mind. It will do me no good.

Chapter Six

"I just don't understand why you did that," I say to Rich. "I mean, you shoved that in the cue cards but why not pick a better place for it than after my sex tape leaking?"

Rich leans back in his couch. It is the same day but the sun has set. We are out on his patio. I couldn't stand the thought of him messing with the cue cards for Rosie and had to ask him about it. Plus I am hoping I can snoop around later if he goes to bed while I am here.

His pool is illuminated, and the pool light changes the colors of the water. Currently it is a bright blue but is slowly shifting to a pink. Rich leans back in his pool chair, rolling his eyes at me.

"Listen, Jenny, I need the word out there for me, too. You understand, don't you? This was a perfect chance for our relationship to get media spotlight. Frankly I am insulted that I wasn't on the list to begin with."

"Amanda didn't think it was relevant for the first interview – "

"It should have been," Rich snaps, his tone suddenly harsh.

I think of Sarah and what he did to her and I balk, trying to mollify him. "I should have. I'm sorry. I was just nervous about the interview."

Rich relaxes and takes a sip of his drink, eying me. "So now people now how strong we are with one another. I'm already getting tons of emails and tweets."

"Since when did you get a Twitter account?"

"A couple of days ago," he says casually, then I realize he must have planned this out since I told him about the Rosie interview.

I feel a surge of anger roll through me and try to shove it down. I try to tell myself that I am working my way out from underneath his thumb but at this moment, watching him smug on his pool chair, I feel nothing but rage. I stand up suddenly.

"Where are you going?"

"I'm leaving."

"You can't leave. You just got here. I think there is a paparazzi outside."

"That *you* tipped off?" I snap as I head toward the inside of the house.

In a flash, Rich is up and yanks on my arm, spinning me around. I am dizzy from the sudden force and find myself staring at his face, which is contorted in anger. I have only seen him angry in flashes that come and go in a blink. I didn't realize I had pushed him so far. Sarah's words flash in my head and I try to take a step back but his grip is tight.

"You are staying here," he says to me through clenched teeth.

"Why does it matter so much? The guy saw me come in," I argue back.

"Because they need to think we are happy together, not just you stopping by to be a bitch."

"I'm not being a bitch," I snap and try to pull my arm away. "Let go of me, Rich."

"Or what? You have to do what I say, Jenny, or I'll leak both those fucking tapes of you. You'll be painted a whore. No one will want to be around you. Everyone will talk about you. Your burgeoning career will be done."

I swear that I am seeing red. Part of me wants to bash Rich's face in. Another part of me wants to make a sneering remark about his failed football career.

Instead, I try logic. "You won't get nearly as much money as you think for leaking tapes of me. You're trying to ride my coattails, but I'm not even as famous as you make me out to be. I'm just starting out – I don't have the name recognition you seem to think I have."

Rich's grip tightens on my arm. I try not to wince or let him know he is hurting me. I have apparently pushed his buttons enough that he is exposing the rage that boils underneath him. I try not to show my fear.

"I told you before that it will be enough to skip town. I'll start over somewhere else!"

"Because that is what you do, isn't it, Rich? You just take off whenever you want, you don't care who you leave behind or what you do to people because the only person you care about is *yourself*," I hiss through clenched teeth.

The slap comes hard and fast. I feel the pain radiate up my jaw as I turn back to look at Rich. I have never seen his face look so blank before. It is devoid of any feeling. There is no expression at all, as if someone has come over and restarted him. My cheek is stinging and my eyes are watering from the contact.

Although I have Sarah's story fresh in my mind, Rich has never actually struck me until now. Part of me knew that it would eventually get to this point. I am sure that Rich has constant plots and plans on his own side, fucking over whoever he can and keeping up appearances. Of course it will begin to leak out and he will take it out on me.

But that does not excuse it. The rage inside of me has quieted down. Instead I pity Rich. I pity him because he is nothing but an abuser who cares nothing about his next score of money. He has earned nothing in his life and won't even pay child support for his own daughter.

"You need to keep your mouth shut, Jenny," Rich says to me, breaking the silence that has shrouded us. "Look at what happens when you overstep."

"Right," I breathe. "It's my fault."

His eyes narrow slightly but he releases my hand and takes a step back. "Stay here tonight."

Rich walks past me into the house. I find myself staring at the pool. My hands are shaking and I try to stop them, taking a deep breath. My cheek is throbbing from the pain of the slap. He hit me hard enough that I am surprised my head didn't start bouncing like a bobble head.

I refuse to give Rich my career on a silver platter. Calling the cops now will only result in the tapes leaking and Rich getting what he wants. He deserves to go to jail but I have to make sure I have all the evidence against him in order.

I step inside the kitchen. I can hear the TV in the living room. I make my way to the fridge and fill a bag with ice, placing it gingerly against my cheek in an attempt to keep the swelling down. I have no idea how I am going to hide this. I know it will swell and look ugly. I hope makeup will cover it enough that no one will notice but I doubt it will get past Jon, Marina and Amanda.

I push that from my mind. If Rich wants me to stay the night, then I will, but I'll be trying to get into his computer. I step into the living room and sit on an opposite chair. Rich does not look at me and the next couple of hours are spent in stony silence.

When it hits ten, Rich stands up and glances at me. "I'm going to bed. Keep the TV down."

I nod and he leaves without another word. I hear him go up the stairs. Does it ever bother him he didn't earn this house? That he just blackmailed Justin for it? Who else over the years has he fucked over? Now that he has left, I feel as if the energy is being sucked out of me. I didn't realize how on alert I was the entire time he was here until Rich went upstairs.

A game show plays on the TV but I find I cannot pay attention. I am itching to try to get into his computer. I want to go through his emails and his documents. Not to mention I can access his cloud from there and delete the back-ups of the tapes of me.

But Rich must have trouble sleeping because I can hear him pacing upstairs. I sit on the chair, rigid, my eyes glued to the TV for a good thirty minutes. Finally the pacing stops and I hear nothing. I tiptoe to the bottom of the stairs and like last time, I hear his snoring.

Quickly I dart into his office. This time I make sure to close the door behind me, although it will muffle the sound. If he comes downstairs to get a drink of water, he might think I went to the guest room to sleep and forgot to turn off the TV.

Earlier Rich had tossed my bag in his office, effectively taking away my cellphone and my own laptop, which I had brought over because I wanted to do some research for *Flower Queen*. I didn't put up a fuss, knowing that it will give me an excuse to come in here.

I quickly check my phone. I have a couple of texts from Marina. I put my phone away and pull out my laptop, opening it up to check my email. I constantly forget to link my email to my phone. I am worried Matt has emailed me and that I will look unprofessional for not having been able to respond. Luckily there is nothing important so I turn back to Rich's computer.

Once again I am faced with his password screen. I bite my bottom lip and try some common things – his birthdate, his last name and the numbers in the address to the house. No luck. Too good to be true that he would give his computer a weak password.

I go through his drawers, attempting to see if he wrote it down somewhere. But his desk is still tidy and full of generic papers, like Internet bill statements. Frustrated, I stare at his computer screen. The glow is giving me a headache and my cheek is throbbing. There is a warning underneath the login screen that says *one try remaining.*

"Fuck," I mumble – I shouldn't have tried the easy passwords.

I get up and pace the office, trying to think of what to do. If I try one more time and get it wrong, it will lock me out. Rich will know that I have tried to get into his computer. I rub my cheek, thinking about what will be the next step after slapping me.

I stop pacing and look at my laptop. My document tab has been left open and on the left side of the box something catches my eye – RICH in big bold letters. I go over to my laptop and realize my laptop is trying to connect to Rich's computer since they are near each other.

Excitedly, I click on it only to have the password dialog box pop up. I curse under my breath. In that one second I had been convinced this was going to be my way to get inside the computer.

Frustrated, I close my laptop and shove everything back in the bag. There is no point in alerting Rich to the fact I had been trying to get in his computer. I'll have to come back with a new plan.

I trod off to the guest room, trying to think what to do next. But I am exhausted and by the time my head hits the pillow, I fall asleep.

Chapter Seven

"What the fuck?" Marina hisses as she steps inside my apartment.

"I know, I know," I tell her, holding up my hands as to ward off her upcoming lecture.

It doesn't work. Marina eyes my cheek, which is swollen and a dark red.

"No, Jenny, this is not okay. This is fucked up. This undercover plan you have going on – it needs to stop."

"It can't," I tell her. "I'm so close. I can feel it in my bones."

"He *hit* you! And you told me what he did to Sarah. What is stopping that from being his next step?"

I run my fingers through my hair. I have a pre-production meeting at 2 P.M. today and am unsure how to work to cover up the mark on my cheek. I asked Marina to come over to help me with my makeup to try to cover it up.

Rich was gone by the time I got up this morning. He left me a note outside the door, stating he has a meeting with the guy who wants to co-finance a small production company with him and that he will need me for a dinner tomorrow night. *And he'll want me to cover up my cheek, I presume!*

"Listen, I just have to get into his computer. Seriously, if I can just get into his computer, I can delete the tapes and I just *know* he will have stuff I can get him arrested for on there. Not to mention his warrant for not paying child support. He has to go to jail, Marina. I can't let him just run around and do this to someone else."

Marina huffs and leans back against the wall in my living room, eying my cheek. "You sound like a superhero or some nonsense. Calm it down, Electra. You don't need to take him off the streets."

"But if he does this to someone else, it'll weigh on me."

"And if you make a mistake or he catches you, he could really hurt you, Jenny. Or kill you."

"Marina, please just help me cover this up."

"Fine but I still think you need to stop this. I get you don't want to be scared anymore like you were of Robbs but this is insanity."

"Maybe," I say, just to placate her.

We spend the next hour working on my cheek. Marina is an expert with makeup. I grow convinced that if she hadn't decided to work on production she could have been a makeup artist. By the time we finish, my cheek looks almost normal as long as no one stares at it too long under direct light.

"That is as good as I can get it," she says, stepping back.

"It's great. I don't think anyone will notice. They aren't looking for it, you know?"

Marina nods and adds a finishing touch and then shrugs. "Okay. You can go to the meeting now."

"Great. I'm actually really excited. I've been researching my role and coming up with a backstory for my character. I've never done that before but I... What? You're looking at me funny."

"Sorry," Marina replies with a small shake of her head. "I don't mean to look like I'm not listening. But I was thinking we need to have a code word."

"A *code word*? Now who is acting like we are in a comic book?"

"I'm serious, Jenny. You can text it to me or even if Rich is around say it to me in conversation so I know you are in trouble and need help." She comes over to me and grabs my hand. "Please. Even if you think it is stupid."

"Okay. It is a good idea," I admit. "Especially if he happens to catch me snooping around."

Marina relaxes just a little. "Okay. What about um... palm trees?"

"Palm trees?"

"It's simple enough. Just text it or even in conversation you can remark about a pretty palm tree you saw or some nonsense."

"I'll sound ludicrous but fine."

Marina smiles and stands up a little straighter. "Great. Okay, you don't want to be late. Let's get you to the meeting."

Even though I know Ayumi is going to be there for the meeting, I still feel nervous about seeing her. I know she has no ill will toward me and has only been kind but every time I see her all I can think about is the fact that she is with Jon and I lost my chance at being with him. I take a deep breath and step inside the meeting room.

The table has been pushed back against the wall and the rest of the actors are milling around, holding coffees and talking in low voices. Matt is in the middle, talking with a producer. I spot Ayumi texting on her phone in the corner. She is dressed down in a button-up shirt and jeans. Her long black hair falls over her shoulders in silky waves. I can understand why she used to model.

Suddenly self-conscious everyone can see the mark on my cheek, I slink inside the room. Matt is a big fan of team-building exercises for the cast. He wants us all to trust one another and form a strong bond before filming. He sees me first and gives me a wave.

"We're going to start in about five minutes," he tells the room.

Ayumi spots me and rushes over. I smell her jasmine perfume, and she smiles at me.

"I'm glad you're here. I have to admit that I am really nervous about filming and it is nice to see someone I know."

"You'll be great," I tell her, smiling. "I wouldn't worry."

"I hope you're right. I'm use to modeling, you know, pose here, move your body like this. But this is going to be new."

"What made you switch?" I ask, genuinely curious.

"Modeling was getting pretty dull. When I went back to Japan to help take care of my mom, one of the last things she told me was to follow my heart. Sounds cheesy, I know. " She gives me a small shrug. "So when I came back, I wanted to get into acting."

I remember it being mentioned that she was in Japan dealing with her family back home and feel a pang of sympathy for her. I give her my brightest smile.

"Well, I don't know what these group activities are going to be. If they are insane, stick close to me, okay?"

"Sounds good," she replies, looking relieved.

We end up partnering up for the group exercises, which start with the corny "trust fall" and end with everyone mock arguing with their partner. Matt runs us through the varying events and by the time we wrap up two hours later, I end up feeling a lot closer to the cast than I thought I ever would.

Afterward, I speak to Matt about thoughts for my character. He actually listens and we work on a backstory together. I am thrilled with how exciting it is to craft a character like this with a director who wants to listen to my ideas and give me feedback.

I shouldn't have been surprised to have my mood soured. As I wrap up things with Matt, someone knocks on the door of the meeting room and pokes their head in. My heart drops in my chest when I see Rich's face looming. *What the fuck, why is he here?*

"Rich, hi," I say, closing my notebook full of ideas.

"Jenny, you're still here," he says in mock concern. "I've been trying to get ahold of you."

"My phone is off," I reply, trying to hide my irritation with Matt next to me. "What's going on?"

"Wanted to see if you will join me for a late lunch. Oh, you must be Matt," Rich says, stepping inside, clearly angling to meet him. "I'm Rich."

Matt shoots me a quick glance that I cannot read and then reaches out and shakes his hand. "Nice to meet you."

"Same here. I've heard a lot about you. It's nice to finally meet you."

Rich and Matt engage in small talk, and Rich makes sure to slip in that he is a casting director looking to get into producing. It takes everything I have not to jump over the table and throttle him. I feel confident that when I look at my phone there won't be anything from him trying to contact me. He just wanted to meet Matt.

When Rich finally stops yammering, Matt excuses himself from the room, saying he has another meeting to go to. I am upset that we were interrupted by Rich. There were still some things that we didn't end up going over because of Rich.

Rich looks at me as if a flip has been switched. His face is blank again.

"Are we really going to lunch?" I ask him.

"No. I'll walk you to your car though."

"Why, did you tip off the paparazzi again?"

The corner of his eye twitches. Yet he cannot do anything to me here, in this public place, so he merely shrugs. I get up and grab my purse, moving swiftly so he cannot try to hold my hand. If the paparazzi are there, I am suddenly nervous my makeup is not up to snuff and go into the bathroom.

Ayumi is at the mirror, reapplying her lipstick. I am surprised she is still here but I saw her chatting to a ton of people after the meeting ended. She is popular and seemingly friends with everyone. My first impression of her in thinking that she will be a stuck up model has been proven wrong each time we meet. I can understand why Jon is dating her.

"Hey, you're still here? I thought I saw your boyfriend in the lobby," she says to me, giving me a small wave.

"Yeah, he's waiting for me," I tell her, wondering how I can hide that I am looking at my cheek without her noticing anything amiss. "Just have to touch up my makeup."

I stop in front of the mirror and try to look at my cheek. I think it is mostly covered but it is hard to look at it without Ayumi noticing. I pretend that I am looking through my purse for something, trying to wait her out. I fish out my lipstick and look back at the mirror. Ayumi is looking at me and clears her throat.

"Jenny," she says to me in a low voice and leans over. "Let me fix it."

I have no idea what she is talking about. She then gently taps on her own cheek. Alarmed, I look back in the mirror. The makeup of the bottom of my cheek has faded a bit and under the harsh lighting of the bathroom, Ayumi has noticed some of the red welt left behind from Rich's hand. *Fuck*, I think, trying to find an excuse to give her.

"Want me to cover it up?" she asks me.

I give her a small nod, and Ayumi takes her own brush and brushes it across my cheek. In one swift movement, the bottom of the mark is covered.

"Hey, that's amazing, what is that?" I ask her curiously.

"Oh, I got it from a shoot I did in Japan for free. It's super expensive, like 150 bucks for this concealer, but they had an extra one and I snagged it. I looked it up online and I'd have to order it overseas to get it here."

"That's a shame," I mumble, looking at my cheek in the mirror. "Works wonders."

An awkward beat fills the bathroom. I can tell Ayumi wants to ask how I got the mark on my cheek but is afraid to come right out and ask. I smile at her.

"I better head out. Talk to you later."

I duck around her and leave the bathroom, relieved at not having to answer any questions. I curse myself for letting her see the mark. I must have rubbed my face in frustration over Rich as I made my way to the bathroom.

Speaking of Rich, he is waiting for me. His arms are crossed and he is smiling at an intern who flutters past him, blushing at the fact he noticed her. When he sees me, he grabs my hand, pretending to be a caring boyfriend. His touch makes my skin itch but I try to ignore it. We step outside and sure enough, a lone paparazzi is snapping our picture from his car. I can't imagine what lame tabloid site he must be working for. I wish Rich would stop calling them. I am sure they probably think I am the one who is setting up these boring photo ops.

We stop in front of my car, and he pulls me in for a kiss. His lips taste faintly of cigarette smoke and for a wild second I think about biting hard on his bottom lip. But I control myself and finally pull away from him.

"I'll call you about lunch," Rich says to me in a whisper. "Like I told you, there is a guy who is interested in starting a company with me. It'd be really small though so I'd be counting on your help."

"What in the world would you want me to do?"

"You'd take on a project or two from us, get the production company name out there."

"I think you are severely overestimating my star power. Yeah *Flower Queen* got me press but not enough that I can get your production company off to a booming start." I cross my arms.

Rich quickly blocks the paparazzi from seeing me and lowers my arms, apparently afraid there will be a photo of me looking cross in the press.

"Listen, don't think about that right now. Just come to lunch. Charm him. He is the only interested investor I have. Everyone else is apparently saying I haven't been around long enough or have anything 'promising' to make them want to go into business with me." His voice is bitter and harsh as he says this, as if it is a personal slight against him.

I want to point out that I don't exactly have a choice in the matter but I bite my tongue and just nod my assent.

"Great," Rich replies. "I really want this production company, Jenny. If I get it, not only does it mean solid and steady money, but I can talk to people who really matter. The elite of the industry."

"Right. Fame," I remark.

His expression darkens only for a second but then he shrugs. "Everyone wants fame and fortune."

When he leans in to kiss me again, I expertly dodge it and get in my car. He gives me a small wave and heads off to his own car. By the time I make it into the

LA traffic, my head is aching. Between Ayumi seeing my cheek and Rich craving his own idea of 'fame and fortune', it makes me want to become a hermit.

Chapter Eight

You really need to start contouring your nose. It looked giant in your interview with Rosie.

I let out a groan and slip my phone back in my purse. Amanda's suggestion to get a Twitter account had been a smart one. Everyone who is trying to create a fan base has one nowadays. But for every nice tweet I got sent my way, there was about five nasty ones. People have no filter on the Internet. I make a mental note to turn off the notification alert for tweets sent to me and glance back up in the mirror.

Paranoid that Rich's potential business partner, a man named Josh Rickland, will notice my cheek, I have been darting off to the bathroom whenever I can to check on it. I am sure I look slightly ridiculous but if Josh has noticed, he hasn't made any indication.

The lunch is dreadfully dull. Rich and Josh have been discussing business ideas back and forth. Josh constantly has a displeased expression on his face while Rich looks like a puppy trying to impress a master with a new trick. By the time he launched into his speech about why he wanted to branch out from being a casting director to having his own production company, a part of me wished I could have been smashing drunk.

My cheek looks okay so I decide it is time to go back to the lunch. As I make my way back to the table, I wonder if Rich is so hell bent on getting this company because he is still craving the fame and fortune he would have gotten if he hadn't blown out his knee.

I hesitate as I head to the table. There is another woman who has stopped by and is eagerly talking to Rich. She looks familiar and it takes a moment to place where I have seen her. Jaime Alexander, who's made her fame on a string of successful reality TV shows and is currently trying to be taken seriously in Hollywood.

By the easy smiles both Josh and Rich are wearing, I can tell she has charmed them already. She is very pretty and a rising star due to the fact she recently broke free of reality TV and has a supporting role on a TV show on a streaming service.

I head over there and Jaime introduces herself as I sit down.

"Sorry to interrupt your lunch," she says to me, a slight Southern accent in her voice. "I just haven't seen Josh in so long."

"That's your own fault, dear," Josh says, clearly checking her out. "You have my number. You should use it sometime."

Jaime smiles and looks back at Rich, who is eying her with the same sort of look that I recognize he used on me back when we met at my casting photoshoot.

"It's really lovely to meet you," Rich says, his voice smooth. "I've heard so much about you."

"You got a real fine man there, Jenny," Jaime says to me with her blue eyes sparkling. "Anyway, I have to run. See you soon, I hope." She directs this last sentence to Rich before giving us a small wave and leaving.

Gross, I think to myself as I watch her go. Her shirt is riding up and when she turns I can see her bellybutton piercing shine from the sun. Rich is looking at her with an expression I cannot read.

As the lunch goes on, I realize I feel unsettled. Whatever Rich is thinking, I am sure I will not like it.

"I think it went pretty well," Rich tells me as I trudge inside his house after lunch, "Josh seems eager to get started."

I want to tell him that I didn't care for Josh just like I don't care for him. Josh seems to be cut from the same cloth as Rich. There is something slimy about him that he expertly hides under cloying words and smiles. Maybe if Rich hadn't fucked me over, Josh would have been able to pull the wool over my eyes. But it isn't working this time. I don't think Rich has noticed the gross feeling Josh gives off and I don't feel inclined to share my feelings. Let him get fucked over if it comes to that.

"Great," I mumble, hoping I sound like I care.

My phone vibrates in my purse, and I pull it out to see a text from Sarah. I glance at Rich but he is rambling on as he makes himself a drink so I open up the text.

My parents mailed me my scrapbook to show you, if you are still interested. Any luck with Doug?

"Who is texting you?" Rich asks me and I quickly press the lock button on my phone.

"Amanda," I lie. "Talking about our next move."

"Well, don't plan anything major," he says, taking a sip of his drink. "With the production company opening up down the line, I want you to have a free schedule. I want you to take on a project or two from us so the word can get out."

"Yeah, sure," I tell him, leaving out the fact that hopefully I will have him behind bars by that point.

"You know what would be major? If you could get Matt to work with us, too."

"What?" I blurt out, taken aback by the nerve of Rich.

Rich sits down on the couch. He pats the spot next to him to sit down and when I don't move, he pats it harder, his features frowning. Not wanting to upset him, I sit down next to him.

"Imagine if Matt Bayblock works for us. It'd put our company on the map. I heard he is fighting with the studio over *Flower Queen* anyway."

"What?" I repeat, feeling idiotic.

Rick gives a small shrug, one that looks as if it is straining to look casual and indifferent but sets my nerves alight. "I guess the producers of the film didn't really want you cast in it."

I bite my tongue so I don't say another 'What?' and instead just look at him. I am trying to figure out if he is lying or not.

Rich keeps talking, "Anyway, filming hasn't technically started yet so…they could still let you go. They don't think you are marketable."

"How did *you* hear this? I highly doubt Matt told you in the five minutes you two spoke to each other."

"Josh knows people higher up. Anyway, if Matt switches to working with us then maybe we can keep you on the project. It'd be terrible if you lost this role, don't you think? It'd be enough to take the wind out of your sails. All anyone would remember is the woman who had a bit part in a reboot of an eighties cartoon franchise who had a sex tape."

His words strike a nerve. I can tell by the smug expression on his face that he knows it. I go to move away from him but he grabs my hand.

"I can *save* your career, Jenny. You just have to listen to me, okay? I'd hate to see you fade away before you even really had a chance to get started."

"Why?" I demand. "Because you care so much about me? As you threaten to leak tapes and tell me that I am going to get fired from the film?"

"I think you and I have a working relationship by now. We have come to a mutual understanding," Rich says.

I yank free of him and stand up. "I'm leaving."

"Fine. I'll see if I can find out more about your job in the meantime."

I turn away from him. My irritation has turned into anger but I can feel it quickly turning into sadness and fear. I need to get out of here. The last thing I need to give Rich is any sort of gratification of seeing me cry.

"Oh, and Jenny?" he says as I reach for the handle of the front door. "You did a good job covering your cheek."

Chapter Nine

By the time I get through the front door of my apartment, my cheeks are stained with tears. My makeup is messed up. If anyone sees my face, they'd see the mark on my cheek from where Rich slapped me. I feel furious at myself for letting him get under my skin and sad at myself for taking so long to pin his ass to the wall.

He has to be lying, I repeat to myself over and over as I pace my living room, *Matt would tell me if the studio isn't happy with me.* Wouldn't he? I would like to think that he would tell me.

I tell myself not to believe a word Rich has said to me but I find myself dwelling on it. I text back Sarah and tell her I would like to meet with her to look at the scrapbook but at the moment, I cannot see the point. As I pace my house, I think to myself that even if I find something in the scrapbook that would embarrass Rich, he will just likely deny it and leak the tapes.

No, I have to get into his laptop. I have to get rid of the sex tapes he has of me and find proof of his blackmailing. As I stare at my laptop in my room, lost in thought, something strikes me. My laptop is still trying to connect to Rich's computer. I go over to it and my cursor hovers over the link to Rich's computer.

Do you want to stop the attempt to connect?

As I am about to click yes, something stops me. It feels as if something is wiggling in the back of my head only I cannot bring it to the surface. I bite my bottom lip. I don't know the password to his computer. There isn't any point to let my laptop attempt to connect to his computer.

Yet before I can delete the connection, my doorbell rings. I am startled by the noise and it makes me jump. I rub my eyes quickly and head toward the front door. I pause to look out at the peephole. The sun is setting, casting an orange hue to everything outside.

For a moment I think I must be dreaming. But no, outside my door is Jon. Surprised, I open my front door. Jon is wearing just a T-shirt and jeans, showing off the muscles in his arms. The fabric of the T-shirt clings to his chest and I can see his muscles taut underneath it.

"Jon. What are you doing here?"

"Jenny. I had to see you."

"Is everything okay?" I ask him, looking at his eyes, which look sad.

"I broke up with Ayumi."

My heart skips a beat. "What? Why?"

"I couldn't be with her. It wasn't fair to her. She deserves someone better than me."

I nod, although I am not following why he is here and why he came all this way to tell me this. Couldn't he have just called me? I want to ask him all of these things but before I can, he speaks again.

"It isn't fair to her, Jenny, because of how I feel for *you*. I can't stand how we keep missing each other. I can't do it anymore. I know you are with Rich but Ayumi – she told me – your cheek…" He trails off and I feel my heart sink into my stomach. I hadn't wanted him to know about that.

"Jon, listen – "

Jon takes a step closer to me. I can feel the heat from his body at this range. My voice catches, and I find I cannot make any excuses for the mark on my cheek. He can see it at this point anyway since I am not wearing makeup.

"I can't let you be with him, Jenny."

"Jon, you can't tell me what to do. Please, it's too hard to explain what is going on with him but you have to trust me –"

"I can't go one more second without you," he says in a strained voice.

I want to protest, to tell him to leave, to tell him all the reasons why I am pushing him away. But with Rich's touch on my cheek and his words in my heart, my voice goes dead. In one swift movement, Jon comes toward me and kisses me.

His lips are hot against mine and together we fall against the wall of my apartment. I kick the door shut with my foot, our lips never breaking as we fall into the kiss. We are both pulsing with desire. Pretending that I didn't care he was dating Ayumi was difficult enough. Now, as he turns up on my doorstep and tells me he needs me, I am too weak to resist him.

I am pressed against the wall. Jon presses his own body against mine as I wrap my arms around his shoulders. Our kisses are hot and hungry, craving each other after too many chances missing out on each other. Jon's hands run up along my sides, gingerly touching my skin. His touch is electric. Goose bumps pop out along my skin as I let him run his fingers along my stomach.

Our lips break only for a moment, to meet each other's gaze, before we kiss again. Our tongues meet and we move from my front door into the living room. We are still clinging to each other as our kisses grow more and more passionate.

Finally we stumble in my bedroom. Jon is peeling his own clothes off and I watch him, admiring his body. He is well fit and toned. Eager to touch him, I lean forward and run my hands along his chest, marveling at his toned body.

In reply, Jon begins to take off my clothes. My shirt hits the floor and goose bumps pop up along my skin. I blush as he looks me over, his hands drifting up my back to unclasp my bra.

When we are both naked and in front of each other, I feel as if my head is spinning. I honestly never thought that we would be together in this way. My own willpower has crumbled. All I want is for Jon to take me in his arms and be inside of me.

I realize I am trembling a little. I am so nervous about sleeping with Jon, as if I am a virgin on prom night. Jon seems to sense this and he takes a step toward me, running his hands down my arms. Then he tilts my face up toward his and kisses me. This kiss is slower, and yet somehow more passionate than the other kisses.

I wrap my arms around his neck and our bodies, fully nude, press against each other for the first time. The sensation sends thrills through me. The electric touch of his body against mine is unlike any feeling I've had before with anyone else. It is as if we are two pieces, matched together perfectly.

Jon gently pushes me on the bed and kisses down along my thighs. Slowly, he parts my thighs and kisses along the soft skin there before stopping just before my pussy. I can feel him blow gently on it and I shiver. Then he moves his tongue down along me. I let out a soft moan, surprised by how good it feels and arch my back a little.

Jon is eager, burying his face in between my legs and working his tongue along my pussy. His tongue flicks gently at my clit, teasing me, as I close my eyes and breathe heavily. The sensations are unreal. Each touch of his tongue leaves me trembling and begging for more.

Finally I cannot take it anymore. My own climax comes to a head and an orgasm shudders through me. Jon grips my thighs as he works on me as I climax. I close my eyes tightly, letting out a loud moan as the blissful feeling enfolds me.

When I come down from it, Jon slides away from the middle of my thighs and positions himself over me. I can feel his organ slowly entering me. My eyes widen in surprise over how thick he is, and I wiggle my hips against him, trying to take the length of him in as best as I can.

When Jon is completely inside of me, he stops moving and looks deep in my eyes. A blush forms heavily on my cheeks and then he gives me a soft smile before he starts to rock his hips. His being fills me up. I wrap my legs around his waist and we move, perfectly in sync, against each other.

Jon buries his face in my breasts, licking and sucking on my nipples as he fucks me. I grip the sheets, moving against him. Both of us are moaning each other's names and our skin is hot to the touch. I move my arms around him and clutch him tightly, my nails digging into his back as he fucks me.

I can feel another orgasm mounting inside of me. Jon is so large and thick that he is hitting me in all the right spots. I can't even think anymore. All I care about is getting to my orgasm and feeling Jon deep inside of me. Jon seems to sense this and in one swoop, he holds me close and rolls over so that I am on top of him, riding him.

His hips buck as his hands grope my breasts as I fuck him as hard as I can, taking his manhood deep inside of me. I close my eyes tightly, moaning loudly. Jon's hands grab my ass and slap it as I ride him.

Before I can utter another moan, my climax explodes. I let out a scream and shudder on top of him. Jon grunts and grips my hips, climaxing as well. We come together and when our orgasms are over, I collapse on top of him, holding him tightly.

We are both breathing heavily. Our bodies are covered in sweat and my heart feels as if it is beating five hundred times a minute. Jon is the same and as he holds me, he kisses the top of my head. I can hear his heart beating underneath me, like a caged bird, fluttering wildly against the side of his chest, trying to break free. I wonder if this was as perfect for him as it was for me.

"Jenny…" he mumbles into my ear, as if in reply.

Sleep is quickly taking a hold of both of us. All I care about is this moment and how perfect it feels to have slept with Jon and now have him holding me. I run my fingers down his chest and peer up at him. He is already fast asleep. I smile to myself and cozy up to him.

Even though I had told myself that I wouldn't go this far with him because of Rich, the bliss from the moment is still hanging over my bed. I feel content and overjoyed to have him all to myself in my bed tonight.

We are just drawn to one another, I tell myself as my eyes grow heavy with sleep. I wouldn't have had tonight go any other way.

Chapter Ten

The morning light is what wakes me up. As I slowly open my eyes, I realize there is a body in bed with me. I stiffen for a moment, suddenly afraid. I don't remember who I let in last night.

When I turn my head, my sleep-fogged memory kicks in. Jon is asleep next to me. He is sleeping quietly. I admire the way his hair falls in his eyes and the stubble that lines his jaw. His chest rises and falls slowly. He is fast asleep, and I hate the thought of waking him up.

Even though we had tried so hard to stay away from each other – me pushing him away so I can get away from Rich and Jon dating Ayumi – we still ended up together like this. I want to be in a relationship with him but I cannot do so while I am still struggling to get Rich out of my life.

The logical side of me knows I have made a mistake in sleeping with Jon. I have done exactly what I was attempting to avoid. Our feelings are just wrapped up together even more now and I am going to have to tell Jon to wait while I figure out things with Rich.

The emotional part of me couldn't be more thrilled. Every part of last night was like a dream coming true. How long have I tried to deny how I felt about Jon?

How long was I telling myself it was time to move on and I had fucked up our chances? Yet Jon still wants me, even after everything we have been through.

I can only hope he still wants me after I tell him what is going on with Rich.

As if he can sense me staring at him, he shifts in bed and slowly opens his eyes. His eyes are fogged over with sleep and he rubs them, trying to wake up.

"Good morning," I whisper in his ear, curling up against him.

He kisses the top of my head, peering down at me, smiling. "Good morning, Jenny. Did you sleep okay?"

"I slept wonderfully."

"Me, too."

Jon kisses me again and the feeling sends fireworks off in my head. Before I know it, we are tangled up in each other again. As he takes me, I cling to him, feeling the way he thrusts in me and matching his movements. We are so perfectly in sync that we climax together.

We collapse in a heap and hold each other. He turns to look at me and I feel for the first time as if someone is truly looking at me to understand me, not in some attempt to use me. The feeling is so new to me that for a moment I am worried I will be emotional and I avert my gaze.

"Jenny," he whispers to me, "I want to be with you."

This is it. I have to tell the truth now. There is no way that I can justify not telling Jon what is going on. I am terrified that the harmony of last night and this morning will be broken by the ugly truth of why I am with Rich. What if I lose Jon?

But there is no way I cannot tell him. So I take a deep breath, and like I did with Marina, explain what is going on. I say it all quickly, and in a rush, so I can brace myself for Jon getting up and leaving.

But when I finish, his eyes are as wide as saucers and he looks horrified. I am worried he is going to yell or berate me over the sex tapes so I keep talking.

"I should have listened to your advice way at the start instead of pushing you away. You wanted me to confront Robbs but I was so terrified of him. So I completely mucked it all up. I didn't even ensure that he didn't have a copy of the tape elsewhere. I was so stupid and I vowed that I wouldn't be again. So when Rich cornered me, I realized I needed to make him think I was going along with it but actively try to escape," I say in a rush, wishing that Jon would say something.

"Jenny, I wish you would have told me," he finally says in a strangled voice. "I would have decked Rich in the face a long time ago."

"You can't. Jon, listen to me, I am so close to getting him. I can feel it. I just need to get on his computer. I know he'll have shit that can get him behind bars. And he owes child support for his daughter. The two of those together can get him in jail. I need to make sure no one else falls victim to him."

Jon runs his fingers gently along my cheek. I can tell he is furious. The anger is boiling just below the surface of his skin, which is now hot to the touch. I am afraid he is going to be mad and yell at me for how I have done things.

But instead he gives a small shake of his head. "I never liked him. And what he is doing to you, Jenny, is disgusting. You get those tapes and you take them to police. Don't just get rid of them. Take everything else you find and get his ass in jail."

I am relieved that he is not angry at me. Instead he kisses me gently and looks at me. I know I am blushing but I don't look away.

"Jenny," he says, "I wish you would have told me."

"I know. I was afraid. I didn't want you to hate me because of Rich having those tapes. Or to think that I was lying. Or a million other things."

He gently moves away a lock of my hair that has fallen in my face and shakes his head. "Not believe you? Jenny, Rich is a prick. And he needs to be stopped. If anything happens, I want you to tell me. I don't even like the thought of you being alone with him."

"I know. And Marina already has me promising if I need her to text or say the words 'palm tree' or something so she knows I am in trouble."

Jon smiles at that and my heart feels as if it is doing summersaults in my chest. He is so handsome. The way the morning light slants on the bed and hits him makes it look as if he is glowing. I don't remember the last time I felt so safe. I wish we could stay like this, forever, frozen in time.

"Well, that's good. I'm going to be incredibly nervous until this stuff ends. You said Sarah has some scrapbook of photos of him?"

"Yeah. Originally the plan was to blackmail him into letting me out of this crap but when I heard Sarah's story…now it just feels wrong to let him run off to do this to someone else. So I don't know what else I would do with her scrapbook."

"Do you think she'd let you make copies?"

"Sure, probably. Why?"

"I think it'd be good if we had back-ups, that's all."

I can tell he is thinking and plotting but I decide not to push it. Jon has other connections that I do not have and he might have a good idea. Besides, at this point, I'll take all the brain power I can get.

He leans over and kisses me again before glancing at the clock. "I have an office meeting at noon. I should probably get dressed. Is it okay if I use your shower?"

"Of course you may" I nod and I admire him as he slides out of my bed, before a thought strikes me. "Jon?"

"Yeah?"

I tear my gaze away from his body and shift in bed, covering my breasts with the sheet. "Rich said this thing last night that has been bothering me, even though I don't even know it is true. He said that the producers of *Flower Queen* didn't want me to be cast. That Matt basically had to fight to cast me and they still don't want me on the cast. I mean, have you heard anything about that?"

The way Jon shifts his gaze from me lets me know that he has. My body stiffens. I am terrified of him deciding to lie to me.

But he just gives a small nod. "Yes, I've heard things. I didn't tell you because there isn't anything really going on besides producers grumbling. I didn't want to stress you out. You were so excited about this project. It seemed wrong to make you worry about something that was just nonsense."

I feel sick suddenly. I am terrified that I will lose my job. This role really means a lot to me and I am worried that even though Matt and I are hitting it off, he will decide the pressure from producers isn't worth keeping me. The thought of actually having to work with Rich makes it even worse.

Jon must see it on my face because he sits next to me. "Jenny, it's okay. You look like you're going to be sick. There isn't anything to worry about."

"Nothing to worry about? Jon, I wish you would have told me."

"I didn't want to worry you."

"I'm vulnerable until filming starts," I point out to him. "If they decide to get rid of me, then what am I going to do? If they threaten Matt, he might get rid of me."

"This is why I didn't want to tell you. I didn't want you to freak out."

"I shouldn't have to hear this stuff from Rich. I should hear it from you," I tell him, crossing my arms.

Jon runs his fingers through his hair. "You have a point. I'm still your agent. I'm sorry."

"If this goes the way I want it to, with Rich in jail and us together, then I should probably find another agent. I wouldn't want this conflict of interest, you know?"

He nods. "Good point." He leans over and kisses me again. "I'm going to shower now."

I watch him go, mixed feelings in my stomach. On one hand, I understand why Jon didn't want to tell me about the producers not wanting me. I even understood why the producers didn't want me. I wasn't an A-list celebrity. Rich's words come back to me about being a bit player in an action film and having a sex tape. My face flushes. Is that going to chase me around forever?

But that doesn't mean that I want to lose out on this role. It means a lot to me and I am trying to take it seriously. This could be my big break into the mainstream. Isn't that what I wanted?

With everything that has been going on, I haven't sat and even figured out what I want for my career. Ever since Robbs and Rich crashed into my life, I had been trying to figure out what the next day would be. I hadn't been giving nearly enough thought to what I wanted to do with my career or even my life in general.

I suddenly felt tired. My good mood from waking up with Jon was fading now that real life was settling back in. I shift off the bed, grabbing a T-shirt and tugging it over my head. I have no plans today besides having Sarah come over to show me the scrapbook. Maybe I should do some soul searching.

Once my T-shirt is on, I go over to my laptop, checking my email. Nothing interesting. I head to my closet to rummage through it to see what I should wear when Sarah comes over. As I move my clothes, I pause. The laptop that Justin has sent me is in the back.

The feeling that I am missing something comes back over me, like a wicked sense of déjà vu. I turn back to look at my laptop and then back at Rich's old laptop.

Suddenly it clicks.

What if Rich's laptop can still connect to his computer at his house? If my laptop tried to connect to it but was blocked by the password, what if his laptop can still connect *and* remembers the password? I would have access to Rich's computer and could get to it through this laptop.

The laptop, which had felt useless since Justin sent it to me, is suddenly full of possibilities. Rich would have assumed Justin still has the laptop. He never would expect the laptop back in his house to connect to his computer.

I bite my bottom lip, the possibilities opening in front of me. This could be the key I need to get into the computer and get what I need. I try to quell the excitement growing in me as I hear Jon turn off the shower. I pull the clothes back over the laptop, grabbing a T-shirt and jeans to wear later when Sarah comes over. All I need now is a plan to bring the laptop over and make sure Rich isn't around.

Jon steps into the room. He has a towel wrapped around his waist. He looks so good that if I weren't distracted by the laptop realization, I would want to tackle him into bed again.

"You okay?" he asks me and I realize he is worried I am still freaking out about the producers not wanting me to work on *Flower Queen*.

"Yeah, I'm okay," I tell him. "I'll figure it out, somehow."

He smiles and I can feel the butterflies in my stomach. I watch him change and when he is finished, he comes over and kisses me.

"I have a meeting but will you call me later? See if you can make scans of that scrapbook, okay?"

"Yeah, okay. I'll talk to you later."

With another kiss, Jon leaves. I watch him depart, sad that the perfect night and morning is now a thing of the past. If I could, I would relive those moments forever. More than ever, I want to get rid of Rich so I can fully be with Jon.

In the meantime, I need to get ready to meet Sarah. I try to push my worry about *Flower Queen* out of my head.

Chapter Eleven

I frown at Rich's text. In an attempt to get over to his house, I had suggested we meet up for dinner tonight. But for the first time ever, he has blown me off. I am thrown by it. Something about it feels off, although I can't pinpoint why. I feel nervous although I am wondering if maybe I just feel that way because of what he said last time we were together.

I can't think of it anymore because the doorbell rings. Right on time, Sarah waits outside. As I invite her inside, I note that she has gotten a haircut since the last time I saw her. It frames her face well and for that second, I can see the sixteen-year-old girl who swooned for Rick, the football player with a golden future.

She holds a book in her hands tightly, pressed against her chest, as if she is afraid that it will vanish.

"I got my parents to mail it to me," she says as she sits down on the couch. "This is a nice place you have here."

"Thanks. I just moved in recently. I'm still getting used to it."

I sit down next to her and she runs her fingers across the scrapbook. "I flipped through this last night. Talk about flashbacks. I feel stupid when I look at it, to be honest. I mean, who makes a scrapbook of her boyfriend with basically just newspaper clippings? There isn't any picture of us at prom or homecoming. Nothing. I was so stupid. But I have Elizabeth out of this and she is my pride and joy." Her tone sounds wistful, as if Sarah had thought her life would have played out differently.

"Everyone makes mistakes. Myself included. God knows I have completely messed up with men," I say, trying not to sound bitter.

"How is Doug? I'm leaving soon but I've given up on seeing him. I was wondering… in exchange for the scrapbook if you can give me his phone number. I won't tell him I got it from you," she says quickly and in a rush. "But it is my last shot."

"You're going to give me the scrapbook?"

"It's silly to hold onto it," Sarah replies. "Nothing but bad memories. And you seem so interested in his past. And I can see the mark on your cheek…"

I touch my cheek gingerly. It is looking a lot better than before but of course Sarah noticed it instantly.

"Things aren't going too well," I admit. "I can give you his number but I wouldn't hold your breath. But I'm working hard to get free of him."

Sarah frowns. "Are you in trouble? Please let me help."

"You are helping," I say quickly, not wanting to drag her back into my muck. "But it might come to a head with him. If he ends up in jail, would you hate me? I know you want your money but I've found out things about him that I cannot just let slide."

Sarah sighs. "I guess expecting him to pay me now is silly. Of course I'll be upset if he lands behind bars if only because of what we had together when I was very young. But I understand."

She hands me the scrapbook. Part of me feels bad for telling her that Rich will land behind bars and not be able to pay her child support. But part of me wonders if then she will truly have to move on from Rich and what he has done to her. The way she cradles the scrapbook makes me wonder if, even though she knows he treated her like shit, she hopes that one day he will come back to her.

I hope that I am wrong and am reading into her actions too much. I imagine that once she leaves a voicemail for Rich, he will change his number in an attempt to shake her. I scribble down his number and give it to Sarah.

"I hope you don't mind, but I don't want to go through it with you. It hurts too much," Sarah tells me as she shoves his number in her purse. "Embarrassing, really. I really don't want to go through that time again."

"I really appreciate what you've told me. I'm sorry I couldn't be of more help to Elizabeth," I tell her and I honestly mean it.

Sarah stands up and gives a small shake of her head. "No, it is fine. Thank you for contacting me. I hope whatever is going on with Doug goes okay. I also hope, for your sake, Jenny, you don't stick around with him. Even with my rose-colored memories of my youth of Doug, I know it would be a mistake to ever get back with him."

"Thank you. I appreciate it. And I'm working on getting away from him."

She hesitates for a brief moment and then hugs me. I am taken aback by her hug but return it. In that moment, I can feel our connection. Sarah, who has broken free of Rich but looks back in the past and wonders what she could have done differently and myself, who is currently in his clutches and wondering how to shake him for good.

Sarah smiles at me and says goodbye. I watch her depart and then slowly shut the door. I don't know if I will ever see her again but as I hold the scrapbook, I know that I will at least have this to go through and try to find information from it.

I sit down at my small dining room table and open it to the first page. It is a letter that Sarah has pasted in from her diary. It details how excited she is to be dating Rich and how she can't believe how lucky she is.

The next few pages are nothing but the entries from her diary. I stop at a newspaper clipping detailing how Rich helped the high school win an important game. Though the clipping is old and the image is grainy, I study it. Rich is holding a football, a smile on his face. I cannot believe it is him. It truly looks nothing like him except around the eyes. Whatever work Rich has done over the years, it has erased the young boy in this photo.

He is youthful and determined, with a proud smile on his face.

I try to compare this to the Rich I know now but fail to see many similarities. The two are too different. I flick through more of the scrapbook. Once I get more than halfway through, I stop at one clipping from the local newspaper.

The story is detailing how Rich blew out his knee. Seeing as he was the star player on the local football team and had colleges interested in him, it was big news that he damaged his knee. Rich even is quoted in the article.

"Doctors are remaining optimistic that I can return to play after I rest. I am hoping I can come back next year on the team and give it my all. I am in recovery right now but don't say I'm out of it yet."

The picture of Rich, with his thumbs up, as if he truly thought he was going to be returning, is somehow depressing. What makes it worse was the young Sarah pasting it in her book, as if this is truly a milestone. Like she said, there is little else in the scrapbook besides journal entries about Rich and newspaper clippings. She even has his yearbook photo on the next page. It is clear that Rich, being hugely popular, was Sarah's first love.

There is the photo that Sarah had told me about. Rich is fast asleep and Sarah has her face in the shot. It is a Polaroid photo. She is beaming, even though Rich has no idea the photo is taken and would probably be furious if he did know about it. Sarah looks youthful and excited, as if she doesn't care or realize that Rich was probably dating other woman while he was with her.

There is another clipping detailing that, unlike Rich's earlier claims, he was not going to be able to return for the new season. Rich's statement in the article sounds a little harsher, as if he knows he isn't coming back but doesn't want to tell anyone yet. I skim through a few more before stopping at the final page. The scrapbook isn't filled, as if someone has decided halfway through that they no longer want to chronicle this mess of a relationship.

The final page is a clipping from the local newspaper, announcing that Rich's doctors say he can no longer play football. It says that he won't be returning back to high school football but he is confident colleges will still retain an interest in him.

There is nothing else after this. I can only imagine that this is where things spiraled out of control and Rich began to hit Sarah. I flip through the scrapbook one more time, looking at the photos of Rich.

I wish I could get inside of his head. I wonder what it was like to have the world at his feet and suddenly lose it all because of a knee injury. It is clear to me that this is why Rich is so dead set on getting that production company open. He hopes it will bring him the fame that he missed out on from his injury.

I close the scrapbook. While I appreciate Sarah giving it to me, I am not sure if Jon will be able to pull anything from it. I push it away from me, mulling over the laptop again. I need to see Rich. Part of me wants to just go over there and see him but I stop myself. He might suspect something is up if I seem suddenly too friendly.

Instead I find myself thinking about Jon. His fingers along my back and his kisses down my neck. After finally caving and having a night with him all to myself, I am greedy for more. I also find myself confirming that the producers wanted someone with more star power on *Flower Queen* and am worried I will somehow lose this big role.

With my head feeling as if it full to bursting, I decide to call Marina. I hope that seeing her and sharing my concerns means I won't feel so full of anxiety.

Chapter Twelve

"What do you mean?"

"It's just a short delay, Jenny. Maybe a week or two while I sort things out with the producers."

Matt does not meet my eyes. In that moment, I've had enough of people not telling me things because they are afraid of stressing me out. This is my *career* that people are not discussing with me. This pre-production meeting ended up being nothing more than telling the cast and crew that the start date of next Tuesday for the first scene has been postponed while things are "sorted" out.

Everyone else has filed out but I am determined to hear it from Matt himself: that filming has been delayed because the producers want an A-list celeb on the film.

"Why don't you just tell me it's because of me, Matt?" I finally say, crossing my arms.

Matt looks alarmed and then bashful. "Jenny, I didn't want this nonsense to affect you or the role."

I want to snap at him that I can take care of myself but I bite my tongue. Matt is still the director and if he is going to bat to keep me on the film, I do not want to upset him.

I soften my tone. "Matt, I appreciate you looking out for me. But this is still my job, you know? I need to be kept up with what is going on."

Matt sighs. "I know. You're right. But this whole thing is about more than just you, Jenny. I thought I'd get freedom with this role. The script they had been so gung-ho about just months ago is now suddenly too 'out of the mainstream' for their liking. They want changes made. Massive changes that go against everything I stand for. So production is halted, yes, but it isn't just because they don't want you in the lead."

I feel a little bit better knowing the production halt isn't only just because of me being in the lead role. Not that I like that Matt's vision is being messed with, but I didn't want the press to label it as it being my fault that production has hit a snag.

I offer him a small smile. "I love the script. I think it's a great story."

"They loved it, too," Matt replies, his tone bitter. "But with a recent string of indie flops on their hands, they are suddenly freaking out mine will just be another in the list. That's why they want you out, Jenny, they think someone else could drum up more interest."

"They might be right," I tell him, hating the fact that it is true.

"Yeah, but you were who I envisioned when I wrote the script. I don't know, you just capture the character so well. I don't know. It's all mucked up."

"I appreciate you telling me and being honest with me," I say to him. "I'm freaked out about being replaced but I know you'll try to make everything stay on track."

Matt nods and we shake hands. On the way out, I feel as if I have a stone sitting on my chest. For one thing, I can't believe that Rich was right about this whole mess. On the other hand, I'm relieved that it isn't just me that is the issue here.

As I step outside, I see Ayumi texting on her phone. I haven't gotten to talk to her since the breakup with Jon. I am suddenly nervous she will see it written on my face that Jon and I slept together and want to avoid speaking to her. Yet at the last moment she looks up and gives me a wave, heading over.

"Hey, this fucking sucks about production," she says to me and I realize for the first time on seeing her that she looks tired and her eyes are puffy. "I was really looking forward to throwing myself into filming this, even if I am just a bit player. This sucks."

"I'm disappointed, too," I tell her honestly. "I've really been throwing myself into this role."

Ayumi shifts her weight in her high heels. "I keep hearing all these rumors about why production has ceased. Apparently producers don't like the script anymore."

"Yeah, that's what Matt was telling me."

"Sucks," she mumbles and looks dejected. "I also heard there are issues with the casting."

In a roundabout way, I know she is asking me about my own role on the film. I don't feel like discussing it with her and give her a small shrug.

"No idea," I lie.

"Well, I better go. I'm meeting some friends for lunch."

"Okay. Nice talking to you."

She gives me a wan smile and I watch her leave, heading off to her car. I am relieved that she made no mention about her breakup with Jon. I don't think I would have been able to keep a blank expression on my face if she ended up mentioning it.

I get in my own car and stare ahead, lost in thought. I still haven't heard from Rich, which makes me concerned. He had been so gung-ho about this production company thing and yet he now seems fine to not contact me at all. Part of me is hoping that he has lost interest in me, but I know that is wishful thinking on my part.

As if in reply to my thoughts, my phone goes off. I look down, half expecting to see it is Rich calling me but instead it is Kathy. I haven't heard from her since she told me about Rich's daughter. I pick up the phone.

"Hey, long time no talk," I say.

"I know. My fault, I've been so busy on the soap opera. I'm actually getting a twin storyline this season, can you believe it? They only give the twin storylines to the popular characters."

"Well, who could not like you? Or your character, for that matter."

"Am I interrupting you?"

"No, just finished a meeting with Matt on *Flower Queen*. What's up?"

"I guess I'm nosey. I wanted to know if you spoke to Rich about Sarah and his daughter yet."

"No. I met with her and we discussed how she wants child support but was trying to avoid sending him to jail for it. I wanted to give him her number but I haven't seen him in a few days."

"Oh," she replies, her voice sounding funny. "I thought maybe you told him and you two broke up over it."

I frown. "Why would you think that?"

"I saw this item on a gossip website. I know, I'm terrible for still looking at them but I can't seem to help myself. Anyway it was this grainy, shitty photo of Rich with a blonde and the article was saying that you two might be broken up and he moved on already." She takes a deep breath. "Anyway, I'm rambling, I'm sorry. I didn't mean to call you out of the blue and be like 'oh you dumped Rich!' but I just assumed…" She trails off, clearly worried that she has upset me.

"No, you're okay," I say automatically, unsure what photo she is talking about. "I turned off Google Alerts for me a little while ago because I got sick of seeing junk about me."

"Have you checked your Twitter?"

I groan. "No. I have all notifications muted on it and just tweet pretty dull stuff. I feel so weird using it. I think my last tweet was about a coffee I had the other day."

"I bet people have tweeted you about it. Anyway, you're telling me you two are still together?"

"Yeah. I haven't really… discussed his daughter with him yet. Not sure how to bring it up. I have no idea what blonde he could be hanging out with."

"Sorry, Jenny, I sound like such a bitch, calling you up to ask about your relationship. I just was dying to know how it went with him in regards to his daughter."

"Sarah went back home about two days ago. Listen, can I call you later? I'm not mad at you either," I say quickly, not wanting her to be worried.

"Yeah, okay. Talk to you soon, okay?"

I agree and we hang up. I find myself biting my bottom lip as I bring up my Twitter. Sure enough, people have tweeted me, asking if Rich is still with me or if he is cheating on me. I search it online and find the story that Kathy told me about.

Is Jenny out a boyfriend? Rumor has it that Jenny and her casting director boyfriend, Rich, who is responsible for landing Jenny her first movie role on Recoil Factor, have broken up. But Rich doesn't seem too cut up about it, as seen from the photo below, where he has his arm wrapped around a mystery blonde!

I scroll down to the photo. It is incredibly grainy. It shows the backs of a man and a woman. The man has his arm slung around the blonde's waist but it is impossible to tell if it is really Rich or not. It could be some random photo and they are claiming it is Rich just for click views.

Regardless, I have a sour taste in my mouth. Something about his radio silence and now this gossip item makes me wonder if all of this is true. If he really has suddenly grown interested in some other starlet, then I am on borrowed time.

I can feel another headache starting up from all of this. In spite of my earlier promise, I call Rich but it goes to voicemail. I hang up before I leave anything stupid on his voicemail.

I'm running out of time and I can feel it.

Chapter Thirteen

"You can almost tell he is an asshole just in this photo alone," Marina remarks, looking at Sarah's scrapbook.

Jon lets out a laugh and then tries to stifle it when he sees my look. "Come on, Jenny. He does look pretty cocky."

"Of course he does," I remark as I put down a cup of tea in front of Marina and a beer for Jon. "He was the local hero of their small town. I mean colleges wanted him to play for them. He had his whole future mapped out."

"So, his knee blew out and now he is a conniving asshole," Marina retorts dryly. "Got it."

Jon takes a sip of his beer and looks at me. "You think he is seeing someone else?"

It is in the late evening and Marina, Jon and I are sprawled out across my living room. It was going to just be Marina and me, but Marina had told me it was ridiculous to tell Jon everything going on and then just assume that he wouldn't want to be a part of anything else to do with Rich.

"But this is why I didn't want to tell Jon and why I lied and told him we were just going to be friends," I pointed out to Marina.

But Marina had shaken her head at me. "No, you told him that because you were terrified of him judging you for how you fucked up with Robbs and then fell into Rich's clutches. The cat is out of the bag and surprise! He didn't have nearly the reaction you were expecting. You can't let him be privy to little bits of information and then shut the door on him."

I realized Marina was right. I had been terrified about how Jon was going to react to the entire story, to where I was ready to give him up because of my choices. I hadn't dared to think I could get rid of Rich *and* end up with Jon but now there was a flicker of light at the end of the tunnel.

As long as Rich wasn't dating someone else and would be bored enough with me to leak the two sex tapes he had.

"Sorry, but isn't this good, Jenny? If he decides now that is he bored of dating you, then isn't that exactly what we want?" Jon asks me, snapping me out of my thoughts.

"Normally, I'd say yes. But what if he decides he's bored with me and still leaks the tapes? He might just leak them and then latch onto someone else. Maybe he won't skip town at all. Not with this production company coming so close to fruition. I don't know."

"I think we are getting ahead of ourselves," Marina speaks up. "I mean, that grainy photo proves nothing.

And it isn't as if he is going to keep in touch with you like you two are really dating. He is using you, after all. He isn't going to call you unless he absolutely needs to."

"Maybe I am overthinking it," I admit. "He has gone a few days before with radio silence."

"See? I think we are all getting ahead of ourselves. You're probably impatient because you want to get over there and try out this laptop idea."

"Laptop idea?" Jon asks, leaning forward.

Marina eyes me, a mental nudge to tell Jon my idea. I quickly recap the laptop from Justin and how it might still automatically connect with Rich's computer. When I finish, he leans back on the couch, nodding.

"That's a good idea. You connect to the laptop and make copies of absolutely everything. Then we can sort through them back here and get what we need to the police."

"Did you mention to Sarah the fact that Rich might go behind bars?" Marina asks.

"Yes. She seemed bummed out because she has been trying so hard to avoid it but she understands. She just wanted Rich to pay his damned child support."

"Their relationship sounded so fucked up," Marina remarks. "Although yours is, too, I guess."

"Rich is a slime ball. I should have known he was lying to you back when he said his parents bought him that house. He told me his parents were dead back when we first met," Jon says.

"They probably are dead to him," Marina says. "I doubt he keeps in touch with them."

"Sarah is going to try to call him. I doubt he'll listen to anything she has to say. He's run from his daughter for this long, why would he pay child support now?" I remark.

"He sounds like a shit. I would have made sure to get the cops after him ages ago. But I'm not a mother. I don't know," Marina replies.

There is a brief silence as the three of us think over what is on our minds. Suddenly my phone rings. I look at it and it is a number I don't recognize. Usually I don't bother picking them up because they are scam calls or robots informing me I won the lottery, but something propels me to pick up this one.

"Hello?"

"Jenny, hey, it's Rich."

"Where are you calling me from?"

"I had to get a new number. Had this stupid spammer calling my phone. And then I was getting things finalized with Josh."

That's all I need to hear to let me know that Sarah reached out to him and he is avoiding her, just like I figured he would. Luckily he does not seem to suspect that I am the one who gave her his number.

"You're finalizing things already? That's fast."

"Well, it'll still be a little bit before it is official, of course, and we need offices to work out of. But we got a project we are in talks in and we'll just work out of our home offices."

"A project?"

"Yeah, don't worry about it. Anyway, put this number in your phone. I gotta go."

The calls ends and I find myself staring at the phone. Jon and Marina are looking at me, waiting for me to explain what just happened. I quickly tell them and Jon shrugs.

"Consider it a blessing then that you're off the hook," he says to me.

"Something just doesn't feel right," I say again. "Maybe I'll just go over there."

Marina puts her hand on my shoulder. "Maybe everything is falling into place and you're just having a hard time with it. You're so used to looking over your shoulder and you can't believe that maybe it'll just resolve itself without you running around like a superhero."

I give her a wan smile in return. I wish I could share their confidence that Rich is simply moving on without me. But I have a feeling in my gut that tells me something bad is going to rear its ugly head and I am running out of time to get into his computer.

<<<>>>

With production on *Flower Queen* halted, I find myself thinking about what I really want to do next in my career. It seems Amanda is thinking the same thing because she calls a meeting with me the next day at a local restaurant for lunch. Amanda, who is incredibly organized and quick to map things out twelve steps ahead, is the perfect person to see in regards to my next move.

I know that it is a topic normally reserved for clients and their agents, but I am going to have to find a new agent anyway. I don't like the idea of dating my agent. The last thing I need is everyone thinking I date anyone who steps in my path, especially after Rich has managed to shove his way into every facet of my existence. I'm still getting a slew of tweets from rabid fans asking me when I am going to leave him. The fact I even have fans, even a small amount, still makes my head spin.

Amanda has her iPad out in front of her when I make it to the table. There is a plate of fresh sushi in front of her that is untouched. She looks up when she sees me and closes the case on her iPad.

"Great, you're here. Sit down, we have a lot to discuss."

"Nice to see you, too, Amanda," I joke as I sit down.

Amanda waves her hand. "Production has been halted on *Flower Queen*. I don't know how much sugar coating you've been getting from Matt, or even Jon, for that matter," she says with a knowing glint in her eye.

"But the producers want to rewrite the entire script and want you out of the main role."

"Yeah, I heard," I reply, trying to keep my voice even.

"There is apparently a couple other investors sniffing around. If Matt goes with them, I can't promise you can keep the role."

"What?" I ask, alarmed. "But Matt said – "

Amanda holds up her hand. "Did you get it in writing?" When I shake my head, she shrugs. "Then Matt can say he will fight for you – and maybe he will, Jenny. But that script is what he considers his golden ticket to Oscar City and if he has to drop you, I am confident he will."

It feels as if she has yanked the carpet out from underneath me. Of course she is right. Matt will choose the script over keeping me. My skin feels itchy, as if I am covered in ant bites. I try to keep my anxiety under control.

"Second thing," she rattles off. "You need a new agent. I love Jon to death but it's clear you two are into each other, don't bother denying it. I am looking at some agents in New York for you."

"Um… New York? What did I miss?"

"Third thing, I got a lead on some auditions out there for plays – "

"*Plays*?"

"Not run-of-the-mill plays, Jenny. It's off Broadway but these are some talented people opening up work out there in New York. You start off in off Broadway productions and you can quickly rise through the rank to get onto Broadway."

The waiter comes by and gives me a glass of water and a plate of sushi that Amanda must have ordered for me before I got here. I blink at Amanda.

"I feel as if we are talking two different languages. Why in the world would I go to New York? I've never expressed any interest in Broadway. Or off Broadway for that matter." I wonder if Amanda is overworked and has a fever or something.

But Amanda shakes her head. "I saw a raw cut of *Beloved* through a source of mine. I don't want to be harsh, but it is terrible. But you're great on screen. You glow. You deserve more than these small roles."

"Right," I reply slowly. "I have *Flower Queen*."

"Do you think that is going to be your big break? Not if you get fired from it. Then you're a girl with a sex tape and a couple of subpar films under your belt who deserves more." I must look hurt because Amanda's expression softens. "I don't mean to sound like a bitch. But you are a natural at what you do and I think you'd shine on stage. I don't think Hollywood is for you. I think you're going to keep getting subpar films and glow in your role and stay stuck."

"You really think they're going to drop me from *Flower Queen*?"

"If these new producers sniffing around make Matt pick between his lead or his script, he'll pick his script, Jenny." Amanda says this softly, as if she's realized she's just thrown a lot at me.

"I have to think about this. You understand. I can't just… make this insane choice to move to New York or go on off Broadway plays or whatever."

"Okay. Think about it. You have some time to decide still."

I push the plate of sushi away from me, suddenly no longer hungry. Hearing *Beloved* isn't that great of a film hits harder than I thought. Amanda, and even to an extent, Rich, is right that I have *Recoil Factor* and *Beloved* under my belt with a slasher flick on the side. If I lose *Flower Queen*, then I am afraid I will languish here in Hollywood forever.

But being on stage, in a play? Even if I try hard to picture something like that, nothing comes to my mind.

"I wouldn't know the first thing about stage acting," I point out to Amanda. "I mean, they are different."

"Right but you'd learn. We'd get you lessons. A lot of actors are making the jump to Broadway in recent years. Surely you've noticed."

"Yes, I have," I admit. "But I can't imagine me on the stage."

"Like I said, Jenny, think it over. And listen, if you stay on *Flower Queen* then don't even worry about it, okay?"

I nod stiffly and the rest of the meal passes by with discussions about off Broadway productions. I feel unmoored. I knew that Matt was under a lot of pressure to conform to what the producers want or he'd lose the budget and their financing. Yet I had thought that truly, by this point, the producers might have warmed up to me on the feature. *If they only saw me in it!* Then I might really have a chance to show them that I can bring what they need to the role.

By the time lunch finishes, I am feeling dejected. After what felt like a promising start to my career, I feel as if I have fallen off the path. Even if I do end up auditioning for off Broadway productions, does Amanda really think anyone would actually hire me?

I am walking down the street, lost in thought, hesitant to get back in my car and drive back home alone, when I see them. I see her first. Her blonde hair catches the bright mid-day sun. I duck behind the side of a building and peek out, hoping they won't see me. Rich is trailing after her. He has a thick pair of sunglasses and a hat on, clearly trying not to be spotted for once in his life.

But Jaime isn't disguised nearly as well. Her blonde hair sweeps over her shoulders and she is wearing big sunglasses as well as a floppy sun hat. But I can peg them both out instantly. And when her hand slips through Rich's, and he leans over and gives her a quick kiss on the mouth before they hop into a boutique, I am spitting mad.

It isn't as if I care that he is with another woman. In fact, if it weren't for those tapes he has of me, I'd be thrilled. I could fully break free of him. But now he is seeing Jaime behind my back and keeping me in his pocket, as if he can't decide which 'rising starlet' he needs the most. I should have known with how she stared at him so openly at dinner that she was interested. And Rich, never one to say no to a beauty, would have snapped her up.

I have lodged the laptop in my car, in case Rich were to call me when I was out somewhere and have me come over. But knowing that he is out now makes me eager to take this moment and get to his computer. I don't know if he will invite me over again at this point.

I walk back quickly and get into my car, driving toward his house. My heart is pounding quickly. I am nervous he will come home while I am there and try to think of an excuse as to why I would have come over. His maid will be there and hopefully let me inside.

After taking a shortcut to miss the afternoon traffic, I am able to pull up into his house thirty minutes later. Rich is not there. There are no paparazzi to be found. Clearly Rich still wants to hide his relationship with Jaime, at least until he has an angle for it and he is sure there is no use out of me. If I get fired from *Flower Queen,* then I am nervous Rich will leak the tapes and be done with me. It'd even give him a boost, to be seen on sex tapes with a rising star.

I glance over my shoulder and get out of the car, clutching the laptop to me. My purse is filled with flash drives I can use to back up everything. My plan is to delete the tapes from his cloud and back up everything else on the flash drive and then delete the tape off his computer.

And then get it to the police before he can figure it out.

I hesitate before knocking, thinking of what to say. Finally, I knock twice and wait. I can hear the maid shuffling inside and then she opens the door, peering out. When she sees me, she looks embarrassed and I realize that Jaime must have been at his house already.

"Hey, I'm sorry for bothering you. But Rich and I just broke up and I have some stuff lying around here I need to get," I lie quickly, hoping it sounds believable.

She nods and holds the door open for me. I step past her and quickly thank her. I know she will be suspicious if I head directly into his office so I go upstairs instead, toward his room.

I can hear her downstairs, moving around the living room. Now that I am in Rich's room, I quickly go through his things, checking to see if there is anything I should grab. I find two flash drives in his sock drawer. Both are labelled with the letter J, which makes me nervous enough that I pocket them, just in case.

The rest of his room is the run-of-the-mill bedroom. There is little in the room that gives it a personal feel, like the rest of the house. I wonder if Rich is even capable of feeling a real emotion toward someone or something. He probably has the house so devoid of feeling in case he has to put it up for sale quickly.

When I see the maid heading to the pool to restack the towels and the bar that Rich keeps out there, I dart out of his room to get to his office. A quick glance out the kitchen window shows me the maid is texting someone on her phone so I slink back toward his office and shut the door behind me.

Now it is time to see if my plan will work.

Chapter Fourteen

Quickly I boot up the old laptop and wait for it to start up. It feels as if this whole process will take ages. I am convinced that every small noise is going to be Rich coming home and bearing down on me. I know if he finds me that it will not go well and there will be no way of reasoning with him or preventing him from getting angry.

The desktop of the laptop turns on. It automatically connects to the house's Wi-Fi, which means that the laptop had definitely been in the house before. My heart is beating so quickly that I am afraid I will have a heart attack. The palms of my hands are sweaty from pure nerves.

I click up the computer box and a new window opens. On the side is Rich's home computer. I hold my breath and click on it.

The laptop is outdated, causing it to run slowly. I feel like I am in one of those hacker movies from the early 90's as I wait for something to happen. Finally, there is a small *ding* and the computer connects to Rich's other computer.

I throw my hands up in the air in some sort of victory pose but at the last second remember to shut my mouth so I don't let out a squeal of excitement. The idea, which was my last hope, actually has *worked*.

But I can't enjoy my victory. I have to back up everything I can from the computer plus get into his cloud and remove the tapes from there so he cannot access it from his phone. I move as swiftly as I can, but the laptop is slow moving through the connection and even slower connecting to his cloud.

I am pretty sure I can feel sweat forming on the back of my neck from nerves. I start making backups of his documents, videos and pictures. Whenever a flash drive fills up, I switch out to another one. The process feels as if it is taking forever. Each second that passes feels like an hour. I wipe the palms of my hands on my jeans.

At one point, it starts downloading a video called *Jenny 1*. The small thumbnail is of us on my couch, somewhat grainy due to the size of it. A sick feeling is in my gut. What a fucking creep. As it downloads *Jenny 2* five minutes later, I tap my fingers against my thigh impatiently.

I hope that the videos, taken without my permission, will be enough to get the police on my side. Coupled with his warrant for not paying child support, I hope it will be enough to get Rich thrown in jail. At the very least, I tell myself, now that he will no longer have the tapes on his laptop or his cloud, I can say goodbye to him. I delete the two videos off his computer when it is finished.

When it has finished downloading the documents, pictures and videos, I shove the flash drives in my purse

and bring up his cloud. There isn't much on it. What is
on it, however, is gross. Backups of blackmailing is on
the cloud. The two videos of me are quickly deleted. I
see he already has a nude photo of Jaime on here as well
and delete that as well, just because I don't want him
deciding to ruin her life out of anger and send it
somewhere from his phone.

With the backup finished and my videos cleared
from his cloud, I turn off the laptop and make my way
to the door. I press my ear against it, waiting to see if I
hear either the maid or Rich. There is nothing but
silence.

Taking a deep breath, I slowly open his office door.
I can see directly into the kitchen from here. I don't see
anyone. I close the door behind me and step into the
living room.

"Going somewhere?"

Rich's voice rings out from the couch. When he
stands up, I can tell he is furious. His face is a dark red
and his hands are clenched. A cold dense fear settles in
my stomach. How did I not hear him? I had been so
quiet, straining at every little noise to see if it was him
or not.

My mouth goes dry. All my plans are crumbling in
front of my eyes. He'll know what I did. I'll be stuck
under his thumb forever.

"Rosa texted me, said you came by to get your
things. She is to alert me whenever someone comes by,
did you know that?"

I think of the maid by the pool, texting someone and curse myself. I should have thought through it better but it felt like my only chance to get inside the house after seeing him with Jaime.

"It's not officially in the press yet but I can give you some other news as well," Rich says, trying to keep his voice casual. "We're going to give funding to Matt's film. Josh knows some investors who are interested."

"That's great," I reply stiffly, finally finding my tongue.

"It really is. Things are moving swiftly. Like I said on the phone, no office building yet, but with Josh's connections and Matt wanting to keep his script intact so badly that he'll side with a tiny production company, we're going to be on the map."

Rich takes a step forward and my hands tighten around the laptop. If I can convince him somehow that the laptop is where I stored his computer information, then he might not even think of looking through my purse for flash drives. Rich thinks I am an idiot. I have to make him think I still am one.

"Of course, we couldn't keep everything. There had to be some bargaining, some mutual things to be agreed upon," Rich goes on. "Luckily with the promise of keeping the script, Matt relented on keeping *you* on the film. So consider yourself let go, Jenny. Jaime is going to be doing the role."

"Jaime? Your new target?" I ask, my voice dry.

"Are you jealous, Jenny? You put up a tough front but I am sure that you loved being with me. It wasn't until I avoided you, waiting for the right time to fit you in my shifting plan, that you came over to my house. Are you thinking you can just take my things and go?"

"Jealous? No, more like I feel bad for Jaime. I know she wants to be famous but she is just making the same mistake I made," I say, taking a step back.

"Mistake? I put you on the map," he growls, and I can tell I have hit a nerve. "I made you, Jenny. No one else cared about you until I got you that movie role and I realized you can serve a better purpose. I helped *you* and this is how you repay *me*?"

I try to keep my voice even and hide any sort of emotion at all. "I know what you did for me, Rich," I say, trying to placate him. "Getting me the role on *Recoil Factor* was kind of you and sweet. And I feel as if I played ball with you long enough, you know? It wasn't as if I ever spoke against you or told anyone – "

"Told anyone *what*?" Rich says, seething, walking directly up to me before I can move away. "That I was nice enough to let you hang out around me? That I still haven't leaked those tapes of yours so everyone knows what a whore you are?"

Something in me snaps. "No, I didn't tell anyone about your failed football career or your daughter."

His face darkens. I know I have gone too far but I am sick of hearing his word vomit and dealing with his insults. If I wasn't holding the laptop, I would have slapped him. I see him connecting the dots in his brain and when he does, he lets out a strange noise of irritation.

"You," Rich says, his teeth so firmly clenched I am afraid that he will crack them. "You gave Sarah my number."

"Yes," I look him in the eyes. "I gave Sarah your number. What will the police think if they were tipped off you have an outstanding warrant for unpaid child support?"

Rich lets out a roar and he shoves me hard. I lose my footing and slam back against the hallway wall. It knocks the wind out of me and for a brief moment I think of falling down the stairs, my hands around my belly, trying to protect Maggie.

The thought of how I curled up in a ball at the bottom of the stairs in pain makes me push off the hallway wall and try to move past Rich. But he is quick and snatches the laptop out of my hands. He raises it high above his head and smashes it down onto the ground. I don't know if he broke it because I am taking off, trying to get to his front door before he gets me.

I am halfway there when I feel a sharp tug on my purse. The strap snaps off and I lose my footing, landing on his marble flooring. My purse's contents scatter across the floor. Yet I have put the flash drives in the inner pocket. They are safely inside the purse, which has slid near one of his chairs. My cell phone's screen has shattered and is out of my reach.

Rich looms over me. His teeth are bared, as if he is a rabid dog. I wonder if this is how Sarah felt the night he beat her so badly she ended up in the hospital.

"What are you going to do, Doug?" I ask, reverting to his old name which takes him aback. "Are you going to kill me? Beat the shit out of me? I’ll go to the cops. I don’t care if you leak the fucking tapes, I’ll go to the police and get you arrested, you piece of shit.”

I am hoping if he considers the fact if he does anything to me that the police will arrest him to be enough to make him stop. It will ruin everything if Rich lets that happen. I don’t want him to know that he is fucked over anyway once I get out of here.

“No one knows you came here except for Rosa,” he says as he yanks me up by my shirt. “I can do whatever I need with you.”

“You’re throwing it all away,” I tell him, trying to keep my fear at bay. “You’re going to do something you regret and you’ll lose it all. Will you outrun the police then?”

I can see my words are slowly getting past his haze of anger. As they sink in, Rich lets go of my shirt and I scramble away from him, trying to get to my phone. But before I can, he yanks me back by the arm. The pain is sudden and I let out a yelp as he spins me around.

“Do you see what you’re making me do?” Rich yells at me. “I’m going to lose everything because of you. Because I have to put you in your fucking place.”

I am now terrified that he is going to hurt me or worse. He is gripping my arm, staring me down, as if I will give him the answers he is looking for.

“I was so close this time,” he hisses at me. “Fame. Fortune. My own company. You’re the only loose end. I’m not letting you fuck this up, Jenny.”

"Rich, what are you going to do – " I say, my voice so high pitched that I barely recognize it

That's when I see his fist coming toward me and then blackness.

Chapter Fifteen

I am running but there is water at my feet. It makes me lose my footing and I seem unable to get up and get ahold of my bearings. I can hear Maggie crying off in the distance and know that I have to get to her. I have to get near her and help her. I push off the ground and try to ignore the fact the water level is rising.

There is a dark shadow at the other side of the room. I cannot tell if it is Robbs or Rich – maybe both of them, combined. I yell at them not to go near Maggie but they do not move. It is as if they are a statue.

The water level is rising faster now. Maggie's cries grow louder. I have to get to her. I have to get to her. I have to –

My eyes open up suddenly and adjust to the dim lighting. My head hurts so much that I feel as if I have been smashing it directly against a rock. I try to move my arms but I realize they are tied together behind me.

I blink a few times, trying to get rid of the double vision. My nose feels cracked and I realize Rich must have broken it when he punched me. As my vision clears up a little, I realize I am shoved in the closet of the guest room. The lights from the bedroom shine in through the slates in the closet door.

I can hear Rich pacing the hallway through the door. I wonder if he has truly and completely lost it. I am terrified that he is going to kill me and hide my body somewhere and just keep on with his life here. He won't want me to go to the cops and he won't want to restart somewhere else. In his quest for fame and fortune, he has lodged himself here in Hollywood and doesn't want to start over somewhere else.

I try to keep the panic at bay but it is almost impossible. If I can get to my phone, then I can call 911 or even shoot Marina and Jon a text for help. First things first is to get out of this closet. I move my hands and feel the rope wrapped around them. I wiggle them to see how loose they are. If I can wiggle free of them then I can untie the rope around my ankles. I am just lucky that Rich did not use anything stronger to tie me up with.

The closet has a couple of boxes shoved in the back and some old clothes of mine hanging in it from when I was actually dating Rich. I run my fingers along one of the boxes but nothing is sharp enough to cut through the rope. I stretch out my feet and they hit a pair of high heels I tossed in here one drunken night. They won't be able to cut through but if I can somehow wiggle the heel in between my wrist and the rope, it might loosen them enough so I can slide the rope off.

I slowly move the heels toward me with my feet. I stop every few seconds to make sure Rich is still pacing the house, muttering to himself. I can't hear what he is saying. I wonder if he is either talking himself into killing me or letting me go. I don't want to stick around and find out.

When the heels are close enough to me, I lay down and wiggle until they are underneath me. I grip them with my fingertips and switch to one side. I start blindly trying to move the heel in between my skin and rope. The whole time I try to control my breathing so I don't go into a blind panic. Each second feels like agony. Rich has tied the ropes tight and trying to create slack is irritating.

I stop and close my eyes. I make myself count to ten slowly to try to fend off a panic attack. I have to get out of this. I refuse to let myself be hurt or killed by Rich. Once I count to ten, I open my eyes again and work on the heel.

Finally, with a painful scrape, the heel is wedged in between my skin and the rope. I wiggle it around madly until I feel the rope begin to give way. Even though Rich tied it tightly, he didn't tie it *well*. Grateful for this lucky break, I give it a hard pull and finally the rope loosens enough that my fingers can curl around it and pull it off.

With my hands free, I move to my feet and untie them quickly. My hands are shaking as I do so and it feels as if a weight is sitting on my chest. Rich is still pacing the house, talking wildly to himself now. Holding my breath, I open up the closet door just enough so I can crawl out. My purse is shoved in the corner, along with the broken laptop and my phone. He must have chucked everything in here until he figured out what he was doing with me.

I crawl slowly across the carpet, terrified that any small noise I make will alert Rich to the fact I am free. I grab my phone and curl up behind the bed. Even though the screen has shattered, it is still on and working. Relief sweeps through me as I bring up my text message screen. It is too risky to call 911.

At that moment I can hear Rich's voice growing louder. It sounds as if he is moving up the stairs to the bedroom. Panicked, I open up a group text to Jon and Marina. I only have time to text ***PALM TREES!!!!*** and hit send and shove the phone under the bed when Rich opens the door.

When he sees me behind the bed, his face contorts with rage. I stand up to face him, not seeing any weapons on him.

"How the fuck did you get free?"

"What are you going to do to me?" I ask him, hoping my voice isn't shaking.

"I have to get rid of you, Jenny," Rich replies. "Either come with me quietly or I'll have to do it here."

"You're fucking crazy," I tell him, trying to delay as much as I can until the police pull up.

"I'm not crazy!" he yells at me. "I've made a name for myself here. I can't leave this behind, not anymore. Not when I'm getting what I deserve. And you are not going to mess this up for me. You give me no choice."

He comes toward me but I duck at the last minute and burst past him. I take off from the guest room, running down the stairs. He is right behind me, bellowing at me. As I head toward the front door, he lurches forward and tackles me to the floor. My mouth fills with blood as I bite my own tongue. Rich's hands are around my neck and I can feel his breath on my neck.

I struggle but Rich is stronger than me and all I can do is wiggle underneath him as he chokes me. My vision is starting to dim and I feel everything in my body going numb. I can't believe that I am so close yet so far…

I think I am dreaming it when I see the flashing lights outside. It is dark outside and the sirens sound as if they are underwater. I feel Rich let go of my neck. The last thing I remember is the police bursting into the house as everything goes dark. As my eyes close, my last thought is *I wonder how Rich will get out of this one…*

Epilogue

"I'm so nervous," I say, staring at the mirror in my dressing room.

"You've done this plenty of times before," Marina points out as she fusses with my hair, even though the hairdresser finished it ten minutes ago.

"Not on *Broadway,*" I tell her, turning around.

"True but you'll kill it. I know you will. You come alive on stage. Movies were just suffocating your true talent."

"That's how Amanda swings it, too," I retort.

Marina grins and I feel a little better. I am waiting for Jon to come by and wish me good luck. He had a business meeting with his new partner in his talent agency here in New York and was running late.

"If this goes well," I tell Marina, "then maybe everyone will finally forget about Rich. I'm sick of answering questions about him."

"Of course you are. It's been a year since he tried to kill you and it's all anyone has been talking about."

"I love how bluntly you word things," I reply but Marina is right.

The media firestorm after the police caught Rich in the act of trying to choke me to death, on top of everything on his computer, like the sex tapes filmed without my knowledge, the blackmailing evidence and his warrant for unpaid child support, meant that Rich was behind bars for a long time and no one associated me with Hollywood acting anymore.

I ended up taking Amanda's advice and moving my life to New York City, just to escape Hollywood. Matt had lost his backing with Rich's production company and crowd funded his project online instead for *Flower Queen*. He had asked me to come back in the role but I had refused. Hollywood had been a learning experience but I needed to move on. I had suggested Kathy for the role instead, since Jaime had backed out of it as well.

Matt had ended up casting Kathy for the role. The movie had done well and Kathy's performance had turned her from a soap opera star to a starlet in her own right. She couldn't make it to opening night tonight of my play but she had sent a giant arrangement of flowers and balloons, wishing me good luck. I was thrilled for her and how things turned out.

Jon moved to New York with me and we began our life together. He started his own business representing people here in the city and I auditioned for plays. Amanda was right – my natural talent shined through better on stage and my career took off. Yet tonight was my first Broadway show and I was nervous.

At that moment, there was a knock on the door and Jon stuck his head in. Relief swept through me as he came over and kissed me.

"Barf," Marina joked.

I stick my tongue out at her and give Jon another kiss. He smiles at me and my heart does a flip.

"You're going to do a great job."

"I love you," I mumble to him as Marina pretends to take a call and leaves the room.

"I love you, too."

When Jon brings me in for another kiss, I know I will have to reapply my lipstick before going out on stage. It is almost show time. But in this moment, through everything that I have gone through, I know it has lead me here. I cannot remember the last time that I have been this happy. Being with Jon and making a name for myself in New York has granted me everything I have searched for in my life.

I have nothing to fear now and everything to look forward to.

Jon pulls away from me and smiles.

"It's show time."

-*The End*-

If you enjoyed this series, I would appreciate your leaving a review of the book. Good reviews encourage an author to write as well as help books to sell. Good reviews can be just a few short sentences describing what you liked about the book without having a spoiler. If you could spend 30 seconds writing a review, I would appreciate it: you can review this title right now at your favorite retailer.

Here is a preview of the **first book of the series** that started it all:

Fifty Recipes For Disaster: A New Adult Romance Series - Book 1

"**ALL RIGHT**, chefs, you have ninety seconds to get your food plated and presented. If your dish isn't ready, you will automatically be eliminated."

My cooking instructor, Chef Michelle Lee, walks through the room, examining our stations. My fellow cooking students and I are competing for the chance to enter another competition. The winner of today's cooking challenge will get the chance to compete for a full-time apprenticeship at Fission, one of Austin's hottest restaurants.

I'm not confident in many aspects of my life, but I know I dominate in the kitchen. I begin plating my dish just as Chef Lee approaches my station.

"Your food presents beautifully as usual, Kiara," she tells me with a smile. "If it tastes as good as it looks, you've got this in the bag," she adds with a soft whisper.

The instructors at *Le Cordon Bleu College of Culinary Arts* aren't supposed to show favoritism to their students, but Chef Lee keeps a soft spot for me. Along with being one of my teachers, she's also my faculty adviser, and she knows the unusual circumstances that brought me to the school.

"Time's up," she calls out to the class. "Place your finished plates on the head table."

I walk my plate to the front of the room and place it on top of the placard that holds my student ID number. My classmates follow suit… several of them glare at me after looking at my dish. I am delighted, knowing they're all both jealous and impressed I was able to execute a well-developed *Cioppino* within the given time frame. My rich seafood stew is accompanied by fresh sourdough loaves. I examine my classmates' dishes and feel my chances of winning are good.

"Clear away your stations," Chef Lee directs. "Chef Lawton will be here shortly to judge your plates, and I don't want any evidence of who made what on display when he arrives."

Chef Lawton is the *sous* chef at Fission and the judge of this stage of the apprenticeship competition. I clear my station quickly and then I take a seat at the front of the room. I want to be able to see Chef Lawton's expressions as he tastes each dish.

As I sit nervously in my chair, my classmates finish clearing their stations. I can tell everyone else is just as anxious as I am… we've received plenty of critiques from our instructors but this will be the first time a professional chef from a restaurant will be tasting our food. The door of the classroom opens and a tall man wearing a black chef's jacket enters the room.

"Chef Lawton, it's so lovely to see you," Chef Lee welcomes him. "I can't tell you how excited we are to participate in this competition."

"We're excited as well," Chef Lawton replies. "We're always looking for new, innovative chefs at Fission. I'm looking forward to tasting the dishes and welcoming one of your students into the final leg of the competition. I see that all of the plates are ready. If it's all right with you, I'll get started."

"Of course," Chef Lee agrees.

I try not to hold my breath as I watch Chef Lawton sample each of the plates. I feel encouraged when he reaches mine. Instead of sampling one bite and moving on, he holds the broth in his mouth for a moment, and then tastes each type of seafood in turn. The expression on his face tells me that my stew is perfect, and I say a silent prayer I haven't been out-cooked by any of my classmates.

"First off, I'd like to say this is an impressive display," the seasoned chef begins. "Everything on this table is up to par with the level of skill and talent I expect to see from second-year students. That being said, there is a clear winner. One chef not only executed a delicious dish, but also added a few subtle, original touches that showed innovation and creativity."

Adrenaline rushes through me as he moves to stand behind my dish. "Who created this *Cioppino*?" he asks.

I blush involuntarily as I raise my hand.

"And what is your name, Chef?"

"Kiara Sands," I reply, trying to mask the excitement in my voice.

"Well, Chef Sands, it's an honor to welcome you to the next stage of the competition. I look forward to tasting more of your food as the weeks progress. I am needed back at Fission, but Chef Lee will provide you with the details of your new position." He turns to the rest of the class. "To the rest of you, don't be discouraged. You all provided me with excellent dishes, and you have bright futures ahead of you."

"Thank you, Chef," the class responds in unison.

Chef Lawton makes a quick exit, and Chef Lee takes his place behind the head table. "Excellent work today, class. You're dismissed until tomorrow," she announces. My classmates gather their things and leave the room... I stay behind to talk to Chef Lee.

"Kiara, I'm so proud of you." She beams once we are alone. "As you know, there will be two other chefs competing with you at Fission. You're the only one who's been selected from *Le Cordon Bleu*, and I know you'll represent us well." She moves to her desk and pulls a large package from her bottom drawer. "Here is your apprenticeship packet. You'll receive your Fission jacket when you report for work tomorrow morning. If you have any questions, or just need someone to talk to, you know where to reach me."

"This seems like a wonderful dream, and part of me is afraid that I'll wake up any minute now," I confess.

Chef Lee gives me a maternal smile. "This is a dream, Kiara. It's your dream. And you're well on *your* way to achieving it."

The information packet Chef Lee presented me with instructs me to be at Fission at 10:00 am. I check my dashboard clock as I pull into the parking lot... 9:40 am. I feel smug, knowing I'm probably the first of the three competitors to arrive. I check my makeup in the rear-view mirror before exiting my car.

Fission is housed in a modern brick building in East Austin, one of the city's burgeoning hipster areas. The

495

area gives off a relaxed, laid-back vibe, but I know the kitchen of Fission will be anything but.

I push open the heavy, solid oak door and am greeted by a pixy-sized hostess with spiked, lavender hair.

"Table for one?" she asks me brightly.

"No," I reply nervously. "My name is Kiara Sands. I'm supposed to start work today."

"Oh! You're one of the newbies!" She says warmly. "I'm Megan. It's a pleasure to meet you. The other two are already here. I'll show you to their table."

Damn it! I'd been so sure I'd make the best impression by arriving first, and here I am, the last of the apprentices to report for our first day.

Megan seems to sense my disappointment. "Don't worry. Paul doesn't give a shit how early people show up. As long as you're here when you're scheduled, you'll be fine. And you haven't missed anything. The other two have just been sitting alone since they got here," she offers reassuringly.

"Thank you for that," I say half-heartedly. As I follow Megan through the restaurant, I'm struck by the eclectic, well-placed décor. All of the tables are made of the same polished oak as the front door. The water goblets on the tabletops are tinted in hues of blue, green, and rose… a selection of art from all around the world adorns the walls. The ambiance is on the right side of the fine line between cozy and overwhelming. The restaurant offers a large main dining room, with smaller, more private rooms on each side.

"This is a beautiful place," I say as Megan leads me toward the back of the main room.

"It is," she agrees. "Paul handled all of the decorating himself. He says that Austin is a melting pot, and he wants all of our customers to feel at home when they dine here."

I'm about to comment on how successfully that goal had been achieved when we arrive at a table occupied by a beautiful blonde woman and a swarthy man with sandy blond hair. A pot of coffee and three cups sit on the table.

"Kiara Sands, this is Jenny Foster and Robbs Martin," Megan introduces us. She checks her watch before speaking again. "It's a quarter to ten, so I imagine that Paul will be out shortly. I suggest you get fully caffeinated and enjoy this time off your feet. It will be the last one for today," she warns with a friendly, knowing tone.

I take a seat in the chair next to Jenny as Megan moves back to the hostess station. "It's a pleasure to meet you both," I offer.

"It's a pleasure to meet you too," Robbs replies. "Congratulations on making it this far in the competition. And I'd like to apologize right now for how thoroughly I'm going to kick both of your asses. This job is mine." He speaks with a blend of arrogance and sarcasm, and I can tell immediately that Robbs and I are not going to get along.

Personal relationships are something I struggle with. In my experience, there's no point in getting close to someone who will inevitably let you down. I prefer to keep my head down and focus on getting my job done. As Chef Lee said yesterday, I have a dream and I'm well on my way to achieving it. I'll be damned if I let Robbs or anyone else get in my way.

"Just ignore Robbs," Jenny advises me. "He thinks that he's God's gift to food... women too, probably." She giggles. "So Kiara, what's your story? Which campus were you plucked from?"

"I'm in my second year at *Le Cordon Bleu*," I answer with pride. In my opinion, *Le Cordon Bleu* is the best culinary school in the area—it's also the hardest to get in to. Jenny seems impressed by my background, but Robbs laughs and dismisses it immediately.

"The *Bleu* is all right, I guess," he snorts, "if you're happy being complacent and doing everything old-school."

"I wasn't aware that being classically trained is a bad thing," I reply shortly. "Tell me, what culinary Mecca do you hail from?"

"*Escoffier*," he answers with a cocky smile. "You know, where all of the innovative, cutting-edge people attend. Three of my instructors were nominated for the James Beard award. So like I said, no hard feelings, but I'm going to kick both of your asses. *Escoffier* specializes in farm-to-table cuisine, so I'm exactly the kind of chef Fission is looking for."

I dismiss his statement with a glare. While the *Auguste Escoffier School of Culinary Arts* is reputed for turning out fantastic chefs, in some culinary circles it's dismissed as a hipster college that prioritizes food trends over basic technique and skill.

I don't feel like debating the merits of my education with Robbs, so I turn to Jenny. "And where do you go?" I ask pleasantly.

"The Art Institute," she replies. "I'm still not positive that cooking is my life's passion. I wanted to go to a college that offers other programs, in case I decided to change my major."

"If you're not sure that you want to be a chef, then what the fuck are you doing here?" Robbs asks hotly. "You should give your spot to someone who knows that this is what they want."

Jenny's green eyes fill with both anger and embarrassment, and I can tell she's fumbling for a response.

"I don't agree with that at all," I say warmly. "What better way to find out if you enjoy working in a real kitchen, than by actually doing it?"

"That's exactly what my instructor said when I won this spot," Jenny says with a nod.

"I see how it's going to be," Robbs interjects with more sarcasm. "The two of you are going to band together in 'sisterhood' and gang up on me."

"That's not how it's going to be at all," a firm voice says from behind me. I turn to see one of the most attractive men I've ever laid my eyes on. He's tall, with broad shoulders, blue eyes, and sandy blond hair. He's also wearing a black chef's jacket, identical to the one

Chef Lawton wore when he judged my dish. He holds eye contact with me for several moments before he speaks again.

"This competition will come down to one thing and one thing only... the quality of your food. Only one of you will be named my new apprentice, so ganging up on each other won't serve any purpose. I'm Paul Weston, and I'd like to welcome you to my restaurant." He extends his hand to me.

I respond with a firm handshake and a smile. "I'm Kiara Sands. Thank you for this opportunity."

"You're here because you deserve to be. No thanks are necessary," he assures me.

If you enjoyed this sample then look for **Fifty Recipes For Disaster: A New Adult Romance Series - Book 1**.

Here is a preview of **another story** you may also enjoy:

Devil's Advocate: A BBW MC New Adult Romance Series - Book 1

KRISTIE LOOKED at the sky as she pulled up in front of the casino. The air was chilly and the clouds were dark and threatening snow, which was the last thing Kristie felt like dealing with. She had been in her car for over ten hours, driving home from college for the holidays. Her back was sore and her legs needed to be stretched out. She wanted a hot bath in a Jacuzzi tub. She'd settle for a hot tub. But who was she kidding? There was no hot tub to be found at her parents' house and trying to have a hot bath without being interrupted was almost impossible.

Kristie had approached the holidays with an ever-growing sense of dread. It wasn't that she didn't want to see her mother, but every time she came home, it was like being suffocated. Her hometown had held more appeal for her when she was younger, back when her father was alive. Since he'd died and her mother had gotten remarried last year, Kristie had delayed going home at all. She had only met her step-father in passing and hadn't met his nephew, who he tried to raise on his own.

Kristie had saved up to stay at a hotel the entire break. It had made the most sense to her. It would cause the least amount of stress during her stay and give her space when she needed it. But when she had mentioned this to her mother, there was no way to mistake the sadness in her mother's voice for anything else. Knowing she was upsetting her mother by refusing to stay at home with her new family, Kristie had cancelled the reservation and agreed to stay at her mother's house instead.

She looked up at the casino where her mother had worked the last five years. Her mother worked in the back offices, far away from the lights from the slot machines and the sounds of people winning money. The casino was a little run down but brought in a steady stream of people who could afford the middle-level slots and risks it provided in a town that was mostly quiet.

The stale smell of cigarettes and alcohol hit Kristie in the face as she stepped inside. She looked around, seeing if anything had changed since the last time she had been here. Nothing jumped out of her. A few of the slots seemed to have been upgraded, but the carpet was still worn down and dirty and the place had an air of despair that made Kristie's skin crawl. She had never been to Las Vegas, but she imagined that the casinos there weren't as depressing.

Kristie made her way to the back and asked for her mother through the grate where an attendant was standing, looking at her cellphone. The woman went off to find her mother, and Kristie was soon ushered into the back offices. The casino décor quickly ended back here. Her mother's small office was near the back, shoved in a corner. The door was ajar, and Kristie peeked her head in.

Her mother was looking at the computer, squinting through her glasses to whatever was on the screen. When Kristie knocked on the door gently, her mother looked up and smiled. Kristie was startled to see she was going gray. The last time she had seen her mother, she had been a brunette. It was odd to see age creeping up on her. She came over to her and hugged her tightly.

"It's so nice to see you again."

"You, too, Mom."

Her mom urged her to sit down as she sat across from her at her desk. It made Kristie feel odd, as if she was interviewing to be her mother's daughter. Her mom didn't seem to notice, however, and smiled again. They made small talk for a while, mostly talking about Kristie's experiences at college. Kristie felt tired. She knew her mom meant well, but she really wanted to go home and nap. She was only here to get the address to her mom's new place.

"How are things with Lionel?" Kristie finally asked, feeling as if she didn't bring up her mom's new husband, she would never get out of the tiny office.

Her mom seemed to relax now that Kristie had brought him up, "He's great. Really, we're just wonderful. There are some issues, though…"

"Like what?"

"Well, it's actually one of the reasons that we wanted you to stay with us instead of a hotel. See, Lionel's nephew, Gray, is a bit of a handful. Lionel still feels responsible for him since he became his legal guardian when Gray was just a little boy."

Kristie wasn't following, "Okay…"

"He tends to run on the wrong side of the law, and we thought it'd be so great if you two could meet and maybe hang out."

The words hung in the air. Kristie felt a twinge of annoyance. She had thought her mother wanted her at the house because she had missed her, not because she wanted her to play nice with her new step-father's nephew. They weren't in grade school anymore. Trying to change someone set in their ways by sticking them with a goody-goody was a useless attempt.

Kristie took a deep breath and held it for a few seconds, letting the air out slowly. Her mother watched, a worried expression on her face.

"What do you want me to do with him?" Kristie finally asked.

Her mom, taking the fact that Kristie hadn't said no as a good sign, started to ramble. "Well, maybe just hang out with him. Show him what you do for fun. Maybe you two can go to the movies or something."

Kristie raised an eyebrow, "Go to the movies? What does this guy do for fun anyway that has you two so stressed out?"

Her mom avoided her stare and sighed, looking tired. "He runs with a bad crowd and doesn't like to listen. He's a good kid though. He's just lost."

"And you think I can fix him?"

"It wouldn't hurt to try, would it, Kristie? For me?"

Kristie sighed and nodded in agreement. How could she say no to her mother? She would always wish that her mother hadn't gotten remarried, but she didn't want her mom to be unhappy either. Her mom got up and walked over to her, hugging her tightly. Her mother's hugs had always reminded Kristie of being a little kid, outside playing till the sun set and running back inside for dinner. Back when her father was alive. Kristie shut her eyes tightly, willing the memories to leave her. She didn't want to think about her father right now.

Her mom finally pulled away and looked at her, smiling, "We'll have to really talk, you know, all about college and everything."

"Yeah, of course."

Her mom's eyes swept down her quickly, so fast that if Kristie wasn't used to it, she never would have picked up on it. She steeled herself.

"Maybe you and Gray can go to the gym. It'd get him out of the house and you could lose a few pounds at the same time," her mom said cheerfully.

Kristie mumbled in agreement and gave her mother one last hug before leaving the office. She should have known that there wasn't going to be any way in hell that her mother would have let an entire conversation go without making some sort of remark to her about her weight.

As she trudged through the casino, her mood lowered with every step. She regretted coming here for the holidays. Before her, they spread out in a bleak landscape. Dealing with her mother's 'helpful advice' in regards to her weight, and trying to show her loser relative by marriage around town. At the very least, she should have kept the hotel reservation.

Kristie dragged out the drive toward Lionel's house. Her mother had given her the address and it was close to the casino. A ten-minute drive didn't seem like enough time to prepare for whatever she was going to walk into. As she turned down the street where her mom's new house was, she found herself taking a deep breath. The first time, she just drove past the house. It was non-descript and had nothing of worth showing that made Kristie even notice it. Her mom had stopped gardening after her father died, and the front yard of this house was plain and dull.

Kristie pulled into the driveway. The garage door was open and a man was underneath a truck, working on it. She could only see his feet. Kristie got out of her car, grabbing her bags, and looked inside the garage. The man didn't look up when she shut the door of her car.

"Hello?" Kristie called out toward the man under the truck.

He didn't answer. Heavy metal was blasting out of a stereo nearby, but it was such an old stereo that the music sounded tinny. Kristie called out again, but the man still didn't answer. She knew that he heard her because he stopped working at one point and went still before resuming. She hoped this wasn't Lionel, because the guy was an asshole. *Probably his fantastic nephew.* Kristie trudged toward the front door, leaving the other guy behind. What a fantastic trip this was going to be.

If you enjoyed this sample then look for **Devil's Advocate: A BBW MC New Adult Romance Series - Book 1.**

Here is a preview of **another story** you may also enjoy:

Romeo Alpha: A BBW Paranormal Shifter Romance - Book 1 by Darla Dunbar

AMANDA WONDERED how the hell she had gotten so far away from home. When she walked, she usually didn't go past a couple of blocks, but she felt so different today. Something was pushing her further and in a different direction, and she wasn't sure what it was. But she didn't care at the moment, because she just wanted to walk.

Not thinking twice about where she was going, she let her gut instinct give her the direction she needed.

Her grandmother had always told her to go with her gut. She'd said human instinct was better than anything. "Intuition is a girl's best friend," she would say, and then they would both laugh. Talks she and her grandmother had always seemed to pop into her head at the strangest of times, like now.

Here she was, going for a walk, and wondering why she wanted to go in a different direction, and there was her grandmother's voice in her head, propelling her along. Amanda missed her grandmother more with every passing year.

Amanda paused and thought about her life thus far. She had just graduated from college and started working in the local animal hospital, but it wasn't quite like she had thought. She didn't see the care and passion she'd hoped to find in the industry. In the city, being a vet was all about how much money you could make, how many pets you could treat. And, at twenty-four, it was hard to be taken seriously.

Her two female roommates were nice, but they all just went their separate ways. They didn't eat ice cream and watch movies like on *Friends*. They didn't share secrets or even laugh or hang out. They really just slept in the same apartment, and they usually weren't even home at the same time. Except Amanda, that is.

Amanda was always at home, it seemed. She had nowhere else to go, really. The other two girls spent most nights out with their real friends or their boyfriends. Amanda lived a lonely life, but she was happy. At least, she was pretty sure she was happy. After all, she had an upstanding career, and she still had money left over from her savings.

Both her parents had been killed in a car accident years ago. Amanda had graduated from high school with no family there that day or on the day she graduated from college. It was what it was, though, and she knew that her parents watched her from Heaven.

The only positive thing was that her parents had been prepared and had made sure they left enough money and a big enough life insurance policy to help her out. They would be surprised but happy knowing how much that money had helped her in the years after their death. She was proud to say that she was able to live off of it through her college years. She'd never even had to get a job like most kids did. Amanda had been able to focus on her classes.

That freedom wasn't worth it, though. She would have worked three jobs at a time while going to school for one more day with her parents.

However, the account was finally starting to dry up, and she needed to think about what she would do. Sure, she had a new job that could pay her bills, but those loans were piling up with interest. Even a vet job only went so far.

Amanda sighed as she began the trek back toward the house.

Amanda liked her walks in the evening. It helped her to relax, enjoying the quiet time alone. And while Amanda wasn't overweight by any means, it helped slim her waistline, which showed those extra biscuits she liked every now and again.

She turned and began to make her way back to the townhouse she shared with her roommates, but stopped as she heard a noise

A rustling came from behind her, and she turned to see the bushes shaking. Looking over to the other side of the sidewalk, she saw those bushes shake as well. Not wanting to wait around to find out what was behind the leaves, she took off at a run. She swore she heard a growl come from behind her, but she didn't turn to see what was chasing her. That would only slow her down. As she reached the door to her home, she quickly turned the knob and went through headfirst. Shutting the door quickly, she looked out the window. She got a glimpse of a long black furry tail as something ran around to the side of her building.

"What in the world are you doing, Amanda?" Betsy stood there looking at her inquisitively.

"Something was chasing me."

"What?"

"I don't know what it was, but something big and furry was chasing me. I saw a long black tail just now when I walked into the house."

"You mean when you dove into the house?" Betsy's grin faded. "I'll call the game warden. If there is a big animal outside, then none of us need to go out there until they find it and get rid of it."

"Well, I don't want them to kill it."

"I know, silly, but if it's a wild animal, they can take it out to the National Forest and let it loose. The city is no place for a wild animal." Betsy turned and picked up the phone from the receiver.

Amanda stood in shocked silence as she listened to her roommate tell the person on the other end of the phone what had happened.

She knew from Betsy's tone that she and the person on the other end of the phone were questioning her sanity. They lived in a big city, and the closest thing they got to a wild animal was a stray cat or two. They didn't even get raccoons. If there was some huge animal like she thought, then it would make headline news.

Shaking her head in aggravation, Amanda turned toward her room. She suddenly felt silly and didn't want to have to explain what she saw to any more people.

"Amanda? Where are you going? They are on their way and might need to talk to you."

"Tell them it was a dog. Now that I'm thinking about it, it kind of looked like that couple that lives down the road's greyhound. Maybe he just got out."

"Are you sure, Amanda?" Betsy asked, turning and saying something into the phone.

Without saying another word, Amanda shut the door to her room tight and then quickly locked the door. She looked over her room and, seeing the window open and the curtains blowing in the breeze, she ran over to push the window pane down and lock it tight. As she stood there, she looked out into the woods that made up her backyard. There, in the distance, two yellow eyes stared back at her.

Suddenly, more eyes appeared, and it seemed the animals went on forever. She was amazed, since the woods behind her house were very dense and small. The dark night was lit with a full moon. A shiver raced through her as she stood there and stared into the first set of yellow eyes. She quickly shut the curtains and went to sit on her bed. She didn't think she would ever be able to fall asleep knowing what was out there. As she laid her head on the pillow, her mind wondered to large beasts with yellow eyes and sharp fangs. But she was soon fast asleep.

Amanda awoke with a yawn. It had been almost a month since the incident with what she now called a dog. She had agreed with Betsy that her mind had been playing tricks on her that night. There were often times when she was sure she felt eyes on her, and she would turn in one direction or another, looking. What she was seeking, she didn't know, but somewhere in the back of her mind, she just wanted to know if the eyes she had seen that night had been real or just part of her dreams that evening. She was still so uneasy about it that her walks seemed to get earlier and earlier each evening.

She was just about to walk out the door when her phone started ringing. She quickly grabbed it and pushed the button to answer it.

"Hello."

"Ms. Walker?"

"Yes?"

"Hello, Ms. Walker, my name is Ernest Montgomery. I am calling to tell you that your aunt has passed away."

"My aunt? But I don't have any family. You must have the wrong Ms. Walker."

"No, ma'am. Your father was Joshua Walker, correct? Mother Maureen Walker?"

"Yes."

"Then, I have the right Ms. Walker. It is your father's sister I am referring to. She unexpectedly passed away from a heart attack. I am very sorry for your loss."

"Oh, my gosh! I never knew I even had any family. I am very sad that I didn't get to meet her."

"Yes, ma'am. I'm sure. She was a nice woman. I have also called you to see if you can meet with me. I need to go over her will with you."

"Her will?"

"Yes, ma'am. Your aunt was a wealthy woman."

"Oh? Um, okay. When would you like to meet?"

"The sooner, the better."

"Okay. How about today?"

"That would be great. I am in Slatesville, in the valley."

"Oh. Okay. That is just forty-five minutes from me. I can be there in a couple of hours."

"Sounds good, ma'am. I am at the *Montgomery Law Firm*. I am the only attorney in the town."

"Okay. Thank you, sir. I will see you soon."

"Yes, ma'am. I'll be waiting."

Amanda fell back on the couch, stunned, for what seemed like forever. Everything was pushed to the back of her mind as she thought about what she had just learned. She had a family. Well, she *did* have a family. Now her aunt was gone. Could there be others in her family who she knew nothing about? She didn't know, but she did know one thing. She wasn't going to find out sitting around here, twiddling her thumbs. She needed to get going fast.

Amanda headed for the kitchen. She wasn't surprised to see that no one was there. Of course her roommates weren't home. They were either in class or with their boyfriends.

Smiling, she made a cup of coffee and drank it slowly, thinking about what she might find out. Then, with a deep sigh, she made her way to her car. She looked at the small Honda with pride. It was a pile of junk to some, but it held a special place in her heart. She hadn't been able to get rid of her father's car. Instead, she had sold her own.

She looked down at the small picture he had taped to the dash near the speedometer. She was about six in the picture, and she had been holding her mom's cheeks in her hands as she kissed her.

She remembered the day like it was yesterday. They had just got to a cabin they vacationed in. She had enjoyed herself so much. The little cabin had one bedroom with a queen-sized bed where her parents slept and a set of bunk beds for her. They had stayed up late roasting marshmallows as her father told her scary stories about wolves and vampires. She had ended up in their bed, snuggled between the two of them. They had spent the next day hiking and walking trails and seeing tons of waterfalls and animals.

She had loved it and had never forgotten. It soon became a family tradition to go camping every year. After some of those trips, they didn't return home. Instead, they moved on to a different location. The constant moving had been hard on her as a kid, but she would have never told her parents that. She had felt like they were hiding something from her. Of course, she had been young back then and had blown it off as childhood curiosity. Now, with this new family member, she wasn't so sure.

Her parents had been very quiet people. They seemed cautious of everything going on around them and were even a little jumpy at times. Maybe there was more going on here than she thought. She needed to find out.

She wiped away a tear and go in the car. The car had a huge dent in one side and was almost fifteen years old, but it got her where she needed to go. She slid the car into drive and smiled to herself.

"Dad would be proud that his car was still running so good, wouldn't he, Trixy?" She and her father had named the car together.

Amanda turned onto the next road and made her way down the narrow two-lane road that led into the mountains. She had never been this way because her parents always went the long way around the mountains. They said they liked to take the scenic route.

She came to a small wooden sign that said *Slatesville—Welcome to your home away from home*. She smiled at the welcoming sign and kept on her way to the town. As she drove, she was amazed at how beautiful everything was. The low-hanging branches of the trees scraped the roof of the car every once in a while.

She was amazed at how many animals she saw. Deer acted as if they weren't afraid of her car. Raccoons were plentiful, and she jumped when a large black snake slithered across the road. There were people all around, and they watched her car curiously as she made her way down the street.

The town reminded her of a long lost western ghost town. It was a little spooky, and she caught herself checking the doors to make sure they were locked. The men nodded at her as she moved forward and many of the people smiled, although they held themselves back a little.

Amanda finally saw the sign that said *Montgomery Law Firm*. She pulled into one of the many vacant parking spots and slowly got out of the car. A handsome man leaned against the building she was about to enter. His brown eyes had flecks of yellow and orange in their deep depths. She smiled slightly, and the man just continued to stare as he looked her over slowly.

"Can I help you, ma'am?"

"I am just here to see Mr. Montgomery."

"Well, you're in the right place, Miss…?"

"Oh, Amanda. Amanda Walker. And you are?"

Something changed in his eyes as he smiled at her and made his way to her side. He held out his hand to her. "Name's Curtis Livingston."

"Oh. Do you live here?"

"Yes. I'm one of the controlling partners here in Slatesville. Well, I have to be going. It was good to meet you."

"You, too, Mr. Livingston."

"Please, call me Curt. Everyone does."

"Only if you call me Amanda."

"That's a deal, sweet lady." She flushed all over when he raised her hand to his lips and gently caressed her knuckles with a brief touch of his mouth. She felt the rise in temperature in her cheeks spread across her upper chest. She stood there and watched as he walked away from her down the street to slip inside a store. She felt foolish and realized that she had been staring. She shook her head, trying to think straight and clear the thoughts that were running through her mind.

Amanda was always aware that she wasn't the Barbie doll type of girl. Although she wasn't fat, she wasn't rail thin, which most men liked, either. Her waist and stomach didn't look like a washboard, although it didn't look like a bunch of bread dough either.

She instantly felt inadequate and quickly turned around to walk to the door of the attorney's office. Knocking, she was surprised when the door instantly opened. The man who opened the door wasn't what she expected. Mr. Montgomery was a short, pudgy man. He didn't wear a business suit, and he didn't seem stuffy at all. He was older and had a short goatee around his mouth. His hair was pulled back into a ponytail at the back of his neck, and he smiled when he saw her.

"You must be Amanda. You look just like your father, except for your eyes. You have your mother's eyes. Let's hope you didn't inherit your father's temper, though," he chuckled.

"You knew my father?"

"Oh, why yes, my dear. We grew up together, Josh and I. Have to say we got into a lot of trouble as kids, and your aunt Mabel was always there to wag her finger and tell on us. You see, there were the three of us; Joshua, Jeremiah, and I. We were called the three musketeers. Mabel wanted to be the fourth, but you know boys. We would never let her, so she always ran and told on us to get back at us for not including her; the little minx." He told the story fondly, and she instantly knew that this man held her family in the highest regard. She also knew he was her ticket to finding out the truth about her family.

"Do I have any more family that I don't know of?" She held her breath, as though she were a child again, asking if Santa Claus was real.

"I am sure you do, my dear. Unfortunately, your aunt was the last of your father's line. She couldn't have any children, and most of the family was killed in a fire in '90. I am sure there is still family on your mother's side, though. However, I must warn you that they are not the kind of people you want to know. Now, if you will come in, I will tell you about everything that now belongs to you."

"What?"

"Oh, my dear, you must know that your father's family had a legacy. You are the only Traverse left to take over the family business."

"What? I don't know what you're talking about."

"They never did tell you who you really are, did they? Oh, you poor child. I am afraid you are going to learn some things about yourself that are going to be hard for you. You must still be a virgin as well."

"I beg your pardon, sir, but I don't see how that's any of your damn business."

"No, my dear, I do not mean to be crude. I was just saying that you have never undergone the Change. It will happen, though. You recently turned twenty-four, and everything changes now."

"What change? What in the hell are you talking about?"

"They hid that from you, too? Oh my gosh. You don't know? Oh, Lord. Okay, first things first. You are now the owner of your family's estate."

"Family estate? So I have a house."

He smiled kindly at her. "Not just a house, my dear. It is what holds the legacy of your family name together. The estate has fifteen bedrooms with their own bathrooms and fireplaces, a kitchen, dining room, parlor, living area, office, library, Carolina room, staff quarters, wrap-around porch with two different sections screened in, pool, tennis courts and 300 acres. It was the pride and joy of your ancestor, Edgar. He was a distant grandfather of yours."

"Oh my gosh."

"Yes, ma'am. How about this? How about I get the keys and directions to the place? You go take a look at it, and then we can talk tomorrow about what you want to do. Stephan has been looking over things, and since your aunt's death, he has given everyone time off until you arrive and decide where to go from there."

Amanda wasn't sure she had the energy to deal with all of this tonight. "Unfortunately, it is very late. Is there somewhere that I can stay for a couple days and then I can go from there and take the day tomorrow to go look at the place?"

"That is perfect. Just give me a second, and I'll find a place for you to stay tonight."

Amanda sat quietly and listened to him talk on his phone. She didn't even hear his words as she thought of what she was going to do.

"I have gotten you a little cabin to rent down the road," he said, drawing her attention back to him. "It is in the woods a little but has electricity and such. On such short notice, I couldn't find anything else. It is only about ten minutes away. The key will be under the mat at the front door. Just go on in and make yourself at home."

"That is perfect. Thank you so much."

"You're welcome, my dear, and we will talk tomorrow. Say ten o'clock tomorrow morning? We will meet here and go to see the house together."

"Perfect. Thank you, Mr. Montgomery."

If you enjoyed this sample then look for **Romeo Alpha: A BBW Paranormal Shifter Romance - Book 1 by Darla Dunbar.**

Other Books by Carla Coxwell

- <u>Fifty Recipes For Disaster New Adult Romance Series</u> (This series precedes "<u>Star Bright New Adult Romance Series</u>")

- Torrid Exposure New Adult Romance Series

- Devil's Advocate BBW MC New Adult Romance Series

- Obsessed Bounty Hunter Romance Series

Get the latest update on new releases from the author at:

https://www.carlacoxwell.com/newsletter

About the Author - Carla Coxwell

Carla has always been a fan of romance novels. To augment what she made waiting on tables to help her way through college, Carla also did some freelance work in the romance genre.

Now she enjoys living vicariously through her characters in her New Adult Romance books.

Connect with Carla Coxwell

I really appreciate you reading my book! Here are my social media coordinates:

Friend me on Facebook:
https://www.facebook.com/CarlaCoxwell/

Follow me on Twitter: https://twitter.com/carlacoxwell

Check me out on Goodreads:
https://www.goodreads.com/author/show/10691544.Carla_Coxwell

Subscribe to my newsletter:
https://www.carlacoxwell.com/newsletter/

Visit my website: https://www.carlacoxwell.com/